FLY-BY-NIGHT

Ruth longs to have her own pony, but the Hollis family have only just moved and money is tight. Ruth is determined and when Fly-by-Night is offered to her for a reasonable price, she knows that her dreams have come true. But looking after a stubborn, frisky pony isn't going to be easy!

A SUMMER OF HORSES

Faith has always been good with animals so why is it that she is terrified of the horses on Beth's farm. As Faith struggles to master her fear, she comes not only to understand horses better, but also herself – as she begins the long ride into adulthood.

THREE TO RIDE

David is determined to ride for England but everything is starting to go wrong for him. He's made some enemies and now he might have to sell his beloved horse, Tornado. Can he achieve his ambition and save his horse?

THREE IN ONE
PONY STORIES

RED FOX

A Red Fox Book

Published by Random House Children's Books
20 Vauxhall Bridge Road, London SW1V 2SA

A division of Random House UK Ltd
London Melbourne Sydney Auckland
Johannesburg and agencies throughout the world

Fly-by-Night first published in Great Britain
by Oxford University Press 1975
Red Fox edition 1990
Text copyright © K. M. Peyton 1975

A Summer of Horses first published by Alfred A. Knopf 1989
Red Fox edition 1990
Text copyright © Carol Fenner Williams 1989

Three to Ride first published in Great Britain by
Burke Publishing Co. Ltd 1958
Text copyright © Christine Pullein-Thompson 1958

This Red Fox anthology first published 1999

Edited and compiled by Charlie Sheppard

Phototypeset by Intype London Ltd
Printed and bound in Norway by Ait Trondheim AS

RANDOM HOUSE UK Limited Reg. No. 954009

ISBN 0 09 940003 0

EDITOR'S NOTE

When choosing and editing the stories for this fantastic pony collection I was faced with a problem. Some of the fashions, prices and practices have changed since these stories were first published. You can no longer buy a horse for forty pounds, hay doesn't cost five shillings a bale, mounted policewomen are an everyday sight, most houses have an indoor bathroom and you would certainly never contemplate riding along a main road without a safety helmet on. So should I delete, modernise or rewrite certain passages?

To me, these stories with their variety of settings, currencies and spellings summarise the appeal of ponies. For generations and across continents, these creatures have captured the hearts and imaginations of many young people. Whether you live in a block of high-rise flats or on an isolated farm, if you catch the 'pony bug' then the need to own, tame and love a pony is hard to ignore.

So I have left these wonderful stories in their original form to remind you of all the other people who share and have shared your love of ponies.

Three in One Pony Stories

Whatever your age or wherever you live, I hope you
will enjoy these stories too.

CONTENTS

FLY-BY-NIGHT

K. M. Peyton

To
Hilary and Cracker

1

RUTH'S DAY OUT

The little green book was very dog-eared. Ruth lay prone on the floor, the book propped up on the fender, studying intently a photograph of a blurry-faced woman riding a horse. The caption to the photograph read: 'This picture shows the horse pushed evenly into the trot by the rider's leg-aids and seat. Note the happy look of the horse, and the true movements of the diagonal legs (the off-fore and near-hind on the ground, whilst the near-fore and off-hind have simultaneously left the ground). Compare with plates 16, 17 and 18.'

'Dinner's ready,' her mother said. 'Get up off the floor, Ruth. It's draughty.'

'It isn't,' Ruth said.

Her seventeen-year-old brother, Ted, home from work for the dinner-hour, peered over her shoulder, grinning. Ruth put her hand over the book. Ted sat down at the dinner-table and as Ruth got up to join him he said, 'Note the happy look of the child, and the true movements of her diagonal legs as she crosses the floor.'

Ruth scowled furiously.

'Sitting down on her well-rounded hind quarters, she picks up the fork with her near-fore – '

'Ted, give over,' said his mother.

Ted said, not teasing any more, 'I passed a lot of kids dashing about on ponies on the way home. In a big field. Pony Club Trials or something. There was a notice up.'

Ruth looked up avidly. 'Where? Near here?'

'Brierley way. Jumping and all that.'

'Oh!' Ruth's scowl vanished and her face became all passionate anxiety. 'If I'd known!' She glanced at the clock. 'Do you think it'll still be on? If I go – '

'I'll drop you there on the way back to work if you like.'

'Yes, of course! Oh, yes, I could!'

Her mother looked at her doubtfully. 'How are you going to get home?'

'Oh, I'll walk or find a bus or something.'

'If you find a bus round these God-forsaken parts you'll be lucky,' Mrs. Hollis said with a sniff.

But Ruth had no thought for afterwards. To get there was all that possessed her. She ate hurriedly, taking no notice of her mother's disapproval. Her mother was disapproving by nature, and did not like the new place they had come to live in, which had made her more disapproving still. Mr. Hollis, a born optimist and peacemaker, said she would get used to it, but Mrs. Hollis said how could she get used to only three shops, five miles to any more and three buses a day to get there? Their house was in the middle of a new 'development of Sunny, Spacious

12

Homes' that had been grafted somewhat incongruously on to the edge of an untidy village in East Anglia. The Sunnyside Estate had a concrete road and concrete lamp-posts and open-plan front gardens, but the rest of the village had gritty tarmac full of pot-holes, or mere mud, and gardens overgrown with gnarled pear trees and sour apples.

'The sooner you go back to school the better,' Mrs. Hollis said to Ruth. 'Moping round all day with nothing to do.'

'But I have something to do now,' Ruth pointed out. She did not like her new school much.

'Hmm,' said Mrs. Hollis.

Ruth finished her pudding and said to Ted, 'Can we go now?'

'Oh, give me a chance,' Ted said, but pushed his chair back from the table in a hopeful manner. 'The old sausages have got to meet the digestive juices.'

'I'll get ready,' Ruth said. She did not want her mother or Ted to see how excited she felt, and she knew it showed. She walked nonchalantly out of the room. She could feel the hot pounding of her joy in her inside: a great flushing of gorgeous anticipation. The unexpectedness of it unnerved her; usually such days, like the never-to-be-forgotten day at the Horse of the Year Show at Wembley, and the day at the Royal Windsor two years ago, were ringed on a calendar weeks before, and approached with a maximum of anticipatory sensation – so great at times as to make her feel sick and almost incapacitate her for the great moment. Her father told her she

13

cared too much. 'Nothing matters that much,' he said to her quite often. But wanting a pony did. Ruth used to cry in bed at night after going to a horse show, because she did not have a pony. 'When we go to live in the country, perhaps you can have a pony,' her father had said. They had lived in the country for two months now, but he had not said any more about it. Ruth wanted to ask him, but she was so frightened that he would dash her hopes that she did not dare to. She was afraid it had just been a prevaricating thing to say, and that if she asked again he would think of something else, like not being able to afford it. But soon she would ask him, Ruth thought, because it was all she thought about. She was nearly twelve, and soon it might be too late: she would grow too tall and need a horse that would certainly eat too much for her father to afford. According to a book Ruth had (a very old one that her father had bought in a junk-shop), people should start riding at ten. If you did not learn to ride as a child you would never acquire a good seat, it said, unless you joined the cavalry and received military training. Ruth realized there was no possibility of her ever joining the cavalry – she wondered if there was such a thing as a mounted police*woman*? – and meanwhile, as far as she could see, her life was being wasted. If she were to say that to her father, he would laugh and say she had no sense of humour. 'Well, I haven't,' Ruth thought. Her only consolation was that, for her age, she was small and thin. Pony-sized for a few years yet.

She pulled her anorak off the hook on her bedroom door. She was already wearing jeans and a blue polo-necked jersey, so getting ready did not take long. Ted started putting on his motor-bike clothes. Ruth fetched the old crash-helmet she wore when she rode pillion, and her mother gave her her bus fare home. '*If* you can find a bus,' she said, 'which I doubt. Now, mind how you go, Ted. You're not in a hurry.'

It was cold on the back of the motor bike. Ruth pressed up close to Ted, her thumbs hooked in his belt, her nose full of the oily smell of his coat. The bike crackled through the village, bounced over the level-crossing, then roared away with the ear-splitting din that Ted loved up the hill and into the country. Through streaming eyes, Ruth saw the Friesian cows, the bare elms and the rolling pastures that fell away to the flat, ditch-seamed marshes and the shining thread of the tidal river. She grinned into Ted's coat, for having come to live in such a place, after London. She saw herself riding along the sea-walls on her pony, a gleaming, eager little beast, ears pricked up, the wind in his tail . . . 'Oh, I must!' she said into Ted's coat.

After some twenty minutes of wild swooping along narrow lanes, Ted turned and shouted something. He was slowing down. Ruth lifted her head and peered over his shoulder. She saw a flag flying at the gateway of a field, purple, pale blue, and gold, and in the field a lot of ponies being ridden, and horse-boxes parked in a row by the hedge.

'Here you are,' said Ted, pulling up by the gate. 'All right?'

'Yes.' Ruth got off, shivering.

'I'll look out for you on the way home, in case you're still walking.'

'I'll manage,' Ruth said. She pulled off her crash-helmet. 'Here, what shall I do with this?' She looked round in dismay. Nothing would have induced her to enter the field wearing anything as inappropriate as a motor-bike helmet. 'Can't you take it?'

'I can't wear two, can I? Stick it in the hedge. Don't leave it behind, though. Cheerio.'

With a blast of noise he was gone. Ruth, nervously fumbling with the helmet, walked through the gate. There was nobody to take any money, or tell her to go away; nobody took any notice of her at all. The field was huge and open, on the top of a hill, and the cold Easter wind swept it. All the adults Ruth could see wore suède coats with sheepskin linings, but they looked cold, and stamped their feet. An enclosure was roped off not far from the gate, which Ruth took to be a collecting-ring, for it was full of ponies and riders, standing or walking about, and from it at intervals a pony would go out and a loudspeaker would give its name and number, and the name of its rider. It would then canter off across the field, jump (or refuse to jump) some rails into an adjoining field, and canter away up this field to disappear over a brush jump and into a wood in the middle distance.

'It's Hunter Trials,' Ruth decided.

She surreptitiously hid the crash-helmet in the hedge, and walked over to the collecting-ring, shivering with cold and excitement. She half expected to be told to leave by one of the cold adults, but she was ignored. The girls on the ponies looked at her without expression. This suited Ruth very well. She did not want to be noticed. She only wanted to look at the ponies.

The ponies were a mixed bag. Quite a few of them, when it was their turn, cantered stickily away from the collecting-ring, refused the first jump three times, and then, on being eliminated, cantered eagerly back to their friends. Ruth's heart bled for their riders, who tried not to look as if they minded. 'If I had a pony,' she thought, 'he would jump that jump.' She was sure she could make him. It was an easy one. She pushed her cold hands into her anorak pockets, and saw herself galloping up the hill towards the wood. 'Like that,' she said to herself, when a boy on a flaxen-maned chestnut did as she would do. The pony went like a tongue of flame over the bright grass. The girls in the collecting-ring watched him, scowling. Ruth heard one of them say, 'Oh, that Peter McNair!'

Peter McNair was better than any of the girls. His pony (Toadhill Flax, according to a programme Ruth caught blowing across the grass) was a Welsh cob with cream feather, like an Agincourt charger, and a white mane that fell down to his shoulder. The course was over two miles long, and the middle part ran through a wood that straggled down the valley just below the collecting-ring. The ponies had to go through it at the top, out into the country and back into it at the bottom before the fast finish over two of the big fences left over from the point-to-point, but squished down in the middle with regard for the smaller animals. Ruth watched Peter McNair disappear at the top end, and ran down across the grass to the bottom end of the wood to watch him come through. There was nobody there except a woman on a folding chair, taking the score, and stamping her feet in the leaf-mould. She took no notice of Ruth, who stationed herself where the course came out of the wood. The way in was through a gate, which had to be opened and closed again, through some trees and over a stream, then round over a log, over the stream again and immediately up a steep muddy bank and out over a rail at the top.

'Tricky,' Ruth thought, imagining. Most of the competitors got off for the gate, but Peter McNair did it all from the saddle. Toadhill Flax skidded to a halt alongside, tearing great streamers out of the grass, and his rider leant down and pulled off the loop of string. The pony, having covered most of the last one and a half miles at a gallop, danced through, quivering with excitement, but Peter McNair held him with one hand, and turned him with his legs, and got him to stand while he dropped the string back. Ruth, watching, thought it was done by magic. Everyone else had had terrible trouble with the gate, pulling their ponies through, and then not being able to get near enough to shut it again, or not being able to remount for the whirling of the excited pony. But Toadhill Flax, as if held on a thread, trembling with excitement, pivoted on his forehand for Peter McNair to put the string back. The cold wind tossed through the wood. Ruth shivered, her eyes riveted on the beauty of Toadhill Flax. She saw Peter McNair just then, easing the chestnut so that from his quivering immobility he leapt into life again, with a great churning of mud, down the bank and over the stream. Instantly he was caught up, to trot neatly through the trees, over the log, and back to the stream, beautifully in hand. Peter McNair pressed him on then, three strides from the stream, and he was over it with a fine stretch and a lifting of the white mane, and up the bank like a trained commando, his rider well forward and with him, ready for the awkward rail at the top. 'Up, Toad!' Peter McNair shouted, and Toad jumped, neat as a cat, springing from his muscled hocks, his tail streaming in the wind. Then out into the open again, at a flat gallop. Ruth ran after them, to watch them finish, entranced by the display of perfect control. 'That's how I would do it,' she said to herself. And, even though her father said she had no sense of humour, she grinned, mocking herself. 'Ruth McNair Hollis,' she thought, 'on Sunnyside Semi-Detached . . . Oh, how can I ever? Without a pony at all?'

Peter McNair, at close quarters, was rather a disappointment. Ruth went back to the collecting-ring, and stared at him. Toadhill Flax stood impatiently, jiggling his quarters and snorting out through wide red nostrils, but Peter McNair just sat without looking excited at all, not speaking to anyone. He looked (was it possible, Ruth thought) bored. He was about the same age as herself, or a little older, a stocky boy, sandy fair. He looked at Ruth, and through her, without his expression changing. Ruth looked at his pony, and thought she would never see another animal as lovely as Toadhill Flax. He was all spring and spirit, yet stood obediently, mouthing his snaffle. When Peter McNair went to get his red rosette, the pony looked more handsome than ever, the red silk clashing against his chestnut, its forked tails fluttering beside the big, inquisitive eye.

The last class was for jumping the course in pairs. Ruth, not missing anything, watched Peter McNair ride across to the girl who had come second to him and ask her if she would ride with him.

'I can't. I'm entered with Jill,' the girl said.

'Jill could find someone else,' the boy said.

Ruth saw the girl with the blue rosette hesitate. But before she could say anything, a girl on a grey pony said, 'Jane, you wouldn't! Just to give the McNairs another rosette!' And she looked at Peter with angry green eyes. 'Cat's eyes,' thought Ruth, fascinated. Peter flushed slightly, but grinned.

'Will you?' he said to Jane.

Ruth watched Jane being sorely tempted. A whole range of expressions ran over her face, from excitement to doubt. But she caught the cat's eyes of the girl on the grey pony, and shook her head.

'It's not fair,' she said. 'No.'

'Good for you,' said Cat's Eyes. She looked mockingly at Peter, and said, 'I'll pair with you, if you like.' Ruth recalled that her grey, a fat gelding with sleepy eyes, had refused three times at the first fence and been eliminated. Peter, obviously not easily ruffled, said, 'Thanks for the offer, which I take great pleasure in refusing.' He wheeled the chestnut round and trotted away towards the row of horse-boxes.

'There!' said Cat's Eyes. 'What a nerve! Typical McNair. He's going home now. Talk about sporting spirit!'

'Oh, well. He can't help it, I suppose.'

'I feel rather sorry for him, in a way,' said Cat's Eyes, maddeningly complacent. Ruth disliked her. 'Anyone could win with the McNair stable to choose from.'

But Ruth, remembering how the boy had ridden the champing chestnut through the gate, holding his electric power with such tact, and skill, did not agree. She did not think Cat's Eyes could have ridden Toadhill Flax through the gate, over the stream and up the bank without hitting the rail, and not lost any marks.

But the intrigue passed, the pairs jumped, the rosettes were awarded. The judges were collected from the far parts of the course by Land-Rover; and the horse-boxes, and strings of riders without horse-boxes, started to filter out through the gate. The cold wind was still blowing, and the grass showed the way the ponies had gone, but the field was empty. There was rain on the wind now, almost sleet. Ruth realized that she was frozen. She turned her head up into the wind, and her black hair blew back from her face. The wine-warmth of joy had dissolved, and she was left with the old familiar ache that would have her crying later, when she was in bed.

'Oh, I *must* – ' she said out loud, into the wind.

She turned round, her eyes picking out the jumps. She was alone in the field now.

'I don't want to win,' she said. 'Only to get round, on my own pony.'

She shivered, hunched against the wind. 'I will,' she said to herself. 'I will. It isn't asking anything much.'

But she knew, to her, it was.

2

MR. HOLLIS AGREES

'All those children on ponies,' Ruth thought, walking home, 'have parents in suède jackets who *know* about ponies.' She had read books about them. They lived in casual old farmhouses full of big dogs and saddles slung over the living-room chairs. They grew up knowing about ponies. Their parents bought them their ponies, and knew what to look for, and how not to be swindled. 'But how shall I,' Ruth thought, 'buy a pony? Not *knowing*?' She was determined now to have a pony. She would not postpone asking any longer. But she knew she could never be one of those casual girls who took it all for granted.

Her mother was right about the buses. There weren't any. Ruth, her head full of ponies, did not mind walking, at first. She was in a complete dream, and did not notice anything. She was thinking about their back garden, which would have to be their paddock, and wondering, as she had wondered many times already, whether it would be big enough. Their 'Sunny Spacious Home' was on a corner of the estate, and had a bigger garden than all the rest, a big awkward triangle. Nobody in their house liked gardening, so it was still all wild and full of half-bricks and lumps of breeze block. Fortunately, being in the far corner of the estate, it backed on to a field, instead of somebody else's back garden, and there were big trees in the hedge which gave a bit of shelter. For there would be no stable for Ruth's pony. No luxuries, Ruth thought. Just the bare pony, if she were lucky.

'I will ask Dad tonight,' she said to herself. Anything would be better than just thinking about it, and being afraid to ask. She wished desperately that her father was a farmer, who would say, 'Of course, lass, you can keep it in Ten Acre. I'll pick you up a useful animal in the market on Friday,' instead of a traveller for Tibbett's Toilet Ware, who would go grave at the thought of spending money and say, 'Ponies don't live on air, you know.'

Ruth walked along thinking about buying a pony. She had forty pounds in National Savings Certificates. Her brother Ted had had sixty pounds, and had taken it all out to buy his motor bike three months ago. It started to rain again, and Ruth plodded on, head down. She pulled the hood of her anorak up and put the crash-helmet on top. There was nobody to see, as she was on a deserted stretch of country lane which ran, undulating, between vast fields whose hedges had been cut out. 'The sort of farmer I don't like,' Ruth thought. It was efficient but ugly. In the burnt-out ditches the rain-water reflected the black grass. The rain started to hurt, with sleet in it, driving horizontally across the bleak lane, and Ruth put her head down against it. Her wet jeans plastered themselves to her legs and the sleet tinned on her helmet. There was nowhere to shelter, not even a tree, so she just had to keep on walking.

After a few minutes she heard the noise of a heavy lorry approaching from behind. She shifted over into the verge, glancing over her shoulder. It was a big horse-box, with 'McNair' painted over the cab. It went past, soaking her still further with spray from its wheels, but about twenty yards farther on it stopped. She walked on. The door opened and a man put his head out into the rain and called back to her, 'Want a lift?'

'Oh, yes, please!'

Ruth ran, and scrambled up into the seat beside the driver. The cab was hot and fumy, with steam on the windows, deliciously comfortable. She slammed the door.

The man put the lorry in gear and eased it into motion once more, and said, 'I don't pick anyone up as a rule, but on a day like this . . .' He grinned. 'Bit wet, aren't you?'

'Yes.'

'Where are you going?'

'Wychwood.'

'I can put you down there, then. I pass it. Bit of luck for you, eh?'

'Yes, I thought there would be a bus, but there wasn't. I went to watch the Pony Club Trials.'

'That's where I've been. Left at three, but had to

take young Peter up to Potton to ride some ponies his father's thinking of buying.'

'What's his father, then? A dealer or something?'

'Yes. You not heard of McNair? It's quite a business he runs, him and the three boys. The two eldest do a lot of racing now, and jumping. Young Peter has to handle the ponies – the others have got too big. They work hard between them – the old boy's a right slave-driver. Wouldn't have got where he is if he wasn't.'

'Have you got Toadhill Flax in the back, then?'

'Yes, that's right. You saw him jumping, eh?'

'Yes. He's a gorgeous pony.'

'Flashy. Done well, hasn't he? Six months ago that pony was as wild as they come, straight up from Wales. And yet today he went round that course and beat the lot of them. That's McNair for you. Work! He never stops. Get a colt like that for twenty quid at the sales, and a year later it's worth two hundred.'

'How does he do that, then?'

'Sheer hard work. Those boys – they're in the stable at six every morning. Peter now – he'd work young Toad (he calls him Toad – says he jumps like a toad) before school, and again when he comes home. Every day. Steady. The old man shouting at him – got a temper like the devil himself, has the old man, but only with people. I've never heard him raise his voice to a horse. He's a right character, I can tell you. Fair, too. You won't get a bargain off him, but he'll not cheat you. He'll not cover faults up. And if he doesn't think you're fit to have a horse of his, he'll tell you straight. Doesn't mind what he says. But work! Cor, he doesn't know what it is to sit in front of a telly. People like that – they deserve to make money, by my reckoning. Good luck to 'em, I say.'

Ruth began to understand what the girls had meant with their sideways remarks about the McNair establishment. No wonder Peter could ride . . . even Cat's Eyes saying she felt rather sorry for him made sense now. Ruth wondered (knowing how she felt herself when she first opened her eyes in the morning) whether Peter McNair really wanted to get up at six every day, to be shouted at by his father.

'I want to buy a pony,' Ruth confided to the cheerful driver.

'Come and see McNair, then. You won't be sorry. He's got some nice little animals, just suit you. We're only three miles farther on from Wychwood. On the Hillingdon road. It's on the right, set back a bit, but there's a notice on the road marking the drive. You can't miss it.'

Ruth, in the steamy cabin of the horse-box, hypnotized by the windscreen wipers diverting the deluge of rain out of her vision, sank into a happy dream of herself buying a pony from Mr. McNair. Having him trotted out . . . running her hands down his legs, like the people in books . . . looking knowledgeably into his mouth. Every now and then from behind the partition she heard a snuffle or the clonk of a hoof from Toadhill Flax, and for a few minutes she had a sense of belonging to the horse world, swishing through the rain with the warm smell of horse permeating the cabin. 'It's lovely,' she thought. 'I am happy.'

'Here you are,' said the driver. 'I'll have to drop you here. I go straight on.'

The dream was over. 'Thank you very much.'

She walked home, head down against the rain.

'Oh, Ruth! What a sight!' said her mother. 'I wondered whatever you could be doing, this weather! Did you find a bus?'

'No, there wasn't one. I walked a long way, then a horse-box stopped and gave me a lift.'

'A lift, eh? What have I told you about taking lifts?' her mother asked crossly.

'Oh, Mother, in this weather, surely? Besides, I told you, it was a horse-box.'

'With a horse driving, I suppose?' Mrs. Hollis said tartly. 'Because it was a horse-box, that makes it all right?'

'Yes,' said Ruth.

'Sometimes, Ruth, I think you're plain stupid,' her mother said. 'Go and get changed and put those wet clothes on the washing-machine.'

'Do you think Daddy will say I can have a pony now? He said we could when we lived in the country. Do you think, if I ask him . . .?'

'There's no harm in asking. But don't expect too much. This house is about all we can afford at the moment. The mortgage is over five pounds a week. Where do you think it all comes from?'

Ruth shivered, and went upstairs to change. 'I

will have one,' she said to herself. 'I will earn some money myself. I'll work in a shop on Saturdays. Or do a paper round. Or – ' She couldn't think of anything else. 'If not I shall die.'

She took her wet clothes downstairs and dumped them in the kitchen. Her mother, smart in towny shoes and a frilly apron, was cutting up tomatoes. Ruth thought gloomily, 'She'd never sit all day on a little stool in a wood scoring marks for a Hunter Trials. She doesn't understand anything about what matters.' She felt uncomfortable thinking such things, but the thoughts came nevertheless. Ruth wanted a tweed mother, with pony-nuts in her pockets.

Ted came in, and later her father drove his car – or, rather, Tibbett's car – into the drive and stamped his feet on the doormat, sniffing the kitchen smells. They all sat down to supper and Ruth ate without noticing, only thinking of what she had to ask her father. 'Tonight I will know, one way or the other,' she thought, and felt sick. She could not get the question out. Her father finished his meal and sat on with a cup of tea and the evening paper. Ted went out. Mrs. Hollis started washing-up, and Ruth had to clear away. She felt cold in her stomach, and the question would not get past her lips. There was a pencil on the table, and she sprawled in a chair opposite her father, drawing a horse on the formica.

'Ruth, for heaven's sake!' Her mother swooped down with a cloth.

'Can I have a pony?' Ruth said desperately.

'Pour me another cup of tea,' her father said, pushing his teacup out from round the newspaper. Mrs. Hollis took the cup.

'Ruth's on about this pony business again,' she said. 'You'd better settle it one way or the other, John, else we'll get no peace.'

'Oh.' John Hollis lowered the paper reluctantly. 'What is it, then?' He knew perfectly well.

'Please can I have a pony? You said I could when we lived in the country.' Ruth looked at him, quivering.

He frowned. 'Well . . .'

'Please. I shan't ever ask for anything else. Not clothes or anything. If I can just have a pony. I'll look after it and everything. You won't have to do anything.'

'Only pay for it,' said her father.

'I'll earn some money. I'll do a paper round. Mary Barker does one, and they want another – there's a card in the shop. I promise. And I could use my National Savings. Ted did for his bike, so there's no reason why I shouldn't. I've got forty pounds.'

'Oh. Would that buy a pony?'

'I don't know. I should think so. I could find out.'

'But then you have to feed it when you've got it. How much is that a week?'

'Nothing in the summer and only hay in the winter. And hay's cheap in the country, almost nothing,' Ruth said recklessly.

'Where would it go?'

'Out the back. There's enough. You wouldn't have

to do any gardening. He'd graze it all smooth and it would look lovely.'

'It sounds a lot too simple the way you put it,' her father said, half serious, half smiling.

'Well . . .' Ruth smiled too, uneasily.

'How do you go about it, then? Buying a pony, I mean. You have to know something about it, don't you? Do you know enough?'

Ruth knelt on the chair, thin eager elbows on the table. 'I met a man today, the man who picked me up in the horse-box, and he works for a Mr. McNair who lives on the Hillingdon road, and he's a dealer. Very straightforward, the man said. He said I'd get a good pony from him. I could go and see him, couldn't I? I mean, it's like a shop. You just go and look round and get an idea. Could I go?'

'You never get a bargain off a dealer.'

'I could look at the adverts. *Could* I look, though? If I *found* one, could I have it? It's no good looking if I can't have one anyway. But if you say I can *look* . . .' Ruth's words tumbled out in a heap. 'If you say I can use my National Savings money, then I could look, couldn't I? Ted used his.'

'Well, his motor bike was for getting to work on. Not just pleasure.'

'Oh, it *is* pleasure!' Ruth said. 'You've only got to look at him – '

Her father grinned. 'He had a wonderful argument for buying it, though. Better than yours, my girl.' But he was too kind to tease her further. 'All right. You use it. In ten years' time it won't be worth much anyway, and as you're so set on this idea I won't say no. You can go shopping.'

'Tomorrow?'

'Tomorrow. Looking. If you find anything hopeful, you must report home. And don't look too keen.'

'*Oh!*' Ruth was speechless with excitement. Her face went red, and then white, her lips quivered. Her father looked at her, and said, 'You are a funny girl.'

Mrs. Hollis picked up the empty teacup. 'While you're in a decision-making frame of mind, dear, how do you feel about my putting my name down with the Council again? We're well settled in now, and I'd like a child about the place again.'

When they had lived in London, Mrs. Hollis had been on the local council's list of foster-mothers, and a succession of small children, one at a time, or occasionally two, had followed each other in the Hollises' spare bedroom. They were children whose mothers had had to go to hospital, or occasionally whose fathers were in prison, or whose parents had been evicted; normally they had not stayed for more than a few months. Just long enough, Ruth had often thought, to get so that they were one of the family. Then, when they went, it was a wrench and a misery; she did not like it.

Her father said, 'All right, dear. If you want to. But past the crying-in-the-middle-of-the-night stage, please. Sixish, say. Tell them your husband is very sensitive.'

'Well, you take what you're sent as a rule. But I'll do my best.'

'Right. Everybody happy?' Mr. Hollis grinned at Ruth. She was sitting in a dream, staring into space. She did not even hear him. Mr. Hollis looked at his wife and shook his head.

'She'll come down to earth,' Mrs. Hollis said. 'When this pony is a reality. It might not be all bliss – all roses. She'll learn.'

But Ruth, if she had heard, would not have believed her.

3

THE FORTY-POUND PONY

Ruth cycled slowly up the driveway that led to McNair's. She wished it was longer than it was, for she was dry-mouthed with nervousness. The great moment had arrived, but perversely she felt no joy: she was too frightened. It meant so much, and she knew so little. Reading her old-fashioned horse-books by the light of a torch most of the night before had done nothing to help. Her head reeled with the fatal diseases of the horse, imperceptible to the inexperienced eye; with the vices that meant doom: from bolting to wind-sucking. She had read about dealers who filed their horses' teeth to pass them off as youngsters, and dealers who injected their horses with sedatives when prospective buyers were trying them out. 'No foot, no horse,' was an adage to remember, and, from the feet up, the possible blem-ishes were legion: curbs, splints, spavins, thorough-pins, windgalls and sidebones on the legs alone. Expressive words with ominous meanings floated through her brain: stargazer, daisy-cutter, herring-gutted, Roman-nosed, ewe-necked, cow-hocked . . . She pressed down on the pedals, standing up, as the gravel bogged her tyres. 'I don't know anything,' she thought in a panic, 'only words.'

But now she was in a yard, meticulously tidy, surrounded with loose-boxes, like a photograph captioned 'A desirable layout.' The loose-boxes were new and smart, with concrete forecourts. At one side was a wooden chalet labelled 'Office'; beyond, behind the stableyard, the roof of a large modern house stuck up. Ruth put her bike against the nearest wall, where it looked very untidy, and went to the door marked 'Office'. Before she got there a man came round a corner from the direction of the house, and Ruth stopped short, feeling like a burglar. Mr. McNair, she thought. He was what Ted would have called very hacking-jacket. He said, 'Can I help you?'

Ruth took a deep breath. 'I want to buy a pony.' Her voice sounded very peculiar.

McNair looked at her carefully. He was smart, almost dapper, in a tweed jacket and well-pressed trousers. His expression was non-committal, his eyes shrewd. He had grey hair and hard, working hands.

'For yourself?'

'Yes.'

'About thirteen hands? Thirteen-two perhaps. How well do you ride?'

'I can't really.'

He smiled. 'That's honest. Mostly they say, "Oh, I can ride," as if the question is an insult. About ten per cent of them can, after a fashion.'

Ruth felt better. If he appreciated honesty, he must be honest with her, surely?

'What do you want it for?' McNair asked. 'Wembley? Or just to keep the grass down at home?'

'Oh, the grass,' Ruth said hastily. Mr. McNair was smiling, but she didn't notice. She was beginning to think that Mr. McNair's ponies might cost more than forty pounds. Everything was so new and expensive, from Mr. McNair's trousers to the first shining bolt that he was pulling back on loose-box 12. There was no rust at Mr. McNair's, no chipped paint, no dirty straw blowing in the evening breeze. Only perfection. Ruth remembered Peter, holding Toadhill Flax on a quivering rein, while he dropped the string. Perfection. 'This isn't my sort of place,' Ruth thought, and in her imagination she saw a stableyard, slightly untidy, with dipping tiled roofs and pigeons, and loose-boxes converted from the old carriage-horse stalls, with cobbles, and cats, and a faithful head looking over the half-door . . . the sort in books. She swallowed desperately.

'Pennyroyal,' Mr. McNair said. 'Nice sort. Six years old.'

Pennyroyal was a dark liver chestnut with no white on him, save a small star. He had a kind eye, and he gave a friendly knucker. Ruth, trying to hold back, loved him immediately, and felt doom descending. She just looked, speechless.

Mr. McNair smiled again. He ran his hand down the hard muscle of the pony's neck, patted his shoulder, and came out into the yard again.

'I don't tell my customers that my horses are what they're not,' he said. 'I don't tell them they're marvellous. They're not marvellous. I just buy horses I like myself.' He was leading the way to loose-box 7. 'I'm hard to please. I've been buying horses for thirty years now. And for every horse I've bought, I'd say I've looked at twenty.'

None of her horse-books had described to Ruth a dealer like Mr. McNair. She was lost, and she knew it. She was far too frightened now to say that she wanted a pony that only cost forty pounds. She looked into loose-box 7, and saw a grey mare, dappled like a Victorian rocking-horse, with black legs and eyes blue-black like best coal. To Ruth she was perfect, utterly desirable, from the bold glance of her lovely eyes to the tip of her frosty tail.

'Sixpence,' said Mr. McNair.

Ruth, in her nervous state, almost jumped out of her skin. '*Sixpence?*'

'Her name,' said Mr. McNair gently. 'The price is somewhat more.'

'Oh!' Ruth went scarlet with horror at her idiocy.

'She's Welsh mountain. I've got her papers in the office. A bit on the small side for you probably. Not now, of course, but in a year or two she would be. Attractive pony, though.'

'Oh, she's lovely!' Ruth's voice was full of misery.

'Most of the ponies are in the field. I'll get Peter and we'll go and see them.'

They left Sixpence and walked down the row of loose-boxes to a gate which led to the house behind and, presumably, the field. Ruth glimpsed aristo-cratic heads, honest hunter heads, and the flashy gold beauty of Toadhill Flax. She paused. Mr. McNair said, 'He takes some holding, that one. I wouldn't offer him to a young girl. I'd lose my reputation.'

They went through the gate, which led down between the new house and a newly planted orchard, to another gate at the bottom. As they passed the house, McNair turned his head and bawled, 'Peter!' By the time they got to the bottom Peter McNair was coming down behind them, a couple of halters in his hand. He joined them, leaning on the gate, and nodded to Ruth, but said nothing.

There were about ten ponies in the field, which was large, stretching away to a line of elms on the top of a rise. Some of them raised their heads and looked towards the gate; two walked towards them in a hopeful fashion; one looked, gave a shrill whinny, and galloped away. Against the ridge of the hill, the gallop looked splendid, wild and free, and Ruth watched admiringly.

McNair said, 'Damned animal!'

The pony was a bright bay, not bold in the way of Toadhill Flax, but with an airy, fine action. It seemed to float over the grass. Its gallop set off two or three of the others, but none of them was in earnest like the bay. They wheeled round a few times and went back to grazing. The bay stopped when it was on the horizon, and stood with its head up, watching.

'We made a mistake, turning her out in this field,' Mr. McNair said to Ruth. 'Woodlark, a Dartmoor, T.B. cross. But wild as they come. There's a lot of work there, to make anything of that one. Peter, fetch Sandalwood first.'

Ruth watched Peter walk away across the field, feeling guilty to be causing all this trouble, when she knew now, with a deep-down, horrid certainty, that none of Mr. McNair's ponies cost as little as forty pounds. Half of her longed to enjoy this feast of ponies; the other half trembled with fear at the thought of telling Mr. McNair of her paltry savings. Even when buying things like toothpaste, she did not like to cause the assistant any trouble. She always took the first one she saw, even if she did not like the taste, rather than ask the person to go to any trouble looking. And now here she was, having all this time and trouble spent on her by the exalted McNairs, and it would be to no avail. In silence she watched Peter approach a group of three ponies talking to them quietly. One came up to him, nuzzling his pockets, but he walked on to a bay that was still grazing, and offered it something out of his pocket. It came up and he haltered it, and one of the other ponies came up, pushing in for a titbit. There was a squeal of jealousy and a great show of teeth and laid-back ears, but Peter disentangled his pony with quiet tact and brought it back to the gate. It was a stocky bay gelding with a thick black mane and tail, a homely pony. Ruth could see him nicely in her back garden, a dependable sort who would go calmly past a dustcart and stop when she fell off. He was not as handsome as the others, but she could love him easily. He looked at her with humble, patient eyes.

'A good beginner's sort,' said Mr. McNair. 'Nothing spectacular, but foolproof. Eight years old.'

'Oh, he's lovely,' Ruth said despairingly.

'Ginny, I think,' McNair said to Peter. 'Then I think that's the lot, at the moment.'

Peter went away and came back with a dark bay mare with a mealy nose and a lot of wild mane. Ruth leaned on the gate, clenching her sticky hands over the top bar, as if she were being tortured. The two ponies stood, heads up, utterly desirable in every way, and she looked at them as if she knew what she was looking for, feeling only this terrible despair, and not able to utter a word of sense. McNair went on talking, but Ruth did not take in what he said. It was no use. They let the ponies go and walked back up to the yard. McNair said, 'Those are the ones that are suitable, just now. In a week or two I may have something else to offer you. We have new ponies in nearly every week.'

Ruth knew it was her turn to say something. They were back in the tidy yard. Peter stood just behind his father, saying nothing, and there was a pointed silence. Mr. McNair looked at Ruth. Gathering up all her courage, and feeling herself going scarlet, she said, 'What – what is the price of – of – ' All the ponies' names completely eluded her. The only one she could remember was Toadhill Flax. ' – of – them?'

'I could let the bay go for a hundred and twenty.

And Ginny, perhaps. The others . . . Pennyroyal, say, a hundred and fifty. He's quite a useful jumper, and is good in gymkhana events. The Welsh mare the same: she's a little winner, and you could get some good foals out of her later.'

Her worst fears confirmed, Ruth felt her scarlet fade, and the cold despair take its place. All her instincts had been right. Not only twice but three times as much as her miserable forty pounds . . .

She said, 'I shall have to ask my father.'

At that moment a large car drove into the yard and Mr. McNair said to Peter, 'Here's Matthews,' and to Ruth, 'Excuse me a moment.' He hurried over to the car and Ruth, grateful to Matthews, whoever he was, was left standing with the silent Peter. Her tumbled emotions no longer disturbed her. It was all useless. She looked down at her feet and mumbled, 'Thank you. I'll go now.'

Politely, still saying nothing, Peter followed her across the yard to where her shabby bicycle was propped against the wall. They passed McNair and his visitor, talking hard on the steps of the office, and McNair called out to Peter as he passed, 'Stay around, Peter. We'll get a saddle on that Woodlark tonight if it's the last thing we do.'

'All right,' Peter said, without any expression.

Ruth picked up her bike. 'Thank you,' she said again, awkwardly. 'Good-bye.'

'I'll come down to the gate. It's supposed to be shut.'

Ruth would rather have shaken off Peter's

unforthcoming company, but was obliged to walk on with him down the drive. It then occurred to her that she would never have such an opportunity again to seek advice. At least to Peter she could admit her forty pounds, if not face to face with Mr. McNair.

'Doesn't your father ever have anything cheaper?' she asked him. 'I haven't got that much money.'

'Well — no. Not unless it's very small. There's never anything under eighty.'

'I've only got forty,' Ruth muttered.

'Forty?' Peter's voice was doubtful, but not scornful. 'You'd only get a young pony for forty, an unbroken pony. Or some old crock.'

'A young pony? Like Woodlark, you mean?'

'Oh, heavens, you don't want a pony like Woodlark! She's not worth anything at all. You want a quiet one. Mr. Marks, at Ramsey Heath, has young ponies quite cheap, sometimes. You ought to go and see him.'

'Mr. Marks?' Ruth fastened on the name, with a great uplifting of her spirits. 'You mean he might have one for forty?'

'He might. A two-year-old. He buys them at the sales, for a sort of hobby. If you get one with a quiet temperament, you ought to be able to manage all right. He lives at Bramhall, the farm on the right past the pub.'

In that instant, Ruth's world was transformed. She turned to Peter with an eager, shining face. 'I shall go and see him. Thank you for telling me. Oh, thank you!'

Peter looked quite surprised. He smiled, which made him look much more human. Ruth noticed that he had freckles, and was quite ordinary, on the ground. She pushed her bike through the gate and he shut it behind her.

'Thank you very much!' she said again, fervently. As she pedalled away down the road, she thought, 'He thinks I'm barmy. But I don't care!' And she started to sing, free-wheeling down the hill.

The next evening she pedalled to Bramhall, and found herself jerking down a rutted lane, with high out-of-control hedges on either side and ditches full of stinging-nettles. Bramhall was a collection of ramshackle old buildings, dung-heaps and picking hens, hemmed in with elms full of cawing rooks. It looked to Ruth far more like a forty-pound place than McNair's, and she liked it instinctively. She liked the faded rose-red of the stable bricks and the thatch with grass growing out of it, and the sour smell of an early elderberry. She was full of hope. She left her bicycle by the gate, where it looked quite smart, and went into the yard. A youngish man was just shutting three cows into a cowshed. He turned round and looked at her with a cheerful grin.

'I'm looking for Mr. Marks, about buying a pony,' she said.

'I'm Marks,' said the man.

He was not frightening at all, and Ruth was able

to say quite easily, 'I want a pony, but I only have forty pounds. Peter McNair said you might have one.'

'Oh, you've been to McNair's, have you? I'll bet Mr. McNair didn't offer you one for under a hundred, eh?'

'No, he didn't.'

'Smart place, McNair's.'

'Yes, very.'

'Somebody has to pay for it.'

'Yes.'

'Let's see what we've got, then, eh? It's for you, is it?'

'Yes.'

'He told you they're only partly broken? You can catch them, and halter them and handle them, but they're only youngsters. Two-year-olds. I got this lot from Beaulieu – the New Forest sales. I got a dozen, last September, but I've sold most of them. There's four left now. They're down in the bottom field. We'll go along. Just a moment.'

He went into a shed and fetched a sieve of oats and a halter, and then led the way down a rutted track between more massive rampant hedges. It was a dull day, and Ruth had a sense of the earth, fed on damp, overwhelming Mr. Marks's property with its swaggering growth. The verges were lush with forward grass, the budding branches tossed over their heads with an uncultivated abandon. The gate to the ponies' field was set deep in rampant hawthorn, with gnarled Constable oaks on either side; the field was not very large, and sloped down to a stream and a thick wood full of crows. Ruth was enchanted with the old-fashionedness of it; the lovely scorn of modern clearance, the encouragement of crows and vermin-sheltering hedges. Later, she could see, it would be all knee-high buttercups and cow-parsley, like a Victorian painting. 'There will be a pony here for me,' she thought. 'It is a "me" place. Not like McNair's.' A little shiver of excitement ran through her.

Mr. Marks gave a shout and a whistle, and the four ponies converged upon the gate. They were all rough and muddy and, after McNair's, definitely of a half-price breed. Except for one. Ruth's eyes went past the thick-legged grey, the wall-eyed skewbald and the nondescript black, and rested on the pony that held back from the others. 'That is for me,' she thought.

It was, in fact, nothing special in its looks: a gelding of an unusual bay-roan colour, like a bright bay that had been left out in the frost. His legs were black and his head was dark, with a small crescent of white between the eyes; the forelock was black and the mane grew whiter as it went down towards the withers where the frosty mantle seemed to have fallen most thickly. The stocky quarters were almost pure bay, and the thick tail black. 'Circus pony,' Ruth could almost hear Ted say. But the pony had a look, a presence, a way of standing which made the other three ponies look like cab-horses. He did not come up, but stood behind, head up, watching Ruth.

'Oh, I like that one,' Ruth said.

Mr. Marks gave a grin and said, 'You watch him.'

He started to give each of the other three ponies a handful of oats out of the sieve, and immediately the little bay roan came up, shouldering the black and the skewbald roughly out of the way. His eyes, large and lively, showed no white, only his ears went back with greed and he plunged eagerly for Mr. Marks's hand. The other ponies moved over for him, making jealous faces. Ruth had seen his cocky walk, the firm planting of his round, rather shaggy feet: it was jaunty, sure.

'He's the boss around here,' said Marks, smiling. 'You're our fly boy, eh? Our smart one? That's what we call him, Fly. He's fly all right.'

'Oh.' Ruth was dubious now. What was fly, as an adjective? As a noun, and a name, it was horrid. As a description, it was rather worrying. Did Fly qualify, she wondered, for Peter McNair's stipulation: a quiet temperament?

'Is he – is he all right? I mean, quiet?'

Mr. Marks pursed his lips. 'Well now, if you're looking for a real quiet one, I'd take the skewbald. Or the black. You can do anything with those two.'

Ruth looked at the skewbald and the black. But beside Fly they were nothing ponies. They were nice, because they were ponies; they had gentle, interested faces. But they hadn't got the – the – Ruth groped for a word and could not find it – the *thing* that Fly had. Fly was a character.

'But Fly – he's quiet?' She had to persist.

'He's got no vices. Wouldn't kick or bite you. But he's got more spirit than the others. I reckon he'll be a more lively ride, when you get a saddle on him. I'll be honest with you, you see. If it's really quietness you're looking for, you should have the skewbald or the black.'

But Ruth could no longer consider the skewbald or the black. She knew already that it was going to be Fly. She only wanted Marks to tell her that he wasn't actually bad.

'Is he forty pounds?'

'Well, yes, I suppose so. If you want him that bad. I was asking fifty really. He's a three-year-old, this one. He's ready to be ridden. But I haven't the time to school him myself. It takes too much patience for me. And my kid's too little yet to ride.'

Ruth, having found that Fly, by the nod of her head, could be hers, was suddenly petrified. She stared at him. She looked for all the things in the books, the faults with the strange names, and deficiencies of conformation, the signs of vice, and the indications of dire disease. And Fly stared back at her, four-square on his black hairy legs, and she could see nothing that the books mentioned, only the pony of her heart, as perfect as Shakespeare's bit in all the anthologies, out of 'Venus and Adonis'. 'Oh, I must be sensible!' she thought to herself. And Fly was looking at her boldly as if it was she who had the faults, knock-knees and rickets and pigeon-toes: it was a straight look, with a glint in it. It was

47

not a look to make her feel sensible. It quenched her fright and her doubts.

'Oh, please, I would like him,' she said to Mr. Marks. 'I've only got forty pounds.'

'Well then, we'll call it a deal,' said Mr. Marks comfortably. He did not strike Ruth as a worrier. 'He's a good pony. The vet's seen 'em all and can't find anything wrong, so you'll be all right there.'

Was it that easy, after all? Ruth could hear her heart thudding, as if it had grown into two. She gripped the top bar of the gate, looking at Fly. She saw him going round the Hunter Trials course at Brierley Hill, and herself sitting easily in the saddle, confident, easy . . . He had bold, wide nostrils, and was wide between the forelegs. But he wasn't common.

'Is – is he New Forest?' she asked Mr. Marks.

'He hasn't any papers,' Marks said. 'But he came from the forest. I'll bring him down your place, if you like – I know a man with a truck. Save you walking along the road. Where do you live?'

'Wychwood. On the new estate.'

They started walking back to the farmyard. Ruth was in a daze. 'I'll have to get my money cashed. It's in National Savings.'

'Tomorrow do you?'

'Oh, yes. But I won't have the money by then. At least, not all of it. I can give you some.'

'No hurry. I'm not worried. What house is it?'

'South View.'

'About six, then.'

'Yes, thank you very much.'

Ruth found she was cycling home. Her head was filled with the image of Fly, standing there with his legs planted out so firmly, the wind in his tail. She thought, 'Fly is a horrid name, if you think of fly like the thing that makes spots over the windows and sits on cream-cakes in the summer. But if you think of Fly as in flying, up in the sky, it is a lovely name. He will be that sort of Fly. Fly. Fly-by-Night.' Ruth was pleased with Fly-by-Night. 'He can be Fly, short for Fly-by-Night. In the Hunter Trials he can be down in the catalogue as Fly-by-Night.' Ruth was cycling through the village and up the concrete road of Sunnyside Estate, her eyes seeing nothing.

'I've bought a pony,' she said to her father, who was having his supper.

He looked up. 'Really bought it?'

'Well, I've got to get the money out. But the man doesn't seem to mind about waiting for it. He's bringing the pony tomorrow.'

'Tomorrow!' said Mrs. Hollis, spinning round from the sink. '*Tomorrow*?'

'Yes.'

'Oh, Ruth, surely – ' Even her father looked rather annoyed. Her mother was speechless, gesticulating out of the kitchen window. 'Where on earth – ?'

Ruth, feeling rather cold, looked out of the kitchen window and remembered that the back-garden, or field, was full of bricks. There was wire-mesh between it and the adjoining two gardens, but

49

nothing round the sides of the house and at the bottom, save a hedge full of holes. She looked at it forlornly, thinking of the lush spring bounty of Mr. Marks's field. Fly would surely find life here a little different.

'Oh, I'll have it all right by tomorrow,' she said.

Her assumption that a fence would grow out of the ground before the following evening made her parents exchange despairing glances. Fortunately at this moment Ted came in with his friend from work, Ron. Ron, like Ted, was seventeen, tall, skinny, and amiable, with a beloved motor bike.

'We're going to work on Ron's camshaft tonight,' Ted said happily.

'I think,' said Mr. Hollis, 'that you're going to build a fence.'

A vast cattle-truck, trailing small clots of dung, laboured up the slight incline to 'South View' and parked incongruously outside.

The driver leaned out of the cab and yelled towards the house, 'Six cows for Hollis!'

Ruth ran blindly down the drive and into the road. 'It's my pony! The pony from Mr. Marks?'

'That's right, miss,' said the driver, grinning. He let down the back ramp with a crash and shower of straw, and from the depths of the big lorry Fly's dark eyes stared at Ruth, wild and shining.

'I'll get him, miss. He's a bit scared like.' The man went into the lorry and untied Fly's halter. Fly charged for the daylight, his hoofs drumming the wooden floor, pulling the driver with him.

'Hey, hey, steady on, my bold fellow!'

He crashed down the ramp, skidded on the concrete, and pulled up, quivering, nostrils wide, held sharply by the rope halter. A quiet one, Ruth remembered, was what she should have had. No animal that she had ever seen, she thought at that moment, looked less quiet than Fly.

4

PROBLEMS

That night, alone in the pock-marked field, Fly-by-Night galloped up and down the makeshift fences, whinnying for his companions. Ruth lay in bed with the pillow over her head so that she would not hear the pitiful noise. When he stopped whinnying she got out of bed to see if he was still there, and saw him standing with his ears pricked up, gazing into the distance, the moonlight washing his frosted back. She kept going to the window, longing to see him grazing, or dozing, but he did not settle. Ruth would have gone out to him, in the cold moonlight, but she knew that her presence made no difference to his behaviour, for she had spent the hours before bedtime trying to soothe him, and he had ignored her, brushing past her in his agitated circling, looking past her with anxious eyes. The neighbours had watched him, amazed, worried about their wire-mesh, and Ruth's parents had shaken their heads and asked her what had possessed her to choose such a mettlesome beast.

'Any trouble and he'll have to go back,' Mrs. Hollis said. 'Thank goodness we haven't paid the man yet.'

'It's all strange to him,' Ruth cried out. 'He'll settle down! He misses the other ponies.'

Shaken with doubts of her own, nothing would now have induced her to admit that Fly was not a wise buy. More than anything her parents could say, the words of Peter McNair, who *knew*, kept repeating themselves in her head: 'If you get a quiet one . . .' But she did not want the grey, or the black, or the piebald. She was possessed by Fly, with his cocky walk and his questing eyes. 'He will be all right,' she said, 'when he's settled down.'

'Tell the man to go and bring this animal's pals,' Ted said, reinforcing his fence hastily with whatever was handy (the dustbin, the clothes-line, two motor tyres, and a wardrobe door that was in the garage), 'before he goes and fetches them himself.'

'He'll be all right in the morning.'

But in the morning Fly was still whinnying, and roaming round the field close by the fences, so that he wore a trodden path. Even to Ruth's eyes the grass in their field did not look very palatable: it was sparse yet, and full of docks. The drinking-water was in an old cistern that Ted had mended with solder. She thought that some hay might occupy the restless pony, and took five shillings out of her money-box, and went on her bicycle to the nearest farm, where a surly old man took her money and dropped a bale on to her handle-bars.

'We ain't got too much ourselves just now.'

'Thank you very much,' Ruth said, full of gratitude for the favour.

She pushed the awkward load home and dropped a precious armload of the stuff on to the ground for Fly. He came up and snuffed it, ate a little, and trampled a lot of it into the mud. Ruth put the rest of the bale into the garage, but when her father came home and put the car in, the hay had to come out. Ruth put it on the porch, by the front door.

'Ruth, for heaven's sake!' her mother said.

'Where else, then?' Ruth asked, in desperation. Her money-box had only another half-crown in it, and the hay was precious. She knew now that she would have to buy a hay-net, and a halter, too, and after that there would be a saddle and bridle, and a dandy-brush, and saddle-soap, and a hoof-pick. And more hay. Fly was still cantering along his track by the wire mesh, and scratching his hind quarters on the posts, which now leaned towards their neigh-bours' gardens. The neighbours on one side told Mrs. Hollis that they didn't like the whole business.

'He'll settle down,' Ruth said. She was white, and had dark shadows under her eyes. She went down to the paper shop and signed on to deliver papers to Mud Lane and the road down to the creek, an unpopular route because the houses were far apart and a lot had nasty dogs. 'Eleven shillings a week,' the man said.

'Oh, thank you very much,' Ruth said, once more deeply grateful. At least, on eleven shillings a week, Fly could not actually starve. She would wear her thickest trousers, and gum boots, for the dogs.

'Look, really,' Mrs. Hollis said, surveying the

motor tyres and the dustbin and the wardrobe door from the front drive, 'we can't go on looking like this. We'll have the estate people on to us. It looks like a slum. You'll have to buy some stakes and wire and make a proper fence.'

The stakes cost half a crown each, and the wire was nearly three pounds a roll. Mr. Hollis bought them, grimly, and handed them over to Ted and Ron to install. Ted had to borrow a sledge-hammer from the builders. That night Ruth was summoned to a serious talk with her father.

'All right, you've got the pony,' he said. 'But it depends on a lot of things, whether we keep it or not. You understand, Ruth, that it's not because I don't want you to have your pleasure. I want it as much as anybody. But it's a hard fact of life that our budget is already stretched to its uttermost limits, and it's only because Ted has started work and things are that much easier that we were able to buy this new house. And the mortgage repayments on this house are going to take all our spare cash for some years to come. In fact,' he added, 'I sometimes wish we'd gone for some old shack down Mud Lane myself – only your mother would never have stood for it. I don't like this millstone round my neck. I wish – oh, but that's beside the point. But you understand what I'm getting at, Ruth? It's not easy, and if we find we have made a mistake, you will just have to take it.'

'Yes, yes,' Ruth said miserably. 'But I will keep him, with my paper round.'

'You're a good kid. But you've just got to know how things are.'

Ruth, quiet and tired, went down into the garden and Fly came up to her, for the first time. She guessed that the change in his life was as much a shock to his system as actually owning a pony was a shock to hers. He stood, and she stroked his neck, and he lipped at her fingers.

'We shall get used to each other,' Ruth said to him. 'And you will be good. You *must* be good,' she added fiercely. She wanted to join the Pony Club and jump round the course at Brierley Hill. She did not want just a rough pony; she wanted a pony that would be obedient to a touch, that would turn on his forehand at a brush of her heel and canter figure-of-eights on the right leg, like a show pony, and jump anything she asked of him, without running out or refusing. Like the ponies in the photographs and diagrams in the horse-books – always beautifully collected, the riders with their knees and elbows in the right places, smiling calmly. She did not know, then, how much she was asking. She only knew that she wanted it, and that she would try. She looked at Fly, at the way he stood, restless, ears pricked up, his rough coat shining over the contours of his muscly shoulders, and she thought, 'I *will* do it. Even if he isn't quiet. I will.' It occurred to her that she could, indeed, start at that very moment, by leading him round the field, and getting him to stop and start when she wanted. Then she remembered that she had not got a halter. 'Not even a halter,' she thought, and all the things she wanted for Fly (expensive items, for all the horse-books agreed that cheap tack was to be deplored) floated in a vision before her eyes, looking like the interior of a saddler's shop, and all her agony came back.

She told herself, 'A halter is only a bit of rope and canvas,' and that evening she made Fly a halter out of some canvas her mother found in her ragbag and a bit of old washing-line that was in the garage. The next day she led Fly round the field, and he was suspicious, but he went, curving his thick mane to the pressure on his nose, snorting delicately. Ruth was entranced.

'He is as good as gold. He did everything I asked him,' she told her mother.

'I thought he just walked round the field. That's what it looked like to me.'

'Yes, that's what I asked him to do.'

Mrs. Hollis gave Ruth a bewildered look, but did not pursue the subject.

Ruth fetched a pencil out of the kitchen drawer and a piece of her mother's writing-paper, and sat down at the kitchen table. She headed her paper 'Things Fly Must Have'.

Underneath she wrote:

> Hay
> Bridle
> Saddle
> Dandy-brush
> Hoof-pick

Round these five items she put a bracket, and printed 'At Once' beside it. Then underneath she wrote 'Things Fly Must Have When Possible'. This was a long list, in three columns, to get it all on the paper:

Headcollar	Hay-net	Curry comb
Rope for tying up	Feed-bowl	Saddle-soap
Body-brush	Bucket	Neatsfoot oil
Shoes	Stable	Pony-nuts

Its length depressed her slightly. The item 'Stable' she wrote without pressing very hard, so that it was nearly invisible. Its ghostliness seemed appropriate. When her father came in she asked him about the saddle and bridle.

'You see, I can't ride him unless I have a saddle and bridle,' she pointed out.

'Yes, I do see,' her father said. His expression was guarded. 'I think the best thing, Ruth, is if we decide on a sum – say, ten pounds – and you can buy whatever it is you want. The day-by-day things will have to come out of your pocket-money, or your paper round, but I will give you the lump sum to buy the saddle and bridle and suchlike. After all, you used your own money to buy the animal with. Ten pounds – oh, say twelve. What do you say to that?'

'Oh, thank you!' Ruth said. 'Thank you very much! That will be wonderful.'

The next morning, in a state of nervous excitement, Ruth cycled eight miles to the nearest saddler's shop.

'I want a saddle and a snaffle bridle, for a pony

about thirteen hands,' she said to the man, who looked politely in her direction.

'Certainly, madam,' he said. 'I'll show you what we have.'

Ruth looked. The saddles were all golden new, pungent with the sour smell of stiff leather, utterly desirable. She stroked one happily.

'Is this a thirteen-hand one?'

'Sixteen inches,' said the man. 'It should fit a thirteen-hand pony. You can try it, and if it's not suitable you can bring it back and try another.'

'I like this one. I'll try this first,' Ruth said.

She chose stirrup irons to go with it, and leathers to put them on, and a white nylon girth. Then she chose an egg-butt snaffle bit, jointed in the middle, and a bridle with a noseband and a plain browband. The man laid all this shining impedimenta on the counter, and Ruth added a dandy-brush and a hoof-pick.

'Is that all, madam?'

'Yes, for now.'

The man totted some figures up on a bit of paper.

'That will be thirty-nine pounds, twelve and eightpence, madam.'

Ruth, having pulled out the twelve pounds in an envelope that her father had given her, looked at him blankly.

'Thirty-nine pounds . . .?' Her voice faded into incredulity.

'Thirty-nine pounds, twelve shillings and eightpence.'

59

Ruth opened her mouth, but no words came out. With a piercing shaft of mathematical clarity, she worked out that the sum the man was quoting her was only seven and fourpence less than she had paid for the pony itself. The man, meanwhile, was looking at her with a severe expression. Ruth looked blankly back at him.

'You – you're – ' She thought, for one sweet moment, that he was playing a joke on her, then she looked at his face again, and knew, quite certainly, that he was not.

'I haven't got thirty-nine pounds, twelve and eightpence,' she said flatly. 'I – I didn't know – ' She looked desperately at the lovely, gleaming pieces all laid out for her on the counter. 'I – I – how much is just the bridle?'

The man totted up the separate parts and said, 'Four pounds, nineteen and sixpence.'

'I'll take the bridle,' Ruth said. She wanted him to hurry, before she burst into tears. His face was tight and sour. He took the lovely saddle away and put it carefully back on the saddle horse, and hung up the girth and the leathers, and put the irons back on the shelf. Then, slowly, he wrapped up the bridle in brown paper and gummed it with plenty of tape. Ruth gave him a five-pound note and he gave her sixpence back.

'Thank you, madam.'

Ruth took her parcel and ran.

That same evening Elizabeth arrived, from the

Council, to live with them. She was a thin, blonde child of six, who took an instant delight at finding a pony in the back garden, and came out to help Ruth while Mrs. Hollis was still talking to the Child Care officer who had brought her. Ruth had been trying to get the bridle on without any success at all. She was just realizing that to accomplish this small task was obviously going to take time and patience. Fly did not, as yet, take kindly to being tied up, so she was obliged to hold him by the halter and at the same time try to put the bridle on. It was plainly impossible. Fly snorted with horror and ran backwards every time she brought the reins up towards his ears, and then she needed both hands to hold him. She realized that, first, she must teach him to stand tied up; then, gradually get him used to the look of the bridle, and the feeling of having the reins passed over his head. Now, having attempted too much, she could see that he was frightened by the new tack.

She stood holding him, stroking his neck, and hung the bridle over the fence out of the way.

'All right, silly. We'll do it very slowly, and you'll get used to it.'

At this point Elizabeth came up and said, 'Can I have a ride?'

Ruth looked at her with interest.

'Are you Elizabeth?' They had learned about the imminent arrival of a child called Elizabeth the day before, when a woman from the Child Care Department had called.

'Yes. Can I have a ride? What's your name?'

'Ruth.'

'Can I have a ride?'

Elizabeth, Ruth decided, was so skinny she must weigh just about nothing at all. Acting on the moment's impulse, she leaned down.

'Put your arms round my neck.'

One hand holding Fly's halter, with the other she scooped up the eager Elizabeth and slid her gently on to Fly's back. He tossed his head and twitched his shoulder muscles as if an insect was worrying him, but otherwise made no move. Elizabeth patted him.

'He's good.'

Ruth grinned.

'He's *wonderful!*' she cried. Had ever 'backing' a pony been so easy? she wondered.

'Go,' said Elizabeth.

'No, not tonight,' Ruth said. She put her arm up and lifted the child down again. 'Tomorrow you can sit on him again. Nobody has ever sat on him before. You are the first person, in all the world, to sit on this pony.'

It was a great privilege, in her eyes, and Elizabeth took it as such, and opened her eyes very wide.

'And again tomorrow?'

'Yes.'

The next day Fly walked round the field with Elizabeth on his back, but it was over a month before Ruth was able to get the bridle on him. It was a week before she could pass the reins up over his head without his running back and looking horror-struck, and another week before she managed to get the bit between his teeth.

'The books say roll the bit in brown sugar. Or jam,' Ruth said to Elizabeth. 'Go and ask Mummy for some brown sugar.'

Elizabeth disappeared at the gallop and came back with a bowl of sugar and a pot of strawberry jam. Ruth took a dollop of jam out with a finger, wiped it over the bit, and rolled it in the sugar for good measure. Then she held it on the palm of her hand and approached Fly, who was watching with great interest, tied to the fence by a halter. Ruth put the reins over his head, held the headstall in her right hand, in the approved manner, and put the bit under his nose hopefully. Fly clenched his teeth hard. Ruth, feeling very sticky, pushed the bit against his teeth, gently, but most of the jam and sugar now seemed to be on her rather than on the bit. Somehow, Fly managed to take several crafty licks, and still the bit was not between his teeth. The bridle was sticky all over. Elizabeth was sitting on the grass, eating the jam by scooping it out on a finger, as demonstrated by Ruth.

Ruth flung the bridle down crossly.

'Oh, he's so stubborn!' she said. She looked at Fly, tied to the fence, and he looked back at her. He arched his neck, licked his lips curiously, and pawed the ground with a neat round hoof. He would stand tied up if she stayed near him, but if she went away he would pull back and whinny and churn about.

Ruth would tie him up and potter about where he could see her, or disappear round the side of the garage just for a minute or two. Gradually she persuaded herself that he was improving. Once he pulled the fence out by its roots – Ted's fence – and once the halter broke, but, these crises apart, progress in this direction was fairly satisfactory. But not with the bridle.

'You need a dozen hands,' Ruth said. She picked up the jammy thing and considered it. Then, experimentally, she unbuckled the bit from one side of the headstall. Then the other. She went over to Fly, and put the bridle on over his ears. She pulled his forelock out over the browband, and did up the throatlash. Then she fetched the bit and buckled it on, on one side.

'Fetch the saucer of sugar,' she commanded the willing Elizabeth. 'Hold it up. Higher. That's right.'

With both hands to work with, Ruth eased the bit into the saucer of sugar and slipped it between Fly's teeth before he knew what she was about. She buckled it on to the other side, and stood back, triumphant. Fly mouthed the strange thing on his tongue, bending to it, tossing his head, curious but not frightened. Ruth was elated, warm with achievement. She stood smiling, utterly happy.

'How's the nag?'

Ted's friend, Ron, having called into the kitchen for some rags, paused on his way back to the garage, wiping his oily hands.

'New bridle, then?' he remarked.

'Yes. I bought it a fortnight ago, and this is the first time I've managed to get it on.'

'Sets you back, horse gear,' Ron said. 'Worse than parts for the bike.'

'Oh yes!' Ruth had given up the idea of ever riding on a saddle, since she had discovered that even second-hand saddles were generally more than the whole sum her father had given her. She looked at Ron with interest, wondering how he came to know about the price of what he called horse gear. Nobody in her family knew about it, and she had not dared to tell her father how much he would have to give her if she was to have her saddle. Encouraged by Ron's interest, she told him about her experience in the saddler's.

'Cor, stone me! I know that bloke. Calls you sir. I bet he called you madam, till he found you hadn't any cash?'

'Yes, he did!'

'Sew their saddles with gold thread, at that place,' Ron said. 'Mind you, new ones are never cheap. Lot of work in a saddle.'

'Yes, but what shall I do? I daren't tell my father how much they cost!'

Ron considered, pursing his lips. He had a thin, amiable, rather spotty face, a lot of untidy hair and, like Ted, smelt of motor bikes. He wore filthy jeans and a black leather jacket with various badges stuck to it and had the same sort of bike as Ted, a twin-cylinder 650 c.c. B.S.A. After they had spent a week polishing their camshafts, they used to ride out and have races along the nearest suitable stretch of road. At week-ends, when they weren't tinkering, they would ride out with their gang. When Mrs. Hollis complained about Ted's obsession, her husband would point out that all his friends were pleasant, well-mannered boys, he was never bored, did not break the law (excepting, on occasion, the 70 m.p.h. speed limit) and wasn't it better than girls? Mrs. Hollis would agree, dubiously.

For all these reasons, Ruth was surprised that Ron knew about saddles – apart from bike saddles.

'Reckon I could find you a saddle,' Ron said.

Ruth stared at him, frightened to say anything.

'There used to be one in an old shed, up Mr. Lacey's place. Pony saddle it was. I remember seeing it, when I used to cut his grass. The lawn-mower was in the shed, and the saddle was stuck up in the rafters. I used to live in Wychwood, you know. Down Mud Lane. Two along from Mr. Lacey. That's why I used to cut his grass.' He looked speculatively at Fly. 'Nice pony.'

'Yes.' Ruth let her breath out.

'When I've finished tonight we'll go along, if you like, and see if it's still there.'

'Tonight?'

'Mmm. When I'm through.'

'Oh!' Not only was the bridle actually in Fly's mouth, but on the very same day it seemed as if she was going to acquire a saddle. To Ruth, after several days of getting nowhere at all, it was as if the day was charmed, bewitched. It was a sort of week described in the horoscopes as: 'Try to be patient. The beginning of the week will be full of minor irritations. But Thursday promises to be an outstanding day, bringing good news and the fulfilment of a long-desired ambition.'

'About an hour,' Ron said.

'Yes.'

Ruth danced back to Fly, still mouthing his bit in exactly the way the books said was to be desired. She hugged him round the neck, smelling the heavenly scent of his thick mane in her nostrils.

'Oh, you are lovely! I adore you! You are *good*!'

'Do you want any more jam?' Elizabeth asked.

'Not now.'

'Can I lick the sugar?'

'Yes. Tomorrow, perhaps, you can ride on a proper saddle!'

'Can we use more sugar and jam?'

'Yes, if it helps him take the bit.'

'I like doing it like that.'

Ruth, having very carefully taken the bridle off, giving Fly time to drop the bit, and not pulling it against his teeth, untied him and took off the halter. He walked away across the bare grass, blowing out through his nostrils. Ruth watched him, glowing with a deep satisfaction.

Her deep satisfaction was shattered when her mother saw the state Elizabeth was in, which Ruth had not noticed, but, after a slight unpleasantness, she was able to escape and join the boys in the front drive. Soon she was up on Ron's pillion and they were scrabbling and roaring through the pot-holes of Mud Lane. The lane, overhung with elms, led down to the creek, and a few tatty weatherboarded cottages sat back from it behind overgrown hedges. Mr. Lacey lived in the last one, just before the lane degenerated into a field track, and the marsh grass took over from the last decaying orchard.

'I reckon no one's cut the old boy's grass since I did it last,' Ron commented, when he stopped the bike on the rutted garden path. Ruth's eyes were already straying to the conglomeration of old barns and sheds behind the cottage. 'What a nice place,' she was thinking. 'Like Mr. Marks's. A "me" place.' She could not take to their smart new house, however hard she tried, when she compared it with the romantic wilderness of Mr. Lacey's abode.

Mr. Lacey came out and recognized Ron, and, after some few minutes of reminiscence and inquiry, he issued a very satisfactory invitation to 'Root out what you please, lad. It's all rubbish.' Ron led the way to one of the sheds, skirting banks of stinging-nettles.

'It was this one, as I remember it.'

The shed was gloomy and full of dust drifting through shafts of the late evening sunlight. Ruth crossed both her fingers and prayed silently, gazing into the dust: 'Please, God, let it be there.'

'Ah!' said Ron.

He was climbing up on an old packing-case, reaching up. 'Look, here we are.' There was a shower of cobwebs and woodrot. Ruth sneezed. Ron swung down and held out his prize, smiling. 'Look, it's no showpiece, but it ought to fit.'

Once, many many years ago, Ruth thought, it had been a good saddle. She took it gingerly, afraid it might crumble in her hands. The leather was dry and cracked, the lining split and spewing stuffing. There were leathers and irons, but the leathers were cracked by the buckles beyond repair, and the irons were rusty.

'No girth,' said Ron, 'and the leathers are no good. But it'll come up all right, I'd say. Neatsfoot oil is what it wants. And the lining renewed, and new stuffing. It won't cost you a fortune, though. What do you think?'

'Oh, if it fits . . .' Ruth, examining, began to see that there was hope. She wiped the seat clear of dust with her elbow, and thought she could see the glimmer of a real saddle's rich shine. In her mind she saw it. She longed to start work on it. 'It's wonderful. If it fits – and it looks as if it should – I am sure it could be made all right.' She was full of gratitude again. She hugged the saddle. She saw herself sitting in it, well down, confident, smiling (as in a diagram captioned 'A good general-purpose seat') waiting to go down to the first jump at Brierley Hill. This was her biggest problem solved. She rode home behind Ron, the saddle on one arm, dreaming.

5

THE GIRL AT 'THE PLACE'

Mr. Hollis went down to see Mr. Lacey about the saddle, and came back looking absent-minded.

'Nice place he's got down there. I mean, it's ramshackle, but – well . . .' He hesitated, considered. 'You could do things with a place like that.'

'Oh, yes!' Ruth agreed avidly. 'All those old sheds you could turn into stables, and all that orchard and field and – '

'Oh, you – !' Her father laughed. But Ruth knew that he was thinking that he would rather have a place like Mr. Lacey's than 'South View' on the Sunnyside Estate. 'There's nothing to do in a new house,' he said, as he settled down to watch the television. Ruth, watching Fly-by-Night searching for grass in the bare plot they called a field, longed for what she called a Lacey-house, with lots of Lacey-grass.

'He'll starve here,' she said to Ron, watching Fly-by-Night. It was summer, and the grass was growing fast, but in the field Fly-by-Night ate it as fast as it grew, and trod it down flat: the field was too small. His summer coat was through, but he was ribby.

'You ought to ask the estate man if you can use the field behind,' Ron said. 'They're going to build on it some time, but not yet awhile. It's doing nothing. Ask him.'

Ruth's eyes opened wide with amazement. She had never thought such a thing possible, and had worried miserably over her lack of grass. She had been taking Fly out in the evenings along the lanes, to eat the verges. She had sat in the cow-parsley, holding the end of the halter, watching him, and worrying. His ribs showing made him look very much a forty-pound pony. On the end of his halter he ate ravenously, pulling at the lush grass, his thick tail switching. Sometimes, when she sat in the grass, she thought she had never worried so much in her life as since she had bought Fly.

'Do you ride him now?' Ron asked.

'Well . . . sort of.'

Ruth looked at the ground, uncomfortably. She had admitted it to no one, but riding Fly-by-Night so far had been a miserable experience. She had cleaned up the saddle and bought a new girth and new leathers, and had accustomed Fly to the feel of it, and to being girthed up. She had got him to accept the bridle, at last, without resorting to jam, and had taught him to stand still while she mounted him. She had then expected to ride off, walking, trotting and cantering to order. But this was where Fly-by-Night's ideas and her own parted company.

'The trouble is, I can't ride,' she said to Ron.

'Well, you'll soon learn, won't you?' Ron said.

'I suppose so.'

'You mean he bucks you off or something?'

'No . . . not really . . .'

It was difficult to explain just what happened when she rode Fly. Every time it was different, so she never knew what to expect. She had got into the habit of leading him down the road and along Mud Lane until she was on her own, in a quiet place, with just the hedges and the trees for company. Then she would mount him.

In her little green book it said, 'He must be encouraged to walk freely forward . . .' According to the book, Ruth would squeeze with her legs and give him plenty of rein, and under her breath, she would pray, 'Please, God, make him do it.' Sometimes Fly would go backwards. The more she squeezed with her legs, the more eagerly would he back, until brought up short by a hedge, or by nearly falling into a ditch. But if he was in what Ruth thought of as his 'freely forward mood' he would leap off as soon as she eased her reins, and continue at as fast a pace as possible. When he did this Ruth had to concentrate on not falling off. She held on to his mane with both hands, and when she thought she had got her balance she would bravely let go to take a pull at the reins. When she did this, Fly would poke his nose in the air and gallop faster than ever. Gaining courage, and getting more desperate, Ruth would pull again, and then again, with all her strength, and the wild progress would generally finish by Fly swerving suddenly to one side or the other, pitching Ruth off over his shoulder. He would then immediately settle down to grazing, and Ruth would lie in the grass, trying not to cry. Not through fear or pain, but with despair.

When, on the rare occasions Fly-by-Night chose to progress at a forward walk, he would proceed on a meandering course to which Ruth's aids would make no difference at all. He would gaze all about him, as if in astonishment at the landscape, and frequently shy violently at nothing at all, so that Ruth often fell off. The only really satisfactory thing about Fly-by-Night, she often thought, was the fact that he did not run away when she fell off. He always started to graze, without even looking for a better bit of grass than that under his feet. Because he's so hungry, Ruth thought.

'It takes a lot of patience, training animals,' Ron said. 'Horses, dogs – people think it can be done overnight. And it can't.'

'No.'

'Training him would be a lot easier if you had another pony to go with him. One that knew. Then this old fellow would just follow along. There's a girl at "The Place" got a pony. She's about your age. Why don't you go and see if she'd give you a hand?'

' "The Place"?'

'Big house opposite the village hall. Pymm, they're called. Father's in beer. Very rich.'

'Oh.' Ron's monosyllabic description was slightly off-putting. She knew 'The Place', but did not know a pony lived there. It was an old house surrounded by belts of thick trees, with wrought-iron gates and a fake gas-lamp.

'You ought to arrange your paper round, so that you can go there. Then you'd meet them. If you're afraid just to walk in, like.'

Ruth looked at Ron admiringly. 'You do have good ideas! I could try that.'

'Oh, I've got it up here.' Ron tapped his head.

'And the field, too. That's a wonderful idea.'

Ron grinned. 'The trouble with you is you don't see the funny side. You make it all matter too much.'

'That's what Daddy says.'

'Looking at you, worrying, no one would say owning that pony was a great joy to you.'

But Ruth, worry or no, could not imagine not owning Fly. She tried, and she thought of all the things she need not worry about, but the picture was one of such bleakness, such a void, an abyss of nothingness, that she could not even consider it.

'It's hard now, and I know I get in despair, but when I think back I can see that I am making a little bit of progress. So as time goes on it will get better and better. Don't you think so?' Ruth wanted reassurance.

'Should do,' Ron said in his amiable way.

'It's so slow, because I'm not very good. I know what I should do, but it's not always very easy to do it.'

'You're a stickler, I'll give you that.'

'The books make it sound so easy.'

'Well, same as books telling you how to take down a motor bike. It's easy, if you just read about it.'

Ruth longed to know the girl Pymm, whose father was in beer. The thought of a friend, a knowing, horsy girl-friend, who would understand her trials and despairs and rare glows of achievement, whom she could ride with and learn with, was a wonderful, warm anticipation. Ruth had made mere acquaintances in the village school, and none was so attractive as to keep her away from Fly-by-Night. Nobody at school rode. But next term, in September, she would be going to the Comprehensive at Hanningham, six miles away, and she thought, with luck, she might meet somebody horsy there.

Fired with Ron's inspirations, she swopped paper rounds by offering the boy who did 'The Place' a shilling a week, and called on the builder to ask if she could use his field. He said, 'Yes, do, dearie. No responsibility taken if he breaks a leg, though, tell your daddy.' He was on the telephone at the time, and spoke to her between conversations to head office, and what meant so much to Ruth meant obviously so little to him that Ruth came out of his office dazed by the ways of the world. That night she cleared a gap into the field and Fly-by-Night galloped through, tail swirling. The field was about an acre in size, with a good hedge all round it. The grass came up to the pony's belly, brushing his thick thighs with its powdery flowers, and Fly grazed avidly. Ruth watched him, filled with the warm happiness that was her reward when things went right.

'Oh, you will get fat and shine,' she said to Fly. 'And be good.'

The bare garden with its ugly bumps and pot-holes and dock leaves and thistles disgusted her.

'Fancy thinking it was good enough,' she thought.

Elizabeth ran down the garden to meet her and Ruth swung her round by the hands. She liked Elizabeth. Now, when everything was right, with Elizabeth laughing and twirling round till they were both giddy, Ruth could see herself jumping round the Hunter Trials course at Brierley Hill, and Fly-by-Night galloping, ears pricked up, and herself riding beautifully, like Peter McNair. 'Oh, Peter McNair,' she thought with a sudden wrench, 'you could show me how to make Fly walk and trot and canter in obedient circles!' She put Elizabeth down, and thought, 'I must find this Pymm girl. I haven't the nerve to go to the McNairs for advice.'

Delivering the papers, it was a week before she set eyes on a Pymm, linger as she might. It was Mrs. Pymm, and she did not look even faintly horsy, as Ruth had hoped, but more like an actress, with dyed blonde hair and tight pink trousers. Ruth was decidedly taken aback and stood on the doorstep clutching the *Daily Mirror* and the *Financial Times* until Mrs. Pymm put out a hand for them.

'Oh, s – sorry.'

Mrs. Pymm gave her a disapproving stare, took her papers and disappeared inside without a word.

Four more days passed and Ruth saw no one but an aristocratic Boxer dog. She felt that Ron's idea was not so brilliant after all, and lost interest. In a few more days she would start at the new school. It was September, warm and golden, and she was alone with her problems.

But when she went up the drive of the Pymm residence the following Sunday morning, a girl was coming out of the front door with the Boxer dog. She was about thirteen, but very elegant, with long pale hair, a pale, sad face, honey-coloured jeans and a white blouse. Ruth was instantly conscious of her feet in their dog-proof gum boots and her muddy jeans and shirt, and shifted her paper-sack nervously on her shoulder. The girl made no attempt to communicate, coolly staring, so Ruth was forced to take the initiative, or for ever regret a lost opportunity. Hot with embarrassment, she fumbled over the papers and said, 'Have you got – er, I mean, someone – someone told me you've got a pony?'

'Yes,' said the girl, not smiling.

'Do you – you keep it here?'

'Yes.'

'I – I've got one, too.'

'Oh.'

'The thing is, mine's not – not broken in, really. I – I – ' Ruth could feel herself getting hotter and hotter as the Pymm girl went on staring without her expression showing the remotest interest. Only for the sake of Fly-by-Night's salvation could she have risked such an ordeal. She finished desperately,

'I wondered if – if – oh, it's just that I wondered if you had a pony, you might be able to help me.'

Afterwards she realized that an appeal for help was the best way she could have thought of for melting the Pymm sophistication. Even this cool girl was not averse to accepting the role Ruth's plea accorded to her. She noticeably unfroze, said, 'Oh,' again, but quite pleasantly this time, and added, 'My pony's round the back. Do you want to see it?'

'Oh, yes, please!'

Ruth dropped the paper-sack on the front doorstep, quivering with excitement. She had never seen round the back of 'The Place', for the house was hemmed about with ancient shrubberies and big trees in such a way as to give no vistas to the casual visitor. But, on following the girl round the far corner of the house, Ruth was pleasantly surprised to see a big garden reveal itself, all shaved lawn and immaculate rosebeds, and, beyond it, a paddock ringed round with old elms. There was a garage for two cars, a lot of gravelled space, and a rose-brick building that was presumably the old stables, for the Pymm girl led the way towards it.

'It's in here.'

A loose-box door looked out over the yard. Ruth went to the open top-door and looked in. 'It' was a grey mare, old enough to be, in fact, pure white. She looked to Ruth to be an Arab, with her beautiful arched neck and wide-apart eyes. A fine silky mane fell down her shoulder, catching the light as she turned her head; Ruth saw the wide nostrils flicker, the eyes shining. The mare, standing just under four-teen hands, was as lovely an animal as Ruth ever expected to lay eyes on. She gazed at her in speechless admiration.

The Pymm girl stood by the door, her face showing nothing. Ruth gathered herself together, trying not to appear imbecile. She felt herself bursting with hot enthusiasm, but the Pymm girl's unexcitement curbed her.

'Oh, she's beautiful!'

'Yes.'

How could the girl, Ruth wondered, not rave with happiness at owning such a celestial creature? But the face showed no pride or joy, only a slightly sulky boredom. Ruth was baffled.

'Is she an Arab?'

'Yes.'

'What's her name?'

'Milky Way.' The girl grimaced. 'I call her Milly.'

Ruth was shocked. Milly . . . not even Milky. 'Have you had her long?'

'Three years.'

'Do you show her?'

'Sometimes. She always wins. She cost seven hundred pounds, so she should.'

Ruth was silenced. She thought of scruffy little Fly-by-Night, her forty-pound pony, and her problems. A hard knot of obstinacy stiffened her; she had not come to be awed.

'If – if you go for a ride, sometimes, perhaps – perhaps we could go together?'

'I usually ride in the field. But I could come with you, I suppose.'

'I ride down Mud Lane and in the fields down there. I live on the new estate. I shall go down there this afternoon if – if you want to come?'

'I'm going out all day. But I could come this evening, I suppose.' The girl's eyes were a pale yellow-green, wary, slightly suspicious. Ruth did not think she ever smiled. Ruth said, 'Would about six be all right? If you want to come?'

'All right, I'll call for you. Where do you live?'

'South View. It's on the left. Seven houses along.'

Ruth finished her paper round and ran home with great leaps, being Fly-by-Night doing the Hunter Trials. Ron and Ted were sitting in the drive, poring over bits of motor bike.

'I've done it! I've met her! She's coming riding with me!'

'Help! Two of them!' Ted moaned.

'What's she like?' Ron asked.

'Well . . .' Ruth hesitated. 'I don't really know, yet. She's queer.'

'You should have a lot in common, then,' Ted said.

'She's a lot queerer than me. I didn't find out what her name is. Do you know it?'

'Pearl,' Ron said.

'Pearl Pymm? It doesn't go.'

'No. It was a joke in the village – Mrs. Pymm being mother-of-Pearl, I mean.'

'Her pony is gorgeous. She said it cost seven hundred pounds.'

'Only six hundred and sixty more than yours,' said Ted.

'Peanuts,' said Ron.

Ruth got Fly-by-Night ready in plenty of time. She tied him to the fence and groomed him with her dandy-brush (that and a hoof-pick were the only grooming tools she possessed). His winter coat was just beginning to come through, giving him a richer look. The bay shone with the health of a ripe horse-chestnut, and the white hair was silvery as Milky Way's own. Ruth stood back and looked at him, the pride of possession upon her. He jerked on his halter and looked back, all impatience and scorn, his little ears pricked up, one round hoof pawing at the turf. His hoofs were getting long and broken, Ruth noticed, with a pang of anxiety. She had put off getting him shod, because of the money, and because he did very little work on hard surfaces, and also because he was bad at picking his feet up and she was afraid a blacksmith would be impatient with the pair of them for their incompetence. But she thought she would not be able to put off getting him some attention much longer. 'I will ask Pearl,' she decided, and the thought gave her a pleasant shock at knowing, at last, someone to ask.

'The Pearly Queen's arrived.' Ted came round the corner of the garage, grinning widely.

'Oh, help!' Ruth felt panicky, reaching for the bridle that hung on the fence.

'She said she'd wait outside.'

'Go and tell her I won't be a minute.' Fly-by-Night, sensing Ruth's urgency, swung about and trod on Ruth's foot. She swore at him, tears of agony blurring her vision. 'Oh, you beast, you beast! Why aren't you – you – *elegant* like Milky Way?'

She scrabbled for the girths, and Fly turned his head and gave her a sharp nip on the bottom. 'I hate you!' Ruth cried out. 'Oh, you are beastly!' But he followed her meekly enough round the side of the house and into the front garden.

At the sight of Pearl on Milky Way, both Ruth and Fly-by-Night stopped short. If Fly was surprised by the sight of the white mare, Ruth was no less astonished at the vision that was its rider. Pearl only lacked a Union Jack on her breast to be fit for competing in the Olympics: she wore an immaculate black jacket, snow-white breeches fitting like tights, and black boots. Her hair flowed out from under her hat in a pale cascade. She sat indolently, holding the mare's head in so that Milky Way flexed her neck uncomfortably, flicking white drops of foam on to her chest. Ruth felt her mouth drop open, and made an effort to recover herself. But before she could say anything, Fly-by-Night let out a shrill whinny and plunged forward with such force that she was nearly lifted off her feet.

'Idiot!' She was out of the gate and on to the pavement, Fly churning wildly in circles, letting out frantic whinnies. Milky Way backed away cautiously and Pearl stared politely. Ruth could only hold on, while Fly's hoofs slithered across the concrete road. She could scarcely hold him and felt herself flung about like a dead mouse with a cat. Her hat came down over her eyes, blotting out the vision of Pearl's derisory snigger. Ruth wished she were dead.

'Here, here, you daft pony.' It was Ron who came to her rescue, his oily hand and wiry strength pulling Fly to a heaving standstill in the middle of the road. The pony was shaking all over, and still letting out high-pitched whinnies which brought all the neighbours out into their front gardens to see what was going on. Ruth felt herself going crimson.

Ron said, 'I'll hold him. Get on. Then I'll lead him for a bit, till he settles. Don't worry.'

'Are you sure it's all right?'

'Yes, of course. He's only excited, after being on his own all this time. I won't let go.'

Ruth scrambled into the saddle and fumbled for her stirrups. 'You go in front,' Ron said to Pearl. 'He should follow all right.'

Milky Way moved off, and Fly-by-Night was pulling madly to get behind her. Ruth, hot with shame, sat grimly down in the saddle, her fingers clenched on the reins. She was frightened, not only of what Fly might do, but of what Pearl was thinking. Fly-by-Night's bare hoofs scuttered over the concrete. Ron, in his oily jeans and leather jacket, a spanner sticking out of his back pocket, hung on to the pony's noseband, forcing obedience. They cavorted down the slope and across the main village street, then Pearl turned Milky Way into the quiet opening that was Mud Lane.

'Down here?'

Ruth nodded, sticky with apprehension. 'It's all right,' she said to Ron. 'I'll manage.'

'He'll settle,' Ron said somewhat dubiously. He turned and looked at her, and smiled. 'Okay?'

'Mmm.'

Pearl was waiting, watching Ron distastefully. She held the lovely Milky Way on a very tight rein, even when she was walking, and Ruth began to wonder if, after all, Pearl knew a great deal more than she did.

'If you walk on,' she called to Pearl, 'he should follow now.'

'What's the matter with him?' Pearl asked. Still holding the mare on a tight rein, she kicked her with her heels to make her walk on, and the mare did as best she could, over-bent and uncomfortable. Fly-by-Night bounded after her and jiggled along, pressed up close to her quarters, giving little eager whinnies. Milky Way was too well mannered to kick, but laid back her ears. Ruth concentrated on sitting well down in the saddle, ready for a buck or a shy, prepared for the worst. A part of her mind, at the same time, was thinking of the picture the two of them made, like a pony-book photograph captioned in big letters: 'BAD'. Amidst all her anxiety, this part of her was already grieving, because she could see already that Pearl did not *know*. She was no female equivalent of Peter McNair, which was the role in which Ruth had cast her. In fact, if she had had Milky Way for three years, and still rode her at a walk on a rein so tight that the poor mare could hardly get her head past a vertical position, Ruth guessed that her ignorance was of the permanent kind, an ignorance in her own character, which did not permit her to admit that she did not know anything. This revelation was so great a blow to Ruth that she almost forgot to worry about Fly-by-Night.

'What's wrong with him?' Pearl asked again.

'Nothing's *wrong* with him,' Ruth said. 'He's not used to being ridden in company, that's all. I'm still breaking him in.' If you could call it breaking in, she added to herself. She felt herself wallowing once more in this mire of frustration that was habitually overtaking her, because nothing went according to the books, and the books, for all their value, had no answer for this abyss that existed inside her which was lack of practical experience. Half of her concentration was always fixed on keeping her insecure seat – on herself, in fact. She sighed deeply, almost groaning.

In spite of her fears, Fly-by-Night did not disgrace himself. Anxious to keep as close to Milky Way as possible, he did not gallop headlong across the fields, nor refuse to go at all, for Milky Way was always moving at an impeccable pace just in front of his nose. He followed her avidly, and although it was plain that his schoolboy ardour annoyed her, she did not show her feelings beyond laying back her ears, because she was so well mannered. To Ruth, the ride was memorable more for the behaviour of Milky Way than the behaviour of Fly-by-Night.

Pearl rode badly. She sat well back on the saddle with her feet thrust forward, and held on by the reins. She had Milky Way in a double bridle, and the mare was cramped with discomfort. In spite of the difficulties Pearl provided for her, the mare's manners were faultless. She had obviously been expertly schooled; she moved beautifully, and obeyed Pearl's ham-handed aids with a willingness to please that roused a great pity in Ruth. Ruth could see that the mare would handle on a gossamer rein and quicken to the merest suggestion from the leg, yet Pearl pulled her about with her impatient, yellow-gloved hands and banged on her sides with her shining black boots as if her lovely Arab were some seaside donkey. And the trusting animal docility with which Milky Way accepted this gross treatment grieved Ruth. The mare had been so well schooled that it never crossed her mind to retaliate. She was all anxiety to obey, her dark eyes fretting and unhappy.

Conversation between the two riders was limited by Fly-by-Night's excitement. Ruth had to concentrate, and Pearl maintained the rather superior, cool reserve that Ruth began to realize was her normal manner.

'Do you belong to the Pony Club?' Ruth asked her when Fly chose to go demurely alongside for a few moments.

'Heavens, no,' Pearl replied, with such scorn that Ruth did not dare ask her reasons. 'I hunt,' she added, without enthusiasm.

'She doesn't seem to be interested in anything much,' Ruth told Ron when she got home. Pearl baffled her. 'Not even riding. Only she did say she would come out with me again. So that's something.'

'You mean she's horrible, but you'll put up with her for the sake of your pony's education?'

'Something like that, I suppose. Not horrible, but – oh, queer. She seems so bored. And her poor pony. It's so lovely, and she's so – so unfeeling with her.'

'She probably rides because it's the thing to do. And she'll come out with you because she's lonely. Half her boredom is being lonely probably. She never went to the village school, because it's free, and now she goes to some tin-pot private school somewhere miles away, so she doesn't know anybody in the village.'

'She doesn't know much – she's not horsy, in spite of having a pony. In fact, I think she – she's worse than me.'

'Good heavens!' Ron looked appalled, teasing.

'But it was a good idea, all the same. Your idea. I should think Fly will stop being so funny if I go out with them a few times. I mean, I can stand her if he improves. She might improve, too, come to that.'

'Or you might meet someone at the new school.'

'Oh, school!' Ruth grimaced.

That was tomorrow.

6

SLOW PROGRESS

When Ruth went to the new school she quickly discovered that there were no depths of horsy talent waiting to be plumbed among her new classmates. Four admitted to having ridden, one on a thirty-year-old Shetland pony, one on a heifer and two on donkeys. But on her fourth day at school, standing patiently in assembly while prayers were read, pretending she was Fly-by-Night lining up in the show-ring, mouthing an imaginary bit, she was startled by the sight of the boy who stepped up beside the headmaster to read the lesson (a dreaded task that she had learnt was liable to fall on any pupil at any time, forecast only by a list pinned up on the notice-board every Monday morning). The boy in his navy-blue blazer, red tie, and dark-grey trousers was fair and stocky, and spoke in a flat, untroubled voice which roused Ruth out of her dream. It was Peter McNair.

It was, of course, perfectly natural that he should attend the same school as herself, but the possibility of it had never entered her head. She felt almost stunned by the shock of his incredible appearance before her very eyes, reading the Bible: quite the last occupation she had ever envisaged him at. But after a few days, having become used to seeing him about, she realized that his presence at school was as remote as it had been at the Hunter Trials. He was in the form above her, which mixed with her own class scarcely at all, and, as a boy in a clique of boys, he was hardly likely to want to make friends with a *girl*. From a few discreet inquiries, Ruth discovered that nobody knew that he rode at all. He was a quiet boy whose only claim to fame seemed to be a second in the 100-metre back-stroke in last July's swimming gala. And his great passion was acknowledged to be butterflies. '*Butterflies?*' Ruth was astonished again.

'Oh, he knows everything about butterflies. And moths.'

At home Ruth said to Ron, 'He knows everything about schooling ponies, too, but how can I get to talk to him?'

'You'll have to get interested in butterflies. And moths,' Ron said.

Ruth made a face. 'That's not one of your very best ideas. I'm just not interested in butterflies. Or moths.'

'I thought it was rather a good idea myself.'

'Yes, well, I should think it is a very interesting subject, if it wasn't that I haven't got time to think about anything else. You see, there's homework now, and it's getting dark earlier. And there aren't any butterflies in the winter anyway.'

'A good point,' said Ron. 'The Pearly Queen's a dead loss, I take it?'

'Oh, Pearl . . .' Ruth sighed.

Having got involved with Pearl was as much trouble as it was help. Milky Way's presence on rides had certainly got Fly-by-Night steadied down and moving in a less erratic manner, but Ruth now worried more about Milky Way than she did about Fly-by-Night.

'She's such a sweet-natured pony, and the way Pearl treats her is awful. And in spite of being pulled about and jabbed in the mouth and completely muddled, she is so anxious to please all the time. It's that that makes me feel so miserable. If it was Fly, he'd buck Pearl off, or turn round and bite her on the ankle like he does me sometimes, or roll on her or something. He'd stick up for himself. But poor sweet Milky Way just tries all the time, and I get sad.'

'I suppose that's what you pay seven hundred pounds for,' Ron said. 'Not to get rolled on, and your ankles bitten.'

'Oh, yes. She's been most beautifully schooled, and she still remembers it. She always leads on the right leg, and never refuses a jump, and she'll do beautiful forehand turns at gates all off her own bat; but Pearl's no idea. I get ever so miserable, thinking of poor Milky Way.'

'That's daft,' Ron said. 'She'll be well fed, and comfortable most of the time.'

'Yes, I know. She's well fed all right. Stuffed with corn, yet she never gets above herself. But sometimes she goes lame, and Pearl takes no notice.'

'What's wrong with her?'

'I don't know. I told Pearl she ought to get the vet, but she says it's nothing, because it wears off after a bit. Which is true. There's nothing wrong you can see.'

'You've got enough to worry about with your own horse, without worrying about someone else's,' Ron said severely. 'You're a born worrier.'

'Yes. I'm worried about buying hay now. And getting his feet done. Money.'

'Oh, we're all worried about that.'

Ruth knew that her father was worried about it, too. The mortgage on the new house was a large strain on the family finances, and Ruth was frightened to ask for anything for Fly in case her father said he would have to go. She had to manage on her paper-round money. By the end of September the field was so bare that she had to start buying hay, and she soon found that Fly could eat a bale in under a week. When she went up to 'The Place' she would see the gardener, who fed Milky Way, measuring out chaff, oats, bran and pony-nuts, and she longed to be able to do the same. 'Not, of course, that it's necessary,' she told herself. For she knew that Milky Way was grossly overfed for the amount of work she did. But she would have liked a bag of pony-nuts. Half a hundredweight was over a pound to buy. She spent two shillings a week on rough carrots, and scrounged stale toast, and cabbage leaves. When the blacksmith visited 'The Place' to shoe Milky Way, Ruth plucked up her courage and led Fly-by-Night round, and the smith pared his hoofs down for ten shillings.

'Nice l'il feet 'e's got. 'E'll do without shoes if you don't do much with 'im. Just around the fields.'

But Ruth knew he would need shoes when he jumped the Brierley Hill Hunter Trials course. She would have to join the Pony Club, too. She found that this cost a pound. She could not spare a pound, or Fly-by-Night would have starved. 'I'll ask for it for a Christmas present,' she decided. 'Every Christmas.' But if she joined the Pony Club she would have to have jodhpurs, instead of jeans. 'I won't worry about that now,' she said to herself, turning over restlessly in bed. Sometimes when she lay there, watching the deep, wintering sky all rashed over with faint stars, she would hear Fly-by-Night whinny down the field. The lonely cry would come on the draught through the bedroom window, with the smell of old grass and ploughed earth, and it stabbed Ruth to the heart.

'He's lonely,' she said to herself, eaten with remorse. She could see him, standing in the frosty dark, whinnying to the stars. Sometimes, if she listened hard and the night was still, she would hear Milky Way reply from her open half-door at 'The Place'. 'Lots of people keep just one horse,' Ruth said to herself, trying to be sensible. She always skipped the pages in the pony-books that started, 'The horse is a gregarious animal . . .' It hurt to think that Fly-by-Night was deprived of something essential to his happiness. 'It's daft,' Ron said, 'to worry.' Ruth thought of Ron's sense, and wished she had as much. 'Don't be *sentimental*,' she told herself. She hated sentimentality towards animals, as opposed to sense, but thought that she verged on it herself at times. If she *knew* more, she thought. She would learn at the Pony Club, and meet people who knew, but she could not take Fly-by-Night to the Pony Club until he could be trusted to do as she wanted. She groaned, turning over again in bed so that the eiderdown fell on the floor.

Ruth guessed that Ron had been right when he had said that Pearl was lonely, for Ruth, having introduced herself to Pearl, now found herself badgered by Pearl's company. Unfortunately, with the best will in the world, Ruth could not get fond of Pearl: Pearl exasperated her, with her sulky moods and her bigoted ignorance, which she would not admit. They rode side by side, along the edges of the winter plough, arguing bitterly.

Ruth, compelled by Milky Way's unhappiness, told Pearl she rode on too tight a rein, to which Pearl retorted, 'I ride her collected. I don't let her sprawl about like Fly-by-Night.'

'But a horse should walk on a long rein, freely,' Ruth said. 'You only collect her up when you're going to do something else, to get her ready. Not all the time. You're ruining her mouth.'

'Who are you telling how to ride?' Pearl asked haughtily. 'Just tell me how many times I've fallen off, compared with you?'

'Just staying on doesn't mean to say you are a marvellous rider. Even I could stay on Milky Way. She never gives you any cause to fall off.'

'That's because I'm riding her properly,' Pearl said pointedly. 'If you rode Fly properly he wouldn't buck you off.'

'He doesn't buck,' Ruth said furiously. 'He shies sometimes, that's all. And I've never pretended I can ride well! But at least I'm willing to learn, which is more than you are. Why don't you join the Pony Club? They would teach you.'

'I don't need teaching!' Pearl retorted, equally furiously. 'My pony does what I want her to do, which is more than yours does!'

As if to prove Pearl's point, Fly-by-Night decided at this moment to take exception to a tractor parked beside the hedge some ten feet away. He stopped, goggling, while Milky Way went placidly on. Pearl turned round in her saddle, smirking. Ruth, white with a seething fury, closed her legs firmly, according to the books, but Fly-by-Night started to go backwards. Goaded by Pearl's amusement, Ruth lifted her stick and gave Fly a belt across the quarters with all the strength of her arm. The pony gave an astonished snort, gathered himself abruptly together and shot off like a cork out of a champagne bottle. By clutching a handful of mane, Ruth managed to keep her seat. She had a glimpse of Pearl's laughter and Milky Way's polite curvetting, and then nothing but the stubble racing under the flying hoofs, and the thick mane flying before her. Her eyes were blinded with tears of humiliation, which she pretended were caused by the wind. She did not attempt to pull Fly up, because the field was big, and she did not want to go back to Milky Way. She sat still in the saddle, still holding the mane, until the pony had topped the long rise and Ruth could see the grey water of the tidal creek lying below behind the seawall, and the cold pastures stretching away on either side of the river. Then Fly-by-Night dropped his head at last, and fell back into a fast, unbalanced trot, and Ruth was able to pull him up by the gate at the top. She turned round, and to her relief saw that Pearl had cantered round in a big circle and was on her way home, alone. The white Arab pony moved like a drifting sea-gull over the grass, easy, obedient. Ruth watched her, bitter at the injustice of it, while Fly-by-Night hungrily cropped at the tops of the sour yellow thistles that grew in the hedge.

When Pearl had vanished, Ruth, ashamed now of her anger, pulled Fly-by-Night's head up and walked back down the field. He went easily, unconcerned, and Ruth could sit and look at the hedges full of wild rose hips and pretend that she was out to enjoy the landscape. At the bottom of the field, where it was flat, she decided to do some schooling, and walked Fly-by-Night round in several big circles. Apart from a tendency to go out in the bottom corner, heading for home, he did these quite well, but when she attempted to do them at a trot he ran out each time at the home corner, and it was only by a lot of hauling and kicking that she was able to get him back on course again. It was her own inadequacy as much as the pony's that distressed her: into her mind sprang a picture of Peter McNair trotting Fly-by-Night in compass-drawn circles, the pony flexed to the bit, his hind legs well under him. The picture had '*GOOD*' written under it. The fact that it was entirely imaginary caused her to weep a little more as she walked back down the lane.

When she got home she gave Fly-by-Night a net of her precious hay and went indoors with her saddle and bridle, which she kept in her bedroom. Elizabeth was sitting at the kitchen table, drawing.

'Was he good?' she asked.

'No, not very.'

'At least,' Elizabeth said, 'he will eat the bridle now.'

And as Ruth went upstairs it was a comfort to her to remember that when Elizabeth first came, six months ago, Fly-by-Night would not even be bridled, let alone ridden in circles. 'Perhaps,' she thought, 'I expect too much. I *am* making progress, slowly.' And the more she remembered what Fly-by-Night wouldn't do, six months ago, the more her spirits revived.

But progress, during the winter, was slow. By the time Ruth got home from school it was dark, and she could only ride at week-ends. During the Christmas holidays the ground was covered with snow, and then frozen slush, and Fly-by-Night remained in his field, tugging at his hay-net. Ruth had to break the ice on the old cistern three times a day. Morosely she watched him out of the windows. Even with the paper-round money, she was only just able to afford to keep him in feed, and only for his sake would she have turned out of bed at six o'clock every morning and cycled, shivering, to the paper-shop for her bag of papers. She was very conscious that money was tight, for her mother was anxious about Christmas, and their presents were dull and necessary clothes, offered with apologies. Her father looked worried, and did the football pools every week, and said, 'This house will be the ruin of me.' To Ruth, the brightest moment of the holidays came two days after Christmas when she met Pearl, when she delivered their papers, and Pearl said, 'I've got a new pair of jodhpurs. Do you want my old ones? I was going to throw them away.'

The jodhpurs were beautiful, with buckskin inside the knees, and Ruth found that riding was infinitely more comfortable. She was full of gratitude, and Pearl asked her to tea once or twice, but Ruth never enjoyed life inside 'The Place' very much, for Pearl's parents were very peculiar, to her eyes, using sanguinary adjectives every time they spoke and quite often shouting at each other with a viciousness that made Ruth wish she could crawl under the carpet. At other times they were very affable and called everyone 'darling'. Their house was furnished with very plushy carpets and satin sofas that engulfed one like great soft clouds. Ruth could never make up her mind whether she liked it or not. Its air of lush comfort overwhelmed her, but a puritan streak in her was repelled by it. On the other hand, she did not like her own house very much, with its cold, functional character. She decided that she must be hard to please, until she remembered Mr. Lacey's place, and its haphazard take-it-or-leave-it air, droopy ceilings, and pear trees looking into the bedroom windows. 'That is how I like my places,' she thought.

Three days before she was due to go back to school she went out to feed Fly-by-Night and found him standing in a corner of the field with his nose stuck in the hedge and his tail clamped hard down on his hind quarters. He did not look up as she approached, which was unusual, for he usually galloped towards her whenever she went near the fence.

'What's the matter, my beautiful?'

Fly-by-Night did not shift. Ruth felt a coldness creep over her. She recognized Fly-by-Night's appearance as that described as 'tucked-up' in all the books; he had little hollows under his hip-bones and looked thin. And as she looked at him she saw that he was shivering. His legs shook, and from his back little spirals of steam rose up in the air.

Her coldness turned to panic. She stood rooted, appalled.

'Fly! What's wrong with you?'

But Fly rolled a miserable eye in her direction and put back his ears. His hind legs started to shake so that all his flanks quivered.

Ruth was alone; her father and Ted were at work,

and her mother had taken Elizabeth to the dentist. She was terrified, for this ailing Fly-by-Night was a stranger to her, all his cockiness extinguished. The shaking, and the wisps of steam horrified her. She ran back indoors, and hunted feverishly through her books under the chapters headed 'Ailments of the Horse'. These chapters, never much studied until now, laid out in horrid detail the symptoms of worms, thrush, strangles, colic . . . She turned from one heading to another, and found that nearly every paragraph ended, 'Send for the veterinary surgeon immediately.' They nearly all said, too, 'Lead the horse into a box well filled with fresh straw and cover the loins with a rug, or sack.' Ruth, having no box, no straw, no rug, and no sack, pulled the blanket off her bed and took it outside. She threw it over Fly-by-Night's steaming back, fastened it at the front with her school-house brooch and round his belly with two of Ted's belts buckled together. Then, pulling her bicycle out of the garage, she cycled frantically round to 'The Place' to tell Pearl what had happened.

Pearl said, 'Well, get the vet. That's what they're for. We had one for Milly when she cut her leg on some wire.'

'Who was it?'

'Richards, he was called. He's the best round here.'

Ruth hesitated. Doctors were free, but she did not know whether vets had a version of the National Health Service for the animal world. Never having contributed anything towards it, she rather doubted whether they did. Pearl, as if divining her thoughts, said, 'You don't have to pay when he comes. He sends a bill later.' This decided Ruth.

'Can I use your telephone?'

'Yes.'

A secretary took her message. She gave her name and address and the secretary said, 'Mr. Richards will be over as soon as he can.'

Ruth hurried home, and spent the afternoon watching Fly-by-Night, who did not move, and rushing out into the front every time she saw a car. The eleventh car pulled up outside the gate. Ruth looked at it, and started shivering herself. The car was brand-new, with wire wheels, the sort Ted and Ron would watch with narrowed eyes, not saying anything. A man got out and said, 'Horse here?'

Ruth nodded. The man was immaculately dressed in a tweed suit and smelt of after-shave lotion. He took a pair of gum boots out of the car and Ruth said nervously, 'He – he's round the back.'

'Lead on,' said Mr. Richards.

Ruth did as she was told, and took Mr. Richards to Fly-by-Night, who laid back his ears and presented his hind quarters, so that Ruth had to hurry back to the house and fetch a halter. Mr. Richards stood waiting, and Ruth had a terrible feeling that he was like a taxi, his fee creeping up while she wasted his time. But when she haltered Fly-by-Night, Mr. Richards just said, 'These ponies are tough, you know,' and after a cursory thumping, listening and peering he laughed and said, 'What's your mother going to say about the blanket?'

Ruth thought the question completely beside the point.

'Is he all right?'

'Of course he's all right.'

'I – I thought – '

'Oh, you women are all the same. Fuss, fuss, fuss,' said Mr. Richards. 'A little cold. He won't die.'

Ruth felt as if she had been run over by a steam-roller. Mr. Richards drove away and she went back to Fly-by-Night and cried, 'How was I to know? And he'll send a bill . . .' Fly-by-Night shivered, and Ruth hugged him. 'Oh, Fly, the money!'

The next day Fly-by-Night was better, but Ruth could think of nothing but the little brown bill that would come through the letter-box one morning, addressed, as likely as not, to her father. Her mother was furious about the blanket. When Ruth told Pearl, she just laughed.

7

PETER TAKES A FALL

By the time the Pony Club Trials at Brierley came round again Fly-by-Night, in Ruth's opinion, was not even fit to take to a Pony Club rally, let alone jump in a Hunter Trials. Ruth longed for the summer, for long evenings, for more riding and – most of all – for more grass. The brown bill from Mr. Richards did not come, but Ruth looked for it every day. Try as she might, she had managed to save no more than five shillings towards paying it, but she thought if she could wait until the grass came through, so that there was no more hay to buy, she would be able to save more. 'Worry, worry, worry,' Ron said. But he did not know about Mr. Richards. Nobody knew except Pearl.

And at school Peter McNair was still an unattainable presence, a quiet boy, lately absent quite a lot. Ruth studied him in assembly, but could see no signs of ill health apart from, once, a black eye. Ruth put the black eye down to Woodlark, but had no way of knowing. She had given up any hope now of ever receiving any advice from Peter McNair, or even of speaking to him, and when she went to the Brierley Hunter Trials she expected – correctly, as it turned out – that he would see her without betraying any sign of recognition.

Ruth went to the Brierley Hunter Trials determined that next year she would ride in it. And it was a sign of her progress to remember that last year, standing on the same ground, she did not even possess a pony, or even dare to hope that she ever might. However unsatisfactory she might consider her schooling of Fly-by-Night, at least she now had a potential entry. 'It's just up to me,' she said to herself, which was in no way a comfort. But she went to Brierley this time, knowing what she wanted. 'Just to get round, next year.' Not even to win.

It was warmer, this year, the air full of the smell of spring. The little wood was full of catkins, and the stream was swollen, the banks soft and peaty. Ruth walked the course, while the stewards were still pushing in the marker flags and the riders were converging at the gate at the top of the hill. The course was basically the same as the year before, but with variations. This year one jumped the course through the wood in the opposite direction, so that one jumped into it over a rail and down the steep bank, and left it by passing through the gate. Having considered all the difficulties, Ruth went back to the collecting-ring to wait for the start. She felt tight and nervous, thinking of next year. 'Whatever shall I feel like next year?' she wondered, and started to shiver.

The girls' faces this year were familiar. The girl

whom Peter McNair had asked to pair with him was there, and the girl on the lazy grey who had objected to the idea. All the ponies looked competent and unworried; the girls sat and talked as if they were quite unconcerned. The ponies did not kick and go round in circles, nor even try to graze. They just stood. 'If Fly just stood,' Ruth thought enviously. It had never occurred to her before that it was something a pony had to learn.

This year Peter McNair arrived in a modest single trailer driven by his father. The pony they unloaded from it was a bay mare of about fourteen hands, more like a show-pony than a hunter. She had a fine thoroughbred head with a white star, and an airy, floating movement that reminded Ruth of Milky Way. She would not have known who it was if she had not bought a programme, and seen the name Woodlark.

'Woodlark!' Ruth stared. She remembered vividly the wildness of the bay filly, galloping along the crest of the big field; she had not dreamed that even the McNairs could have tamed such a creature so quickly. The day after she had seen Woodlark she had bought Fly-by-Night. 'They have had exactly the same time as I have had,' she thought. And Fly-by-Night would not even trot in a circle!

She would have been acutely depressed if Peter McNair had mounted and ridden away to sit unconcernedly in the collecting-ring. But her spirits lifted a little when she saw that the McNair magic was not so potent as she had supposed. Peter, in fact, looked unhappy, and seemed to be having a bitter argument with his father. Mr. McNair stood at the mare's head while Peter saddled her, and his hands were full keeping her still: it was obvious that she was far from composed.

Ruth heard McNair say, 'Of course she'll go round. I haven't brought her all this way just for the drive.' His voice was very curt, the sort one would not wish to argue with, and Peter said no more. His head was under the saddle flap as he did up the girths and Ruth could not see his expression. She was fascinated, eavesdropping from a discreet distance.

When the mare was saddled, Peter mounted. He sat very still in the saddle, not saying anything, his face closed up and showing nothing. His father led the mare for a few paces and then let go, and Peter kept her walking, away from the crowd and the horse-boxes. Ruth thought, 'From the way the mare goes, it must feel like sitting on a volcano.' She thought, too, that Woodlark was one pony that would not stand still in the collecting-ring. Peter made no attempt to bring her near any of the other ponies, but kept her out of the way, walking and trotting.

'Perhaps she's not so different from Fly after all,' Ruth reflected. 'Except that she's got Peter, and Fly's only got me.'

She had not attempted to jump Fly-by-Night yet, except over poles on the ground and small ditches, which did not trouble him. Some of the jumps on the trial course looked quite big to her eyes, although very clean and inviting. She thought the nastiest was the jump over the rail and down into the wood, and decided to stand there, in the same place as last year, so that she could see most of the course. A man sat on a camp-stool in the wood, with a score-sheet on his lap. Ruth stood by the hedge and waited for the first pony to come, glad of the warm sun.

Some of the ponies did fast competent rounds, but many of them were not at all marvellous, and Ruth, as is the way with competitors, felt very cheered. This course was a thing between oneself and one's pony: half the time one was alone, out in the country, and there were no spectators apart from one's fellow competitors, who knew what it felt like, and the adults scoring on their camp-stools. 'I *shall* get round,' Ruth said to herself. 'Oh, I shall do it!'

Woodlark jumped last in the class for twelve-to fourteen-year-olds, having been kept out of the collecting-ring until it was nearly empty. Ruth recognized her by her gallop: she went up the hill as if on wings, twice as fast as any of the other competitors. Whether Peter had her under control or not Ruth could not tell, until she appeared on the far side of the wood, still galloping, and Ruth assumed she must have cleared the intervening obstacles. Peter was just sitting there, not pulling at her nor seeming – from a distance – in any way alarmed; in fact, as they flew a fence out in the country it looked to Ruth so easy that for a moment she wondered why she was so worried about trying it

106

herself. And why Peter himself had seemed unhappy about the idea. But as the mare circled for home and came at her floating gallop across the field to what Ruth thought of as 'her' jump, Ruth began to change her mind.

The jump into the wood was cramped between trees and the bank down to the stream was poached and steep. Most ponies had slithered down it on their hocks, or gone down in surprised and unseating bounds. It was not an obstacle to take fast, and Peter was pulling Woodlark up in plenty of time. As she came nearer, Ruth could see that, although Peter had her collected, she looked very wild, and anything but an easy ride. Peter was watching the dark hole into the wood, frowning, and Woodlark, held back, was taking great bounds up into the air like a Lipizzaner stallion. Peter eased his hands. The mare plunged forward, fast, and galloped at the rail, but at the last moment she decided she didn't like the look of it, and stopped.

Unfortunately she had left it a fraction too late. Skidding in the mud, she cannoned into the rail and pitched right over it in a spectacular cartwheel. Ruth saw her shoulders drop, her tail fly up in the air. There was the splattering of mud clods and a crashing of branches, then some anguished snorts, a cry of anger, or pain, and a lot more splashing. Ruth ran forward, more by instinct than inclination, but as she got to the splintered rail Woodlark came bounding back up the bank, wild-eyed. She hesitated at the top, quivering, too frightened to jump out, and too frightened to go back. Her reins were over her neck and trailing between her forelegs.

Ruth knew she ought to try to catch her, and tried a soothing address, but her voice came out anything but soothing. Woodlark, churning about, saw her, swung away – but the man taking scores was coming up the bank behind her. Woodlark, cornered, swung round again and jumped, clean and high.

'Catch her!' the man bawled at Ruth.

Ruth made a rugby tackle at Woodlark's head, and caught a handful of mane. She gripped tight and Woodlark pulled her off her balance. She cried out as Woodlark trod hard on her foot, groped up with her other hand for something better than mane, and fell over as the mare stumbled, treading on her reins. Fortunately, as Ruth fell she caught the vital rein, and held on tight. Woodlark started off with a great bound, but was brought up abruptly. Ruth felt herself dragged across the grass, but somehow managed to get to her feet again, winded and unable to utter a word, soothing or otherwise. But at this moment the man caught up with her and Ruth saw his hairy tweed arm reach over beside her own. Woodlark was captured. Ruth let go, shaken.

'Well done, my dear,' said the man. 'It was misguided of me to shout "Catch her", but I know this mare. We wouldn't have got our hands on her for a fortnight if once she'd got away.'

Ruth nodded, still panting. Even the large man had his hands full holding Woodlark. She turned round to see what had happened to Peter, and saw him emerging from the wood, climbing the rail. Ruth expected him to look shocked and pale, but, apart from the fact that he was covered in mud, he looked as if nothing untoward had happened at all.

'Is she all right?' he asked.

'Seems to be,' the man said.

There seemed to be no question of Peter's not continuing, in spite of the severity of the fall. After a brief examination of the mare's forelegs, he went round to the near-side to mount, while the man endeavoured to hold her. Woodlark was in a frenzy of nervous excitement, swinging round in circles, her hind legs bunched beneath her. Peter stood patiently, waiting his moment, then was up and in the saddle with one movement, so that the mare scarcely knew it.

The man grinned and said, 'Your father selling this as a child's first pony?'

'More like tenth, I should think,' Peter said.

'Wait till I get back to my seat.'

The man let go and hurried away, and Peter turned the mare away and cantered her in a tight circle. Ruth went back to her spot in the hedge, not envying Peter at all. He went to the bar slowly, holding the mare in, so that she was almost cantering on the spot. Peter's face showed nothing but intense concentration. Ruth held her breath for him, more nervous than he. She could see the wildness in the mare's eyes, and the curbed energy in her pirouetting hind legs. With a lesser rider she would have run

109

out, or stopped, but, by what seemed a miracle to Ruth, Peter got her clear over the bar and down the bank in impeccable style. He rode her through the wood, twisting and turning through the trees, but when she saw the way out through the gate, and the open field beyond, she fought for her bit, pulling like a train. Peter managed to stop her, but then could not get her to approach the gate at all. Thwarted in her desire to do as she wished, Woodlark started to go up on her hind legs.

Ruth groaned to herself, watching the exhibition with a sweaty feeling, as if she were personally involved. 'Suppose Fly-by-Night does this next year?' she thought. But immediately she knew that Fly-by-Night was no Woodlark, exasperating as she might find him at times. Peter was on his own with Woodlark, fighting a personal battle, for Ruth could see that the stewards up the hill were getting ready for the next class, having given up waiting for the reappearance of the little mare out of the wood. The scoring man was waiting, but impatiently, knowing that his score-sheet was wanted up the field. Presently the girl Ruth called Cat's Eyes came cantering down the field on the grey pony to collect it, and the man climbed up the muddy bank to hand it over.

'Major Banks says please will you clear the course,' she said.

The man turned round and bawled through the wood, 'Will you retire, please, Peter!'

As Peter had been trying to get out of the wood

110

for the last five minutes, Ruth did not see that the instruction was going to alter anything for him. Woodlark, covered with sweat, was still napping sulkily, but with less vigour, and was appreciably nearer to the gate. Given time, Peter was going to win, but his orders to retire altered the situation. Ruth, watching, and thinking, 'Whatever will he do?' did not guess that the problem could be so easily resolved. Peter turned Woodlark away from the gate and cantered her back some forty feet along the path. Then, turning her sharply on her hocks, he sent her off at a sharp pace towards the gate. She flew the obstacle with at least two feet to spare and galloped away back to the collecting-ring.

Ruth went back up the hill, tired, as if she had confronted all Peter's problems herself. Every time she thought of herself doing it all on Fly-by-Night she went hot and cold with fright. 'If I feel like this now,' she thought, 'what will I feel like on the actual day?' It was a daunting thought, to be countered with scornful, Ron-like opinions to put the whole thing in its proper place: a potty Pony Club competition without even any spectators . . . as if it mattered whether one fell in a ditch or won a red rosette. It was a nothing . . . fun for the kiddies . . .

Obviously Mr. McNair did not think it a nothing. When Ruth got to the top of the hill she saw that Woodlark was already unsaddled and ready to go into the trailer. Mr. McNair stood by her with a sharp look in his eyes, smoking a cigarette and not looking at all sympathetic. He was talking to Peter and, although Ruth could not hear what he was saying, she could tell that it was nasty. She watched from a distance, pricking with indignation. McNair ought to be glad that Peter was alive, after a fall like that, she thought. But Peter, coming out of the horse-box, did not seem to be upset. His face, as usual, showed no expression, but Ruth thought that, if he had any feelings at all, he must be fed up.

She hoped, after catching Woodlark in that spectacular fashion, Peter might remember her face and acknowledge her the next time they passed at school. But when school started again, Peter, in blazer and flannels, was as remote as he had ever been.

It was spring, and the grass was growing; the sun had warmth again. Ruth decided to start learning about butterflies.

8

'IN NEED OF CARE AND PROTECTION'

Ron, the ever-helpful, said he had a good book on butterflies which he would lend her. Ruth did not think the idea was likely to bear fruit, and could not help getting the giggles when the boys inquired politely how the lepidoptery was going.

One spring evening, when Ruth was leaning on the kitchen window-sill, thinking how nicely the grass was growing, the familiar racket of the motor bike came to a crescendo in the drive outside, shutting out the noise of next door's lawn-mower. Mrs. Hollis automatically went to the oven to get Ted's dinner out, but when the door opened it was Ron who stood there, not Ted.

'Oh, Mrs. Hollis,' he said in a queer voice.

Ruth looked up sharply. Ron was as white as a sheet.

'What is it?' her mother said.

'It's Ted. He – he's – '

'He's had an accident?'

Ruth felt herself go cold all over. Her mother stood by the oven, tense, bright-eyed.

Ron nodded.

'How bad is it?' How sharp, how cool her mother

was, Ruth thought, amazed. Just as if she had expected it all the time. It was Ron who looked terrible. Ruth was shivering.

'He's not – not dead. I don't know how bad. They've taken him to Burnt Wood casualty.'

'Sit down,' Mrs. Hollis said to Ron. 'Here.' She pulled a chair out for him, and took his crash-helmet. 'The kettle's boiling. I'll make you a cup of tea, and some brandy in it.' She sounded completely matter-of-fact, as if Ron had come to tell her that Ted would be late for tea. Ron buried his face in his hands and said, 'I didn't know it could happen like that, so quick. Oh God, it was awful.' He was almost crying.

Mrs. Hollis was very gentle with Ron, as if what had happened to Ted was of no importance. Ruth, enormously impressed by her mother's self-control, could not stop crying. Nothing like this had ever touched her before: the evening remained fixed in her memory ever afterwards as the blackest thing that had ever happened. When her father came home he took her mother to the hospital, where she stayed all night and the next day as well. The hours passed like days. Ted was critically ill with concussion and several fractures. Ruth, like Ron, could not believe that the irrepressible Ted could possibly be extinguished so simply, in spite of the fact that the newspapers were full of tales of fatal accidents every day; she prayed stubbornly, as up till now she had only prayed for Fly-by-Night, and every morning woke to the feeling that she came to think of as 'a dark cloud'. The house seemed quite different without Ted in it.

Ruth thought that if Ted merely went on living her dark cloud would dissolve and life would, by comparison, become rosy and sweet once more. But life, of course – she realized rather bitterly a few weeks later – is not so simple. Ted was pronounced out of danger, but the consequences of the accident now spread a different sort of gloom through the house.

Ruth, washing up in the kitchen, heard her father say to her mother over his cup of tea, 'It's only when a thing like this happens that it comes home to me how much we've been counting on Ted's money. It was all wrong, of course, but knowing his tenner a week was there was always a nice thought. It's been nothing but worry since we saddled ourselves with this mortgage.'

Ruth heard her mother say something about going out to work and her father replied, 'That would mean giving up Elizabeth.' There were a few more sentences she did not catch, and then she heard her father say, half-humorously, 'Poor Ruthie will be selling papers to feed herself, let alone that darned pony of hers.'

'You'd like to give up this house, wouldn't you?'

'I'd like to stop having to worry about money.'

Ruth went on washing up, with a cold feel in the pit of her stomach. Fly-by-Night was so vulnerable, when her parents talked about money. Keeping him on the paper money was desperately hard as it was, and was going to be a lot harder when she started getting him shod. And next year he would need to be in hard condition for the Hunter Trials, which would mean more expensive food – not to mention the Pony Club subscription. Ruth knew that if she started thinking about all this, she would feel sick. It had happened before.

Later on, before she went to bed, her father said to her, quite gently, 'Ruth, this pony of yours . . .'

'I pay for him all myself,' Ruth said frantically. 'I've never asked you for anything, not since the saddle!'

Her father put down a little brown envelope on the table. It was addressed to him. Inside was a bill for three pounds, thirteen shillings and sixpence.

'But he never even did anything!' Ruth wept, incensed by the tactlessness of Mr. Richards's timing in sending out his bill, as much as by the bill itself. 'He only said I fussed!'

'He came,' her father said sadly. 'That's what they charge for, just coming. You don't make a habit of this?' he added, waving the bill.

'Only once. And I shall pay it. It's not for you. It's mine. He addressed it wrong.'

'I shall pay it,' her father said firmly.

'But you – '

'Look, things may be difficult, but I'm not so hard up that I can't pay this bill. Now stop crying. I'm not angry. But if this happens another time, I want you to tell me, not keep it secret.'

'Yes.'

★

Thank heaven, Ruth thought, that summer had come, and the field was bright with new grass. There was no more hay to buy, and she could save her money, get a hoard in for next winter. She wondered, now, if she was desperately selfish, to want this thing so badly. With all the family troubles.

'But what difference would it make if you gave him up?' Ron said very sensibly. 'It wouldn't pay off the mortgage, what you would get for him.'

'No one would buy him, the way he is,' Ruth said.

'Things'll come all right,' Ron said optimistically. 'They usually do. Ted's coming along fine.'

That was the main thing, after all, Ruth remembered. Ted was going to be in hospital for three months, the doctors said. Ron and Ruth went to visit him on the nights her parents didn't go (on the motor bike, but slowly, in deference to Mrs. Hollis's instruction). He had been put on to basket-making, to while away the time, and had been carried away with creative fervour, weaving baskets five feet high.

'What are they *for*?' Ruth asked, amazed.

'Waste-paper baskets,' Ted said happily.

'But nobody's got that much waste paper,' said Ron.

One evening, when Ruth was waiting for Ron to pick her up, a woman arrived at the door. Ruth, answering the bell recognized her as Mrs. Challoner, the Child Care woman, and asked her in.

'I hope you don't mind my calling at this time,'

the woman said to Ruth's mother, 'but something urgent has come up, and I've come to see if you can help me out. It's only a short-term case, a child we think would be better away from its parents for a month or so. Needs a stable atmosphere, just to be accepted into a normal family, carry on at school, no fuss. The psychiatrist passed it on to me, and I wondered if you could possibly help.'

Ron called at this moment, and Ruth left her parents discussing the situation with the woman in the living-room, and went out into the kitchen with Ron. She repeated what she had heard to Ron, and Ron said, 'It'll get a stable atmosphere here all right, if you've got anything to do with it.'

Ruth smiled. 'Of course, Ted's room's empty now, so I expect Mum will agree.'

They went to the hospital and told Ted that his bed was being taken over. 'You'll be out in the garage when you come home,' Ron told him. 'Better start weaving yourself a bed.'

'They're out of cane,' Ted said sadly. 'The old girl says I've used up six months' stock. I've sounded her out about having the cylinder head in here so that I can polish the parts – but she wasn't very keen. She's starting me on tapestry tomorrow.'

'Very nice, my boy, very nice. Knitting's next on the list, after tapestry. And when you've used up six months' stock of wool there are a few bales of crochet cotton down in the storeroom.'

When Ruth got home she found her parents watching television.

'Are we having that child?' she asked curiously.

Her mother nodded. 'Yes. It's only for a month or two. Mrs. Challoner is bringing me all the details tomorrow morning, and says she'll deliver the child in the afternoon. How's Ted, by the way?'

'He's doing tapestry.'

This evoked some amusement, and Mrs. Hollis said she would take him socks to darn the following evening. 'You see that this new child has a pleasant evening tomorrow, Ruth. It's a pity we've got to go out the first night, but the sister wants to speak to us. I told Mrs. Challoner how we're fixed, but she seems to think it will work out all right. So we'll give it a trial.'

Ruth went home from school the following evening, curious, and a little nervous. It was a warm evening. The children were playing in the road with tricycles and skipping-ropes, and soon the open-plan fronts would whirr to the noise of lawn-mowers. She thought of Ted, imprisoned in his bed for the sake of a moment's over-impetuosity on the motor bike, and was sorry for him. 'He should have done it in November, if he was going to do it at all,' she thought.

She went in through the kitchen door.

'Oh, Ruth,' her mother said. There was a boy sitting at the table, reading a newspaper. 'This is Peter, Ruth, who's going to stay for a bit.'

It was Peter McNair.

RUTH WATCHES TELEVISION

Ruth was so shattered by the unexpectedness of the situation that she could not speak. She opened her mouth, and no words came out. Peter looked up and said, 'Oh hullo,' without much interest, and Mrs. Hollis said, 'I suppose you two know each other, if you're at the same school? By sight, at any rate.'

'Yes,' Peter said.

Ruth shut her mouth, as it would not work, and dropped her satchel on the floor.

Mrs. Hollis said to Peter, 'Do you like liver and bacon?' and Peter replied, 'Yes, I don't mind it.'

'Pick up your satchel, Ruth,' Mrs. Hollis said. 'Are you sickening for something? You look blotchy.'

'No,' Ruth said dimly. She groped for her satchel, and fled out of the kitchen. She ran upstairs, and locked herself in the lavatory. She was shaking all over, and felt an insane desire to laugh out loud. In her satchel she had a book on butterflies. 'But he's downstairs! Here to stay! *Him!* Of all the people in the world . . .'

'Ruth, are you being sick or something?' her mother asked outside the door.

'No, I'm all right.'

'Well, before you come down, just make up Ted's bed, will you? I don't seem to have got anything done today, and the dinner's cooking now. I've put the sheets out.'

Ruth did as she was told. Ted's room was impersonal without Ted's untidiness stamping it. Ruth spread the sheets and felt herself coming back to earth, warm, elated. The shock dissolved into a feeling of utter satisfaction at the ways of the world. By the time she was smoothing the quilt the satisfaction had given way to a feeling of extreme curiosity as to why Peter McNair had come into the Child Care Department, and why he was better parted from his parents. As far as she knew, he did not have a mother. But from what she had last seen of his father it did not seem unreasonable to suppose that Peter would be happier away from him. Who had interceded for him? she wondered. She had noticed that he had been away from school for the last three days, but it had never entered her wildest dreams that he could be the urgent case Mrs. Challoner had been talking about.

She went downstairs slowly, back into the kitchen. Elizabeth was laying the table with a lot of clatter; the bacon was spluttering noisily under the grill, and Peter stood staring out of the window with his hands in his pockets. Fly-by-Night was out of sight in the field, but Peter showed no interest in the hoof-marked back garden. Always a reserved boy, it occurred to Ruth that, during the time she had known him, he had got gradually more and more withdrawn. Because he rarely showed any emotions, it did not mean, she realized, that he did not feel any, and what was happening to him now could scarcely be less than a personal crisis in his life; yet he did not look upset. He had the slightly watchful expression in his eyes that Ruth now knew was his normal expression; his whole attitude was one of observing, recording, and passing no opinion. But Ruth saw now that it was not because he had no opinions to pass. For the first time it occurred to her that, under his stocky, unrevealing shell, he was very much aware, and as sensitive to hurt as any more normally extroverted child, if not more so. And really, when it came to the subject of problems to solve, he had more troubles by far than she had. It was more to the point now that she should try to make things come right for Peter than that he should make things come right for her. This change of outlook came to Ruth in the moment that it took her mother to pull the grill-pan out from under the grill, and say, 'Ruth, make the tea.'

'Elizabeth, wash your hands. They're filthy,' Ruth said, from force of habit, going to the tea-caddy. How strangely things worked out, she was thinking. Her mother put out the meal for the three of them, and they sat down to it. Peter had a good appetite, whatever his spiritual starvation, and there was no need to force a conversation when they were all so healthily occupied. When he had finished Peter said to Mrs. Hollis, 'Can I go and have a look round before it gets dark? Isn't there a creek at the bottom of the lane – the lane that goes to the right, off the estate?'

'Yes, there is,' Ruth said.

'You can go,' Mrs. Hollis said. 'But be back by seven, before I have to go out.'

'Can I come?' Elizabeth asked Peter.

'I don't mind,' Peter said.

Elizabeth leapt eagerly from the table and fetched her gum boots. Peter went out with her, apparently quite happy that she should accompany him.

'I'm glad she wanted to go,' Mrs. Hollis said to Ruth, pouring herself a cup of tea and sitting down rather wearily. 'She'll keep tabs on him. He's not likely to throw himself in, with her around. And I didn't want to say no to him, the first night.'

Ruth looked at her mother, shocked. 'Throw himself in? Surely it's not that bad?'

'Well, no normal, happy child presents itself at a police-station and says it refuses to go home, and please could they find it somewhere to live. Which is apparently what he did.'

'But very sensible, if you feel like that,' Ruth couldn't help pointing out. 'Better than running away in an aimless fashion. And his father is beastly.'

'So I understand. Mrs. Challoner had to do some investigating, and went to see him, and said that he was absolutely flabbergasted at what Peter had done. He said if he came back it would all be all right, but Peter flatly refused to go. It seems that since the mother died, three or four years ago, the father more

123

or less drowned his sorrows in work, to the exclusion of all else.'

'The horse-dealing business,' Ruth put in.

'Yes. I realized it was the same McNairs that you went to see last year, when Mrs. Challoner was telling me all this. Apparently Peter was expected to go along with his father, and submerge himself in the horse business, too, but Peter had other ideas. It seems he's not the slightest bit interested in horses. He didn't worry very much at first, but as he got older, and presumably more competent, his father expected him to be riding all the time. He started keeping him away from school, just to ride. And Peter got fed up. The last straw was apparently when his father stopped him eating bread and potatoes because he was getting too heavy. So he just walked out.'

'Good for him.'

'Mrs. Challoner thought it would just be a matter of talking Peter into going back home, and smoothing things over, but when the psychiatrist fellow looked into it, he said Peter was on no account to go back. So that's how we got landed with him. Mrs. Challoner knew about Ted, so knew we had a spare room. And round she came.'

'Queer,' Ruth said. She was still bemused by the way things had worked out. 'He's a marvellous rider.'

Her mother looked at her sharply. 'After what I've told you, I hope you'll have more sense than to start talking horses to him. I told Mrs. Challoner that she might not have chosen a very good place for him, what with you and your horse-nonsense, but she didn't think that merely seeing a pony out of his bedroom window would be more than he could bear. But you're on no account to trouble him with your pony problems, Ruth.'

'No, I won't.'

'That's the one thing that really wouldn't do him any good at all. He has to go and see the psychiatrist once a week, so they must consider he needs watching. I don't want you to upset him.'

'No, I wouldn't!' Ruth said indignantly.

'We've enough problems to get on with at the moment. We don't want any more.' Mrs. Hollis finished her cup of tea and looked at the time. 'Your father will be in in a minute. I must put his meal on.'

Ruth started to do her homework on the cleared end of the table. But she could not concentrate on what she was supposed to be doing. She kept thinking of Peter being under her nose all the time, and herself not being able to ask him about Fly-by-Night, when everything went wrong. 'Torture,' she thought, digging her pencil deep into her notebook, making an agonized doodle. 'Cruelty to children.' She drew a little girl, transfixed by an arrow. 'It's me that will be going to the psychiatrist when Peter's finished.' She longed to tell Ron what had happened, and see the expression on his face.

All her tack was dirty and needed cleaning, but she spent the evening watching the television. Peter sat on the other end of the sofa, staring at

the screen. The only conversation that passed
between them at all was a few desultory remarks
about school.

10

PEARL MAKES A BET

It was a hot summer, the hottest for years. The ground was baked hard, and big cracks opened up in the clay down by the creek. Ruth rode Fly-by-Night along the dry paths, her thighs sticky with heat against the saddle, flies singing in a cloud round the pony's head. If it hadn't been for the goal she was working for, she would have been very content. Fly-by-Night had stopped bolting with her; he trotted and cantered when she asked, and nearly always stopped when she wanted. But he had a definite mind of his own, which was still a match for her riding. There were days when she had battles with him, long-drawn-out miserable affairs which she won by patience rather than skill. She could not rely on his obedience; she could not be sure, when approaching even a small ditch, that he was going to jump it. The fences at Brierley were as impossible as mountains, by his present standards.

Ron said, 'If you take him to a Pony Club meeting, they will teach you how to do it. Isn't that what it's for?'

Ruth agreed that it was. 'They only meet in the school holidays. I'll go to the first one in August.'

She did not want to admit to Ron that the thought of going to the first meeting terrified her. She was afraid Fly-by-Night would make a fool of her in front of all those competent girls.

Even if she had not been given definite instructions about not troubling Peter with her 'nonsense', Ruth realized, as she got to know Peter better, that her own instinct would have stopped her from opening the subject. It was as if Peter, normal in all other respects, had put up a sort of barrier where horses were concerned. He never passed a comment on Fly-by-Night, seeming almost not to see him. When Ruth passed him out riding – which she did quite often, for he went down to the creek a lot to swim, or look for butterflies – he would just nod his head to her, but never linger, or stop to watch, or pass any remark. He never mentioned any of his riding experiences, or his home, or his father, or his brothers, as if none of his past life had ever happened. Ruth supposed this was a symptom of the disturbance that the psychiatrist was interested in, but when she asked him what he did at the psychiatrist's – having pictured him lying on a couch recounting his life-history – he said, 'Oh, we go to Lyons and eat chocolate éclairs,' which did not help Ruth at all.

But in all other respects Peter became a normal member of the family. He was no trouble at all, quiet, obedient, perfectly good-natured. At first he hardly spoke at all, but gradually he thawed out. He smiled more often, and at school, Ruth noticed, was far more lively than he had been. When the time came for Ted to come home from hospital Mr. and Mrs. Hollis decided that he might just as well stay. They had got used to having him around, and there was room for another bed in Ted's room. Mrs. Challoner was very pleased with their decision. 'He's settled down so well with you. It would be such a shame to have to move him just at the moment. His father's gone abroad, you know, so perhaps the change will do the gentleman good. I hope so, because Peter will have to go back to him eventually.' Ruth hoped the nasty Mr. McNair would stay abroad for a long time. She liked Peter, and was still hopeful that, after a few more sessions eating chocolate éclairs, he would get round to talking 'horse-nonsense' with her.

As the first meeting of the Pony Club approached at the end of July she tried to convince herself that she had nothing to worry about, but she was not very successful. She tried to tell herself that this meeting would, in fact, solve her problems, because that's what the meetings were for, but she dreaded her introduction to the ranks of those capable, cold-eyed girls. She longed to ask Peter about them, and about what happened at the meetings. She got as far as saying to him, 'I'm going to a Pony Club meeting on Wednesday,' but Peter only said, 'And the best of British luck,' which did nothing to make her feel any more optimistic. If he thought she needed it, it was no more than she felt herself.

Having prevailed upon Pearl – in vain – to join

the Pony Club and accompany her, Ruth resigned herself to the awfulness of this first experience, and spent most of Tuesday on a marathon cleaning operation, of her pony, her tack, and her shabby clothes. As the day went on she got gloomier and gloomier, so that in the evening Ted and Ron kept passing remarks about the joy of owning the most faithful of man's servants, a horse.

'If I were you, I'd take up basket-weaving instead,' Ted told her. 'You could get a fair old load of cane for the cost of that brute.'

But the brute, when she had finished, did look lovely. Ruth was cheered when she went out again in the evening, and saw him grazing under the trees in the last of the sun, the golden light adding an extra burnish to the work she had put in on his coat during the afternoon. He had filled out beautifully since the spring, yet was not too fat, for Ruth had been keeping him in the garden all day, where the grass was very spare, and only letting him into the builder's field at night. And his extra inches were muscle, not flabby fat; his shoulders and quarters were hard and strong, his eyes bright with good health. When he saw her at the fence he came cantering up, as he always did now, and pushed his nose at her eagerly. She rarely gave him titbits, for he had taken to biting when she had given him too many. Now, at least, he never bit, but he still gobbled his lips at her in his thrusting pony way, all bounce and push. Fly had never been a pony to just stand and let himself be stroked.

'Be good tomorrow, please,' Ruth whispered, and sent up a little prayer to the first star.

Having ridden very little on roads, Ruth had worked out a route to the meeting mostly through lanes, and when she had to go where there was traffic she got off and led Fly-by-Night. She supposed this was all wrong, but she did not want to be landed under a car for the sake of principle. As he was not shod, she had always put off taking him on roads, but now she realized that it was a part of his education that she would not be able to put off much longer.

Fortunately for her pride, she was mounted and progressing quite satisfactorily when four girls on ponies clattered out of a turning just ahead of her. She felt Fly-by-Night gather himself together underneath her; she sat down tight and took a firm hold on the reins, and was just able to prevent him in his mad rush forward from cannoning into the hind quarters of the last pony. The rider turned round and gave Ruth a surprised look, as Fly-by-Night let out an excited whinny. Ruth, crimson, said, 'I'm sorry.' She could feel Fly-by-Night's excitement, the very thing she had dreaded; he was bouncing beneath her, snatching at the bit, swinging his quarters about.

To her great relief the girls ahead of her turned into a field gate, and she found, following them, that she had arrived at her destination. She was committed now. Whatever happened, she felt, was now out of her hands. She could but do her feeble best.

Beneath her, Fly-by-Night, taking in the scene,

trembled with excitement. There were about thirty ponies in the field and a middle-aged, military-looking man with a fierce black moustache – whom Ruth remembered was Major Banks – was bawling at them all to assemble in the middle and circle round him. With him there were two or three older girls, more or less grown-up, and an elderly man sitting on a shooting-stick. She had just arrived in time. Without dismounting, she cast off her shoulder bag with sandwiches and her headcollar in it, so that it landed under a convenient bush, and headed Fly-by-Night hopefully towards the circling riders.

He went like a coiled spring, in bounds of excitement whinnying loudly. Ruth was preoccupied with keeping him from getting out of control; she knew from the way he fought her hands that at any minute he would get his nose up in the air and rush off headlong. Major Banks was eyeing her nervously, but Ruth's eyes were fixed on Fly-by-Night's amazed ears, flexing backwards and forwards.

'Steady, steady, you little idiot!' she muttered, but her voice was as nervous as Fly's progress.

She managed to join the circle, with Fly dashing and darting, crowding the pony in front, and still letting out his frantic neighs. The girl behind wisely kept her pony at a distance, for which Ruth was greatly relieved, for she was afraid Fly would kick.

Major Banks was picking out the competent riders for the more advanced training, and the ones left circling, Ruth concluded, were the ones for the elementary class. Just as she was thinking that perhaps the worst of Fly-by-Night's astonishment was giving way to acceptance of this strange new game, the competent group was sent away to tʰ other side of the field. As the riders set off at a fa t trot, in a big bunch, Fly-by-Night took off in pursuit, whipping round out of the circle and breaking into the wild canter that Ruth had been dreading. She pulled at him, but he put his nose up, snatching at the bit.

Ruth heard Major Banks roar something at her, but she knew she was on her own. She sat down as firmly as she could to the lurching, unbalanced pace, and heaved desperately on the left rein to circle Fly back to where he had come from. With his head pulled round he galloped on as best as he could, but Ruth's brute strength gradually prevailed, and he started to slow up, in big jerks, showing the whites of his eyes.

Ruth, bitterly embarrassed, turned him round towards the group she was supposed to be with, but he refused to go in this direction, and napped round to face the other way. With brute force once more Ruth hauled him round again, and drummed him with her heels. He faced the right way, but would not move, except backwards. By the time Major Banks reached her, Ruth was biting back tears of humiliation.

'What's all this, animal?' Major Banks said quite cheerfully, reaching out a hand to Fly-by-Night's bridle. 'You want to be with the others, do you? Well, we want you over here.'

He put a hand on the reins and led Fly-by-Night,

who went without any more trouble. Ruth sat still, sick with despair. The two groups of ponies were now circling with one of the other girls in the centre of each; everyone was occupied, and Major Banks halted Fly-by-Night and looked at Ruth, stroking Fly's neck.

'You didn't manage that too badly,' he said. 'Don't look too worried. Young, is he?'

'Yes, he's four. I had him when he was three.'

'You had him unbroken, I take it?'

'Yes.'

The Major shook his head and tut-tutted. 'Same old story. These so nice but quite crazy parents will buy their children a sweet, wild pony, and expect them to grow up together.' He smiled at Ruth quite pleasantly. 'Hard, isn't it?'

'Yes,' said Ruth stiffly. 'Only I bought him myself. My parents had nothing to do with it.'

'Even worse,' said the Major cheerfully. He stood back, surveying the now resigned Fly-by-Night thoughtfully. 'I'll say this for you, you've an eye for a nice pony. Very nice.'

Ruth's spirits rose a notch.

'We've had wilder animals than this in the Pony Club.'

Ruth's spirits rose another notch.

'Join the others,' said Major Banks. 'He'll be all right.'

Fly-by-Night, having fastened his eyes on the right set of ponies, joined them without any further trouble, walking in a circle round the instructor, a dashing-looking girl of about twenty slashing a crop against her gum boots. Ruth could feel vibrations of amazement still coming up through Fly, but his demeanour was now more subdued. She began to think she might be able to cope.

For an hour and a half they rode in circles, walking and trotting, first all together, then one by one, then in a long row over a very low cavaletti, then one by one. Ruth, concentrating hard, never had time to wonder what the others were thinking of her; they all had their problems, too, she came to realize. And most of them didn't have such a handsome pony as hers. On the other side of the field the more advanced riders were doing much the same thing with Major Banks, only their jumps were bigger and their circles were smaller, and the performances were altogether more polished.

At lunch-time Ruth had hoped to talk to some of the girls and perhaps find the understanding friend she was always hoping for, but Fly-by-Night, tied to the hedge, kept getting his feet tangled up in his headrope because he was still excited, and she had to untie him after a few crises and spend the lunch-hour holding the end of the rope herself. As he kept darting about every few minutes, and she was trying to eat sandwiches at the same time, it was not at all restful. She was very envious of the girls whose ponies stood dozing, and who were able to picnic on rugs with bottles of pop and no troubles. She realized that there were things Fly-by-Night had to learn that she had not even thought of yet.

When it was time to tack up again, Fly threw his head about every time she tried to get the bridle on, and while all the other girls calmly trotted off to the centre of the ring, Ruth was left fighting and dancing round in circles by the hedge. But the instructress came over and, with the same cheerful nonchalance that Major Banks had used, offered help.

'Little beggar, aren't you?' she chided Fly, and had the bridle on instantly. Then she said, 'Nice pony. New, is he?'

'It's his first Pony Club meeting.'

'They all have to learn.' Ruth's only consolation lay in the fact that nobody seemed to think that her troubles were anything out of the ordinary.

When she got home, Ted, Ron, and Peter were eating beans on toast in the kitchen. Ruth came in feeling exhausted. With an excess of chivalry Ron offered to hot up the beans for her, and Ruth was able to flop down at the table and pour herself a cup of tea.

'How was it?' Ted asked.

'Oh, bits were all right,' Ruth said cautiously. She felt she had learned a lot, if only a more exact knowledge of what she could do. 'It's those gym-khana games,' she added. 'We did games in the afternoon. Fly just doesn't know about games.'

'Fly's always playing games.'

'Not these sort of games. Bending and things. You have to go in and out down a row of bamboo canes. All the good ponies canter and turn on a sixpence and come back again. Fly just trod on them, or missed them altogether, and went half-way across the field before I could turn him round.'

Ruth ate her baked beans, and told the humiliating story of how Fly had bolted across the field and she had had to be rescued by Major Banks. Ted and Ron made sympathetic faces, and passed a few facetious remarks about horseplay, then went back to discussing a magazine which they had laid out on the table showing the specifications of the latest Metisse frame. Ruth reached for the sugar, and realized that Peter was watching her, saying nothing as usual. In her preoccupied state she had forgotten all about him and now, seeing his politely inexpressive look, she wanted to throw the sugar-basin at him. She hated him for knowing so much, and herself for knowing so little.

Ron pushed his chair back and closed the magazine. 'You won't go again, I take it?' he said to Ruth.

'I jolly well will,' Ruth said fiercely.

Ron grinned. 'A martyr to the cause.'

The next day was hot again, with a sweet breeze blowing up from the river. It was the sort of day to be utterly content, yet Ruth could not feel it. She was all ruffled up inside, and rode down over the stubble fields to the creek without hearing a single note of the skylarks' music cascading from the sky, or the summer purr of the distant combines. The tide was high and Peter was drifting about in an old inner tube with another boy from the estate. They kept tipping each other out, ducking and spluttering. Ruth rode along the sea-wall and watched them, aloof from their enjoyment. She knew she was in a bad mood, and felt no better when she saw Pearl trotting down the hill towards her on Milky Way. Milky Way was trotting lame, as she often did. The ground was very hard, and Ruth frowned. She rode off down the wall and went to meet her.

'Hullo,' Pearl said. 'What was it like? Do you know how to make your pony behave now?'

Ruth's eyes sparked. She felt anger fizzing up inside her, but was very careful when she spoke.

'I know enough not to ride my pony when it's lame,' she said shortly.

'Riding her doesn't make it any worse,' Pearl said. She was holding Milky Way in so tightly that the mare took a step backwards. Ruth looked at the perfect animal, her gleaming white coat, the flexed neck with the fine mane blowing out in the breeze, the black Arab eyes and wide nostrils, like a horse in an old painting, and felt her bad mood pricking her like a pair of spurs. What could you say to anyone like Pearl? she wondered in despair. Pearl's long hair blew out; she wore a white polo-necked jersey and spotless jodhpurs. Ruth hated her.

They rode on together. 'What did you do?' Pearl asked, and Ruth told her, leaving out all the humiliating bits.

'It sounds terribly dull. And do you mean to say that Fly really did all those things, bending and all that? I didn't think he could.' Pearl's pale green eyes slid round to look at Ruth, slyly provoking.

'Oh, didn't you?' Ruth said sharply. 'Well, he did.'

Under her breath, and to herself, she added, 'After a fashion.'

'Let's canter,' said Pearl.

Not wanting to continue the conversation, Ruth cantered, seething, after Pearl. Pearl did a large circle of the field and Fly-by-Night followed, snatching at his bit, bouncing horribly. Ruth remembered the girls at the Pony Club cantering small circles, very collected, very slow. She lifted her face up to the hot sun and knew that, today, nothing would please her. Her bad mood had been encouraged by Pearl. Pearl rode with her toes down and gaps under her knees. Major Banks would shout at her, Ruth thought.

Milky Way pulled up, dropping one shoulder, on the path that ran up to the sea-wall. Peter and his friend were lying on the sea-wall, sucking grass. The friend had a radio playing. The inappropriate row, all mixed up with the skylarks, exacerbated Ruth's ill temper.

'Let's go back across here,' Pearl said. She hauled Milky Way round so that she faced a broken gap in the fence that ran up from the sea-wall, separating the grassy ride from a field that had been recently combined. The straw bales were still lying on the red-gold stubble. Pearl stopped beside the gap and turned round to Ruth. 'After you,' she said maliciously.

Pearl knew perfectly well that Fly-by-Night would not jump the gap without a lead from Milky Way. She sat there, grinning, looking at Ruth, and

Ruth knew that she was being paid out for lying about Fly-by-Night's prowess at the Pony Club. Ruth realized the justice of the situation, and the neatness of Pearl's trap, and knew she was helpless. If she was to turn up the path and say, 'I'm going home this way,' it would be as obvious an admission of failure as if she went through with the fiasco of trying to make Fly-by-Night jump.

Pearl said in a loud, clear voice, 'I bet you my new pair of jodhpurs your pony won't jump that fence without Milly leading.'

Ruth almost snorted with rage. She would gladly have seen Pearl drop dead in that moment. All her bottled anger and frustration came to boiling-point, and she snatched Fly-by-Night's head up from the grass with a wrench that was worthy of Pearl herself. She looked at the gap, which consisted of a bar about two feet off the ground, and a tiny ditch, and knew that Fly-by-Night would no more jump it for her than take off and fly, but such was her blind anger that she was no longer capable of retiring from the argument. She turned Fly-by-Night round so that he was facing the gap and pressed him forward.

'Hey, Ruth!'

As Fly-by-Night, sensing what was in store for him, was already going sideways instead of forward, Ruth had no difficulty in stopping him at the interruption. She looked up and saw Peter coming down the sea-wall, still sucking his grass. He came over to her and said in a low voice, 'That was a jolly good offer. Get off.'

Ruth just stared at him.

'They're Moss Bros.,' Peter said. 'Come on, let me have him.'

Ruth slid out of the saddle, too amazed to say anything. Peter took the reins out of her hand, and Fly-by-Night stood like a rock while he mounted, ears pricked up. The stirrup-leathers were too short, but Peter just crossed the irons over the front of the saddle.

'I say,' Pearl said. 'That's not fair.'

Peter turned Fly round so that he was facing the gap squarely and grinned at Pearl. 'You said the pony. We've got witnesses.' With no indications to Fly at all that Ruth could see, he then put him straight into a canter and jumped the gap. On the other side he pulled up, turned on a sixpence and came back, jumping it again and pulling up beside Pearl.

'One pair of jodhpurs,' he said.

Pearl was white with anger. 'You cheated!' she said furiously. 'You've got nothing to do with it! I was talking to Ruth!'

'You said "I bet your pony won't jump",' Peter said. 'You didn't say anything about the rider. Isn't that right, Biffy?' he called up to his friend with the radio.

'That's what she said,' Biffy agreed.

'You owe Ruth those jods, then. And if you don't give them to her, we'll come up and debag you in person.'

'Oh, you beast! My father would throw you out!'

'I bet your father doesn't make bets he doesn't

keep. You jolly well owe Ruth those pants, and I'll tell him so. And you shouldn't ride a pony as lame as that. I'll tell him that, too.'

'You mind your own business, you interfering – oh!' Words failed Pearl. She wrenched Milky Way round and disappeared up the hill at a flat gallop, all pale flying hair and tail. Ruth stood watching, acutely happy. Even Biffy's radio now seemed to be playing celestial music.

'There,' said Peter, looking rather pleased. 'That showed her.' He slid off Fly-by-Night. 'You make sure she sticks to what she said.'

'Look,' Ruth said, 'how did you get him to jump that?'

Peter looked surprised. 'What do you mean?'

'He won't jump it for me.'

'Oh, they get to know what they can get away with, I suppose.'

'You mean it's me, all the things he won't do?'

'Well, I don't know.'

'Look, I won't ask you ever again, but just this once, while you're in the mood, would you just see if you can get him to jump that again, and go up the field in and out of the bales, as if it's bending, and canter a circle and – oh, you know, the Pony Club sort of things? Will you?'

'Well, if you like.'

Peter got on again, and lengthened the stirrups. 'One dressage display coming up.'

Fly-by-Night went over the gap again, jumping big, his ears pricked up. To Ruth, never having seen him being ridden before, he looked magnificent, all shining bounce and jauntiness. He flexed his neck to Peter's hands, carrying himself with the same boldness that she had once admired in Toadhill Flax. Peter seemed not to do anything, just sit there but Fly-by-Night went up the lines of bales, in and out, at a canter, without once poking his nose or even attempting to run out. At the top he turned and came back, first at an extended trot, then at a collected trot, then at a slow, collected canter. Opposite the gap once more, Peter cantered him in a circle on the correct leg, then changed direction and sent him off in a circle on the other leg. He then halted and got him to stand out, show-wise, all collected and square on his four legs. He reined back four paces, did a turn on the forehand, and jumped back over the gap to halt in front of Ruth.

'There. I'd do a levade, too, but I haven't got my cocked hat with me,' he said.

Biffy shouted from the sea-wall, 'When you've finished assing about down there, we were on our way to look for a Comma, if you remember.'

Peter got off again and handed Ruth the reins. 'He's nice,' he said. 'Reminds me of Toad, only smaller.' He picked another piece of grass to suck and ambled away to join Biffy. Half-way up the sea-wall he turned and said, 'Those jods are yours, remember. Biffy'll be a witness.'

'Come on,' Biffy said. 'Wasting blooming time with girls' stuff.'

The two of them disappeared over the sea-wall,

and the strains of the radio faded away across the saltings. Fly-by-Night put his head down and started to graze, as if he had never seen grass before, and Ruth stood looking at him, in a daze. She felt as if something had come out of the sky and hit her. There was nobody in sight at all, just herself and Fly-by-Night on the edge of the stubble-field, and the distant hedges all shimmering in the heat.

'Fly-by-Night,' she said.

Fly flicked an eye at her, pulling at the grass. Then, just like a pony in one of her books, he lifted his head and gave a little flutter of his nostrils, and rubbed his head against her arm in a friendly way. Ruth felt weepy all of a sudden, elated and weepy altogether, in a strange, dazed way.

'It's the heat,' she said to herself, and mounted Fly-by-Night. He cleared the gap in one bound, and cantered away up the stubble-field.

The next morning, when Ruth did her paper round, she found a brown paper parcel on the doorstep of 'The Place', addressed to herself. Inside were the jodhpurs, with the Moss Bros. label still new and unsoiled.

11

RIDING AT HILLINGDON

One afternoon at the end of August when Ruth came in from her ride she found her mother in the kitchen drinking cups of tea with Mrs. Challoner.

'Do you know where Peter is?' Mrs. Hollis asked Ruth.

'He's down the creek somewhere, I think. Do you want him?'

The two women looked at each other warily, and Mrs. Hollis said, 'No hurry, I suppose.'

Mrs. Challoner, looking relieved, said, 'I'll leave it to you to tell him, then?'

'Yes, all right.'

When Mrs. Challoner had gone Ruth said nervously to her mother, 'Tell him what?'

'That his father's married a Neapolitan opera-singer.'

Ruth looked at her mother to see if she was joking, but she did not look particularly amused.

'Do you mean it? It doesn't sound – er – well – ' Ruth was at a loss. Neapolitan opera-singers did not ride horses, nor stand in cold collecting-rings in sheepskin-lined jackets calling out the numbers.

'They want Peter to go home.'

'Oh, no!'

'He'd have to go back soon, in any case,' her mother said. 'I only hope he'll find a new mother an added attraction.'

Amazingly, Peter did. 'What's she like?' he asked cautiously.

'All Mrs. Challoner told me, dear, is that she's rather fat and speaks no English at all, but smiles all the time.'

Ruth listened to the conversation, wondering if it was real. It didn't sound like the sort of thing that actually happened to ordinary people. Afterwards, when she was alone with Peter, she said to him, 'Do you mind?'

'It can't be worse than it was before,' he said.

'Why, what was it like before?'

'Well, at least someone smiling all the time will be nice to have around, won't it?'

He did not say any more, but his remark seemed very reasonable to Ruth.

She had known that he was going back when his father came home, but had put off thinking about it. It was not that he had, in fact, helped a great deal practically in schooling Fly-by-Night since the day he had ridden him down by the creek, but his having shown Ruth what was possible had helped her immeasurably. Her confidence had increased, which Fly-by-Night had seemed to sense, and the better the pony did for her the more sure she became, so that she felt that their mutual progress was like a snowball, steadily building up. They still had plenty of bad patches to put it all in perspective, but these did not cast Ruth down with the same force as they had earlier in the year. She was more philosophic about it all.

'You'll get fat at this rate,' Ron said approvingly. 'Nothing to worry about.'

The Pony Club no longer held her in awe, expecting the worst. After two or three more times, Fly-by-Night stopped his whinnying and displays of astonishment, and settled down to doing what he was told (even if it was only because all the other ponies were doing the same thing). Ruth made some tentative friends, but none who lived within riding distance, so that her love-hate relationship with Pearl continued as far as riding out was concerned.

'Why do you go out with that horrible girl?' Peter asked her.

'Because she calls for me. And she *was* honest about the jodhpurs.' Ruth felt bound to defend poor Pearl.

'She couldn't have wriggled out of that,' Peter said. 'She made the offer in a loud enough voice, so that everyone would have to take notice.'

'Take notice of me not being able to make Fly jump the gap.'

'Yes, well, we fixed her, didn't we?' Peter said with great satisfaction. 'Has she got the vet yet?'

'No.'

Milky Way was still a source of grief to Ruth. 'I would give anything,' she said, 'to own Milky Way.'

'She's not worth anything, the way she is,' Peter said.

'That's not the point. It's her nature that I love.'

Peter said, 'There's only one pony that I've ever liked. I mean liked as – as – oh, you know. More than just something to ride. A pony that was like somebody.'

'Who was that? Woodlark?'

'Woodlark? Ugh! No, it was Toad.'

'Toadhill Flax? What happened to him?'

'Dad sold him,' Peter said. 'He said I could have him for my own, then a week later someone offered a good price for him, and he sold him.'

'Your father's horrible!'

Peter grinned. 'But I've got a lovely mother – a big, fat, enormous, spaghetti-eating, smiling opera-singer.'

Ruth was shocked.

Peter went home, and Ruth did not see him until she went back to school. Even then they did not have much opportunity to talk, but Ruth gathered that Peter thought his home vastly improved. 'My father's a new man,' he said. 'You won't recognize him. He's taking singing lessons. And we have spaghetti every day. Truly. All oozing with lovely, greasy gravy, and garlic in it.' Ruth did not know whether he was making it up, or whether he meant it. It still just did not sound quite real to her. She went home and told her mother, and her mother was pleased.

'Just what the place needed, I should imagine. Mrs. Challoner told me, when she first went there,

148

that the house was just like an extension of the stables, all littered with gear and sale catalogues, and linseed on the cooker, stinking the place out. No fires, just a bit of old cheese in the pantry. No wonder Peter got fed up.'

Ruth missed having him at home dreadfully. They all did. Ted, not yet fit enough to go back to work, was morose with boredom. The first coal of the winter was delivered, and Ruth heard, with a familiar feeling of dread, the mutterings of her father over the bill. She realized that he had got steadily quieter over the past year, more and more worried looking, and less given to making the jokes that had made them all laugh. She heard him say to her mother, 'This winter will find us out. I really think we'll have to move before the next one. But heavens know where to.'

'A flat would do us, now the children are growing up,' Mrs. Hollis said.

Ruth could not bear to listen. She did not think anything so bad could happen. 'That's what you thought when Ted had his accident,' she reminded herself. 'And that happened.'

Ted went to the doctor to get permission to go back to work, but the doctor would not hear of it. 'Come the New Year, and we'll consider it,' the doctor said. Ted, who was still under treatment at the hospital for the injury to his back, was not surprised, but his frustration increased. Always an active person, the enforced idleness came hard, and the fact that his disability was adding substantially to the family's financial difficulties gave him a guilt complex that made him gloomy and pessimistic.

Ruth, having gained new confidence with Fly-by-Night, now found that her season of content was doomed.

'It can't happen!' she said desperately to Ron. 'I can't give him up now, when everything is beginning to come right!' She did not dare let her parents see how much it mattered, because she knew that they had enough to bother about as it was. There was only Ron, the universal comforter, whose presence invariably cheered Ted, and whom everyone was pleased to see.

'Well, it hasn't happened yet,' Ron said steadily. 'And if you do move to somewhere without a field, perhaps Peter could help you out? Your parents did a lot for him, after all. Mr. McNair might keep Fly-by-Night for you.'

'But without paying? I couldn't afford to pay.'

'What your mother did for Peter is worth years of a pony's keep.'

'But, if it's a flat, that means a town, and we'll be miles away from Hillingdon – how shall I be able to go over and ride him often enough?' Even to Ron, Ruth could not explain that she would have to see Fly-by-Night often, almost every day, or life would have no point at all. In fact, she could not imagine herself without the pony. Life without Fly-by-Night was like a thick fog in her imagination. It was a nothing. Even sensible Ron would not understand how utterly committed she was.

His idea was a straw, and Ruth clutched at it. One night her parents drafted out an advertisement to put in the paper, to sell the house, and the next day Ruth waylaid Peter at school, after lunch, and told him what was happening.

'I'm sure we could keep Fly-by-Night for you,' Peter said gravely. 'I know my father wouldn't mind.' He pondered, and looked at Ruth's tight, miserable face. 'It'll be difficult for you, getting over to ride him.'

Ruth nodded. 'About three hours' bike-riding, to a couple of hours' pony-riding.' It was better than selling him, but the prospect was heart-chilling.

Peter grimaced. 'Rather you than me.' He paused, then said, 'Look, why don't you come over on Saturday and see my father about it? Come over on Fly, then you can try him round our course.'

Ruth's heart leapt at the invitation. Simultaneously she thought of all the snags. 'It's a lot of road, to get to you. He's not shod.'

'Haven't you had him shod yet? Why ever not?'

'I can't afford it,' Ruth muttered.

'Oh, but you must,' Peter said. 'Then you can come up whenever you like, and use our jumps. I bet you won't move for ages yet, if your parents are only just writing out the advertisement.'

Ruth was silent.

Peter said, 'If you ride him up on Saturday, you can leave him at our place, because the smith's coming next Monday. Then he can be shod with ours, and you can take him back again afterwards. You won't have to pay anything. How about that?'

Ruth was silent again. The prospect was so inviting that her puritan streak made her feel she must refuse. Then she thought of Ron's sense, and grinned, and said, 'Yes, that would be marvellous.'

The house advertisement was in the paper on the Friday and on Saturday morning, as Ruth left home on Fly-by-Night, a man and a woman had already arrived to view. Ruth rode away down the concrete road, trying to keep her mind on the marvellous day that lay before her, but her stupid wits kept wandering, and all she could think of were the grassy tracks down to the creek where the skylarks sang, and the red-gold stubble where Fly-by-Night had cantered through August and September. 'Don't be *stupid*,' she told herself. 'What's the good of thinking of that?'

Now, early November, the fields were all ploughed again, and the elms baring, like ink drawings against the sky. The tarmac gleamed with rain. Fly-by-Night's coat was thickening, the frosty roan working over the movement of his shoulders as his unshod hoofs padded along the verge. 'When you come back,' Ruth told him, 'you will clatter. You'll frighten the wits out of yourself.'

But today he was good, and they reached the McNair drive without incident. Ruth felt Fly stiffen with excitement as he smelt the other horses. Peter was in the yard waiting for her.

'We'll put him in a box for now, and you can come indoors and meet my big fat momma. Then this afternoon we can ride.'

'What, you too?'

'Why not?'

Ruth realized that the chocolate-éclair sessions must have had good effect after all. 'Fly-by-Night's never been in a loose-box before – at least, not that I know of,' she said. 'I don't suppose he'll like it.'

'Time he learnt,' Peter said. 'Do you want to look at the horses?'

Ruth felt herself shiver with pure pleasure. A place like McNair's, with Peter now her personal friend, was her idea of paradise. The boxes were all immaculate, full of clean straw and shining animals. Fly-by-Night, appeased with a large net of hay, stood looking about him with amazed, excited eyes – no less amazed and excited than Ruth's. She followed Peter down the yard, looking in at each half-door, and Peter told her about each inmate. 'Jason. He's nice, but he's been spoilt.' Jason was a fourteen-and-a-half-hand chestnut with a lovely head and a bold eye. 'And this is Prairie Fire. He's won two point-to-points. My eldest brother is riding him in a National Hunt race next week.' Prairie Fire was dark bay, a raking, powerful gelding with scars on his legs. 'You can't stop him once he's going. But can he go! This grey is Seashell. She's as mild as milk, lady's hunter. And this is Rustum. Half-Arab, nice, very green ... ugh, Woodlark. You pretty little devil! This is beastly Woodlark.'

153

'Why is she so beastly?'

'You can have a ride on her, if you like. You'll find out. She's got a nasty female mind.'

'Better than a nasty male mind.'

'Oh, no, give me a gelding any day.'

Ruth followed Peter round to the house, in a warm, horsy dream. The house was warm, filled with delicious cooking smells. In the kitchen, Mr. McNair was sitting in front of a blazing fire, reading *Horse and Hound* and drinking coffee, and at the cooker stood the Neapolitan opera-singer. Ruth thought she was like a great sun. Well-being emanated from her like the warmth from the fire. She beamed at Ruth, and immediately produced steaming mugs of cocoa, and Ruth was fascinated by the vastness of her; yet she was so neat and quick and strong with it, and so happy. She sang while she cooked, and spoke in torrents of beautiful Italian, which nobody understood, but Mr. McNair and Peter nodded and smiled and said, 'Si, si,' and after a little while Ruth found herself doing the same. Ruth could see the change that had been wrought in Peter's father, for he had an air of contentment about him like a domestic cat on the hearth-rug. Ruth would not have recognized the same man who had nagged Peter on the day of the Hunter Trials. After a delicious lunch, Ruth left the house almost regretfully to go riding with Peter. She had offered to wash up, but had been refused with a cascade of shocked surprise and an embrace.

'Nice, isn't she?' Peter said, as they went back to

the stables. 'You can't imagine the change she's made in everything.'

Ruth looked at Peter, remembered the night he had arrived in her own home, pale and silent, and thought how strangely things worked out: now it was her turn to be hurt by what was happening, and Peter's turn to be made happy. They seemed to have no control over anything at all.

Peter decided to ride his beastly Woodlark, because he said she needed it, so they saddled the two ponies and rode side by side across McNair's fields to the woods beyond. There were no woods where Ruth lived, and as the ponies left the open fields and turned on to a peaty track that led away into an unfamiliar, cathedral-like gloom, Ruth was aware of a new dimension in her riding. Fly-by-Night's hoofs rustled in brittle leaves; trailers of wild clematis tangled in her hair. It was silent and secret. When a pair of wood-pigeons clattered suddenly, heavily, out of the branches above their heads, she was as startled as Fly-by-Night, and shied with him in spirit. Peter turned and laughed, and Ruth saw Woodlark break into a trot and start twisting through the trees, Peter bending low to miss the branches, yet quite easy and still in the saddle. Fly-by-Night, anxious not to be left behind, followed eagerly, and Ruth felt herself whipped and whacked by the trees. She bent down like Peter, but bounced and slithered and bit her tongue. She had no control over Fly-by-Night at all.

155

'A bit different from the sea-wall!' Peter said, pulling up to wait.

Fly-by-Night barged into Woodlark's quarters, but Peter turned the mare instantly, before she had time to think about kicking. 'We've made a Hunter Trials sort of course through the rides here. All the jumps are very low. I bet Fly-by-Night will do it, if Woodlark gives him a lead. Do you want to try it?'

Ruth, getting her breath back, nodded. She was frightened, and longing to do it at the same time. She felt as if the trees were pressing down on her. It was like being indoors. There was a cracking of dry twigs and Woodlark was away, cantering over the thick, soft humus. Ruth felt Fly-by-Night go, without her telling him, and she sat there, head down, her throat dry with fright, but all her instincts up over the jumps ahead of herself. This, she recognized, was the very stuff of her dreams: Peter giving Fly-by-Night a lead and herself learning what it would be like at Brierley.

The jumps came at her at all angles; she just got a warning in time by the flick of Woodlark's black tail ahead of her. Fly-by-Night crashed through regardless, carrying away loads of brush on his thrashing hoofs. Ruth had a vision of Woodlark disappearing suddenly, as if over a precipice, then herself teetering on the edge of a peaty bank, looking down on Peter. She saw Woodlark stretched out, bounding away from her, then she was flying through the air as Fly-by-Night plunged in pursuit. Amazingly, at the bottom, she landed back in the saddle, although she was convinced that she had come down the bank quite independently of her pony. There was a jolt; she clutched a handful of mane, and stayed with him as he went over a log and away down a stinging ride, hoof-fuls of peat from Woodlark's hoofs flinging up in his face. For a moment she had time to enjoy it, the muffled ground running beneath, the smell of wet bark and pungent leaf, and the sourness of fungus and decay; then Peter had turned right-handed ahead of her and they were flying a bank into a thicket. There was running water below, and the clutching of brambles. Ruth shut her eyes. Fly-by-Night stopped suddenly.

'Still there?' she heard Peter say, and they were out on the edge of the open fields again, pulling up on familiar slippery grass. Woodlark's nostrils were red as she curvetted to a standstill, all feminine elegance, Peter's hands taking her up, strong but not rough. Fly-by-Night stopped in three bounds, tearing up streamers of turf. Ruth landed up his neck.

'Oh, heavens!' Ruth muttered. How did Peter have time to think? she wondered. How would she ever do it, alone?

'Lots of that is what you want,' Peter said. 'It's very good for getting them handy. If you came up every week-end, he'd soon be going round without any trouble.'

'Oh, if I could – !'

'But why not?'

Wracked with fears, longings, and doubts, Ruth

left Fly-by-Night in the McNair paddocks and cycled home on Peter's bike. She had half-expected to see the removal van outside and all their possessions on the pavement, but when she asked her mother, 'Did they buy it?' Mrs. Hollis looked at her in amazement, and laughed. 'Gracious me, you're in a hurry! We've had three lots of people to see, but nobody's falling over themselves to give us a cheque. These things take time, as a rule.' Ruth, without Fly-by-Night in the garden, felt bereaved. 'This is what it will be like if we move,' she thought. What good would a pony be to her half across the county, a Saturday pony? A pony was for talking to when you went out of the back door, and for looking at out of your bedroom window, and riding even if you only had half an hour before tea. What good would Fly-by-Night be, left in a paddock, even a McNair paddock, if nobody bothered with him except at week-ends? Now, just when her dreams of Peter helping her were coming true, satisfaction was bludgeoned by all the other circumstances. Ruth wept. 'What's the matter with you?' her mother asked.

'It's her age,' Ted said, which was a family joke to explain the unpredictable.

Fly-by-Night was shod and Ruth rode him home. In his field that night he whinnied for his lost companions, and roamed up and down the hedges. 'He'd have friends if he lived at McNair's,' Ruth thought. 'But he wouldn't have me.' She didn't think he would mind terribly, not having her, but she minded. She wept again. Her mother gave her two aspirins and a drink of hot lemon.

Peter was right about the house not being sold very quickly. Ruth, Ted and Elizabeth got used to putting everything away and keeping the place excruciatingly tidy for the couples who would call inconveniently in the evenings and poke round their bedrooms and in the airing-cupboard and the bathroom. Mr. and Mrs. Hollis went to look at flats, and came home with long faces, saying nothing. Because she was going to leave it, Ruth loved the grassy tracks down to the creek more and more. The stubble was ploughed, snow fell on the saltings and piled up in big drifts against the sea-wall. The winter was as bad as the summer had been good, and there were only a few Saturdays when Ruth was able to ride over to Hillingdon. Even then the wood was bogged down and the ground too wet for jumping. She would hack through the fields with Peter and they would come back into the house for platefuls of steaming risotto round the fire, then Ruth would hurry home along the darkening roads, wincing at the sluicings from passing cars. But Fly-by-Night had enough to eat, because Mr. McNair came down in the estate car and left sacks of pony-nuts and some bales of good hay.

One Wednesday evening a middle-aged couple who had looked at the house earlier called back and left Mr. Hollis a deposit on it. 'They don't want to move in any great hurry,' Ruth heard him say, 'but

I suppose we'd better decide what we're going to do.'

'The flat over the butcher's shop, next door to Woolworth's was the best of the last batch,' Mrs. Hollis replied.

Ruth felt sick. Her parents asked her if she would like to go and see it with them, but she shook her head, white and silent. Ted went, and came back and said, 'It's all right. There's a good yard round the back for a motor bike. Near Ron, too.'

It was snowing softly. In the field Fly-by-Night's back was melting the snow as it fell, but his roan made it look as if it was lying on him. He whinnied impatiently for his nuts, shaking drops of moisture off his muzzle hairs. Ruth stroked his hard neck. Under its roughness, his coat was shining with Mr. McNair's good feeding, and he was fit, and his hoofs shapely from the blacksmith. Ruth went up the garden and cried again, over the washing-up, and her mother said sharply, 'Ruth, for heaven's sake! At least you can *keep* him – what more do you want?' But the flat next to Woolworth's was fifteen miles from Hillingdon.

Three days later, when the thaw set in, Ron called. As he unwound all his layers and wrappings in the kitchen, his nose shining red in his good-natured, unhandsome face, Ruth put the kettle on to make him a cup of tea.

'There was an ambulance going down the lane at the bottom. Asked me for Mr. Lacey's. So I went along to show 'em the way. He's got his daughter over there from London, but she said the cold was too much for him. He's got pneumonia. He looked bad. I wouldn't be surprised if that's the finish of him.'

'Oh, poor Mr. Lacey!' Ruth said. 'I didn't know.' And even as she spoke the words, an unworthy thought came into her head. She looked at Ron and saw that the unworthy thought was in his head, too. Flushing slightly, she turned away to fetch the tea-caddy. They neither of them said anything more about Mr. Lacey.

It snowed again the next week, and Ruth, unable to resist the temptation, went down the lane and walked up Mr. Lacey's garden path. The pear trees, loaded with snow, seemed to lean against the dilapidated lean-to kitchen. Big puddles lay on the stone flags inside. Ruth could not see her mother there, somehow. With a set face she peered in through the living-room windows. The ceilings were cracked and flakes of plaster lay on the carpet like indoor snow. She could see the narrow staircase curling up, and the brick floor. At the back there was a conservatory with a vine in it. Ruth turned her head away and walked on down the garden. The old fruit trees made arched roofs of snow over her head; every move on her part brought a rushing avalanche. Beyond the trees were the old sheds, a line of them, with sagging roofs, cluttered about with old water-butts and rolls of wire-netting and rotted rabbit hutches. Beyond again, a gate, and two acres of virgin snow, quilted with birds' feet, stretching towards the marshes. Ruth stood in the snow and squeezed her face up with longing. 'Oh, God, *please*! Please could it happen? He needn't die; he could just go and live with his daughter.'

But when she got home her mother said Mr. Lacey had died that afternoon.

12

A DAY OF DECISIONS

'Oh, the messiness of it!' Ruth said to Ron. 'The not knowing. The misery of it!'

She sat at the kitchen table, with the Hunter Trials entry form in front of her. There was a month to go, and a smell of spring in the air outside.

'Woe, woe, woe!' Ted wailed. 'Oh, misery me!' He reached over for a box of crisps that stood on the table and ducked his hand in.

'Hasn't she made her mind up *yet*?' Ron said.

'Oh, reely, I don't know what to do for the best, Mr. 'Ollis,' said Ted in a mimicking voice. 'George says sell the place and Edie says keep it, it'll be worth a lot of money for building one of these days. And our Ada says we could use it for a summer cottage. And Joe says keep it in the family; our Tom has hankerings after being a farmer, and he's only a year more to do at school and we could set him up in tomatoes, like, if we had a bit of ground. And our Ethel says – '

'Oh, shut up,' said Ruth. She wanted to buy Mr. Lacey's house so badly that she could not bear Ted to joke about it. Her father wanted to buy it, too, and her mother, not at all enthusiastic, at least agreed that it could be made into something habitable. But their own house was sold and in six weeks they were going to have to move out, and Mr. Lacey's only daughter could not make up her mind whether to accept Mr. Hollis's offer or not. Ruth prayed for her every night, prayed for the woman's addled mind to clear, for her to agree to sell it. If it had not been for the Hunter Trials coming so close, so that they now filled her mind largely to the exclusion of everything else, she did not think she could have stood the suspense for so long. Mr. Lacey's place was paradise, and Ruth felt as if she were standing at the gates, looking in, and Mr. Lacey's daughter was fumbling in her large untidy handbag for the key. For weeks and weeks she had been fumbling. Ruth had gone thin again, and edgy, and her father said, 'It doesn't matter that much, Ruth,' as he had once said about buying a pony, but this time he did not say it with any great conviction, because he, too, wanted to buy Mr. Lacey's cottage almost as much as Ruth. 'You really could do things with a place like that,' he would say, standing dreamily in front of the fire, jingling his money in his pocket. 'You'll need to, believe me,' Mrs. Hollis would say, rather sharply. 'I'll sweep it up for you,' Elizabeth told her. 'It only wants dusting. It's a nice house.'

Ted, looking for another motor bike to buy with his insurance money from the accident, had earmarked one of the sheds for a workshop. He was back at work again, and happy. Ruth had hoped that even if they didn't get Mr. Lacey's house they might

164

have stayed where they were now that Ted was working again, but her parents were not going back on their decision to move.

'We must get a cheaper place,' Mr. Hollis said firmly. 'I'm not changing my mind.'

He did not like his work very much, Ruth knew, so she supposed it must be a poor life for him to work without joy merely to pay for necessities like a roof and food, and with no money left over for having a bit of fun. Sometimes in the summer he would walk down to the river to watch the sailing, and come back very quiet, and rather short-tempered. Ruth knew he would like a boat, although he never said so. Even a holiday, which they had not had now for five years.

But Ruth, when she got to thinking about it too much, had only to turn her mind to the Brierley Hunter Trials to know what real apprehension was. The days were drawing inexorably nearer. If she had thought – as she had thought last year – that she had no chance at all of getting Fly-by-Night round the course, she would not have bothered; she would have admitted her failure. But she knew now – thanks to the McNair schooling grounds – that he had a chance. He was not hopeless. If he was in the right mood he would go like Woodlark herself. Peter no longer had to give him a lead. Anyone else but herself, Ruth thought, would be looking forward to the date with a pleasurable anticipation, but she could only face it with near panic. But she was going.

'Will you be going?' she had asked Peter at school.

'Oh, I might. When is it?' Peter said, very off-hand. Ruth told him the date and he said, 'If there's nothing else to do I might.'

When Ruth rode out with Pearl, Fly-by-Night could give the Arab mare a lead over the gap into the stubble field. Pearl, unwilling to accede that Fly-by-Night had improved, said, 'It's Milly being off colour, with this stiff leg of hers.'

'Haven't you got the vet *yet*?' Ruth asked her.

Pearl shook her head, but looked rather chastened. 'I will,' she said.

Two days later she came round to Ruth's on her bicycle and said, 'What do you think? Mr. Richards came round today to look at Milly, and he said she's got navicular. Apparently it's incurable, so Daddy's buying me a new pony.'

Ruth looked at Pearl in astonishment.

'But what will you do with Milly?'

Pearl shrugged. 'I don't know. She's useless, according to Mr. Richards. He said it never gets better, and the pony stumbles a lot and is unsafe to ride. So Daddy says I can have a new one!' She was obviously far more excited about the new pony than concerned about the fate of Milky Way. Ruth looked at her coldly.

'Will you keep Milky Way?'

'Mr. Richards says we should breed a foal from her. But we shall want the stable for the new pony. I don't know what we'll do.'

'A foal . . .?' Ruth's eyes opened wide at this

entrancing idea. 'You won't sell her? You *can't* sell her! Oh, it would be lovely to breed a foal!'

'Yes, but I want something to ride, don't I?'

At school the next day Ruth reported to Peter. 'What is navicular anyway?' she asked him. 'Is it as bad as she makes out?'

'Yes, it gets gradually worse with age, so a horse with navicular disease isn't really any good. It's always liable to go lame. It's a sort of inflammation of one of the bones in the foot. My father wouldn't touch a horse if he thought it had navicular.'

'I wonder what they'll do?' Ruth mused.

'They could sell her to someone for breeding. She'd still be quite valuable – that's the big advantage with mares, when something like that crops up.'

Ruth drifted through the next lesson in a dream, choosing a sire worthy of Milky Way, seeing the mare grazing peacefully under summer trees with her Arab foal. Her head was full of dreams: of Fly-by-Night winning the Hunter Trials, of her father buying Mr. Lacey's house . . . 'Ruth Hollis, stop biting your nails,' the teacher said acidly.

There was a fortnight to go to the date for Brierley . . . a week. Ruth started to worry about getting there, because it was a long way to hack, all on the roads. Her mother was worried about moving, because they had nowhere, as yet, to move to at the end of the month. 'You must give that woman an ultimatum,' she said to her husband. 'We can't wait for her to make up her mind for ever.'

'All right,' said Mr. Hollis. Ted was completely involved in buying a new motor bike, going round looking at machines with Ron every evening. Pearl's father was driving all over the countryside looking at expensive ponies for Pearl.

'What a mess it is all at once,' Ruth thought again. 'So many things going on, everything so untidy . . .' But just then, in her mind, only the Saturday of the Hunter Trials mattered. All the other things could wait until afterwards. Triumph or disaster would happen on Saturday, and all the other things would sort themselves out, too, shortly afterwards . . . triumph or disaster. 'One thing at a time,' Ruth thought.

On the Thursday Peter said to her at school, quite casually, 'We're taking Woodlark to Brierley on Saturday. We'll pick you up if you like. It's not out of the way.'

'Fly-by-Night, you mean? In the horse-box?' Ruth wanted to get it quite right.

'Yes. We'll take the big one.'

'Thank you. That would be a terrific help.' Ruth spoke calmly, but the offer was such a relief that she could quite easily have embraced Peter on the spot.

'By the way,' Peter grinned suddenly, 'Father-of-Pearl called yesterday, to see if we had any animals suitable for his dear daughter.'

'Oh, and did you?'

'They fancied – wait for it – get ready to laugh – you'll never guess – '

'Woodlark?'

'Right first time!' Peter was grinning. 'That's why we're taking her to Brierley, as Father-of-Pearl wants to see what she'll do. Of course, she'll go round like a bomb, so we're not worried. Father tried to tell Father-of-Pearl what an absolute beast she was, but he kept saying, "My girl's a splendid little rider. She can handle anything." So after a bit Father piped down. And Pearl was doing her uppity act, treating Father like a shop assistant, so he came in hopping mad and said, "Let them buy her, and good luck to 'em." It was a real laugh. I enjoyed every minute of it.'

Ruth could not help smiling, picturing Peter taking it all in with his non-expression on his face, not saying anything.

'If she rides Woodlark like she rides Milky Way, she'll get bucked off in double-quick time, splendid little rider and all,' Peter said.

Ruth knew that Woodlark was a pony who would stick up for herself; she was as bold, and crafty, as Milky Way was sweet and kind. Ruth had no wish that Pearl should come to a bad end, but she hoped more that Milky Way would be made happy.

'Everyone will be at Brierley on Saturday,' she thought, without enthusiasm. Besides Pearl's family, her own mother and father had said they would like to come and see her 'jump round', and Ted and Ron had said they would 'drop in'. None of this comforted Ruth at all. Now it was so close she wished desperately that it was over.

On Friday night she cleaned her tack, and

groomed Fly-by-Night in the field. The weather was dry and sharp, the evening sky pink and ploughed and calm. Fly-by-Night now stood tied up without protesting, but he still did not stand in the resigned way that Ruth so desired; he still fidgeted and gnawed the post, or tried to graze. But he did not bite her any more, and he never kicked. His feet were shapely, newly-shod (at McNair's, as before), and his winter coat had thinned, and shone when the mud had been removed. 'You're not bad, for forty pounds,' Ruth said to him, and he looked at her, four-square, cocky, his little white crescent shining in the dusk. To Ruth, he looked so marvellous she felt a lump come into the throat.

That night she felt that she never slept at all, although she supposed afterwards that she must have done, on and off. She got up feeling sick, and thought how blissful it would be if she didn't have to go. 'Talk about a glutton for punishment!' Ted remarked. 'What time does the tumbril start rolling?' Ruth tried to laugh, but it was impossible.

She knew that her attitude was ridiculous, but it made no difference.

She went out and groomed Fly-by-Night again, getting the mud off his feet as best she could. The day was damp and grey, fairly warm, but not very exciting. Somewhere there was a sun that suggested it might come through later. But it had not rained again, and the ground was fairly dry. 'Thank goodness,' Ruth thought, 'I am going with the McNairs!' The thought of setting out alone made her shiver.

She fed Fly-by-Night and let him loose again, and went indoors and changed into Pearl's jodphurs, and the jodphur boots and grown-out-of black jacket that Peter had lent her for the occasion. She had her own hat, shabby but serviceable, and a white school blouse and a rather frayed Pony Club tie – also Peter's. She pulled her hair back with a rubber band, and looked at herself in the mirror, and thought she looked like someone at the Horse of the Year Show. 'Hope we jump like it,' she said to her reflection, and smiled and held out her hands for the silver trophy, like a photograph in *Horse and Hound*. But there would be no silver trophy for her, however well Fly-by-Night did, because she was in the same class as Peter. It was a wild dream indeed that made her think of rosettes, but, of course, dreams will rise to anything. When she went downstairs everyone remarked how smart she looked.

'Do you want to take your sandwiches with you? Or shall we bring them in the car?' her mother asked.

'Oh, you bring them,' Ruth said, not interested in food.

'Tumbril's coming up the road now,' Ted said, from the kitchen door. Ruth gave a little shriek and hurried out to catch Fly-by-Night.

Mr. McNair came in for a cup of coffee, and Peter and Ruth boxed Fly-by-Night, with Woodlark rolling a wild white eye at him over the top of the partition, and all the neighbours peering. Peter, too, looked strangely smart in a black jacket and tie; the decorum of his garb after jeans and polo-necked jerseys with holes in the elbows, emphasized the essential seriousness of the day, and Ruth felt a little more hollow inside. 'I feel dreadful,' she said bleakly.

Peter said, 'You're mad! About a potty thing like this? We wouldn't have bothered if Woodlark hadn't got to be shown off.'

'What if she does what she did last year?'

'Last year she was scarcely broken in! Green as grass. It was daft to try it. That's when Father was a bit off his rocker, between you and me and the gatepost.'

Mr. McNair, no longer off his rocker, came cheerfully down the garden path and said, 'Got everything, girl? Saddle and bridle aboard? All set to go?'

Ruth nodded, and squashed into the front of the horse-box between Mr. McNair and Peter. Her parents came out and waved and shouted, 'See you later!' and the horse-box rolled away down the concrete road.

'It's started,' Ruth thought, but now she felt calmer and more cheerful. After all, no worse could happen to her than happened to Peter last year, and he didn't seem to think it mattered at all. He and his father were talking about a knock in the horse-box engine.

For the third time Ruth passed through the gate on the top of Brierley Hill where the Pony Club flag fluttered out on its flag-pole by the gate. They were in plenty of time. The stewards were still trundling about in the Land-Rover and pegging out the collecting-ring.

'You can go round the course now, before we unbox the ponies,' Mr. McNair said.

'Oh, heavens, all that way!' Peter groaned. 'I know it.'

'Don't be so cocky, young fellow-me-lad,' said his father. 'How do you know it isn't quite different this year?'

Peter groaned again, but climbed down and started plodding off across the field, a white-faced Ruth at his side. Several figures could be seen in the distance, doing the same thing, climbing laboriously over the fixed timber that they all hoped to fly faultlessly an hour or two later. It was downhill from the collecting-ring, to a ditch and fairly low fixed rail in a hedge, then a long gallop up the other side to the top end of the wood.

'Take him away fast, as if you really mean it,' Peter said. 'Because a lot of them refuse the first jump, because they don't like going away from the others. Once over, you've got lots of time to get sorted out, going up the hill. Golly, what a bore, hiking all this way!'

At the top of the hill was a tiger trap into a wide ride through the wood. From this ride there was a detour through a very tangled part of the wood, over a large rotted tree-trunk, and back to the ride.

'You'll get your head knocked off here if you don't duck,' Peter said.

At the end of the ride there was a tricky jump

out which involved jumping up on to a bank, and out over a ditch with a rail fixed over it.

'Woodlark takes things like this in one if I don't watch out,' Peter remarked.

After a long plod round the adjoining fields, where the jumps were all fairly straightforward, the course led back into the wood again, through the gate.

'I think I'll get off for this,' Ruth said.

'If I get off I'll never get on again,' Peter said. Ruth thought the same thing might happen to her, but decided to take the risk. 'He ought to be getting a bit weary by the time he gets this far. *If* he gets this far. He might be glad to stand.'

The course-builders had apparently decided to give the bank where Woodlark had fallen a miss this year, for from the gate the course led up a narrow twisting path through the wood to the lip of a different bank which dropped some five feet into a bit of a stream. On the far side, so that the pony had to take off straight out of the stream, a big pile of branches had been thrown across the path to make an obstacle.

'It's easier than the other bank,' Peter said. 'Not so steep.'

'Ugh,' said Ruth.

'You've done worse banks than this at home.'

'Sometimes I have,' Ruth said. 'But sometimes I haven't.'

Peter grinned. 'All part of the lovely fun,' he said.

The course led out of the wood over an easy fence and back to the start on a parallel course to

the way out, down the long hill, over the ditch and
another rail some fifty feet away from the first jump
of the course, and back up to the collecting-ring.
By the time they had got to the bottom of the hill
again they had caught up with several of the girls
doing the course ahead of them.

'Hullo, McNair. How many red rosettes are you
picking up today?' The girl who spoke was the one
with malicious eyes who Ruth always thought of as
Cat's Eyes.

'More than last year, I hope,' Peter said shortly.

Cat's Eyes laughed, jeeringly. 'Of course, I'd forgotten!' She remembered now, with obvious glee.
'Instead of going over the rails and through the gate
you went through the rails and over the gate.'

'Yes, that's right.'

The girl who was walking up the hill with Cat's
Eyes said, 'You needn't be so clever, Mercy. The day
you get over the first jump will be more memorable
than the day Peter doesn't come in first.'

Ruth thought, 'Bully for you.' The girl who spoke
was called Jane Withenshawe, and had come second
to Peter the year Ruth had first watched. Ruth,
noting that Cat's Eyes was really called Mercy, was
amazed at the inaptness of it. As they made their
way back to the horse-box she said, 'Why is that
girl so beastly?'

'Born like it, I suppose,' Peter said. 'Jane's all right.
And her pony's a cracker. Dad sold it to her three
years ago.'

Jane's pony, Ruth remembered, was a bay gelding,

very like Woodlark in looks, called Clipper. She remembered Peter asking Jane to pair with him, two years ago, and Jane showing in her face that she had wanted to say yes, but nobly refusing.

By the time they had unboxed the two ponies the class for the youngest children, twelve and under, had started. Ruth's stomach felt cold again as she fetched Fly-by-Night's tack and started to saddle him up. There was no sign of her family as yet, for which she was profoundly grateful, but the Pymm Jaguar was parked inside the gate. Mr. McNair went across to intercept them, in response to Peter's muttered plea.

Peter mounted Woodlark, and waited for Ruth to tighten her girths. Woodlark pivoted impatiently, flexing to her curb, her fine black mane lifting in the breeze. By comparison Fly-by-Night was sturdy, tough and masculine where the mare was all female elegance. Side by side with Peter, Ruth realized for the first time that Fly-by-Night was quite small, and that she had grown quite a lot during the last year. To give him the aids now she had to put her legs back to find his sides. She had an instant's panic: 'I am growing out of him!' but as quickly she thrust the thought from her mind. There would be time, later, to worry about that. But the thought added to her nervousness.

They walked and trotted up and down the top of the field, out of the way of the course. Ruth felt Fly-by-Night eager and bouncing beneath her, and herself stiff with nerves, her fingers like wood. Peter did not appear to be at all concerned, but he was riding Woodlark with considerable attention, not just passing the time away chatting, like most of the girls. When they eventually went down to the collecting-ring Ruth noticed several curious glances sent in her direction, and it occurred to her that being with Peter had given her a sort of standing already, although she had not done anything yet. It frightened her, and yet was a comfort at the same time. Being with Peter, she did not have to think for herself, just follow Woodlark, stand still when she stood still, and walk about when she walked about. Only, when her number was called by the steward, she would be on her own.

'I wish I could go first and get it over!' she said miserably to Peter, as the steward started checking them over. She knew she was about three-quarters of the way down the list, five behind Peter. This would be the longest hour of her life. The first girl was already away, cantering crabwise down the hill.

'We'll walk round a bit more,' Peter decided. 'It's too cold just to stand.'

Walking round a bit more, Ruth remembered all sorts of things she didn't know.

'Does the fastest round win?'

'No. Speed doesn't matter, unless you're so slow you exceed the time allowed. I shouldn't think that would happen to Fly-by-Night.'

'How do they score then?'

'Five for knocking anything down, ten for first

refusal, twenty for second, thirty for falling off, ten for not shutting a gate, two for hitting a marker.'

'Oh.' The words went out of Ruth's mind as soon as Peter had spoken them. She could see Pearl, looking very elegant in jade-green tweed, with her long hair blowing in the wind, talking to Mr. McNair; she could see Jane Withenshawe out in the country going at a terrific lick on the bold Clipper; of her parents there was still no sign. The wind was cold and it looked like rain. Ruth felt very sick.

'I'd better go back. There's only three before Woodlark now,' Peter said.

Ruth followed him back. Mr. McNair came over with the Pymms and Peter had to be polite. Ruth was under no such obligation, which was fortunate, as Pearl said to her, 'Golly, you don't think you're going to get *him* round, do you?'

Ruth glowered at her. She had no wits to think of a reply, so rode off to the other side of the collecting-ring. Peter came past to go to the start, and for one awful moment Ruth could not stop Fly-by-Night from following Woodlark.

'Not you!' the steward shouted at her, and she managed to turn Fly-by-Night round just in time, before Peter put Woodlark into a canter. She hustled him furiously back into the ring, and saw Pearl grinning.

All the parts of Peter's round that she could see were faultless, and he came back very fast down the hill and flew the jump at the bottom as if it were six times its actual size. When Woodlark came back she was very excited, and Peter had to take her away and walk her about to cool her off, so Ruth did not get a chance to hear how he had done. Mr. McNair was looking very satisfied, and smoking cigars with Mr. Pymm, so Ruth assumed that all was well.

Several of the rounds, from what one could see from the collecting-ring, appeared to be faultless, but what went on in the wood, where all the tricky bits were, was not revealed. The steward, a smart woman in sheepskin and suède, said to her, 'You're the next. Don't go away, will you?' She checked out the next departure, which was Cat's Eyes', and said, 'You're new, aren't you? I haven't seen your pony up here before.'

'Yes – er – no – '

'Don't look so frightened!' the woman said. 'Your pony looks as if he could do it standing on his head.'

Her few kind words wrung a grateful smile out of Ruth. She watched Cat's Eyes' grey gelding canter very slowly down from the start to stop at the first fence. She realized that she probably would not have to wait much longer, for the grey did not look as if he intended to go any farther. The steward apparently thought so, too, as she said, 'Are you ready, dear?'

Ruth nodded. At the same moment, a yell of 'Ruth!' rent the air, and she turned round, startled, to see Ted and Ron standing at the ropes, looking very out of place in their motor-bike gear and crash-helmets. Ted did a boxer's hand-clasp over his head and shouted, 'Attagirl!'

'Go down to the start now, dear,' said the steward. 'Mercy is eliminated.'

Ruth gave Fly-by-Night a panic-stricken kick with her heels and he bounded forward into a fast trot, nearly cannoning into the returning grey, who came home at a far more eager pace than he had left.

'Sorry,' she muttered.

She steered Fly-by-Night for the flag where Major Banks was standing, and managed to pull up in the right place. He checked her number, glanced at his stop-watch, and said, 'Off you go, then.'

Ruth, having somehow expected a roll of drums and a flash of lightning to herald her performance, was amazed to find herself cantering down the hill, completely on her own. The short grass was smooth and inviting, the rails at the bottom looked piffling; beyond, the hill stretched up to the tall elms on its crest where the rooks were cawing and a gleam of sunlight was passing. There wasn't a soul in sight. Ruth no longer felt frightened. She felt excited, and fantastically happy.

She knew Fly-by-Night was not going to refuse the rails, by the feel of him. She knew, too, that when she felt like she did now refusals did not happen. She had not waited two years merely to refuse the first fence. Fly-by-Night went over it like Woodlark herself, so big and bold that Ruth almost lost a stirrup, and had to take a clutch of mane to steady herself.

After the jump he steadied himself, and Ruth

could feel him wondering what he was up to, galloping across this strange countryside with no Woodlark beside him.

'Come on, Fly. This is in earnest,' Ruth said to him happily, and he flicked an ear back at her, from deep in his thick mane, and Ruth saw the steam of his breath and the shining edge of his eyes, and leaned forward in the saddle, feeling invincible.

The tiger trap into the wood was solid, and Ruth felt the pony's momentary surprise, and instant's doubt. To dispel it, she closed her legs hard. Fly gave a little grunt, and jumped it in a rather unpleasant popping style, which left Ruth up in the air when he was already down. But Peter had said nothing about marks for style. Ruth had a glimpse of a man on a shooting-stick making a mark on his score-sheet, then the roof of the wood closed over her, and Fly-by-Night's hoofs were muffled by the thick, soft ground. She looked up, and saw the marker flag for the left turn just ahead. She pulled up sharply, in a soft smother of leaves, and Fly-by-Night turned on to the narrow detour that led to the fallen log. He was at home in the wood, after all his pounding round the McNair estate; he had learned to do sharp turns through the trees, and scramble under the scrub while Ruth leant close over his withers, ducking for the branches. They came upon the log suddenly. Fly had no time to hesitate; he was over, and Ruth swung him round for the open ride beyond. She had forgotten the tricky jump at the end of the ride, and after the pleasant ease of the canter down the wide path she came to the bank with a lurch of fear. Fly-by-Night went up on the top with more of a scramble than a jump, and then stood there, boggle-eyed, staring into the ditch. Ruth unashamedly took a large bunch of mane in both hands, gave him plenty of rein and drummed hard with her legs.

'Come on! You *must*!'

Her urgency communicated, for after a moment's uneasy pawing at the ground, he jumped out over the ditch and rail in one almighty bound, with such suddenness that only her handfuls of mane kept Ruth aboard. With only a slight pang at her lack of professional poise, she headed Fly-by-Night out across the open grass, and as his shining hoofs flung out beneath her she was full of a sense of exhilaration at what they had already achieved. Even if she did not look smooth and calm like Peter, she got there just the same — so far. At least Ted and Ron and Pearl would see that she had managed half-way; she was not disgraced, whatever happened.

Fly-by-Night seemed to have understood what it was all about now, as if he was enjoying himself, for he flew the first jump out in the open without a moment's hesitation. There was a short stretch across the corner of a field, a jump out over a gap and a bundle of brushwood, then round in a circle, over some straw bales and back towards the wood again. The gate was the next obstacle, and Ruth felt a moment's qualm. She thought perhaps Fly-by-Night wouldn't fancy anything fussy now, after his unimpeded progress over the countryside.

He pulled up in front of the gate because he had to, coming to a halt in long skidding slithers where the ground was already cut up and slippery. Ruth slipped down and took the string off the gate, shoving it open with her foot. Her legs felt all trembly.

'Come on, Fly!'

She was in front of him, pulling him, which he (as if knowing that this procedure was captioned 'Bad' in Ruth's book) did not like. He did not move, but stared at her, his nostrils all wide and red with galloping. Ruth came round to his side and led him properly, and he went through, with a snort of suspicion. Ruth had to heave at him to stop, and managed to get the string back over the post by stretching both arms out to their fullest extent, one holding Fly and one dropping the string. It was not a polished performance, but they had been quite quick.

When she came to mount again she realized immediately that her girths needed tightening, as the saddle started to slither round when she put her weight on the stirrup. She cursed and struggled, with Fly-by-Night going round in circles, heaving up the inch of loose with her clumsy, excited hands. Fly-by-Night trod on her foot, and lunged away into some brambles, and she half hopped, half fell after him, trying to keep him still. The mud was up to her ankles.

'You beast! Wait!'

He waited long enough for her to get half-way

183

back in the saddle, but while she was still in mid-air he set off. Ruth pitched back on the cantle, the reins slithering through her fingers. A branch knocked her cap down over her eyes so that she could not see where she was going: she only knew that there was a great crashing of undergrowth all round her and that twigs and brambles were clawing at her like live animals. Suddenly there was a sharp blow and a pain down the side of her face that made her cry out. A branch seemed to break off with an explosion right in her ear. She thrust her cap back, but could still see nothing but a blur of clutching branches through which Fly-by-Night was forcing his way in a series of excited bounds. Whatever had hit her face was agonizing; she realized that she could not see for blood. When she put her hand up it came away all red.

'Fly, stop it!'

She pulled him to a halt by brute force, tears of sheer rage adding another impediment to her reeling vision. She wiped her face with the back of her sleeve, and peered round for a way out of the predicament Fly had landed her in. There was no sign of a track anywhere, only impenetrable jungle.

'Fly, we're *lost*!' she sobbed. She was outraged – nobody got *lost* in a Hunter Trials! She thought of Pearl, and choked with grief.

'You idiot pony! You beastly idiot pony!'

She mopped frantically at the blood and tears in an effort to see, and kicked Fly on into the thinnest bit of her surroundings that she could find. He crashed through and she bent down, choking and muttering, looking desperately for the salvation of a yellow flag. Suddenly, they were in the open. There were no flags, but at right-angles to their wild stampede through the bush a hoof-churned track appeared. Ruth's sense of direction had become so confused since her blow on the head that she did not know which way to follow the path, but with what she afterwards thought of as a stroke of genius, she thought to look at the hoof-prints. Sunk deep and fast, they showed the way.

Fly-by-Night set off at a canter again, and Ruth tried to sort herself out. She could feel nothing in her face now, and had no idea what had happened, but she did not seem to be feeling in any way indisposed. Rather she felt humiliated and a trifle damp, more with baby tears than blood. 'Oh, you *fool*!' she said to herself, cantering along the path, ashamed and angry. Getting lost, and *crying* . . . she was so incompetent it wasn't true. Reviling herself for her stupidity, she came to the bank without expecting it. Fly-by-Night skidded to a halt and teetered on the lip of it, snorting. Ruth had a glimpse of a startled face staring from the far side, then Fly-by-Night went down in one bound, landing with a great splash in the stream. The person scoring shouted something, but Ruth had no idea what. She was too busy keeping her seat. Fly went through the brush, scattering it with a cracking and a crunching all across the ride, and they were flying away towards the jump out into the open. 'The lovely open!' Ruth thought. She felt as if she had been in the wood for ever, carving her way through, and wondered if she had been given up for lost. All sense of time had left her. She felt she had taken well over the time allowed already. Her eyes stung, and she still could not see very well, but she no longer knew why.

Fly-by-Night, going now as if he would never stop, flew over the fence out into the field. Ruth had to turn him down the hill, but otherwise there was nothing to do, only sit there, and see the people in the collecting-ring on the opposite slope, and think, 'Here I come! I've done it!' She felt wonderful. She did not feel as if she belonged to earth at all. She felt that nothing in the whole world could ever worry her again, nothing could possibly go wrong, nothing could detract. Fly-by-Night went over the ditch at the bottom as if he was Woodlark herself, and then she was back beside Major Banks, who was clicking his stop-watch 'Steady on!' called the Major.

Ruth heaved, wondering if Fly-by-Night was all set to go round again, but the pony got the message, and dropped into an unseating trot. Ruth bounced and pulled again. Someone came up and took Fly-by-Night's rein and said, 'Whatever have you done to your face?'

'I don't know.' She didn't say it, but she didn't care either. She felt wonderful. She saw Ted and Ron coming towards her, and grinned at them idiotically.

'I say, whatever have you done to your face?' Ted said.

Major Banks came up with the woman out of the collecting-ring and said to her, 'Mrs. Marshall will take you to the First Aid, dear.'

'I think she ought to be put down,' Ted said. 'It's the only humane thing to do.'

Major Banks stared at Ted, and Ted said hastily, 'She's my sister. I'll take her to the First Aid, if you like.'

'Oh, good,' said the Major. 'We can't really spare Mrs. Marshall for a minute or two. It's that van by the Land-Rover. There's a St. John's man there. He'll see to her.'

He looked at Ruth again, rather doubtfully, and went off back to the start. Ruth looked round for Peter, but saw that he was trapped by the Pymms once more, over by the horse-box, so decided she had better get the First Aid chore over. She slid off Fly-by-Night on to her trembly legs, and patted his damp neck.

'Wasn't he marvellous?'

'You did jolly well, from what we could see,' Ron said. 'No more than we expected though. I'll hold Fly if you like, while you go with Ted.'

'Yes, come on, you're losing gore like a stuck pig,' Ted said. 'Come to St. John, where Mercy is eliminated.'

'Where *what*?'

'That's what that woman said. Mercy is eliminated. Didn't you hear her? We liked that, we did.'

Ruth could see that Ted was in one of his dotty moods. They all went to the St. John's Ambulance van, where the man looked very pleased to have something to do. Ruth discovered that her borrowed jacket and tie were all spotted with blood, which worried her more than the wound itself, which, when she was cleaned up, was discovered to be a small but deep cut just below her right eye. It was swelling fast, which was the reason she couldn't see very well.

'You're very lucky, my dear,' said the St. John's man. 'Very lucky it missed your eye.'

Ruth thought it a matter of opinion as to why, as the only injury of the day, she was to be considered lucky, but did not say so. Ted said, 'Very lucky. Mercy is not eliminated after all.'

Ruth was decorated with a sticking-plaster that obscured her vision still farther, and given a cup of tea, then she went back up the hill with Ted and Ron, leading Fly-by-Night. The sun, having struggled hard all morning, was just coming out. It had a summer warmth in it, which fitted in: Ruth knew that this was a day when nothing now could go wrong. She was in a stupor of warm, deep-seated bliss. The excitement and the sickening nervousness had given way to a radiance she had never experienced before. She could feel her face smiling idiotically. She could not stop it.

They were almost back at the horse-box when Ted spotted their parents coming across the grass towards them.

'You've missed the act of the century,' Ted greeted them.

'Oh, whatever have you done to your face?' Mrs. Hollis said to Ruth. 'What happened? Did you fall?'

'No.'

'You got round all right?'

'Yes. A branch hit me, that's all.'

'Oh dear. Never mind. I suppose it was lucky it wasn't your eye. We're terribly sorry we missed you, dear – '

'But you won't be sorry when you hear the reason why,' her father interrupted. Ruth looked at him. He looked quite different from how she had ever seen him before. He looked just like she felt. And she knew the reason why.

'The house?' she said. 'It's all right? She said we could have it – Mr. Lacey's house?'

'That's right. She made up her mind at last. We can move in whenever we like.'

Ruth said nothing. All she could see was the two acres under its covering of snow, the sun shining on it, and the bird marks making lace patterns. She saw Fly-by-Night turned out there, and another, shadowy pony, a companion for Fly. In her dreams, it was Milky Way, in foal to an Arab stallion, never to be hauled about by Pearl again. (Because she knew now that miracles happened.) There was a stable for Fly-by-Night, and a yard paved with bricks . . .

'Say something,' said Ted.

'Please give us your opinion, Miss Hollis.' Ron was grinning.

Her father gave her a little pat on the shoulder

and said, 'Leave the child alone. Her constitution isn't up to all this excitement in one day.'

'Her constitution needs a few sandwiches, by the look of it,' her mother said. 'Can't you tie that pony up somewhere, so we can have our lunch?'

Ruth noticed, for the first time, that the event was over and the ponies were all tied up and their owners picnicking. She saw Peter coming up the hill on Woodlark, carrying a red rosette in his hand, and behind him was the bay, Clipper, with a blue rosette tied to his browband. Peter saw her and shouted across:

'Go on! Are you dreaming?'

He came across, grinning. 'Major Banks wants you, over by the Land-Rover.'

'Oh.' Ruth turned to set off for the Land-Rover, but Peter said to her, 'Take Fly, you idiot.'

'What for? Why does he want to see me? My face is all right.'

Peter made a despairing face. He spoke to her very slowly, as if to a foreigner: 'He – wants – to – give – you – a – rosette.'

The miracles were coming in shoals. White as a sheet, Ruth tightened Fly-by-Night's girths and mounted, and followed Peter down to the Land-Rover. (Her parents said to Ted, 'Do you think she's all right? She does look queer.' Ted said, 'She probably thinks she's been killed and has arrived in heaven.' 'Don't talk like that, Ted,' his mother said severely.)

When Major Banks saw Peter he said, 'What,

you don't want another one, do you? Wait till this afternoon.' He was standing with all the score-sheets spread out on a little table, and a boxful of rosettes. He looked very cheerful.

'No, sir, it's Ruth. You said she had won one.'

'Oh, that's right. You came sixth, dear. Very good show. How's your face? All right?'

'Yes, thank you.' Ruth took the white rosette he handed her.

'Lucky it wasn't your eye, eh?'

'Yes, sir.'

'That's the lot, then. Go and have your lunch. Well done.'

Ruth rode slowly back towards the horse-box with Peter. She was speechless. Peter looked at her, smiling.

'Shock too much for you?'

She nodded.

'You'll ride pairs with me this afternoon?' Peter asked.

'Me?'

'Yes, you.'

'Not Clipper? I can't see out of one eye.'

'What does that matter? The other eye's enough, isn't it? Fly'll take you.'

'All right. Yes.'

Ruth rode back to her parents, and Ted and Ron, who were eating sandwiches in the car. When she glanced behind she saw Peter giving his red rosette to Pearl, as if it were a discarded programme. She looked down at her own, shining white in her fingers, and started to count the miracles that had happened that day. The radiance was still spreading. The white rosette would be her dearest treasure until the day of her death.

'Have a sandwich?' said Ted.

A SUMMER OF
HORSES

Carol Fenner

This book is for Esther singing to birds
And Faith with her honest eloquent eye
For Beautiful Grace who always ran fastest
For Beth with her shoulder against the sky

I would like to thank by goddaughter, Jessica Rowe, who suffered through a tediously long draft of this novel when it was called *The Animal Person*. A hundred and a half dog-eared pages of a typed work can look pretty dull to a young girl. I thank, too, Jessie's mother, my good friend Susan, who helped her tackle it. Appreciation to Lynette Vinton who, encouraged by her mother, Mary, also read the manuscript in its early stages. The reactions of these mothers and daughters to the story gave me fresh insight.

This book would still be called *Horse Story — Working Title* but for my husband, Jay Williams, and my editor, Jenny Fanelli. On the same day 750 miles apart they each came up with *A Summer of Horses*. How could I protest such plottings of fate?

I am also indebted to my horse, Hail Raiser, who taught me how to listen.

Carol Fenner

1

No one was there to meet them. After scrambling to collect their luggage from the compartment under the bus, the two girls hauled their suitcases into the waiting room. There they stood in desolate silence watching the other passengers leave the station. The big room with its fluorescent lights seemed to grow colder and damper as it emptied.

'I think we should have gotten off at the last stop,' said Gem, her voice hissing with worry.

Faith glared at her older sister. 'No way,' she snorted. But she was worried too. They were supposed to be met by their mother's old college friend, and Faith couldn't remember what Beth Holbein looked like. The woman was a rare visitor to their home in the suburbs of Chicago. She never talked much at their chatty dinner table.

'She might be late,' Faith's mother had warned them. 'She tends to pile too much into her day.'

Their mother often talked about her quiet friend. Beth could lift enough bales of hay to load a truck. She drove tractors and a big horse trailer. If her old pickup truck broke down, she could lift up the hood and fix it. Faith's father said the reason Beth didn't get married was because . . . 'Ye gods! She scares men away!' Beth could do many things that often only strong men do.

Perhaps this Saturday was one of the piled-up days, thought Faith. Or perhaps they *were* at the wrong station. Resentment that she had been holding in check rose up in her. She didn't want to be in this dismal, ugly station in the middle of rural Michigan. She wanted to be home, where her mother's fine voice hummed and sang through the tall rooms of their comfortable old house. She wanted to help her father do chores – empty wastebaskets and fold laundry, pick up twigs from their neatly tended lawn. She wanted to be home, where her brand-new twin baby brothers were just beginning to belong. They were tiny as puppies, with miniature fists and little curled toes.

I could have helped with the twins, she thought for the hundredth time. And Dad and I could have fixed the meals all summer. Gem would've been at the beach or on the phone. There's no way we could have been any extra trouble.

'Why isn't she here?' hissed Gem angrily and Faith snapped back to the present.

'Ye gods! What a place!' Gem's sour gaze swept the barren room and stopped at a door marked WOMEN. 'I think I'll try the ladies' room,' she announced and stalked off, her big canvas bag slung over her shoulder.

Faith watched her go with a mixture of envy and disdain. 'Trying' the ladies' room meant her sister would comb her hair and brush her eyebrows and adjust her makeup. Gem was beautiful, with a lion's mane of sandy gold hair. Her real name was Grace Marie, after a great-grandmother, but nobody called her that. She was fourteen, a track star and a flirt. If there was no place to jog and no one to flirt with, Gem combed her hair.

Faith deserted the luggage to walk to the door and look out through the screen. It was late afternoon and the mid-June sun was soft in the parking lot. A gas station-store across the street had a dog-eared sign, OPEN, in the window. But no one seemed to be around. Down the empty street Faith could see a crossing where a dirt road met the paved one. Gem was right. What a place. Not even enough traffic to pave all the roads.

Gem came back more sour than before. 'I hate this *farm* idea of theirs,' she ranted. 'I *hate* animals.' She glared at Faith as if it were her fault instead of their parents'. 'You should get along fine, you're such an animal lover. But *me* – I won't have any company except for a ten-year-old mouse brain.'

'What about me?' cried Faith. 'I've got a boy-crazy sister with bulging muscles and toilet paper wadded down into her bra. Some company!' Then she added maliciously, 'I think it's going to be great. You're such an athlete. You probably can do *chores* and stuff like that . . . clean out stalls full of *manure*. I think it'll be a perfect summer for you. Eleven weeks of horse manure!' The sisters glared at each other in the empty waiting room.

'You might just hunt up that number we're supposed to call in an emergency,' Faith said, spite still nasty in her voice. 'That is, if you haven't packed it in with your high heels and perfume!'

Gem slipped her hand into the depths of her canvas bag, rummaged around and haughtily produced a folded paper.

But there was no answer when they called the number from an old-fashioned pay phone. Faith had a dismal image of a faceless Beth waiting at another station in some distant town.

An hour passed. People began to arrive for the next bus. And Beth arrived, too. Faith recognized her from the window. She recalled the shining pony-tail – hair the color of dark honey pulled back from the tanned face. But she also knew for certain it was Beth because she clopped into the parking lot in a horse-drawn buggy.

'She's here!' Faith yelled back to Gem, who had just begun to size up a tall, freckled guy wearing a basketball jacket.

Faith slammmed out the door, her pale, thin legs flying, red hair floating out behind. The horse – a real, trotting, breathing horse! She'd loved horses ever since, as a little girl, she'd seen the mounted police parade in downtown Chicago.

'Hello,' said Beth. 'Thought you'd like a different sort of ride.' She smiled a quiet smile and climbed down from the seat.

Faith's eyes were all for the horse, a chestnut – hair the color of her own. 'Like new copper,' her father always said. The horse's red coat had a burnished shine that deepened into shadows under smooth muscles. He stood quietly, but Faith sensed a readiness in his waiting. She sent him a silent greeting with her mind and eyes – as one animal to another. He tipped his head and slid her a sidelong glance.

Gem, who had finally torn herself away from the basketball jacket, came out the door with her snappy, self-conscious walk. Then she saw the horse and buggy. She stopped. Her mouth dropped open.

'Faith, Gem,' said Beth, 'meet Shinyface.'

The chestnut's ears perked forward. People gathering to meet the bus stared with pleasant curiosity. This ordinarily would have embarrassed Faith. But Gem, the aggressive and daring sister, stood so dumbfounded that Faith was oddly comforted.

The buggy was old, but tidy. Its leather seats were worn. Beth grabbed the three biggest bags and hoisted them into the back seat. She was wearing old blue jeans, really old, not bleached out or faded on purpose but jeans with real holes in them, and big, thick boots. Faith noticed for the first time that, although Beth was slender with a narrow waist, she had hefty legs and strong, smooth arms.

Faith had never paid much attention to Beth when she had visited them. She had accepted her father's view when he claimed Beth was 'crazy living all by herself – ye gods! – doing a man's job – never sure of where her next dollar's coming from.'

Now, at this bright, exciting moment, Beth didn't

seem at all crazy. She was the herald of lovely surprises.

The ride to the farm was splendid. Forgotten were the new baby brothers wiggling in their pretty blankets. Beth let Faith hold the reins. The power and pull of the big animal pulsed through Faith's thin arms as his great shifting hindquarters plunged them forward along the road. They drove beneath huge trees. An early summer breeze brought fresh meadowy smells across their faces.

'Fortunately, we've plenty of unpaved roads,' Beth told the girls. 'Dirt roads are much kinder to a horse's feet than pavement and a good deal less dangerous than our busy highway.'

'You've got a highway somewhere?' asked Gem with an edge of sarcasm in her voice. She sat, surrounded by luggage, in the wide back seat.

Beth's answer was cheery. 'Oh yes. Not too far. Civilization is within reach.' Then she added seriously, 'But far away enough to forget most of the time.'

'Where do you go to the movies?' Gem asked in dismay. Faith wanted to add, 'She means, where do you find the boys?' but she was feeling too good to bug her sister.

'We've got a movie house in town.' Beth spoke over her shoulder. 'It's open on Wednesday nights and Saturdays.' Gem groaned.

'And I'm afraid my television is sort of sick.' Beth didn't sound sorry. 'But you'll never miss it.'

The buggy rattled and sprang along. Gem slumped, sulking, in the back.

'Don't let the reins go slack,' Beth told Faith. 'Keep a light feel on his mouth.'

Faith tried to sense the horse's mouth through the reins. Her special gift with animals had never included control over them. She had a fine ear for listening to animals – hearing speech in their voices. Part of her listening was noticing their movement, the expression on their faces, their eyes. She could creep up close to rabbits; she could scold back at a squirrel. Her father called her Dr Doolittle.

They passed fields of new corn, a cattle ranch and more fields bordered by great oak trees. Faith kept trying to tune her listening in to the horse. But it was a bit overwhelming. Shinyface was so large and powerful. She contented herself with keeping her hands firm.

'How far do we go?' asked Faith. She felt an unfamiliar sense of command and she could have gone on forever. The summer spread before her, alive with promises.

'Almost there,' Beth told her, holding out her hands for the reins. At a break in the line of trees, Beth slowed the chestnut and manoeuvered the buggy on to a drive. Gem sat up, interested in spite of herself.

They approached a rattly, wooden bridge. Water sparkled and chortled beneath. Beth spoke soothing sounds to the chestnut, who drew his head down and arched his neck sideways at the busy water as they started across.

'Easy, Shiny, easy . . .' Beth murmured over and over. The buggy veered dangerously close to the bridge rail. Gem gasped. Faith knew an instant of panic. With high, tense steps, the horse pranced and twitched over the bridge. Now Faith had no trouble hearing the big chestnut. The signals were strong. She could almost see through Shiny's eyes – the water flashing and quivering like a great snake. A thrill of danger slid across Faith's skin.

Once on the other side, Shiny calmed down and trotted out quite smoothly. They passed a field with sheep in it. A big, old farmhouse came into view perched on a grassy rise. Faith noted it needed a coat of paint. Beyond the rise poked the top story of a barn, dark red with a sturdy roof. As they drew closer, Faith saw smaller buildings scattered about, all freshly painted. A stretch of grassy hills dotted with horses rolled up to the horizon.

Somewhere from these hills, Faith heard a wild, high-pitched whinny and the lower, calmer answer from a distant horse. She felt, beneath the sudden goose bumps on her skin, the stirrings of adventure.

2

Holbein Farm was bigger than Faith had expected. Beth proudly informed the girls that the sheep they had just passed were hers and that the farm also supported many cats, three dogs and a donkey. Somewhere among the hilly fields were a small lake and several acres of woods. Her nearest neighbors, Beth told them, were a couple of miles away.

They drove past a corral where a gleaming dark horse trotted nervously. 'That's Apollo, my stallion,' said Beth. She explained that he was kept separate from the other horses 'because he gets sort of crazy whenever a mare is in season.'

'What's "in season"?' asked Faith.

'When she's ready to conceive,' said Beth. 'And sometimes more than one mare is ready at the same time. We isolate Apollo to protect him as well as the other horses – and ourselves.'

Faith was just beginning to find the discussion fascinating when it ended. Beth's attention focused on easing Shiny into a turn towards the house. She halted the buggy by a sagging back porch. A huge, woolly white dog came joyfully padding to greet them. Gem stayed nervously in the buggy, but Faith slipped down from her seat and clucked and mock-growled. The dog's tail wagged furiously. She stroked his ears and scratched above his tail.

'Wolfie usually terrifies people with his friendliness,' remarked Beth. She took a long, approving look at Faith before she turned to hoist the luggage from the buggy. Gem climbed down uneasily. She didn't care for dogs. She usually relied on Faith to keep one busy until she got away.

While Beth led Shinyface and the buggy down toward the barn, the girls lugged their suitcases into the kitchen. Wolfie panted eagerly at Faith's heels. 'You stay here, Wolfie,' said Faith, closing the screen door gently in his face.

Beth's house was a crazy mess – 'chaos' their father had called it. 'You girls should get along fine in Beth's chaos, judging from the condition of your bedroom,' he had said.

The kitchen floor was crowded with various kinds of boots – tall riding boots, muddy work boots, fat moon boots. Magazines, catalogs and unopened mail were piled on the kitchen table. A tangle of harnesses hung over the back of one chair. Dishes from past meals were balanced precariously in the sink.

Does our room look like this? thought Faith. She herself was rather inclined toward neatness. Her chair in their bedroom back home was piled as high as Gem's with soiled clothes, but hers were all folded. When she sat in the chair, it sort of pressed them neatly together. Gem created chaos around her, changing in and out of clothes and hairstyles until she only had time to drop her discarded things on the floor. 'Dump and dash,' their mother said of the older sister. 'Miss Dump-and-Dash.'

Now, at Beth's house, Miss Dump-and-Dash was looking for the bathroom, where she could lay her makeup and colognes. Just off the kitchen was a large, modern, half-finished bathroom. Gem gasped and Faith followed her in. The bathroom was a mess. Back home there were rules about picking up towels and putting toothbrushes back where they belonged. I guess Beth doesn't have any rules about the bathroom, thought Faith. Gem moaned.

The short laugh behind them made them turn around. Beth explained that one of her sheep had been sick during a spring frost and she had brought her in to keep her warm. The sheep had lain on the bathroom rug, messed on the floor, eaten from the bathtub and drank out of the toilet bowl.

'I cleaned up the worst part,' said Beth. 'I keep meaning to get to the rest, but I haven't found the time.' The sisters just stood there speechless until Beth suggested, 'Best to use the old bathroom just across the kitchen.'

My, my . . . *two* kitchen bathrooms, thought Faith.

'Ye gods!' said Gem when she saw the other bathroom. A doorless linen closet was piled full of dirty laundry which spilled out into the room. A tall avocado plant sat in the tub, its leaves green and perky. Faith giggled. She wasn't fond of baths. Gem found the mirror to her liking and calmed down.

'You can explore the farm a little bit today, if you

want,' said Beth. 'You'd better put on some boots.' Then, noticing the confusion in both girls, she said sneakers would do. 'Did you bring any old ones?' she asked, eying their soft leather flats.

Faith and Gem changed into old tennis shoes right out of their bags, opened in the kitchen, and set out to explore the farm. Beth stayed behind to answer a ringing phone.

The girls, joined by the strangeness of a new place, stuck close together. They found a path down to the barn. It was a huge, old barn built into the slant of a hill. A short distance away was a fenced rectangle similiar to Apollo's corral. There were no horses in it, just standing sections of fence, crossed poles and barrels on their sides. Faith grew excited. This must be the ring where riders practised. They probably rode around those barrels − or jumped their horse over them! The ring looked as if it was used a lot.

They entered the barn into a room which Faith noted with surprise was clean and tidy. Saddles sat on wooden racks in neat rows. Bridles hung on the wall beside them. Passing through a narrow door between saddle racks, they discovered the stable. The odor of damp wood, manure and hay filtered warmly from a row of stalls. Faith peered into the nearest one and was disappointed to find it empty.

A ladder in the ceiling led into a giant hayloft overhead. The girls ventured up cautiously and climbed out on top through a square hole.

Hay was stacked in neat bales almost up to the two-story ceiling. Light came dustily through little, high-up windows. Cats sat about, some of them stretching, some of them crouching, one of them clawing its way into a large bag of cat food. Faith thought this would be a cozy place to come with a book on a rainy day.

Next they wandered off to a field where they had seen some horses. 'They must live out-doors in summer,' Faith reasoned aloud. A number of them were grazing in the middle of the field. The girls climbed the fence and sat on top. The horses, after first looking up, bent their heads back to the grass.

'Let's go nearer,' suggested Faith with a confidence gained from her ride in the buggy.

'Forget it,' drawled Gem. 'You're the big animal lover. Besides, Mom said to take it slow with big animals. And she meant *you.*'

But Faith slid down from the fence into the big field. Immediately she felt smaller; a faint chill of apprehension cooled the back of her neck. This was *their* field. But the horses continued to graze.

She stood for a while watching them in their field, trying to feel their life. Not one of them looked up.

Near her a butterfly flickered out of the grass. The sun shone down. Faith could feel the warmth rising from the earth beneath her. Insects hummed. She began to walk towards the group of horses.

Nearest to her was the big chestnut, Shinyface. On his neck and hindquarters his hair was ruffled up and drying. He seemed enormous now that Faith was on the ground. Beyond was a small, pretty brown mare with a shaggy mane. A black horse bent his long neck quietly to the grass. The closer Faith got, the bigger the horses loomed. She hadn't realized just how big they were. Tails switched at flies, horse skin shivered. The sun surrounded them all in a lazy peace.

Faith walked on a little slower, feeling her way. The black horse lifted his head and looked at her. She stopped and sent him her special signal, a little trembly with a strange nervousness. *Hello, horse.*

His gaze reached into her eyes, an alien stare. A quietness seemed to radiate from his body. His tail flickered. Faith could see, from the corner of her eye, the other horses raise their heads. They were all silent, looking at her, the intruder in their field. The sun beat down. The air seemed to grow thick.

Suddenly, without warning, the black horse spun up and around. His tail spread and his neck arched. His energy was like the crack of a whip among the others. There was a flurry and a springing and a lightning thrust of hooves. The horses bolted, twisted. Their necks tossed, manes flaring. A wild, shuddering cry came from the black horse. He stood up on his hind legs and pawed the air. His mane was like a flame behind him.

Then he plunged and bucked. His hind hooves struck out at the air. Faith froze in her tracks. Behind her, Gem screamed. Faith heard a thundering as the horses began to spin and wheel towards her. The earth seemed to heave beneath. The pounding of hooves sent a beat up through her legs. Her body was rooted into the ground. Her scalp went cold.

The herd came boiling towards her. The air was full of the frenzy of their huge bodies. Faith heard a terrible wail rise up from her own throat, an awful sound she hadn't known she owned.

The sea-wet chestnut was upon her. He wheeled and, flicking his hooves, passed by so close she could feel the warm wind he caused. Her arms flew up. As if at a command, the rest of the herd turned and raced in the other direction.

On weak legs, Faith ran lurching back to the safety of the fence. 'Some animal lover,' snorted Gem. Her face was so white that the few freckles on her nose stood out like crayon spots.

Later that evening, after a pizza supper, and after the dishes were all piled on top of the dirty ones in the sink, Beth said, 'Tomorrow we'll have a riding lesson.' Gem and Faith exchanged looks of horror. Faith felt an awful coldness coil in her stomach.

Never before had she been frightened of an animal. But these horses seemed so unlike the groomed and bridled animals of the mounted police. Even Shinyface in the field had not been the same horse Faith had known harnessed to a buggy. She could not understand what had happened in Beth's field of unfettered horses. Their great size and uncontrollable wildness had filled her with terror.

'I don't think the horses like me,' she said to Beth. 'There's a big black one who didn't like me at all.' She described how savagely they had behaved.

'Oh,' Beth said, unconcerned, 'they were just

feeling good, showing off for company. The black one is Thundercloud. He was probably just welcoming you.'

Faith was quiet, thinking about Thundercloud's welcome. His name alone was unsettling. He could have trampled her without even noticing it. She knew danger when she saw it.

That night she dreamed she was in an empty field full of the smell of horses. The air was heavy with danger. Suddenly the horses were there, pounding and thrusting towards her. She tried to make the right sounds – a whinny, a snort – but her throat was stopped. She turned and lifted one heavy foot after the other, pushing through the thick air with all her strength.

And woke up sweating and whimpering in the big bed with her sister. 'Will you *stop* wiggling?' hissed Gem. 'You're *ruining* my hair!'

Gem's irritation drove Faith's nightmare away. Comforted, she settled down in the bed and fell back to sleep.

3

When Faith woke up, the only trace of her fear was a vague uneasiness. The sun was sifting into the girls' room through pretty eyelet curtains. Except for two boxes of books in the corner, the bedroom was as neat as a pin.

Almost as orderly as the tack room, thought Faith. She was warmed by the idea that Beth had made a special effort for them.

Gem was still sleeping soundly – her beauty sleep, their father called it. She tried to stay in one position all night so her hair would be manageable in the morning.

Faith thought she smelled French toast. She put on her slippers and followed the smell down the narrow, steep old stairs.

The grandfather clock by the door at the front of the stairs said 6:35, early for Faith. It's Sunday, she thought, and was struck with a wave of homesickness. Their father cooked breakfast on Sunday – pancakes poured into the shape of their initials. She wondered if her mother was awake yet. Were the twins sleeping?

Beth was at the stove when Faith wandered shyly

into the kitchen. She looked as though she'd been up for hours. Her 'Good morning, lazybones' was bright and crisp. A rich, nutmeg-y smell came from a grill next to the stove burners. It *was* French toast for breakfast. Faith's spirits lifted.

'Thought you'd be first up,' Beth told her then went to the foot of the stairs to holler up at Gem. 'Wake up, Sleeping Beauty!' She sounded like their father. 'You're getting old in bed!'

'I don't want to ride today,' announced Faith while the three of them were eating breakfast. 'Mom said take it easy at first.'

Beth pushed her French toast around the plate after the syrup. Gem tried to look cool.

'We won't do much,' said Beth calmly. 'Besides, Harold wouldn't hurt a fly . . . even a horsefly.' She smiled at her own joke. 'You'll see.' There was something unbending as iron in her pleasant manner.

Beth got up and balanced her sticky plate in the sink. 'Put on your jeans and sneakers and I'll see you down below.' Her voice was cheery but Faith sensed beneath it was no room for argument. Without waiting for a reply, Beth left them at the table and headed for the barn.

Their suitcases were still in the kitchen, except for Gem's makeup case, which had displaced everything else on the counter of the old bathroom. They pulled out their jeans, clean socks and shirts and shoved their suitcases back underneath the kitchen table.

'I don't want to do this,' muttered Faith as she

dressed by the refrigerator. Her mother never insisted Faith do something against her nature and always seemed to know when not to push.

No matter how she lagged, Faith was finally clothed. Down below meant the stable in the lower part of the barn. The girls took their time getting there. Faith noted that the stable looked freshly swept. The smells that yesterday had filled Faith's nose comfortably, wood and manure and hay, now had a dangerous heat in them.

Beth was standing just inside the big stable doors with two saddled horses. One was the dainty brown mare with the shaggy mane and the other a big, strong-looking horse whose name, Beth said, was Harold.

'Harold is a bay. Bays are brown with black manes and tails and black legs.' Faith noticed with alarm the great size of Harold's sturdy black legs, the huge, rock-solid hooves. 'Harold used to be a hunt horse,' Beth continued. 'He really loved the chase.'

'He's *big*,' said Gem in her fussy voice which meant she was worried.

'He's old,' said Beth. 'And smart and beautiful.' She leaned into Harold, her cheek against his shoulder.

Faith's body was growing formless with dread. Beth, who had seemed a new ally yesterday, was now a stone stranger.

'He's big,' repeated Gem.

'But,' said Beth stepping away from Harold,

213

suddenly all business, 'Gem will ride Vixen. Faith will ride Harold.'

Faith's stomach did a slow, horrible flopping. She would have to get on that monster. Beth handed her the big bay's reins and instructed Faith to follow her out to the ring. I was right, thought Faith, that *is* where riders practise. But no trace of her earlier excitement was there to comfort her. Harold was huge beside her, warm. She could feel him breathing.

'Don't let him step on you,' called out Beth crisply. She walked out the door, followed by Gem leading Vixen. Faith leaned away from the big horse, reins loose in her trembling hand. She sidestepped out the barn door and banged her shoulder painfully. Harold's feet seemed enormous, his body tanklike as he plodded beside her.

In the ring, Gem was standing on a small platform next to Vixen. A black riding cap sat snugly over her heavy hair. ' . . . left foot in the stirrup. Swing your right leg over the saddle,' Beth was saying. Her voice came to Faith as if through a fog. 'Hold the reins with your thumbs on top.' Gem looked as if she'd done it all before. Faith wondered where her sister's fear had gone. She watched in surprise as Gem walked Vixen on out around the ring.

'Pick a hat that fits,' instructed Beth, pointing to a bin full of worn riding caps. 'For your protection.' Faith was not reassured. Protection? With trembling hands she settled a hard, velvet-covered shell over her head. It didn't feel right − but *nothing* felt right.

'Lead Harold to the mounting block,' Beth urged a bewildered Faith. 'To the right of the steps – to the *right*.' Then she added strongly, 'Always – *always* mount a horse from his left side. Is that clear?'

'Why?' asked Faith, stalling for time. But Beth didn't answer her question. She took Harold's reins from Faith and led him to the right of the mounting block. 'Get on the block,' she ordered. 'Come on, don't waste time, Faith.'

Faith, stung into action by Beth's sharp tone, mounted the steps. Harold didn't seem so big from this new height. It wasn't difficult to place her left foot in the stirrup and swing her other leg over the saddle. But once perched on the horse, she felt disconnected from herself, helpless. A warm, dusty odor rose from the powerful body. She could feel Harold's breathing, the readiness of his muscles. She herself had no muscles to speak of.

The big horse bent his head down and she felt as if she would pitch down his long neck to the ground. She clutched the front of the saddle. I'm not an athlete, she wanted to tell Beth, who was making quick adjustments in the stirrup leathers so they would fit Faith's ten-year-old legs. Everything was moving forward with Faith caught in the motion, her speech trapped in her throat.

Beth's firm voice came to her as if from a distance. 'Now, just walk Harold around the ring after Gem.' She clucked at Harold and gave him a quick slap on his rump. The muscles beneath Faith jerked and the huge animal walked.

Gem was proudly strutting about on Vixen. Sweat broke out on Faith's forehead and in the palms of her hands. The steady rolling heave of the horse made her feel sick to her stomach. All of her natural instincts, the parts of her that could exchange signals with animals, were smothered in a blanket of fear.

'You mount from the left because it's traditional,' Beth's faraway voice continued. 'The cavalry wore swords at their left side and couldn't swing that leg over the horse.'

Ordinarily this information would have interested Faith, but she couldn't use it to eliminate the veil of fear she moved through. And Beth didn't seem to notice her fright. She just kept up a patter of facts about the cavalry and how they started the English style of riding and Faith no longer heard at all.

The hour lesson was torture. Faith felt shapeless astride the huge horse. First Beth had them go clockwise around the ring. 'Keep out to the rail!' Then they had to turn their horses and go the other way. Faith watched her sister learn how to post up and down as Vixen first walked, then trotted around the ring. Why standing up in the stirrups and sitting back down over and over enabled you to ride was a mystery Faith didn't even question. 'Grip with your legs, Gem. Clamp those legs in and push up out of the saddle,' Beth called out. 'Up . . . down . . . up . . . down.' Faith watched from the back of a slowly plodding Harold, hoping to be ignored. Now added to her fear was a rush of thick envy. I'll never catch up, she thought miserably.

Gem's face was serious with concentration. Up . . . down. Around the ring she posted, bobbing and bouncing unevenly to Vixen's quick trot.

'That's the idea,' said Beth. 'When you're posting correctly, the horse's trot won't bounce you all over the saddle. Feel that, Gem?'

Posting felt *impossible* to Faith when it was her turn. Even when she tried it at a walk, her legs chafed against the saddle. She couldn't rise up into the post without her upper body collapsing. Bored, Harold kept stopping.

'Keep him walking!' shouted Beth. 'Cluck to him.' The hair at the back of Faith's neck and around her forehead was wet from the effort and anxiety.

Finally, with a sigh, Beth turned her attention back to Gem, whose athletic body responded easily to her direction. Faith sat rigidly on Harold and watched as her sister now posted evenly around the ring at a trot, her bright hair lifting and falling. Gem had the elating look she sometimes wore when running. Faith sat hoping Beth would soon call it a day. Walking Harold was awful enough. She didn't want him trotting.

But after Beth showed Gem how to halt Vixen, she turned to Faith. 'Let's try posting at a trot, Faith,' she said with brisk cheeriness. 'It's often easier than at a walk.'

As if he understood the words, Harold moved into a trot. Fear swept over Faith. The quick, lurching movement shot her all over the saddle like a drunken puppet. The bouncing hurt her crotch. She hunched over the saddle, clutching the ridge in front of her. The reins dangled uselessly.

'Pick up the reins. Let go of the pommel!' called Beth. Faith barely heard. Whimpering, she bounced around the ring atop the huge animal. Her hands were glued to the front of the saddle. She couldn't obey Beth's shouted commands of 'Look up! Look up!' Finally Beth told her, 'Okay, Faith, let's walk for a while.'

But now Harold didn't want to slow up and Faith couldn't make him obey.

'Pull back with the reins! Back with the reins!' Beth shouted. But Faith's brain was frozen. She could only clutch the pommel and whimper 'Whoa . . . whoa' in a weak little voice. Her feet had been shaken from the stirrups. Her long, thin legs slapped against the horse's sides. Harold came to a halt in front of Beth.

Faith expected Beth to help her out of the saddle, but Beth just said matter-of-factly, 'Why don't you walk him around a little? I'll work Gem and Vixen some more.'

Harold plodded dutifully out along the rail. Faith watched her sister on Vixen. Gem had that greedy eagerness on her face that came over her when she was excited about something.

She's forgotten all about boys for an entire morning, Faith thought miserably.

At the lesson's end, Faith inched her way fearfully

from the broad back, sliding down Harold's side, toes searching for the ground. Her legs ached. Her crotch was sore. But worse, she was shrunken with despair over her failure at riding. She led Harold back to the barn easily, though. Leading him was now less frightening than being on top of him.

'Cheer up,' said Beth, seeing Faith's forlorn face. She unbuckled the girth and hauled the heavy old saddle from Harold's back. 'Tomorrow you'll do better in a regular class.'

Faith lay awake in bed that night next to her soundly sleeping sister. Gem had been too tired to do her nightly exercises or even chatter about 'guys'. Faith missed her mother, who would never have made her get on a horse. She felt somehow betrayed. Here it was, only the next to last Sunday in June. She had two *months* plus two weeks to go before she would be back home where someone understood her. Gem's phrase, 'Some animal lover,' burned like a brand in her mind. Faith staunchly resisted the urge to suck her thumb.

4

The next morning Faith woke at half light. It was too early to get up but she couldn't get back to sleep. Aside from the birds chirping sleepily, the farm was quiet. She lay there for what seemed like ages worrying about the day ahead. Then the sun began to slip through the curtains and she heard Beth running water in the kitchen. Monday the real world begins, she thought.

Without enthusiasm, she pulled on yesterday's jeans over the same underwear. She didn't bother to change her socks. Before going downstairs she poked Gem.

'Wake up, Sleeping Beauty,' she said loudly at her sister's blinking face. 'Time to clean out stalls.'

She thumped down the stairs with Gem yelling after her, 'You little rat!'

There was no French toast this morning. Beth was on her way out the kitchen door with a great bag of cat food in her arms and a cup full of coffee hooked by one thumb. She pointed with her elbow to the cereal boxes on a shelf. 'Juice and milk in the refrigerator. Jam and butter, too.'

She let the screen door slam, calling over her

shoulder as she went, 'Come down to the stable when you're finished.'

Faith ate slowly, trying to hold the day still until she found her balance. She considered doing the dishes before she left the homey comfort of the kitchen. It would be a legitimate delay. She wasn't ready to be thrown on a horse again.

Gem bounced into the kitchen, jogged by the table and grabbed the piece of toast Faith had just loaded with strawberry jam. She banged out the door hollering, 'Touché!'

Faith scrambled after her, forgetting the dirty dishes. She was furious at Gem. It made her feel suddenly brave and full of purpose.

But her purpose was deflated by the surprise of lively activity outside. Cars were pulling into the driveway, discharging kids of various ages in riding clothes or jeans and sneakers. Students for the regular classes, thought Faith. There were a few boys but mostly the students seemed to be girls. Faith remembered Beth saying that riding was one of the few sports where women could compete on the same level as men.

At the stable, Gem was finishing Faith's toast and sizing up a group of teenage girls in well-fitting breeches and long black riding boots.

'They're in the advanced class,' she whispered as Faith came up. 'We're only in the beginners.'

Any of the remaining anger Faith felt toward her sister dissolved in a wave of panic. Before she could plan a quick disappearance, Beth handed her Harold's reins — attached to Harold.

'Beginners first,' Beth said and added jokingly, 'You can warm him up for the advanced riders.' Faith, numb with worry, didn't even smile.

As she led the giant Harold down to the ring, her stomach churned. Mothers were sitting in their cars on the hill above the ring and more mothers were down leaning on the fence. Riders for the next class were chatting in groups. Someone's father stood with his foot on a rail, watching.

The warm face of Faith's own mother slipped into her mind. Tears began to collect behind her eyes. But Beth was now directing beginners to the mounting block, adjusting stirrups and clucking horses and riders out into the ring. There was no time for sorrowing.

Once Faith climbed on to Harold's broad back, her legs felt slack and useless. Added to the feeling of helplessness was embarrassment at being out there in front of all those parents. She felt naked and foolish on the giant horse plodding slowly around the ring.

Fortunately, there were seven other students besides Faith and Gem. Beth spent the entire first part of the lesson just getting some of them used to walking around while trying to post up and down. They all seem to catch on so quickly, thought Faith as she struggled in the saddle, following behind the only boy in the class.

'Posting smooths out the bumps when you're

riding at a trot,' Beth called out. 'You don't tire as easily. You can cover long distances in comfort.'

'Cover long distances?' Faith asked herself, imagining a prairie, a desert, endless hills. Around the ring was too long a distance for her.

But before the end of the lesson, four students, including the boy, were trotting and posting with Gem. Beth spent most of her attention on these riders. Faith and the other three were instructed to walk their horses around at the rail while standing up in the stirrups.

Faith's crumpled stance in the stirrups felt unnatural and foolish. 'If it doesn't get worse than this, I'll live,' she said to herself. 'But who wants to?'

Toward the middle of that first week at Holbein Farm, Gem stopped describing to Faith the merits of all the boys she knew back home and began to talk about horses.

She doesn't even like animals, Faith thought dismally. Animals are *my* specialty.

Gem's conversation was now full of terms like 'noseband,' 'throatlatch' and 'diagonals.'

Diagonals became one of Faith's nightmares. She could barely lift herself into a posting position at a walk. At a trot, she jiggled all over the saddle and her brain went cold. Now Beth was asking that she recognize diagonals.

'At a trot, horses' legs move in *diagonal pairs*,' shouted Beth from the center of the ring. 'Right foreleg with left back leg. And vice versa.'

Faith's legs ached from the effort of trying to post.

'Notice when the horse's outside leg moves forward,' instructed Beth. 'Post *up* in rhythm with his outside leg.'

The other riders seemed to be getting the idea. Of course the horse had only two forelegs – there was only fifty percent chance of being wrong. But Faith *always* seemed to be on wrong diagonal.

'Sit a bounce, Faith,' cried Beth from the center of the ring. 'Come up on the correct diagonal.'

There was no time to think. It happened too fast. Faith couldn't distinguish one bounce from another. Desperately she tried to open her animal-listening ear, tried to feel Harold's legs. But she had lost connection with her *own* legs except for their twin throbbing.

'Slow down, Faith. Let him walk. You need to strengthen those legs,' called Beth at one point.

With a sigh of relief, Faith pulled Harold down to a walk. That, at least, she could now do. She checked Beth's face as she and Harold walked past. Was she angry? Disappointed? The tanned face was quiet.

'Drop your stirrups and practice lifting yourself into posting position without them,' said Beth reasonably. 'Use the inside of your thighs and your knees. Twice around the ring. Cluck to him! Make him move out!'

Faith urged Harold into a faster walk. She strained and struggled to lift up without the stirrups to brace against.

'That's right, Faith, keep it up,' said Beth. It didn't feel right but Faith felt she should get a Brownie point for fooling Beth. She couldn't raise up more than half an inch from the saddle. Still, she forced herself to keep at it. Twice around the ring seemed like forever. The insides of her knees felt raw.

When she dismounted to lead Harold back to the stall, her thighs shook uncontrollably and she felt close to tears.

Back in the ring she could hear Beth's crisp instructions as the riders went around one more time.

It seemed to Faith as though she were slipping into a dark and bottomless hole. Far up, at the edge of the hole, in sunlight, posted Gem on the right diagonal.

At suppertime, Faith was surprised at how Gem gobbled her pizza. She was usually finicky about food. She didn't want to gain weight. But that night Gem put away three pieces before Faith had finished her first.

'I think you're getting fatter,' said Faith spitefully. 'You'd better take it easy on the pizza.'

'Mind your own business,' snapped Gem, but her hand paused in mid-pounce over the fourth piece.

Thursday afternoon, Beth brought Vixen in from the field to show the sisters how to groom a horse properly.

'You girls can be a big help before lessons,' she said, 'if you know how to groom and tack up the school horses.' Faith clenched her teeth and hung back.

'First, use the currycomb,' said Beth. She rubbed deeply into Vixen's coat, circling against the hair growth with a tooth-edged rubber disk. Dust surged to the surface.

Faith found herself interested despite her nervousness. Beth showed them the various brushes, the different strokes to use to pull up dust and brush it away. Vixen stood quietly.

Beth had them each work on the mare.

'Don't be afraid to really brush hard,' she said. 'It stimulates the oil glands. Makes a shiny coat.'

Faith hated getting that close to Vixen. But she couldn't brush hard standing stiffly away from the horse.

'She won't bite, Faith,' said Beth a little impatiently. She took the brush from Faith and began to finish the job. 'Vixen's been good,' she said. 'You can get her a carrot.'

Relieved to get away, Faith hurried to the cool, shadowy part of the tack room where a big sack of carrots was kept. She had seen students giving carrot treats to horses before. She picked out a good-sized carrot and took her time getting back. Beth was knocking dirt and hair from the brushes. 'You can give it to Vixen,' she told Faith. 'Careful of your fingers. Hold your hand flat.'

Timidly Faith waved the carrot near Vixen's

mouth. Vixen's teeth snapped open and caught it. Faith shrieked and snatched her hand away as the carrot disappeared, *Crunch, crunch*. Gone.

Could've been my fingers, thought Faith, rubbing them. They felt dangerously like carrots. Can't even feed them right, she thought, sinking deeper into the hole.

She stood back when Beth showed them how to tack up Vixen. First Beth hoisted the saddle on and buckled it up. Then she picked up the bridle and slipped the reins over Vixen's neck.

In spite of herself, Faith edged closer. She was fascinated and horrified at the task of putting the bit into the horse's mouth. Beth stuck her thumb and fingers into the sides of the great rubbery lips. Vixen's mouth opened. Wet bits of grain and carrot slid out. Beth pushed the bit in between the big teeth and pulled the crown-piece in place over Vixen's ears.

It had taken only a few swift movements, but Faith didn't know how Beth made sense out of the noodle-tangle of leather straps she joined and buckled. Gem made a yuck-face when she tried putting her fingers into Vixen's mouth. Faith backed away, her brain closing off on the image of the big, wet horse teeth.

Beth sent her a long glance. Then, sighing, she suggested that Faith only be responsible for helping groom the horses and carry the tack. 'You're not quite tall enough to pull the bridle over even Vixen's head,' she said. Faith felt relieved and, at the same time, somehow cheated.

The next day, Gem bridled Vixen without a wince. Then, showing off, she bridled Harold for Faith. Faith was surprised and envious.

But in the days that followed, Faith did help with the grooming. Early every morning, before lessons, she worked hard, moving guardedly around the big animals with the currycomb, then the brushes.

Gradually she relaxed a little, no longer arching away from their warm bodies. Brushing became easier. She found herself enjoying the closeness and the healthy odor. Her animal-listening ear perked up. She began to murmur to the animals as she brushed. 'Good fellow' she said to Harold. 'Guh-uhd fellow.' She forgot about being in a hole.

When she put away the brushes, her arms would be sprinkled with horse hair, her hands darkened by dirt. She always felt pretty accomplished until Gem handed her Harold's reins, saying with unctuous good will, 'Have a good ride.' Faith's spirits would sag. To get past the morning, to lunchtime and the easy afternoon, she would have to go through another lesson.

After lunch was the time that Faith enjoyed most. Things slowed down for her. Sometimes she visited the sheep, Wolfie panting at her heels.

Despite their blunt, stupid pushiness, Faith felt no

fear of the sheep. She learned to call them, 'Baa-aa,' from way back in her throat. She began to notice their individual shapes and markings. When new-weaned lambs pressed to the fence, bleating for their mothers, she ached with sorrow.

At feeding time, she helped Beth carry pails of grain. She hoped Beth would notice how unafraid she was of the sheep. While Beth strode ahead of her, Faith chattered loudly about how she and the sheep were 'pretty good friends'.

Beth didn't wait when Faith had to stop and set the heavy pails on the ground to shake out her cramped fingers. Still, Faith thought she detected the stirring of a special bond between them. She longed to suggest that they hitch up Shinyface to the buggy and let her hold the reins – as she had long, long, a hundred years ago. But whenever she had the words in her mind, Faith felt shy and told herself it wasn't the right time.

Some afternoons she helped Beth weed the vegetable garden. There were a lot of weeds but they came up easily from the dark, rich soil. 'You're a better worker than your sister,' commented Beth once. Faith turned her head to hide the surprise of tears in her eyes.

One day, Beth suggested Faith help Brady, too. He was a quiet, white-haired old man who Beth hired to clean stalls, saddles and bridles.

Faith, pleased at being such a help to Beth, didn't mind the hard, dirty work. Since some horses were brought in at night the stables needed daily cleaning. She swept out the aisles and tack room while Brady wordlessly shoveled out stalls and pushed wheelbarrows full of straw and manure outside.

Faith asked Beth what would happen to the manure pile. Would it just keep getting bigger and bigger? Beth was amused. 'Oh, we use that to fertilize the alfalfa fields – and the garden.'

Faith thought of the dark, rich soil around the thriving tomato plants, the growing corn and creeping squash vines. And the abundance of happy weeds. Everything went round in circles: alfalfa to the horse to the manure pile back to the alfalfa. Nothing ever really ended.

The lessons didn't end either. The second week, her sister was moved into a class with more advanced students. Faith had to stay with children so small their feet couldn't touch the stirrups.

Beth now required that Faith bring Harold from the field herself. Fortunately, he was always standing by the gate waiting for the carrot Faith brought. She didn't have to step in among a cluster of horses to get him. The carrot Faith warily thrust at Harold served to occupy his attention while she snapped a lead line on to his halter.

Beth didn't approve of giving carrots *before* the lessons.

'That's bribery,' she said. 'Save carrots for a reward *after* the lesson.'

But Faith always sneaked Harold the bribe. To her mind, she was rewarding him early.

Beth spent more time now urging Faith into a trot on Harold. Faith hated being with the babies who couldn't trot at all. She hated the wobble of her body in the saddle. But most of all, she hated the curling, sick feeling in her stomach that accompanied each lesson.

In the afternoons, she continued to escape to the sheep or the other animals. She spent some rainy afternoons in the hayloft with the cats, a book and a peanut butter sandwich. She went for walks with Wolfie.

She talked with the orphaned baby raccoon who lived in the lambing shelter. His name was Rackity and, at first, he cowered in a corner of his cage. She sat on an old milking stool and watched him for a long time. Soon she was able to coax him up to her hand. Rackity would let her stroke him. He got so he would take raw vegetables from her long, gentle fingers. Beth joked, 'You must be part raccoon – a red-haired raccoon.'

But Faith's pleasure in these other animals seemed somehow diminished. Her magic touch didn't extend to the huge, beautiful animals with their great, wet nostrils and heavy necks. Occasionally she wandered off by herself down to their field. She stared into it, leaning against the fence.

Beneath the peaceful appearance of distant horses grazing lay the powerful thunder of hooves, the uncontrollable strength of charging animals . . . lay

231

violence and death. But here, too, Faith sensed, was some kind of an answer. She had about eight weeks to discover it — or avoid it. She wasn't sure which she could do best.

5

In early evening, traffic on the dirt road past Holbein
Farm virtually stopped. The quiet lengthened with
the shadows. The sun eased down behind the woods.
There was a comfortable munch from the feed
troughs as most of the animals nudged noses to grain.
It was the time Faith counted the days left of the
summer.

Usually she sat on the back porch, scratching mos-
quito bites and listening to her sister splash in the
tub inside. Gem's baths were as predictable each
evening as the pizza. They were a kind of comfort
to Faith. Wolfie always came and plopped down near
her by the steps. That was also a comfort. Sometimes
Beth came too, and sat quietly with them whilst the
pizza baked. Then Faith felt as if she and Beth were
connected somehow to the fields and hills, the
animals, the softening sky. She forgot to count
the remaining days.

Though Beth had finally gotten her television
fixed, the girls had gotten out of the TV habit. The
few times they did turn it on, the screen images
were no longer compelling. The color seemed
dimmer. 'It's her set,' said Gem. It's the horses,

thought Faith. Beth herself never stayed awake in front of the TV very long.

Daytimes were a different story. Beth seemed to have endless energy. Activity was everywhere. Neighbors came to help build fences. Their voices and saws and poundings criss-crossed the air. Interesting strangers pulled up in cars to look over Beth's horses. People came with mares to breed with the beautiful, frenetic Apollo.

Faith observed the horse people with the detachment of an outsider. Serious young riders arrived with their fathers or mothers, wanting a well-bred horse to show at jumping events. Fox hunters from Midwest hunts and lean endurance-ride competitors came looking for horses with stamina. Sometimes they took a horse away, leaving Beth richer and sadder.

But Beth was too busy to be sad for long. She even taught classes on the Fourth of July. Faith and Gem didn't expect a celebration but Beth grilled hot dogs outside for supper. Afterward they lit sparklers and sat around watching them sizzle and die. Fireflies glowed here and there in the darkness. Faith wondered only briefly if her father had been fussing over his barbequed spareribs all afternoon.

Then Faith noticed Beth had fallen asleep, head on her arms, right where she sat. Beth's life doesn't pause for the Fourth of July, she thought. She was touched that this busy woman had made the extra effort to celebrate the holiday. Faith decided right then to find more ways to help at Holbein Farm.

★

There were plenty of things to choose from. Besides the grooming and helping Brady, Faith took over clearing dishes and cleaning up after each meal. She began to enjoy keeping the kitchen picked up. She organized the books and catalogs and magazines into several crates she had found in the unused chicken house. She kept Beth's mail piled neatly on her desk whether Beth opened it or not.

Gem caught the cleaning fever and began to organize the old bathroom, removing the avocado plant and dirty laundry. She arranged the towels by color and put the toothbrushes in pretty glasses. She wasn't feverish enough to actually *do* the laundry, but she sorted it and put it in baskets in the pantry.

'Now I won't be able to find things,' said Beth, smiling.

'But you pick up the stables,' protested Gem. 'We can easily find bridles and lead lines because they're all put back in place.'

Beth gave her thoughtful look again, faintly tinged with embarrassment. 'Well,' she said finally, 'I'm only one person. Brady's only here a few hours a day. There is work here for at least three, maybe four. I have to choose the most important things as I see them. The horses can't clean up the stables or their bridles and saddles.'

'You need a housekeeper,' said Gem

'You need a cook,' said Faith, who was beginning to foresee the time when she would grow tired of pizza.

235

Beth sighed.

'You need a husband!' exclaimed Gem.

'Who can cook!' added Faith.

Beth began to laugh. 'I see you two have it all figured out,' she said, wiping her eyes.

'*What kind of guy,*' *Faith's father had snorted, 'wants to move way out to a farm and be put to work by Beth, ye gods!*'

Or maybe to ride Harold, thought Faith, silently agreeing with her father.

One day a young couple who had come looking for a carriage-driving horse hauled the high-stepping Shinyface away. They left behind a check for twelve thousand dollars. Gem was impressed. 'No wonder Beth wouldn't let any of us ride him,' she commented. Faith was sad when the couple drove off. They'd never hitch Shiny to the buggy now, she and Beth, and rattle along a dirt road. She watched the bright chestnut tail sway gracefully from the back of the couple's horse trailer as it disappeared down the drive.

Beth didn't see them leave. She had gone hastily into the house. When she came out later, her eyes were red and swollen. She didn't say a word to Faith but strode out to the field with a lead line and brought back Thundercloud. Faith watched her from the porch. The black horse followed, light and eager, behind the walking woman. There was something relentless about Beth's movements as she tacked up

Cloud by the fence. She swung herself into the saddle from the ground.

Gem came out on the porch, waving fresh-painted fingernails. Together the sisters watched Beth ride through the field, up over the hill, and disappear. 'What's wrong with Beth?' asked Gem. 'I thought I heard her crying in the sheep's bathroom.'

'I don't know why she sold Shinyface if it makes her feel so bad,' said Faith.

'She needs the money, dumb-o,' grumbled her sister. 'Dad says she always falls in love with her best horses and won't sell them and that she's broke all the time. Once she almost lost the farm because she wouldn't sell her favourite jumper to a famous rider for umpteen thousands of dollars.'

'But she teaches,' protested Faith, 'and people pay her to board their horses here.' And other things, thought Faith. Beth kept horses that were ready to foal and she helped in the birthing. Faith had never known anyone who worked so hard.

'She sells wool – and lamb meat, mutton and stuff,' she reminded Gem.

Gem snorted. 'Peanuts,' she said. 'Big money comes from selling her best horses. Dad says she has to shell out for fencing and roofing and haying and farm equipment. And taxes. And vet bills.'

Faith watched the spot on the hill where Beth had ridden from view. She saw the woman in her mind's eye . . . legs grown into the sides of the horse, a centaur, waist supple, hands easy. Why didn't she sell that damn Cloud instead she thought.

Strangely enough, Faith began to get used to Harold and his big bumble of a trot. The huge bay nuzzled her for a carrot and sniffed her hair while she snapped on the lead line. Other horses now recognized her as the carrot kid and edged closer for a treat too. Faith learned to throw pebbles at their legs to keep them away from the gate as she brought Harold through.

Although Faith still did not put on his bridle, Beth now insisted she saddle Harold after grooming him. At first it made Faith uncomfortable. She was afraid of angering the horse in her clumsy effort to heft the heavy old saddle on to his back. But Harold quietly tolerated her struggle.

She began to notice, brushing his round sides, that her listening ear seemed more alert. Not quite the way it was with dogs and sheep. But she saw with new eyes Harold's smooth coat, his mane, the long muscles of his shoulder and thigh.

It was with surprise and a flash of fresh terror that she learned one morning that she would not ride Harold.

'He's sore in the foreleg,' explained Beth. 'You can ride Cloud.'

Faith's heart stopped. Thundercloud! Her knees went weak. 'Go get him,' instructed Beth. 'Go on . . . and *smile*,' she added, seeing Faith's pale face.

Cloud wasn't standing near the gate. Holding a carrot stiffly in her fist, Faith walked slowly out into the field, a lead line over her shoulder. Her sensitive listening ear was filled with a low roaring. Cloud grazed off by himself, but Faith kept a nervous eye on the other horses, too. The big black animal looked at her curiously as she approached him.

'Cloud?' she said, her voice trembling. She stopped a distance away.

'Hi, remember me? I don't need any welcome today.' Cloud dropped his head and looked at Faith out of the side of his eye. She took a deep breath and walked slowly up to him. He didn't move. He eyed the carrot. She reached gingerly up to his halter and clipped on the lead line. He sniffed the carrot, then bit the end off daintily.

Surprisingly, the big black horse came in easily, almost eagerly. His eagerness itself was frightening. All her former discomfort around a horse returned as she was grooming him. His neck arched. His nostrils blew in and out. Warily she placed the saddle pad on his dark back, half expecting him to bolt. But he stood quietly as she hoisted the saddle on. After she had buckled it up, he stood staring out the door, ears alert.

When Beth came to put on the bridle, Faith was grateful. She still couldn't bring herself to put her fingers into a horse's mouth.

Once astride Cloud she immediately missed Harold's big, round sides. Cloud was leaner and there was a lightness about him – almost the opposite of Harold's solid steadiness.

'Hold on. Hold on a minute,' Faith wanted to say. 'Wait!' But part of her grew alive and excited. She didn't have to cluck to Cloud to get him to walk out along the rail. His walk was firm and easy. No lumbering here. His body coiled beneath her. And his trot, when Faith asked for it, was high and smooth as butter.

'I can still see a lot of daylight between your knees and the saddle,' observed Beth loudly from the center of the ring.

'Hug that leather! Knees in! Heels down! Grip with your *whole* leg.'

During the lesson Faith found, to her delight, that she was posting up and down, working Cloud, at Beth's command, into a figure-eight pattern. She could almost *feel* the diagonal on Cloud and she tried to post up with his outside foreleg. Sometimes it worked. Faith smiled. She sat a bounce when they reached the center of the figure eight and sent him around the other way on a new diagonal.

'Good!' shouted Beth. 'You've got it!'

Cloud was doing what Faith was trying to tell him. He felt wonderful. Visions of surpassing her older sister, trotting easily and with perfect control, filled her head. Her hands would be light, her legs would be stronger. She ignored the flash of panic the vision stimulated.

'Heels *down*!' hollered Beth. 'That's better. Now, give with those hands a little. Make them light. Pretend Cloud has eggshells in his mouth. Don't lose contact. Feel his mouth. And *relax*, Faith, relax. Loosen up that back. You're sitting stiff as a soldier . . .'

Beth hollered the entire lesson. She spent more

of her attention on Faith than the four other students, little kids with astonished eyes. But when Faith was through it seemed like she had only been working ten minutes.

'That was much better,' said Beth with a little smile. Faith slid down Cloud's side, enjoying for the first time the contact along the length of her body with the firm sides of the horse. The animal person in Faith blinked its eyes.

Later on, with no Beth around, Faith watched Thundercloud in his field. He flirted wildly with the other horses, plunging into their midst until they were all scattering and chasing each other, charging the air with an electric frenzy.

She was relieved when Beth put her back on Harold for the next lesson. Although she couldn't feel diagonals on the big bay, she was surprised at how much easier it was to ride him after Cloud – not smooth, but strong and steady.

There were only three other students in the class that day. They were all younger than Faith, and she felt pleased and confident to be way ahead of them.

'You're getting there,' Beth told her. 'You've come a long way. Time you learned to canter.' She ordered the others to the center of the ring and Faith to ready Harold. 'You'll go counterclockwise,' Beth said.

Nervously Faith listened to Beth describe the leg and rein signals that would make Harold surge into the strong, ground-covering pace. 'Outside rein. Outside leg. That'll be your right. *Don't* yank the rein. Just a light pressure.' But Faith's right leg couldn't work without her left leg. She couldn't give a strong signal with just one. Harold continued to plod around at a trot.

'I see daylight!' yelled Beth. 'Hug that saddle . . . Knees in! Knees in! Use your *whole* leg!'

Faith was mortified to be failing before the three younger students. They sat openmouthed astride their horses. There was so much to remember: knees in, outside rein, press with the outside leg. Which was outside?

Beth grew more irritated. She accused Faith of not wanting to canter and therefore not giving the signal in the right manner.

Finally Beth plucked a crop from the bin of hats. She cracked Harold across the rump with the little whip. He gave a huge lurch that almost unseated Faith, then shot around the ring at a canter. Fear flapped wildly in Faith's stomach. She leaned forward and clutched Harold's tough mane.

'Sit up! Sit BACK!' shouted Beth.

Harold's speed increased, his power exploding beneath Faith. All her control left her. Fear choked the scream back down her throat.

'Sit BACK! You're telling him to go faster! DON'T lean forward!'

But Faith no longer heard. Harold thundered toward the fence, swerved, and Faith slid half way down his side.

'Sit UP! SIT UP! DON'T FALL! SIT UP!'

But down she went into the dust of the ring.

Harold's great, plunging hooves narrowly missed her head.

She lay curled in a ball while the dust settled around her. Through a heavy numbness she heard Harold's hoofbeats as he headed toward the other end of the ring.

'Are you okay?' Beth was crouching beside her, looking at her intently. Then she seemed satisfied and said, 'Just stay there a minute. Don't move. You didn't land very hard.'

But I'm not okay, Faith wanted to say. I must have broken something, she thought. But at the same time, she knew she was not badly hurt.

Beth jogged after Harold to tie up his reins and pulled up the stirrups. He stood in the corner, snorting and blowing with excitement. Beth led him back to where her fallen student lay.

'Well, you've had your first fall. That puts you ahead of your sister.'

My first fall? thought Faith. There's more to come? She stood up carefully. Her face was burning and her whole side felt stiff and aching. She was trembling and slightly disappointed that there was nothing worse with her.

'We all fall,' said Beth lightly.

'Even you?' asked Faith faintly. She didn't believe it.

'Yes,' said Beth, 'when I'm not being smart.' Then she asked briskly, 'Now, do you know why you fell?'

'He was going too fast,' said Faith. 'You hit him too hard.' She became aware of the three younger students, faces pale and wide-eyed, at the other end of the ring. Harold stood obediently, but his body radiated eagerness.

'No,' said Beth. 'You fell because you *expected* to fall. You wanted to be on the ground instead of on the horse.'

'I was just scared. He wouldn't stop,' said Faith. She was beginning to feel belligerent.

'You were asking him to go,' said Beth. She sounded exasperated. 'You were telling him to go faster and faster.'

'I was not,' said Faith in astonishment. 'I wanted him to stop.'

'Now, we'll try it again,' said Beth. 'This time you'll do it right.'

'No,' said Faith, 'I *won't*. This is no fun. There's no reason why I have to learn to ride if I don't like it. And I don't.' She thought of the three frightened faces watching them – felt she was speaking for them, too. Like an avenging angel, she cried, 'This isn't school. I don't need a grade in horseback riding. It isn't *necessary*!'

Faith's mother always left her daughter alone on the rare occasions when Faith balked or complained. Beth showed no such mercy. Her face was pale. Her mouth was straight.

'It is important that you get back on Harold *right this minute*,' said Beth. There was nothing soft or gentle in her voice. But her hands were gentle. Her fingertips were soft on Faith's shoulders as she turned her to face the horse.

'Ready? One . . .' She bent and took hold of Faith's left leg. 'Two . . .' And hoisted her . . . 'Three' up to the saddle. Faith had no choice but to swing her other leg over the horse. It was a comfortable, easy movement. Angrily she sat, staring through the big bay horse, through the dirt of the ring.

'Now walk him, around the ring once,' said Beth lightly. 'Then give him the signal to trot.'

Faith's face burned along the spot where the fall had bruised her cheek. Tears seeped from behind her eyes. Unwillingly she clicked Harold into a walk. She didn't want Beth to crack him with her crop again, so she pressed him into a trot. He was surprisingly eager, springing forward as though still inspired by Beth's earlier swat.

Sweat dampened the back of Faith's neck and grew wet tents under her arms.

'Twice around the ring,' commanded Beth. 'Don't let him walk. Keep him trotting.' But after one turn, Harold stumbled back into a walk.

'I said TROT!' hollered Beth. 'I want two full times around the ring at trot. Start again.'

Faith was furious. She hated Beth. But now, every time Harold showed signs of slowing down, Faith dug into him with her heels. Her knees felt raw. So did her throat from holding back her anger. Sweat was sliding down her spine and her shirt was sticking to it.

Faith finished trotting two times around the ring. She stopped in front of Beth and glared at her, daring her to make her do anything else.

245

Beth's face had a cold, closed look. She took a deep breath and sent it out sighing. 'You can untack Harold and put him back in the field.' Then she turned toward the other students, dismissing Faith, and said in a cheery voice, 'Out on the rail, everybody. We're going to walk and then canter. Now, who can tell me why Faith fell off?'

As she left the ring, leading a quiet Harold, Faith strained her ears to hear what went on behind her. One student, a thin girl of about seven, piped up in a baby voice, 'She didn't sit up.'

'Little liar, nosesucker,' said Faith fiercely to herself. She felt betrayed. It wasn't fair. The tears spread up again behind her eyes. 'I will never get on a horse again,' she vowed out loud, not caring who heard her, her voice slapping the air.

Harold seemed placid while she removed his tack. When she opened the gate to let him into the field, he hesitated, then nudged her shoulder gently, breathed into her hair. Faith burst into tears.

'Oh, Harold,' she whispered as he moved off toward the other horses, 'oh, Harold, why did you dump me?' She hung over the gate, watching him amble away. 'What's wrong with everything?' she mourned, half aloud.

Faith couldn't look Beth in the face that night. Beth didn't seem to be angry with her but the quiet easiness between the two of them wasn't there. Beth was coolly cheerful. She had made a delicious chicken pie for supper.

Afterward Faith and Gem helped carry grain to

the horses and the sheep and paint one of the new jumps that would go into the ring. The anger inside Faith eased away, leaving a little rock of determination half buried inside her. 'I will not ride.'

6

Beth was getting ready to host a mid-July schooling show. The ring received a new coat of paint, fresh sawdust and bright pots of geraniums. Beth was preparing her students, too. They would be judged on how they trotted and cantered, how they started, halted, how they sat. They would be asked to ride a horse in patterns – a figure eight or a cloverleaf. Advanced students would take a course of jumps as well.

There was plenty to do without even getting on a horse. After her fall from Harold, Faith managed to disappear at lesson time for a few days. Her absence went unnoticed, or at least unquestioned, during the bustle. She pretended to be so busy stamping and banding the show announcements that time just slipped by her. But she knew she would have to confront Beth sooner or later, and she watched and waited for the smartest time.

Gem would ride in the schooling show. Eagerly she helped bring in horses for the lessons. She planned on riding in nearly every lesson Beth taught. She was 'in training,' she said. She wanted to do well against riders from other schools.

At night in bed, watching Gem do her nightly exercises, Faith listened to her endless chatter about the coming show. Gem worried about posting on the correct diagonal. Faith was surprised. She had thought Gem had diagonals down prefectly.

'The judge for the show rode with the Olympic team,' Gem announced each night. In the same breath, she fretted that new boots, ordered two weeks earlier, had not yet arrived.

After her sister fell asleep, Faith would lie awake for a long time. She wished she were home. Weekly letters came from her mother but they were addressed to both girls and talked about how the twins were growing. The funny lines her dad penned at the bottom made her feel lonely. She missed her mother's quiet 'good mornings' and orderly break-fasts. At home she could enjoy the squirrels and rabbits in their wide back lawn without being res-ponsible for them. Here she was *forced* to spend time working around horses she didn't even like. Work, work, work. And Gem's whisperings at night, which used to bore her into sleep at home, now made her feel somehow crippled.

Two days before the show, she decided to approach Beth when she came upon her lying beside the lawn mower with the toolbox. A perfect time, Faith reasoned. Beth wouldn't want to spare any energy on Faith right now. There was mowing to be done.

'I'm not riding anymore,' she said to the body bracing itself by the mower. Beth's face was contorted with concentration. Faith steeled herself and said stoutly, 'I've decided I don't want to ride horses anymore.'

'Just a minute . . .' grunted Beth. She gave her wrench one last turn and sat up, wiping her forehead with her sleeve. Then, to Faith's dismay, she turned her full attention on her.

'That's your decision,' she said. 'You're not an athlete like your sister. Your legs aren't strong. And you're not competitive.'

That's settled, thought Faith, relieved and insulted at the same time.

'But,' continued Beth, 'you've a fine rapport with animals.' She settled back thoughtfully on her elbows. 'You recognize most of the sheep. Dogs follow you like children. You are easy with new mamma cats and you're the only one Raccoon will come to.' She looked intently into Faith's face. 'Why not horses?'

'I can't listen to horses,' said Faith. It pained her to say it out loud. 'I know they're saying things, but I can't hear them.'

'You've got it backward,' said Beth firmly. 'Horses are supposed to listen to you. You tell them what to do and make them do it.'

'I can't talk to them either,' said Faith.

'Part of talking to a horse is riding him,' said Beth, standing up. 'A horse listens to leg pressure – the shift of your body – your control of the bit in his mouth.' She turned to go, the conversation ended.

Faith was silent, dissatisfied. Then Beth turned back to her.

'You ought to learn to lunge a horse, if you want to speak so they'll listen.' Faith gasped as visions of forcing a horse to the ground, the way a cowboy twists a steer, leapt into her head. But Beth said, 'You do it from the ground. With a long rope. It's a way of exercising a horse without getting on to him.' She turned back to the lawn mower. 'Not now – after the show.'

So, thought Faith, I'm not through with horses after all. A knot of worry lodged itself inside her, but she pushed it away. Beth had said 'after the show.'

That night, Faith watched her sister run silently in place, knees chopping up high. 'Does that really make your legs stronger?' she asked, sitting up in bed.

'I don't know,' said Gem without missing a beat. She wasn't even breathing hard. 'I just like to do it.' She checked her stopwatch, though. Faith knew she believed in getting results from her efforts.

Faith got out of bed and tried a few jogs. Her feet slapped noisily into the floor. The bureau jiggled, shaking Gem's bottles and jars.

'Elephant!' hissed Gem. 'Keep your weight up! Don't drop it. How can anyone light as a bird sound like a mammoth?'

Faith *slap-slapped* a few more steps.

'Tiptoe it, mouse brain! Tiptoe it!'

'Tiptoe your big mouth!' cried Faith and flung herself back into bed. Gem began to do hamstring stretches, leaning her weight into her palms against the wall.

'That's why you're a good rider,' said Faith. 'Your legs are strong from running.' She looked down at her own thin legs.

'Wrong,' said her sister. 'Different muscles for riding. You keep your heels *down*, remember? Sergeant Beth's yell? *Heels down! Heels down!* You need to lengthen the back of your legs.'

Faith watched. 'This exercise is good for that,' said Gem. 'Or maybe walking upstairs with your knees in and letting your heels push down over the edge of the step . . .'

'Ye gods!' said Faith. 'That sounds stupid.'

But the next morning, while Gem was getting her beauty sleep, Faith tried running in place. She found to her surprise that, in trying not to wake her sister, she could 'tiptoe it.' She didn't last longer than forty seconds by her sister's stopwatch. She tried it again. She had never realized how long a whole minute was.

She decided, as she descended the stairway to breakfast, that she would run in place every morning before her sister woke up.

That night, she climbed the stairs with her knees together, her heels pushing down over the edge of the steps. It was awkward and she felt like an idiot. It took her forever to get to the bedroom, causing her sister to ask, 'Where *were* you?'

'Nowhere,' answered Faith, which was exactly where she felt she had been.

*

The Saturday of Beth's horse show they all rose earlier than usual, even Gem. Faith skipped her tiptoe jogging. They had horses to get ready. All week they had been mowing extra areas for parking vehicles from other stables. They had been laying down fresh straw in the stalls and cleaning tack.

Around 7:30 that morning, vans and horse trailers drawn by dusty big Buicks, jeeps and trucks began rolling into the farm. Faith had the job of guiding them to a proper parking spot according to a plan she had helped Beth work out the night before over a hasty pizza supper.

By midmorning she was high on her own importance. There was a circus bustle of people and horses about the place. Faith barely minded sidestepping the great, sleek bodies being led or excercised or groomed next to the various vans and rigs in the parking lot.

Guests from other stables, recognizing her as the red-headed parking attendant, asked her for directions. 'Where's the water for the horses?' 'Where's the bathroom, miss?' 'Where do I find Beth?' 'Don't suppose you'd have an extra lead line.'

She ran back and forth, finding a clothes brush for riders in their formal jackets, answering the telephone.

Gem looked elegant in a pale blue jacket with a dark velvet collar, but she pouted. Her hunt cap had a rip in it. Beth had assured her that the judge wouldn't notice it, but Gem had seen Beth's best rider in a brown jacket and matching velvet cap. Her name was Cora and she was a talkative show-off.

There was also a handsome boy from the LilJohn stables riding in the jumping class. He was tall and lean with very black hair. Gem tried to keep the ripped part of her hat away from his view of her. Faith told her, 'He's not even *looking* at you.' She wasn't quite telling the truth. The black haired boy *was* checking her sister over. Boy crazy, thought Faith derisively. But she noticed that Gem was nervous and part of her sympathized with her sister.

Now Gem was fretting about making Vixen change leads when cantering the figure eight. 'Vixen favors her right foreleg no matter which way we circle,' moaned Gem. Faith knew, from hearing Beth holler it, that the inside foreleg was supposed to lead when the horse was cantering in a circle. The rider couldn't look down to check but had to *feel* whether it was right or not.

'I can never feel the lead,' worried Gem. 'I have to sneak a look down to see which shoulder is forward.' She demonstrated, sliding her glance down without moving her head. 'Could a judge notice my eyes?' she asked.

'I can hardly tell you're looking down and I'm standing right next to your face,' Faith reassured her.

When Gem rode into the ring, Faith watched with Beth. 'Wrong lead, wrong lead,' muttered Beth when Gem turned in a figure-eight canter.

But her sister took a yellow third-place ribbon and carried it out of the ring with a triumphant smile. 'If I can learn to feel the leads, I can take a blue ribbon next time,' she boasted.

Part of Faith cheered her sister while another part mourned, 'She's not even an animal person. She doesn't even *like* horses.'

That evening, after the last dusty vehicle had pulled away and Beth's last tired horse had been turned out to pasture, Faith resumed the custom she'd forgotten the last few days. She counted the weeks until she could go home. But now there was a new, disquieting feeling. It won't be the same, she thought. Something is changing forever here this summer and nothing will ever be the same.

7

The morning following the schooling show, Faith's legs were stiff and sore from all the running around of the day before. But by lunchtime they felt supple and surprisingly strong. She went with Beth to bring in the horses for grooming and lessons. Together they climbed the long hill into the back field where the horses had wandered, grazing. Faith's fear at being deep in a field of horses was manageable with Beth along.

'I think I have more breath,' she told Beth, bragging a little. 'I don't have to stop to catch it.'

'That's good,' said Beth. 'You can help me bring these fellows in more often.'

Faith groaned inwardly. Why can't I keep my big mouth shut she thought.

But as the days slipped toward August, Faith helped bring in the horses. Flies were thick about the stable. At the woods' edge their forest brothers, deerflies, lurked ready to feed on warm horse bodies. The big animals stood in groups in the fields, whisking insects from each other's faces with their tails.

Each morning Beth broke through the clusters of horses to cull the ones she wanted for a lesson. She led three or four together back to the stables. Faith could manage one at a time. She still sidestepped nervously when leading an eager Cloud or any of the other high-spirited horses.

In the back of Faith's mind flickered Beth's promise to teach her how to lunge a horse. Faith ignored it. Helping bring in the horses, grooming and saddling them was adventure enough. She also ignored the tiny spark of interest that glowed inside her like a small forgotten star. Lunge a horse?

Beth didn't forget. One cloudy afternoon, she asked Faith to meet her in the ring with Harold. He didn't need to be tacked up, just groomed she said.

When Faith led the big bay down, she found Beth was standing in the center of the ring. Around her like the rim of a wheel trotted a frisky new dun horse, playfully shaking his head. Beth turned like a hub in the center, keeping taut the long line attached to his halter. With her left hand she trailed a lengthy whip in the dirt behind the trotting horse.

'This is a lunge line,' Beth called to Faith. 'The trainer's tool.' She clucked to the horse and said, 'Caan-ter.' The dun horse moved from a trot into a slow canter. Beth kept the whip trailing behind him. The horse shook his head and sent out a playful buck. Calmly Beth brought him back down. 'Tro-oh-t,' she said. He slowed to a brisk trot.

Faith stood outside holding Harold by his lead line.

'You lunge a horse to exercise him,' said Beth. Once more she clucked a canter at the dun, who

257

tossed his head but began to canter again. He thundered in his wide circle about Beth while she turned herself slowly, following his movement.

'You lunge a horse to discipline him, too,' said Beth. 'You try and keep him balanced – keep his rhythm even.' Faith watched the turning figure with a mixture of awe and worry. It looked easy enough. But then, so did riding.

'I want you to come in here,' said Beth without taking her eyes from the horse moving about her. 'Tie Harold to the hitching ring and come in here next to me.'

Faith felt chills of panic cool her stomach. As she tied Harold up, her mind furiously planned how to dodge the circling horse to get to Beth. She sweated as she watched but, when the dun pounded past her for the third time, she dashed for the center.

'You lunge a horse to observe him,' continued Beth as if nothing unusual had happened. 'You also lunge a frisky horse to take some of the zip out.'

Faith found herself turning beside Beth. With barely a change in movement, Beth handed the line to Faith. 'Just keep it up,' said Beth.

The transfer happened so smoothly that Faith had no time to panic. She kept turning while the dun cantered around her. He seemed not to notice the change. Beth trailed the whip.

'Now – gently – ease the line toward you,' said Beth so quietly her words barely moved the air. 'Don't pull or yank – just close your hand on the line, ease it in and say "trot – easy, now".'

Faith closed her hand, her eyes fixed on the horse. His movement was hypnotic: *tha-thud, tha-thud.* She chose a moment.

'Trot,' she said clearly, aiming the sound and easing the line toward her stomach.

The dun slowed down into a trot without a break in rhythm. A sweet wave of pleasure swept through Faith.

There was silence except for the soft thud of the trotting horse. They all turned together, the horse and Faith and Beth. Then Beth let out her breath.

'That was perfect,' she said. 'That was quite – perfect.'

Harold was tougher to lunge, stubborn. It was hard to get him started. 'Be patient,' said Beth. 'He knows the signals so well, he'll teach *you.*'

But there was no repeat of Faith's success with the dun that day. The whip was difficult to drag while using the other hand.

'The whip just provides a frame. It's not to use on the horse – just to give him a boundary,' Beth told her.

The entire process felt awkward to Faith. But gradually, in the days that followed, she learned to cluck Harold into a jerky trot around her. She also lunged Vixen and Cloud, a brown horse named Hobo and the dun. They were easy to work at a trot.

Cantering was another matter. The surge of power, the hooves pounding about her, touched the memory of wild horses plunging toward her in the field on that first day. She circled a thundering horse about her in a wash of dust and fear. Eventually, after many hours and many a horse, she learned to ease the big animals into a canter. But she had to steel herself each time she gave the *canter* command.

As her skill increased, Beth had Faith lunge high-strung horses before lessons. Sometimes Beth needed an older horse loosened up.

Faith walked and trotted them around and around. She never felt fully in control when they cantered, so she avoided calling for it unless Beth was watching.

'They can warm up fine at a trot,' she told herself. But another part of her whispered scornfully, 'Chicken.'

Once in a while, the lunging exchange between Faith and the horse became dreamlike. It only happened when no one else was about. The horse moved in hypnotic circle around Faith and her commands came from her mouth like music.

'It's like we're dancing,' she told Brady later. 'And I lead.' She had taken to talking to Brady though he seldom answered her. But this time he said, 'Wouldn't catch me messing with them birds. No sir, I don't tell 'em what to do an' they don't mess with me.'

Brady's afraid too, she thought. She felt bold by comparison. Safely on the ground she could use her voice. She used her hands, too, caressing as she brushed the horses' smooth neck and sides.

She finally learned to put the bridle on the easy

ones, working nervously beside the big, breathing bodies. Cloud took the bit with no fuss at all when her fingers pried into the sides of his slippery mouth. She remembered, in spite of herself, the feel of his eager response when she'd been astride his back.

'If you're really good, a horse sees out of your eyes – sees where you want him to go – while you use his legs to get there.' Beth had said that, but it still didn't make sense.

What was it she had felt way back then on the eager black horse? Had Cloud seen through her eyes? Had his vision been clear and brave? *Could that have been her on Cloud?*

Except for five straight days of record-breaking heat toward the end of July, the Michigan weather was comfortable. There was a lot of rain, which made the grass and the trees lush and thickly green – and nurtured the flies.

Beth let Faith take care of the new litter of kittens in the barn, which included naming them. She hadn't suggested Faith take a lesson again.

Fine with me, thought Faith, but she did feel a twinge of jealousy and awe as her sister began to learn to jump a horse. Faith watched Gem on a small, gray horse first go over low cross poles and then over barrels.

She grew impatient with her sister too, when Gem fell in love with the feisty little gray, whose name was Rambler. All Gem talked about was Rambler this and Rambler that. 'He never pops a fence, that Rambler, he stands right off and goes over so smooth. And he's so *cu-u-te* and gentle, you'd never imagine he could jump that way.'

Ye gods! thought Faith. But she could no longer say spitefully to herself that Gem didn't like horses. She just 'lu-u-ved' Rambler.

Gem was also very excited over phone calls from the black-haired boy from LilJohn stables. His name was Owen. They talked for hours on the phone until Beth had to make a house rule about phone calls – twenty-minute limit or stall-cleaning penalties. This was very effective for, although Gem 'lu-u-ved' Rambler, she didn't love mucking out his rich, odorous leavings from a stall. She began to set the kitchen timer when Owen called.

But if Gem had Rambler and a new boyfriend, Faith had seven kittens. At first they were kept in the pantry off the kitchen. The kittens were as good as twin babies, Faith thought, maybe better since they were tiny and furry and easy to cuddle. One in particular, the smallest and weakest, a black one with a white mask across its face, was her favorite.

The other kittens were strong and pushy. Blackie Whiteface, as Faith named the little one, couldn't fight its way to its mother's nipples through six other struggling bodies. Beth gave her a medicine dropper – 'the nurse's tool,' she said, and Faith used it to feed Blackie Whiteface watery milk with a little honey in it.

Beth gave Faith vitamins and other supplements to mix into the milk. Soon the kitten began to fill out and grow, and Faith could tell that Blackie Whiteface was a boy.

Whenever Faith entered the pantry, Blackie Whiteface would come springing and wobbling in his dizzy little walk to climb all over her feet and claw her socks. She would pick him up and he would crawl across her shoulders and back and grab at her hair. Once he wet on her shirtfront. Faith didn't really mind. Her animal ear was charmed by purring. And Beth seemed to be pleased.

Even after the mother and her kittens were moved into the barn, Blackie Whiteface continued to follow Faith. The first night he was away, Faith heard him mewling at the back door. There stood little Blackie Whiteface wanting to get in. He was so happy to see Faith that he clawed halfway up the screen door until Faith opened it and dragged him off.

Beth told her that, if she got Gem's okay, Blackie Whiteface could sleep in their bed. 'Just one night,' agreed Gem. But she was very agreeable these days.

The kitten wet in the corner of the room next morning and Faith hurried to clean it up. She spread some of her sister's cologne over the spot, hoping to discourage Blackie Whiteface from using the same place again.

Next night, Gem didn't say a word when Faith crawled into bed with Blackie Whiteface on her shoulder. 'It's nice seeing you smile again,' said her sister. 'You've been so glum this summer.'

Gem was having a wonderful summer. Excitement glowed in her face. She had never looked so pretty, and Faith felt only a little jealous. She had a cuddly kitten and she had noticed, as she did her hamstring walk up the stairs, that it was quite effortless. Her legs were strengthening, she was sure of it. Perhaps she would surprise her parents when she got home. She wouldn't be able to ride a horse – but she'd have legs like a ballet dancer.

8

Early in August, Beth began to prepare her students for another horse show. Her patience was short during the lessons and she tolerated few mistakes.

'Now you *know* what diagonal is! Why are you ignoring it?' Faith would hear her yell. Or to her prize student, Cora, who looked down at a fence while jumping it, 'Where should your eyes be looking? Eyes up! Eyes up!' Sometimes Faith would hear her from as far away as the kitchen. 'Relax. RELAX! Say that to yourself. OUT LOUD! I want to hear you say it.' Faith could never hear the students from the kitchen, but she knew they were riding around the ring mumbling, 'Relax . . . relax . . . relax . . . relax.' Washing up the breakfast dishes or watering the garden, Faith felt a little like Cinderella – doing all the unexciting chores while Beth's students were dressing for the ball.

'Easy with those reins; you're on his MOUTH! You're guiding a HORSE, not sawing down a tree!'

The lessons themselves, usually an hour, some-times went on and on, lasting nearly two hours. The students were exhausted and downcast. Gem, whose smart new boots were rubbing her sore ankles, was doubly miserable.

This horse show was a big one at an elegant fox hunt stable near Detroit. Riders from many Midwest states, the East Coast and even Canada were coming. Beth would have to truck the horses a long distance and they would not return until after midnight. Beth said Gem was ready to compete in a jumping class as well as on the flat.

As the show date grew closer, Faith too was caught in the fever of preparations. She cleaned and oiled tack, washed saddle pads and helped the riding students with the daily grooming of the four horses that would be used in the show.

Faith admired clever, quick Cora, Beth's best rider. She was nervous and funny and talked as she groomed about riding disasters – falls she'd had and bad habits of horses. Faith wondered how she could keep riding in the face of so much danger.

At night Faith went gradually to sleep amid the restless, excited chatter of her sister. Gem was trying to hypnotize herself into the correct jumping position. 'Hands forward, eyes forward – heels down.' She repeated it over and over to herself. As her voice droned away, sleep came slowly and deliciously to Faith, snuggled next to Blackie Whiteface.

They rose at four on the Saturday morning of the show. They loaded the four horses into the trailer and were on the road hauling in Beth's old pickup by five. They watched the sun come up from the highway into Detroit and stopped for doughnuts at a truck stop filled with silent truckdrivers warming hands around mugs of coffee. Then they hit the highway once more.

At the show grounds, they unloaded the horses and tied them to iron loops on the trailer. Cora and two other students who would ride for Beth showed up with nervous mothers. Then began the laborious grooming. Not only must the horses be shining and clean, their manes and tails had to be braided with colored yarn, their hooves polished. They all worked. Even two of the mothers helped. The other mother paced and smoked.

A nervous Cora, grooming Cloud, began a litany of terrible falls at horse shows, ones she'd seen or read about. Faith shuddered at grisly accounts of broken necks over jumps, broken legs of horses and riders. She was delighted when Gem told Cora, 'Stop polluting my space.' After that Cora worked in abused silence.

The horses sensed the excitement in the preparations. The more elegant they began to look, the prouder they stood. Their nostrils widened and their eyes rolled back. After the horses were ready, Faith helped Gem put her hair in a French braid caught in a blue silk ribbon. Then Beth called her riders together to distribute the hunt caps. Gem grabbed quickly the new cap of dark blue velvet. She crammed it on her head. Although it was too small for her French-braided hair, she insisted it fit fine.

Cinderella's sister, thought Faith smugly. She

walked away from the group, suddenly lonely and missing Blackie Whiteface.

There were riders and trailers and horses all over the grounds. Faith wandered about, amazed at how many people wanted to risk their necks. The grass of the show ring was velvety and there were flowers beside all the jumps. Banners fluttered from the tall, white-painted judges' stand perched high beside the ring. Dressing up danger, thought Faith.

There were spectators sitting in bleachers and a well-dressed group under an awning at decorated tables. A good rider could earn points to ride in the big show at Madison Square Garden and events in Washington, D.C., and Pennsylvania. Faith felt a surprising tug of sympathetic terror for her sister, riding in such an important event.

But in the first two Equitation on the Flat classes, Gem took third-place yellow ribbons, while Faith gaped from the sidelines.

Then she was lonelier than ever and wandered off by the food tent. She waited in line for the hot, oozing sloppy joe sandwiches everyone seemed to be eating. Ahead of her stood a tall man in a cowboy hat. The way he stood reminded Faith of her father and she felt a rush of homesickness. She peered around the man to see what he looked like.

He had a blondish beard and smile lines at the corners of his eyes. He didn't resemble her dad at all. He was chewing on a toothpick. He smiled down into her face.

'What's doin', Red?' he asked her.

Faith was so pleased, she blushed.

'Looks like you been working hard.' He nodded toward her dirty, straw-covered jeans. Faith blushed again and hid her hands behind her back. She knew her hands were grimy from grooming horses and her nails were black. Suddenly she realized she was going to have lunch and she hadn't remembered to wash her hands. That was a rule back home – clean hands or no meal. Beth, too, reminded them before eating.

'Excuse me,' she whispered and fled from the line to search out the washroom.

Later, after she'd eaten her sloppy joe underneath a tree, she saw the cowboy leaning against the stairs by the judges' booth. She wandered over to him, drawn by his big worn hat and the easy way he stood. He was still chewing a toothpick. She wondered what he was doing at an English hunt-seat show. Cowboys didn't ride the same as English-trained riders. Even their saddles were different.

She leaned against the white rail of the ring, sighing as she looked at the preparations for the next class.

'You scare real easy, miss,' remarked the cowboy. Faith's heart went cold. Who had told him she was a coward? But the cowboy added, 'What did I say t'make you run off?'

Faith was so relieved she giggled. 'Just went to wash up before lunch.'

'You ride?' asked the cowboy, shifting his weight against the railing.

'I used to,' replied Faith. That was at least half

true. 'But horses aren't my favorite thing.' She waited for him to ask about her favorite thing. She would tell him about Blackie Whiteface or Rackity or the rabbits in her backyard at home.

But he drawled, 'What're you doing here?' Faith looked up at him, hesitating. He smiled. 'This is a heck of a place for somebody who's not into horses.' His eyes were tan colored and warm. Like his skin and beard and his smooth, taffy-colored boots. She liked the soft way he spoke.

'I'm visiting,' said Faith. 'And I help with the horses.' She nodded. 'There's work for two or three at Beth's farm.'

'Is that Beth?' asked the cowboy. He fanned his chin toward the line of horses and riders waiting outside the ring.

It was Beth, giving last-minute words to her riders, dark-honey hair straggling down out of her ponytail. She had her stall mucker boots on, which made her feet look like Beetle Bailey's in the comics. Her face was sweaty.

Faith realized he had been watching Beth for some time, not Gem, beautiful in her blue velvet hunt cap.

'That's Beth,' she answered. 'She's talking to my sister.' Faith watched the cowboy's face. 'My sister is a pretty good rider even though she just learned this summer. She still has to look down to check her leads, but Beth says she has a good chance to place. Beth says judges are biased.'

The cowboy looked at her with interest. Encour-

270

aged, Faith went on. 'Some judges don't like boy riders – or fat girls – or Appaloosa horses . . . no matter how good they are. Beth says most judges love thin, blonde girls on big grays or blacks.'

'Is that a fact,' said the tan man. He switched his toothpick. 'Probably so.'

'The class my sister rides in won't be the real big jumps,' she continued to inform him. 'They change the course and raise the fences later for the real good riders.'

'Yeah,' he agreed.

Faith didn't usually talk at such a rate to strangers. But there was something about the cowboy, a kind of warm excitement that seethed from his skin and clothing. And he liked her, she could tell.

He smiled around the toothpick, showing nice, strong, even teeth.

'Where do you live?' asked Faith.

'Oh, anywhere,' he said, his eyes turned back towards Beth. She was still talking to Gem, stroking Rambler's neck. 'Everywhere.'

Nowhere, I bet, thought Faith. A wandering cowboy. She edged nearer along the rail, drawn by his pleasantness, and looked up at his face.

'What do you do?' she asked.

He looked down at her, amused. 'Are you nosy?' he teased, 'or just careful? How many questions you gonna ask before I get to tell you my name, my age – and how much money I make?'

'How much money do you make?' asked Faith,

delighted with her new sauciness. She saw herself flirting like Gem.

The cowboy spit out the toothpick, threw back his head and laughed.

'You're quite an ol' gal, Red.' Faith smiled. The cowboy had a wonderful laugh. She noticed that his hands were fine, with very clean nails. Perhaps he was a movie cowboy. Most people who rode horses had tougher-looking hands. Who cared? A warm excitement fluttered in her throat.

She glanced hastily over at Beth, talking now to Cora, who sat on Cloud. Beth's hands were gentle on the neck of the big, black horse, stroking. Faith knew that Beth's nails were chipped and dirty, the palms calloused. She tried to look at Beth through the cowboy's eyes and, for a brief instant, Beth came into focus as Faith had never seen her. Her serious face, intent upon her student, blooming rich with color. There was a vast quiet beneath her hands against the dark horse. Her strong arms were smooth and tanned. Why, she's beautiful, thought Faith.

A flash of jealousy shriveled her briefly. Then she pushed it away, thinking, he's not going to wait till I grow up. But I could give him to Beth. *Like a carrot.* Maybe she'd be grateful. Maybe he'd visit a lot.

Then the loudspeaker interrupted her dreaming. They were calling riders up for the next class. There was excitement along with dust rising in the air as horses and riders approached the ring.

'Gotta go,' the cowboy said. He turned and

mounted the ladder into the judges' booth. 'See ya later, Red.'

Surprised, she watched him enter the booth. Then, afraid of losing him, she called up, 'What's your name?'

'Ben,' he called back, 'Ben Warren from Pennsylvania. Your Beth has heard my name before, I betcha.'

Pennsylvania? Faith was disappointed. She had hoped for Montana or Wyoming.

But the real surprise came when she began to realize that Ben Warren was in the judges' booth because he was one of the judges.

Over the loudspeaker came the announcer's voice. 'Afternoon, ladies and gentlemen. Most of you are already pretty familiar with our judge for the Equitation over Fences events. Mr Ben Warren comes to us from Green Valley, Pennsylvania . . .'

From below, Faith let this new knowledge sink in. The cowboy was a lot more than a cowboy. Then embarrassment came. What had she said to him – about judges being biased? And about her sister looking down for the right lead? Oh no! She had even explained to a *judge* about the raising of the fences.

In a hot glow of shame, she fixed her eyes on the activity ring. She was barely able to enjoy how well the first rider fenced. She couldn't appreciate the tremor in the spectators when Cora, the star rider, went off course, forgetting the correct order of jumps. Cloud still pranced and snorted eagerly under the tearful girl as she left the ring, disqualified.

The next horse refused a fence, sending the rider catapulting through the air to land on the far side of the jump. Faith was too preoccupied to even gasp.

Then the announcer called Gem's name and number, and Faith was finally able to focus on the ring. Her sister rode beautifully, turning corners with confidence, eyes up over the fences, hands forward and light. Faith couldn't tell if she looked down for her lead as she rounded her turns. Rambler flew over each obstacle and Gem settled him back nicely for the next fence. There was a round of applause when the pretty girl trotted off, her back proud and straight.

When the winners were announced, Gem had earned a first-place ribbon for the event. Faith stopped hating herself for bad-mouthing judges to an actual judge. She wondered, briefly, about Mr Ben Warren's choice. Her sister had certainly ridden as if she had years of experience under her narrow belt.

When the cowboy climbed down from the judges' booth, she accosted him. 'Is my sister really that good?'

Ben Warren chuckled. 'I must admit, Red, I'm a little partial to black or gray horses and lean riders. Don't have to be pretty, but they have got to move in harmony and the rider must not make mistakes.'

'Can't fat riders ever win?' asked Faith, a little spite lifting her voice.

'If they don't make mistakes, sure,' answered Ben Warren. 'And if their weight doesn't hinder the horse.' His eyes crinkled when he smiled at her. Faith dropped her head, embarrassed before his niceness.

'First-place ribbon probably would've gone to Cora What's-'er-name if she hadn't gone off course. But, who knows. Your sister rode well. I caught her checking for her leads once or twice but she was the best in the Novice Ridden class. She earned her ribbon.'

Faith looked back up into the cowboy's smile. He was the nicest man outside her father she had ever known.

'Can you cook?' she asked.

9

'I invited someone to dinner tomorrow,' said Faith to Beth on the long drive home. 'Okay?'

It was growing dark and Beth's face was in shadow.

'Hope your friend likes pizza,' said Beth tiredly. 'I've got a lot of catching up to do. We shot the entire day today.'

'He's bringing the whole dinner!' announced Faith triumphantly. 'He can cook. He said just to set the table, have the wine glasses chilled and fill the water glasses two thirds full.'

There was a long silence while Beth digested this news. Faith could feel the truck slow up almost imperceptibly. Then Beth asked tersely from the shadows, 'Wine glasses? *Whom* did you ask, young lady?'

'The judge,' said Faith slowly, savoring the interest she could feel coming from both Beth and her half-dozing sister. Next to her, Gem stirred and sat up.

'Mr Ben Warren, the judge. The judge of the Novice Ridden Hunter class – and the Baby Green over Fences and . . .' She frowned in the effort to remember. 'All the Novice Hunter division. I don't remember them all – but the whole last half of the show was judged by Mr Ben Warren, the one in the cowboy hat.'

The silence that grew in the cab of the truck was finally broken by Gem. 'You've got to be kidding! He's gorgeous! I can't believe it.' But she knew Faith wasn't kidding. 'The fox in the cowboy hat?' Gem's voice grew shrill with excitement. 'He looks like a country-and-western star!'

'How very interesting,' commented Beth. But she no longer sounded so tired. Faith couldn't tell if she was pleased, but Gem certainly was. Her sister began to plan out loud what had to be done to prepare for Mr Ben Warren.

'We've got to vacuum. Faith, you vacuum. I'll dust.' She rambled on and on. Did Beth have a tablecloth, a real one − and napkins? They simply couldn't use paper napkins when they were having wine. And couldn't they have just a little − Gem and Faith? Faith's could be mostly water − but just for the show of it? They'd have to launder the towels. 'And oh!' Gem squeaked. 'The bathrooms!'

Faith smiled to herself in the growing darkness of the cab. Squeezed in between Gem and Beth, she remembered the cowboy's slow grin when she'd asked him if he cooked. He had offered to prove it. Then, made bold by his delight with her, Faith had brazenly suggested he come over the next day and fix Sunday dinner.

'How many?' he had asked. 'How many eatin'?'

'Just me and my sister. We don't eat much. And Beth. She eats a lot.'

He had laughed then and asked for the address. Faith could only remember the phone number of the farm. He pulled out a little gold pencil and a tiny notebook and wrote it down.

'Maybe he won't come,' she said interrupting Gem's excited planning. 'He only has the phone number.'

'Well, we'll see,' said Beth calmly. 'It's either a grand feast for four or pizza for three.'

Both Faith and Gem groaned. The time had come at last for a change.

The next day, Faith was wakened by an insistent Gem, who was ignoring her beauty sleep for once.

'If we're going to get this place presentable, we'd better get started.' Her voice was excited and driving. 'Get up so we can make the bed.'

Grumbling, Faith eased Blackie Whiteface to the floor. She would have to do her secret jogging later. She helped Gem shake the sheets up and make the bed.

'I want my breakfast,' said Faith stoutly, more to resist Gem's bossiness than because she was hungry. Grudgingly she had to admire her sister's energy but Gem was taking over the idea – her gift. It was a bigger and better gift than being a blue-ribbon or a good weeder.

'How can you be hungry?' asked Gem. 'I'm not hungry.'

'He's not coming to see *you*,' hissed Faith. 'He doesn't even know you exist! I invited him. He's *my* friend. And he's coming to see Beth more than anyone.' When she said this, it stung a little. She thought wistfully of the cowboy's smile and his fine hands.

Gem paused, looking hurt. Then she said, 'He gave *me* a blue ribbon so he must know I exist.'

'Well, all you had to do to get a blue ribbon was to be blonde and ride a gray horse, that's all,' Faith lashed cruelly. 'He *saw* you looking down!'

But her sister had recovered her composure. She said reasonably, 'Come on. We've got to straighten up the bathroom and the kitchen – and find the wine glasses and real napkins.' Faith sourly acquiesced. Gem's plans were wonderful embellishments on her own daring idea.

'Animals first,' Beth reminded them. 'It'll go faster if we all help.' She aimed the last remark at Gem but looked surprised when Faith groaned along with Gem.

'Even in emergencies?' Faith asked. She wanted Beth to understand that she wasn't shirking.

'Animals *are* the emergency,' said Beth firmly.

So they spent the next hour feeding horses, the donkey, sheep, dogs and cats. It took another hour to medicate a kick wound on Hobo's shoulder and knock a leaning fence post back in.

Faith itched with impatience. Gem looked as if she would explode.

Finally, farm chores finished, the girls attacked the kitchen. It had served as a catchall during the preparations for the show. Beth seemed amused at their furious activity, but she quietly picked up the living room and began to run the vacuum.

'She's pretty laid back for a prospective lover,' whispered Gem to Faith. But later on, after Gem had discovered linen napkins neatly tucked in the back of the cupboard, Beth appeared with a sturdy carton containing some beautiful crystal glasses that had been her grandmother's. There were seven wine glasses and six water goblets.

'I've never used these,' she mused, taking them out of the straw they were packed in. She held one up to the window. The light leapt and shimmered like a shattered rainbow trapped inside the glass.

Oh, I hope he comes, thought Faith and, as if she had signaled Ben Warren, the phone rang. When Beth answered, it was the cowboy asking for directions

After that, Beth disappeared upstairs to change her clothes. Faith and Gem stuffed the remaining clutter into the hall closet – sacks of cat food and kitty litter, looping reins of broken tack and a bag of unsorted laundry. The door would barely close and it took the two of them, throwing themselves against it, to finally latch it shut.

'If anyone knocks the doorknob, it'll explode,' giggled Gem, which sent them both into a storm of laughter.

Then it was left to Faith to set the table with the mismatched silver and old flowered plates. She polished each plate as she set it down. She worried a little about Beth falling asleep right after dinner as she often did, sometimes nodding in her chair right at the table.

Gem disappeared, first into the bathroom to rim her eyes with blue mascara. Then she scurried upstairs to put on her faded, skin-tight cutoffs, rearrange the stuffing in her bra and pull on a beautiful silk sweater. 'The contrast will be smashing!' she had informed Faith.

Faith did not believe the contrast would be so smashing. But, she thought grudgingly, Gem will probably look beautiful anyway. For a moment she considered asking to borrow a blouse from her sister. But she was comfortable in her white T-shirt and her jeans were clean. She hoped Gem wouldn't out-shine Beth – or the crystal glasses, either.

She ran outside to the garden to pick marigolds and daisies and a pretty blue-flower weed.

She was standing with an armload of flowers when the yellow van pulled into the long drive. She could see it slow down at the bridge and lurch up past the sheep field, a foreigner feeling his way in a new place.

It was a big van. She noticed that it was very clean, not like Beth's old truck or her dust-coated Horizon with its 'I Brake for Animals' bumper sticker. He really can live anywhere, thought Faith. Delight at his coming flooded her.

The screen door banged but she barely noticed Gem come out, or Blackie Whiteface curling around her legs. Wolfie bounded barking to meet the visitor. Beth peered briefly from an upstairs window.

Faith waited, holding the flowers, feeling like a queen welcoming royalty from another country. The big yellow van pulled smoothly to a stop by the back porch.

'Hi, Red,' said Ben Warren, sliding out of the driver's seat. He walked up and smiled down into her face. He wasn't wearing the toothpick. The wrinkles deepened warmly around his tan eyes. 'You look like a bride with those flowers,' he said, and smoothed his hand over the sheen of her red hair. 'Might pretty.'

Faith was so flushed with delight that she didn't even mind Gem posing on the back porch with her lion hair flung back. But then Beth came out of the door, and it wasn't any Beth she knew.

Faith had never seen Beth in a dress and hadn't known she even owned a pair of high heels. She looked uncomfortable and unsteady. The dress she wore was a faded yellow with drooping shoulders, cut simply, but somehow belonging to a half generation earlier. It had creases running across the skirt as if it had been folded a long time. The short sleeves were too tight around Beth's round arms. Her ponytail, now pulled to one side, gave an unnaturally jaunty look.

After a frozen minute, Beth wobbled over to the porch steps. Her welcoming smile was drowned by the worry on her face.

She's worried about falling down the steps, realized Faith. Gem shot her a look of wide-eyed, exaggerated horror which usually made Faith want to laugh. Now, it merely increased her discomfort. She wished fiercely that Beth would go inside and change back into her jeans.

To make matters worse, Ben Warren's face assumed a false look of heartiness. He strode up to where Beth stood and said in an uncomfortable voice, 'This must be Beth.'

'No, it isn't!' erupted Faith. 'She usually looks much better!'

There was a shocked silence. Faith could hear the tail of her sister's gasp. And then Beth laughed. It was a big, deep laugh. She had come back among the living. She stopped wobbling and leaned against the old, peeling porch column. Her face relaxed and smiled.

'You were right, Ben Warren, yesterday when you told Faith I would know your name. I know you.'

The genuine ease flooded back into the cowboy's manner. He chuckled, put one boot on the lower step and leaned into his knee.

'I sure know *you*, lady,' he admitted. 'You're a legend. Turning down fifty thousand green ones for the fine black thoroughbred of yours. That right?'

Beth looked startled and then blushed.

'I've watched you ride many a time,' continued the cowboy. 'Now I watch your students ride.' He paused, then said softly, 'The dynamite lady, Miss Beth Holbein. Pleased to meet you at last.'

He smiled a real smile into her face. There was a kind of burning in the air between them, like electricity. Gem shot Faith a knowing look but Faith ignored it. They really like each other, she thought a trifle sadly. But she comforted herself that this was her gift to Beth, her cowboy.

They all helped Ben Warren carry bags of groceries into the newly cleaned kitchen. Faith steered him carefully past the hall closet. Then she arranged the flowers on the table, letting them spill and trail from an old milk pail.

It was a lovely evening, despite some minor setbacks. Beth's high heels menaced her walking. A sheep got loose and wandered around outside the house. Ben Warren had to sharpen the dull kitchen knives before he could begin cooking.

'Dull knives are dangerous knives,' he said as he slid the newly sharpened blade into a chicken breast, neatly severing the flesh from the rib bones. 'You wind up forcing the blade and you can slip and cut yourself.'

Faith watched, entranced. He arranged the chicken in a baking crock with tiny new potatoes and artichoke hearts. Faith had never liked artichokes much. But when she saw them, hot from the oven, nestled next to chicken and potatoes in a bubbly sauce, she could hardly wait until they sat down to eat.

Gem was allowed a half glass of wine and Faith a mineral water with a dash of wine. There were hot rolls. Beth had picked fresh lettuce from her garden to toss with tomatoes, sweet onions and Ben Warren's homemade dressing.

'Oh,' breathed Faith as they all sat down and spread the napkins in their laps. 'Oh . . .' A phrase of her grandfather's came to mind. 'What a sumptuous repast!' she said.

They all clinked glasses while the escaped sheep peered through the dining room window.

The rest of the evening was wonderful, too. Beth took off her shoes and walked barefoot in her old-fashioned dress. She did not flirt like Gem flirted. She blushed and beamed. They all did the dishes. Ben Warren insisted. 'You have to get this stuff over with or it just hangs on,' he said.

Then he gave them a grand tour of his van. It was neat as a pin. Up front he had a tape deck and a citizens band radio. Behind the front seats was a little kitchen with a real sink, a stove and a miniature refrigerator. There was even a tiny bathroom with the towel and washcloth neatly in place. In a narrow closet hung his clothes, shirts all facing left. Faith thought of the hall closet back at the house and shuddered.

In the back of the van was a bunk bed on which sat a guitar. Faith was rapt when Ben Warren picked it up and began to hum.

He played 'Harvest Moon' and they all sang. He played 'The Ash Grove.' Then Gem sang 'I'm Bidin' My Time' in her very beautiful, clear soprano voice and Faith hated her only briefly.

Faith had never seen Beth smile so much. Nor had she ever seen her so awake at this hour of the

285

evening unless there was an emergency with a sick horse or a broken water pump. Tonight Beth's eyes were bright and merry. She didn't seem the least bit tired. Nobody, in fact, was tired, and it was midnight before anyone realized how late it was.

Smiling, Beth suggested that it was time to 'hit the hay, girls.' Faith and Gem went reluctantly up to their bedroom, but they left the stairwell door open a crack. After they had changed into their night-clothes, they crept back down the stairway, smothering giggles, and crouched near the bottom, trying to hear what Beth and Ben were saying to each other in the living room.

Blackie Whiteface came tumbling down the stairs, his toenails clicking against the wooden steps. Faith hushed him and he curled up in her lap, licking her fingers.

Bored by the long pauses between the soft conversation in the living room, Faith fell asleep in the stairwell, leaning against her sister. She was startled awake as she and Gem and Blackie Whiteface rolled, *bumpidy-thump*, down the last couple of steps and thudded into the stairwell door. They had all dropped asleep against each other and collapsed like a house of cards. Ben Warren, who had leaped to his feet at the crash of bodies, ran to the door and yanked it open. It was not the door to the stairwell, but the hall closet door.

There was a clatter and thump and the cowboy's shout of alarm. When the girls peeked around the doorjamb, they saw an amazed Ben Warren covered with loops of tack, dirty laundry and kitty litter. Beth was leaning against a wall, her hand over her mouth. Faith couldn't tell whether she was laughing or just plain mortified.

'Well,' said Ben Warren, waving his arms to disentangle himself. Then he saw the sisters and a frightened kitten peering from behind the door and began to laugh. 'You sure need some organizing around here,' was all he said.

10

Faith was so high on the overwhelming success of the dinner party that she floated about for a week, absorbed by Beth and Ben's interest in each other.

When Ben Warren wasn't off judging a horse show, he lived in his van parked next to the garden. There was a new atmosphere about the place.

Beth was warm with Faith these days and smiled often. She was amused that Ben Warren had cleaned up her kitchen spick and span and she couldn't find anything anymore. He had even straightened up Beth's closet, and all her shirts and blouses were now facing left.

The cowboy had begun to finish up the sheep's bathroom, too. In the evenings, he and Beth talked over where the new shelving would go and whether the shower should be separate from the tub.

Faith basked in her own virtues. She whistled as she shoved damp clothes into the dryer. She hummed as she did the dishes. Ben Warren called her Cinderella, but she could tell he admired her sense of order. Once he watched her lunge a horse in the ring. She showed off by calling for a canter, something she was still reluctant to do, and then she brought the swift-moving animal back down to a smooth trot. Ben Warren tipped his hat to her. 'Pretty good stuff,' he said. Sometimes the world is wonderful, thought Faith.

One morning, in the tilting mirror of their bedroom, Faith was startled out of her happy satisfaction. Something had happened to her thighs. At first, she was horrified. I'm going to have a bulge in my thighs, she thought. I'm growing up into a person with bulging thighs. Her calves, she noticed, were rounded out too. She decided against the striped shorts she had pulled from the drawer. Instead she dragged on a pair of dirty jeans.

It seemed impossible that her tiptoe jogging in the morning could be responsible for the new shape of her legs. Nor could the hamstring toe-walk up the stairs at night. True, she did her exercises easily and automatically. She now jogged five minutes in place without breathing heavily.

Faith was desperate to wake her sister and discuss her legs. But she knew Gem would be impossible to talk to this early. Later, she thought, she would ask Gem about her thighs. Her sister had definite opinions about beauty. She was somehow always mysteriously aware of the right 'look' in a person. 'That's a cool jacket,' she would whisper to Faith, nudging her. Or, 'Did you see his *haircut*? It's atrocious! He looks like a fish.'

Faith ran downstairs and into the kitchen. Beth was already outside, feeding stock. Ben Warren's van was gone. The cowboy had a show to judge in

Indiana. A few flies buzzed by the window and Faith swatted one out of existence with the swatter. Now that Ben Warren had repaired the screen doors there were only a few flies in the house.

Faith ate some cereal and carefully washed up her dishes, putting them away on the newly lined shelves. Gem would be getting up soon. She never slept past a riding lesson but she was often late to help Faith with the grooming.

Faith did most of the grooming and tacking up for the beginners' class. Beth had a lot of new students too small to do it themselves. The broad backs of horses seemed easier to reach with the brush these days.

On some days she actually enjoyed being close to the horses, slipping underneath their heavy necks to get to the other side. She could bridle them all now, wiggling her thumb and fingers into the sides of their mouths until they took the bit. Then she would spray them with fly spray and help the little ones mount.

Often she watched the lessons with a careful eye, listening to Beth's directions, looking to see if the riders followed them. She checked to see if she could 'see daylight' between their knees and the saddle. New riders' knees always stuck out. The relief she had once felt at the beginning of each lesson – relief *not* to be riding – had been replaced by a vague envy.

The morning of her new-shaped legs, Faith left the kitchen with a firm purpose, ignoring the chill that cooled her heart. For several days she had been contemplating a daring move. Today, she thought, maybe I'll do it. Just sit on one of the horses when I bring him down to the ring. Just sit in the saddle. The chill moved into her middle.

She bounded from the porch, scattering a few barn cats. Cars were pulling in with students. She met Beth leading Rambler toward the stable.

'Good morning, lazybones,' greeted Beth with a mild smile. 'I've already tacked up Vixen and Hobo. I'll need Rambler here and the other four regulars. They're in the stalls.' She handed the gray's lead rope to Faith. 'You look ready for anything today.'

'I am,' said Faith, and led Rambler off. He went easily into his stall.

She was a little nervous tacking Harold up. Flies had invaded the stable and all the animals were jumpy. But she led the big bay outside to a stump and mounted easily. On the way down to the ring, from the high vista of his back, she felt such a rush of excitement and power that Harold surged momentarily into a trot. The old panic returned. She sat back and pulled him down into a walk, heaving a great breath. 'Don't you dare, Harold,' she muttered.

Beth was in the ring with students when Faith rode Harold up. When she turned to take the horse from Faith, her eyebrows lifted. 'What have we here?' was all she said.

Faith swung out of the saddle and slid down Harold's warm side to the ground. She handed the reins to Beth trying to appear casual. 'I'll ride all the others down.' She ran back to the barn, flinging a friendly wave at the gathered mothers. Her back felt loose and strong and she wondered briefly how tall she had grown this summer.

But when she was grooming a restless Hobo, pestered by flies, he stepped on her once. Then, when she slapped his rump, he dangerously waved his hind leg. Cautiously she led him down to the ring, limping as she went, her foot smarting. 'He's in a rotten mood today,' she informed Beth.

She changed her mind about riding the others down. But later, Faith bragged to Brady in the barn that she had 'taken up riding again.' Brady just grunted and kept right on working. Faith realized she would have to look elsewhere for proper appreciation. In a way, she suspected she had told a lie to Brady. She wasn't sure she'd try riding a horse to the ring again.

But, several days later, she delivered first Harold, then Vixen by riding them down to the ring. She felt that, one of these days, she would take on Hobo, too.

The muscle roundness in Faith's calves and thighs didn't astonish Gem. When asked, she said, 'Well, it looks like you're going to have *legs* after all, not those pale sticks you've been walking around on.' It wasn't a whole lot of comfort. Still, Faith felt able to wear her shorts again, even though they were a little tight in the leg.

★

One evening, after the dishes were done and Ben Warren was cleaning his fingernails, he suggested to Beth that they go out dancing. 'Found a nice place, Lady Beth, with some good music. It'll be somethin' new.'

Gem looked up with interest. 'A disco?' she asked. Ben laughed.

Beth was standing by the kitchen table cleaning tack. 'I don't have time for *new*,' she said impatiently. 'Or discos.' But then she joked, 'I've got six more of these to do. If you want something new – here, clean some tack.' She tossed a bridle at him. There was a long dead pause.

She meant it to be funny, thought Faith. Into the silence between the couple, Faith dropped an uneasy laugh. Then, quickly, she offered, 'I'll do it Beth.' She grabbed the bridle from Ben's lap. 'This is Cinderella's job.' But Ben Warren did not smile. He got up and left the room, saying, 'See you later.' They heard the van start up and drive off.

Beth stopped rubbing oil into the bridle looped over a chair. Gem paused in her perpetual nail polishing. Faith felt the air lie heavily on them, gathered about a table full of tack.

Gem finally shrugged and said, 'I guess the honeymoon is over.'

'No!' said Faith. When Gem and Beth looked at her in surprise she mumbled, 'Honeymoons last two weeks. It's only been eleven days.'

After that, small arguments constantly erupted

between Beth and Ben. They were about trivial things. 'If you put your blouse back the same way you took it out, your closet would stay neat,' Ben would protest.

At first, Beth nodded and smiled, chiding him, calling him 'Mr Perfection'. He called her 'Willie Workhorse'. Gradually, Beth stopped smiling and began to frown whenever the cowboy protested the way she did things.

Faith couldn't understand it. Couldn't they tell when they would irritate each other? Couldn't they take the same kind of care with one another they had at first? In the beginning it had amused Ben that Beth went out of her way to use dirt roads instead of the nearby blacktop and highway. Now he criticized how dirty her car got. 'Take the highway,' he told her. 'You're always late for things.'

Now, during lessons and chores, Beth appeared distant, preoccupied. She didn't seem to notice Faith's efficiency with horses, how easily she groomed them.

'I call for a canter all the time now,' Faith told Beth one afternoon as they brought in horses to be lunged.

'Good,' said Beth – but she didn't seem to have heard.

Gem didn't appear worried about Beth and Ben when Faith tried to voice her distress. She was more concerned about when Owen was going to call next.

Gradually the arguments between Beth and Ben Warren became more intense. Bewildered, Faith gave up trying to intervene. The perfect relationship seemed to have turned upside down.

One afternoon, the cowboy stormed out of the house and into his van. He drove off in a fury of dust and spitting gravel, his van narrowly missing the corner of the bridge.

The atmosphere inside the house was grim. Beth sat in the kitchen cleaning another bridle with a cold, determined expression on her face. Faith felt defeated and lonely. She left to seek the quiet comfort of the barn, hoping Blackie Whiteface would be there. She wanted to cuddle him and nuzzle into the fur behind his neck. It always made her feel good.

She called his name into the barn loft. 'Blackie? Blackie Whiteface? Hey!' He usually skittered out when he heard her voice. But he was not in the barn. Faith wandered down to the sheep pen. There was a bristling commotion in the ram section where two rams were challenging each other. Beth and Ben, thought Faith. Stubborn. Plain bullheaded.

Blackie Whiteface was there, perched atop the railing of the sheep pen watching the rams. His little white face peered down into the activity. He leaned so far forward into the pen he appeared to be glued by his hind feet to the top rail. The fury in the pen increased, raising dust. There was the thud of heads and horns, a jostling of woolly bodies.

'Blackie, get away from there,' scolded Faith. The rams backed off from each other and lowered their heads. Their mean little eyes grew smaller.

Their charge was furious. They lurched. When they hit, their bodies plowed into the fence. Horns locked.

'Blackie!'

She cried out as the kitten was knocked from his perch. He fell like a stone into the pen – into the angry, blind activity between the rams.

Then she was screaming, 'Blackie! Blackie!' She struggled over the fence, waving her arms at the rams. They backed off in astonishment at the power of fury.

His little body lay in a crumpled heap. Faith knelt and touched the sprawled ball of fur. He was alive, his breathing slight.

Very gently, she eased her hands beneath the little form. With great care, she walked with him to the back porch. She sat down on the steps and cradled the warm little body in her lap. Blackie Whiteface mewed faintly and tried to lick her hand. She could feel his heartbeat through her palms . . . so faint. *Beat, beat*, and a long pause.

'Blackie? Blackie Whiteface?' she whispered. *Beat, beat.*

She knew when he left her. The beat was so faint, she held her breath. And then it was gone.

They planned a funeral for Blackie Whiteface. Beth lined an old shoebox with soft flannel. 'We just want to ease him gently back into the cycle of life,' said Beth. 'Soon he'll be back in circulation again.' She smiled sadly. 'Part of a flower here, part of tree . . . grass . . . part of a horse, part of you and part of me.'

Faith was numb with misery. She didn't want a flower or a tree. She wanted the little black and white kitten who had slept curled against her every night.

Ben Warren returned in the late afternoon in time to help dig the narrow little grave. They buried Blackie Whiteface near the woods under a big old hickory tree.

In the evening Ben held Faith in his lap as if she were a baby again. Faith leaned into his clean-smelling shoulder and let herself be that baby for a while.

Beth and Ben were gentle with each other too, speaking in soft, low voices. Gem held Faith's hand and offered to sing her any song she wanted to hear.

'Just hum,' said Faith. 'I think I'd like some humming.' So Gem hummed *Ave Maria* getting only a little carried away on the high notes. It was a very good evening in a way. When she went to bed, Faith plunged into sleep immediately and slept deeply all night.

The next day it was sunny and warm and seemed too bright. Faith's body felt heavy and slow. She went through the motions – cleaning up the dishes after breakfast, bringing the horses in for Beth's classes and helping groom and tack them up. There was not even the luster of fear around the horses anymore. She poked at her food at lunchtime; Ben's succulent meals didn't tempt her. She avoided the sheep and kept out of the barn loft where the mother and sisters of Blackie Whiteface romped and fought.

She wondered listlessly if the rest of her life would drag on this way, colorless and dull.

In the late afternoon, she plodded down to one of the horse fields. Gone was the sharp edge of anxiety she had always felt approaching it. She could hardly believe she had ever been that scared of anything, had *cared* that much.

She sat on the top rail of the fence in the warm sun. Horses grazed, switching at flies. She stared off over the fields and the strangest feeling came over her. She saw the sunlit fields as if through a gray veil. She felt them fading from her, everything slipping away, no longer hers. An emptiness invaded her so terrible that she clutched the rail beneath her.

'Why so quiet, Red?' asked a voice near her elbow. Ben Warren leaned against the rail next to where she sat. She could not answer. His voice came to her through the grayness.

Then he reached his big, neat hand gently to the top of her head and smoothed her hair.

The awful emptiness welled up.

'I don't want to die,' whispered Faith. The hum of insects came muffled through the veil.

'Who says you have to?' asked Ben Warren.

'Everybody dies,' said Faith dully. But she looked into his face near her shoulder. She felt the faint stirrings of hope.

'You won't die, Red,' said Ben Warren. He tucked his finger under her chin and turned her face to his.

'Sometime, a long, long time from now, so far away neither of us can believe in it, a real old lady with your name and lots of memories you don't even have yet will die. But she won't mind.'

He spoke slowly. 'She'll be going on a new adventure, one you can't go on until you die – and she'll be ready. You can't go there until you're ready.'

'Was Blackie Whiteface ready?' asked Faith, pulling away suspiciously. With the suspicion came a sharp bite of pain.

'I suspect he was,' said Ben Warren. 'It's just that you weren't ready for him to leave, is all.'

'No,' said Faith softly. 'I wasn't.'

Then Ben Warren hugged her again, quick and short, lifted her in one sweep from the fence and spanked her lightly on her bottom.

'Come on, Red,' he said. 'We gotta feed livestock.'

Dutifully she followed him back to the barn, her gaze fixed on the taffy-colored boots and the grass slowly lifting back from his big footsteps.

That night, lying next to her sleeping sister, Faith stared into the darkness of their room. The hollow by her shoulder where her kitten had curled every night felt cold. I don't have to worry about rolling on him, thought Faith. With that freedom came the memory of his little round belly, breathing in and out as he slept.

Tears ran silently from her eyes and into the hair

by her ears. She lay that way for a long time, shaking with silent sobs, curbing her misery to keep from waking her sister. She stared into the room half the night and finally drifted into a choppy sleep filled with shards of dreams. She dreamed Blackie White-face was still alive and scratching on the screen door wanting to be let in.

Toward dawn she fell deeply, dreamlessly asleep. They let her sleep late. She woke up several times during the morning, then finally sat up. She found it odd that sunlight was pouring into the room, slanting bright and yellow across the floorboards. She climbed out of bed and went to the window.

In the fields below, horses grazed. She could hear the faint clatter from the kitchen where Ben Warren was washing dishes. Gem's trill of composed laughter told Faith her sister was on the telephone with Owen. Down by the barn, Beth emerged carrying grain for the stallion. The world was turning and turning. Faith leaned her head against the cool glass of the upper window.

The faint clean smell of outdoor horses and sun-warmed grass drifted past her face. She stretched her arms to the top of the window frame and took a deep breath.

She was growing hungry, but she wanted to wait a little before she stepped back into the world.

11

Late in August, the weather in lower Michigan was perfect. Occasional brief rainstorms kept the meadows lush. Although the flies persisted, the nights were now cold enough to kill off some of the pesky insects.

Tomatoes and courgettes reached their peak in the garden. Faith helped Beth harvest them both. Beth made vats of tomato sauce and they all ate courgette forty different ways.

The loss of Blackie Whiteface made Faith more quiet and thoughtful than before. She fell back into the routine of the farm, but fragments of the kitten's lively spirit came to her at unexpected moments. When she went with Beth to bring in the horses, her mind would fly unbidden to the big old hickory tree by the woods. She welcomed the tears at these times but went off by herself to shed them. Once, alone with Cloud, she dropped her brush and wept loudly against his warm neck.

The horses were in peak shape, despite the daily torment of the flies. Their coats gleamed with health and cleanness. They frolicked in their fields. They wandered from fly-switching groups to graze.

Watching them from her quietness, Faith saw the horses with a different awareness. She saw how they spoke with movement and stance, arguing and challenging. They raced. They scratched one another. They stood close, inhaling information. She watched them tease and nip each other. She was surprised their speech hadn't been clear to her before.

The stream of life at the farm gathered Faith in. One Saturday, a crew of neighbors came over in the morning for a tree felling. All morning Faith's ears were filled with the angry buzz of power saws. Four huge, dead oaks at one end of the biggest field were cut down. Great limbs were trimmed off, cut and stacked for winter firewood. Then Faith watched the crew wrap chains about the giant trunks and haul them with a tractor into the middle of the field.

In the stillness of the afternoon, they piled brush heavily about the trunks. Faith helped stuff newspapers inside the branches. Then Ben Warren touched a match to one of the crumpled newspapers and stood back. The newspaper flared up. The dry wood caught and leapt into flame. Like a neon decoration the flames ran along the trunk. The people standing about clapped and cheered as the twigs crackled wildly.

All afternoon they fed the fire, until finally the old, dried-out trunks caught. The flames settled into the crumbly wood of the great prone trees and glowed there, burning slowly.

That night, the slow fire lit up the field. The neighbors gathered there. They cooked thick steaks, speared and held over the fire with green branches. They toasted slabs of Ben Warren's homemade bread on long forks and slapped them on to cardboard plates to soak up the juices. There were ice hampers filled with lemonade and beer.

They toasted fat, dusty marshmallows, burning the skins crisp over their oozing insides, and ate them pressed in between melting chocolate graham crackers.

Ben Warren got out his guitar and played a rousing song. With sticky faces, everyone sang, wiping hands on their wads of gummy napkins.

Then Ben struck a mellow sweet chord and played a song no one had ever heard before. 'About this gal I know,' he explained.

Faith knew it was Beth he was singing about, although Ben didn't look at her right away. He sang about her smooth strong arms and her little waist.

Faith glanced hastily at Beth to see if she was listening, but Beth's face was in shadow. Faith couldn't see her expression.

> *And she can't lie − that gal o' mine,*
> *and a promise she will keep.*
> *She's honest as day is long*
> *and stubborn as her sheep.*

There was clapping and some good-natured ribbing from the people gathered there. Beth's face moved out of the shadow into the glow from the fire. Faith could see she was smiling in a funny, shy way.

The heat of the fire held them all together in its slow burning. Now the great logs seemed lit from inside, their outer shape held together by the glow within. Like long lanterns on some strange planet, Faith thought, and we are travelers, unafraid.

The night was very black and clear, no moon but crisp stars. Everyone lay on blankets, talking quietly. Gem sat with Owen on a blanket. They held hands. Faith lay, sleepy, with her head in Beth's lap while Ben Warren smoothed her hair. She thought of Blackie Whiteface for the first time without the yawning ache. There seemed to be no loneliness or sadness anywhere in the world.

Problems aren't solved by one magical night, thought Faith several days later. It had been raining, off and on, all morning. There were puddles around the back porch and Wolfie had tracked mud all over the kitchen floor. Thunder rumble still hung in the sky, now near, now distant.

Beth couldn't teach on a rainy day, but she had been exercising horses in between thunder showers since breakfast. 'They're getting sloppy from being ridden by too many novices,' she explained when Faith questioned the purpose. 'They need to be shaped up.' And out she strode before it could rain again. Faith recognized the determined expression on her face. It meant: *Stay out of my way; there's too much to do!*

Faith sensed something stormy in the air besides the weather, but she couldn't put her finger on it.

That afternoon, Faith had just started clearing off the lunch dishes when Beth and Ben began one of their arguments. Faith could hear their voices in the living room. Their quarreling was easier for Faith to take when her sister was around, but Gem had gone off for a drive with Owen and his mother. Owen was practising for his driving test. Even Brady was gone, visiting family in Ohio.

Faith sighed. She could tell this argument was going to be a long one. Beth had lost several phone bills somewhere among her scattered mail and forgotten to pay them. Now the phone line had been disconnected. Ben Warren couldn't make some calls about a horse show in Canada. The quarrel, which had started with Beth's messy desk, had progressed to the messy condition of her closets.

'Lady, I can't function in chaos,' the cowboy was saying. His nice, soft tones were gone, gone the slow drawl.

Beth muttered something about having horses to exercise. Ben interrupted. '*You* can't function in it either, by the looks of things,' he said. 'All those emergencies of yours are your own doing.'

'I do all right.' Beth raised her voice, cold as the edge of a knife. 'I *function* best without interference.'

A terrible silence. Then Beth continued, slow and stubborn. 'While you are lining up boots and organizing bills, horses get out and run all up and down the road – or the donkey eats up half my garden or a sheep drowns! What good are boots in a row while horses are waiting to be exercised? Or when my sheep is struggling to get out of a water tub?'

That's not Ben Warren's fault, objected Faith.

'Proving my point,' roared Ben Warren. 'Anybody with just a tad more brains than a sheep knows enough not to sink the watering tub in the same field with them!'

They're not being fair. Not fair. Faith tuned out the voices, running the water full blast in the kitchen sink, churning up the suds. She scrubbed furiously at a frying pan.

Then she realized it was quiet in the living room. She couldn't stand it and slipped into the doorway to have a look.

Ben Warren sat on a stool by the old-fashioned desk. His shoulders were slumped forward. 'What's the use,' he said quietly.

Beth was at the window, looking out. Her face was closed and pale.

'What's the point?' He wasn't really asking a question.

It wasn't the usual argument after all. It wasn't slam-the-door anger where Ben Warren stalked off forgetting his cowboy hat, leaving everything behind in his angry dust. And came back later for it. And made up.

This was cold, quiet, giving-up anger. The cowboy got up from the stool. Slowly he went from room to room gathering his belongings. He didn't forget his socks and his blue work shirts in the laundry basket – or his toothpicks or the special coffee cup over the sink. It didn't take him long. He had most of his stuff in his van anyway, neatly hanging or filed away.

'You can keep the food in the freezer,' he said quietly to Beth. He was stuffing things into a blue denim bag. Beth still stood by the window looking out, a statue with fists gripped, face of stone.

She didn't turn. Faith felt a rush of despair. Ben Warren smiled wanly at her as he opened the screen door. 'Bye, Red,' he said. He didn't even slam the screen door when he left.

Faith ran out behind him, tagging after his heels. He swung himself in the side door of the yellow van.

'Ben?' asked Faith.

He turned and looked down at her from the doorway.

'You coming back?'

'Don't think so, Red.' His drawl was heavy and serious.

'Can I write you a letter? Someplace?' asked Faith. 'Do you have an address? Anywhere else, I mean?'

'I'll send you a card when I get somewhere.' He looked at her for a moment. Faith felt tears coming on. Then he said, 'Don't make it harder, Red.' He turned, closing the van door gently behind him.

'It's going to rain,' Faith said to the closed door.

She waited for the van to pull out. He must be

putting things away, she thought. Even when he's mad, he's neat.

Then she turned and ran back to the house. Beth wasn't in the living room anymore. Or the kitchen. Faith hurried, calling through the house, 'Beth! Beth!' No answer from upstairs either. She felt meanness spreading through her body.

'Don't you like Ben Warren?' she wanted to ask her. *My cowboy? I gave him to you. Is that what you do with a present?*

She slammed out on to the porch. The van was still there. Then she saw Beth striding down to the barn. She's just going to keep on working, thought Faith.

She watched Beth disappear into the stable and then reappear, lugging a saddle with a bridle over her shoulder.

From the distant sky, a faint rumble of thunder seemed ridiculously appropriate. Up to the rain-green field strode Beth, hardly slowed by the weight of the heavy saddle.

Nothing stops her, thought Faith in dismay. Beth hoisted the tack on to the fence rail and marched into the field. Faith watched her catch Cloud without so much as a greeting or a pretty please.

She's already exercised Cloud, thought Faith, and then remembered how Beth had ridden out her sorrow when Shinyface was sold.

Dark clouds were re-forming overhead and the low rumble of thunder growled nearer. Faith felt a fresh surge of anger. They would all have to sit around oiling down wet tack tonight so it wouldn't stiffen from being rained on. And if somebody didn't do something, Ben wouldn't even be there, his easy presence warming the room. She'd have to make Beth see. She jumped off the porch and began to run down to the gate. Beth had finished tacking up Cloud by the fence.

'Its going to rain, Beth,' hollered Faith, hoping to make her pause. But Beth swung neatly up into the saddle. She turned the big black horse and trotted past Faith, leaving a wake like electricity. Off across the big wet field they went. Faith watched her fall into the quick rhythm of the horse, her honey-dark ponytail bobbing in time with Cloud's tail. The long motion of her back as she posted up and down was easy and sure, as smooth as breathing. Over the crest of the hill they disappeared, heading toward the woods.

'You can clean the tack yourself!' Faith shouted after her.

She looked back and Ben Warren's van was still in the driveway. She had the feeling he was waiting in there, not wanting to leave. If she could just get Beth to stop for a minute.

She crawled through the fence and began to run across the wet field. Grass soaked her sneakers. Her feet sank into the soft earth. It took ages to reach the top of the hill. Once there, she paused to catch her breath and get her bearings.

She could see Beth and the black horse, dwarfed by distance. Thunder rumbled again and Beth leaned to pat Cloud's neck. Faith could almost hear the soothing, 'Okay, sweet boy – okay.'

Beth eased Cloud into a canter and he moved out gradually faster, until they were flying toward the woods.

How beautiful she is, thought Faith. The half light of the approaching rain cast no shadows. Everything stood out clearly, the blades of grass, the perfect miniature of horse and rider against the darkened trees. Ben should see her, Faith thought. He wouldn't be able to leave.

Even the small brown rabbit showed clearly, and Faith saw him with pleasure. Her animal person eyes caught the movement as he darted out of the brush, startled by the activity in the field. His little body plunged in a zigzag pattern into the pattern of the thundering horse.

Faith cried out. Cloud stopped short. He spun up and around. Beth hurtled from his back, somersaulting through the air. Faith heard her land with a muffled crunch. The crumpled figure twitched against the rubble of wood and stones. Then she lay still.

Faith was running before she knew it. Then she stopped, half-turned toward the house. Shouted, 'Ben! Ben!'

No sign of life about the van. Wolfie lay by the back porch. She cupped her hands at her mouth. Yelled at the top of her lungs, 'BEN! HELP! BEHHHHHHNN!' Nothing stirred except Wolfie. He got up, stretched and yawned.

Faith whirled about and ran again toward Beth.
When she reached the fallen figure, she was out of
breath. Beth lay on her side. One arm twisted oddly
beneath her. Her face had no color. Protruding from
her torn shirt by the collar was what Faith at first
took to be the handle of something – a screwdriver
– grayish with a jagged end. Then a bleat of fear
slipped from Faith's lips. It was a bone. A little circle
of blood stained the shirt collar. The bone glistened
wetly.

Had Ben heard her call? Where was he? She had
a momentary vision of him folding a T-shirt and
closing a drawer.

Faith knelt down in the rubble and put her head
carefully against Beth's chest. She could hear the
healthy thud of Beth's heart.

She stood up and looked back toward the distant
driveway. Her own heart skipped a beat. The yellow
van was disappearing, the *purrumble* of its motor
thinning out as it got farther down the drive. She
hadn't even heard it start.

'Oh, *no*!' she moaned. She moved to run toward
the van, the house, the phone. And caught herself.
Wasted motion. Too late. No Ben. No phone.

The nearest neighbors were too far away. Lightning flashed a jagged opening down the sky. A
terrible helplessness seized her, and the old, familiar
smallness. She heard herself moan a long whimpering sound. At the same time, questions whirled
in her head.

How long would it take Ben Warren to reach the

highway? How much time? Could she cut him off some way?

She felt a tug at her sleeve and turned in panic. It was Cloud, looking contrite. He nosed her shoulder.

'Oh, Cloud,' she breathed, and the helplessness dissolved. She straightened his reins. Her eyes scanned the distance where fencerow trees thinned out. Beyond the next field and meadow was a faraway blacktop road. It was Ben Warren's usual route from the farm and connected with the highway. He would be at the bridge now. A minute or two and he would reach the dirt road. He still had to drive past Beth's big sheep fields and an abandoned farm before he turned on to the blacktop.

'Stay there!' she commanded Cloud. She ran to Beth's half dismantled mower and yanked off the tarp covering it. She dragged the tarp across the grass to Beth. Gently she spread it over the prone body, making a little tent over her face. Beth moaned but did not move or awaken.

Then Faith straightened out Cloud's stirrup irons. She guessed at the correct length and pulled them up three notches to fit her legs. Then she led the horse to a great rock where she could stand and hoist herself into the saddle. Her sneakers squished in the irons and her feet felt heavy. The stirrups were still too long, but Beth moaned again. There wasn't time to fumble with buckles.

In Faith's mind was forming the only plan she could think of. She would have to be quick and cut across Beth's two fields then across the neighbor's meadow. She just might cut off Ben Warren's van before it turned from the blacktop on to the highway.

Lightning flashed again with an accompanying roll of thunder. Cloud's ear shot forward. Faith could hear the quick breath that signaled the big horse's panic. 'Easy,' she said. She stroked his neck. In quieting the big animal, she felt herself grow calm. Now. She turned him and pressed her legs into his sides.

Cloud lurched into a frightened canter, unsteady. Fear and the familiar wobble returned to chill Faith briefly. Then she sat back and gave a light tug on the reins. 'Easy, Cloud,' she said. She could feel him relax. She patted his neck. 'Easy.' She guided him toward the line of trees that marked a long-gone fence.

Now Cloud settled into a swift, light canter, comforted by Faith's voice and the direction from her legs. It's not all that far, she kept thinking to herself.

It began to rain, heavy and sudden, big drops. Before they crossed over into Beth's next field, horse and rider were both drenched. Faith could not see, through the curtain of rain, any sign of Ben Warren's van.

She leaned forward now and urged Cloud into a gallop. Across the field they flew, swallowing up the wet ground. No holes, she prayed, no holes, please. Briefly, the brown rabbit slipped in and out of her mind. Rain stung her eyes, blinding her. All the stray ends of her panic joined with the force of the great horse into a strange excitement. *So this is how it feels.*

She marked her direction now, eyes squinted

against the arrows of rain, by the dim outline of a white shed in the distance. Ben Warren would have to turn at that point.

As she neared the end of the field, she suddenly noticed the wooden fence. Now she remembered. It separated Beth's field from the neighbor's meadow. No quick way round. She knew she would have to jump.

Into her mind came the several commands Beth shouted most in her jumping classes. 'Hands forward. Eyes up. Grab mane! Ask him! With your legs. *Ask him!*'

It was too late to stop and there was no time to think. She aimed Cloud at the fence. Could he see it through the downpour? The rain whipped at her face. The pounding of hooves filled her ears. The fence seemed to come at them. Cloud's powerful body gathered beneath her and she moved her hands forward. She raised her eyes into the stinging rain, into the drenched meadow beyond. She asked him. With a great surge, Cloud soared over the fence and landed with a satisfied snort on the other side. A yelp of alarm escaped from Faith. She felt herself slipping from the saddle. '*Sit up! Don't fall!*' said Beth in her mind. She struggled back into the wet seat. It took her several gasping seconds to settle Cloud down and find his rhythm again.

The blacktop road, a short distance beyond the white shed, was empty. The image of the bloody bone protruding from Beth's shirt grabbed her mind. Cloud's firm sides were warm through her sodden pant legs. She urged him on. They tore across the meadow and then alongside the blacktop. The curve ahead told Faith nothing. But when they reached and rounded it, she could see, not far away, Ben Warren's van slowing down for the highway access road.

'Ben!' she yelled. 'Ben!' Cloud sensed the urgency and pressed on faster.

'Ben, WAIT!' The van turned on to the access road.

No! She was losing him. The yellow van, wheels spattering along the wet surface, began to speed up to join the highway traffic.

'Ben! BEN!' Cloud's hooves clattered on the blacktop. They were too far away. She strayed to the left behind the van, praying Ben would check his rearview mirror.

And he must have. Gradually, because of the slick pavement, Ben Warren slowed down.

And stopped. The van's hazard lights went on, blinking dimly through the rain. Horse and rider raced toward the blurry shape.

As long as she lived, Faith would remember the look of astonishment on Ben Warren's face through the rain-spotted window.

The sun came out as the rescue squad gently eased Beth on to a stretcher. Ben had used the emergency frequency on his CB. Help came almost immediately. The ambulance had driven partway into the soggy field and, after Beth was securely placed inside, worked its way carefully back through the gate and out the drive. It was several minutes before Faith, untacking Cloud by the stable, heard them switch on the siren.

'Nothing we can do right away, Red,' said Ben Warren. 'Best feed the animals.'

By the time Faith and Ben Warren reached the hospital, Beth had already had a CAT scan and X rays. A young doctor told the pair that Beth had broken her collarbone, fractured her upper arm and suffered a concussion.

'We're putting her in a clavicle strap,' he said. 'It's to keep her shoulders back so the collarbone can mend properly.'

When Ben and Faith were allowed to visit Beth's room, she was lying with her eyes closed. There was a strap hooked under her arms which disappeared behind her back. Her left arm was in a sling. She opened her eyes and stared groggily at them in a funny, cockeyed way.

'Who painted the spill?' she asked. Neither Ben nor Faith laughed. Does she mean 'Who spilled the paint?' Faith wondered.

Ben Warren just put his hand on her shoulder and said in a quiet voice, 'Beth.' Then Beth smiled gently and went back to sleep. Her face was bruised but it made her look pretty, as if she were wearing rock-star makeup.

The next time she woke, she tried to get up, saying, 'Apollo didn't get grained.' Ben jumped up from his chair and said, 'It's all taken care of, darlin'.' Then Beth sort of flicked her eyes like she'd been slapped and eased back against the pillow.

'Oh, Ben,' she said softly and went right back to sleep again.

The third time she woke, she sounded like her old self. 'Did anyone feed?' she asked, meaning the animals. She never worried as much about whether or not humans had eaten.

Ben said, 'Yes, we've eaten.' Then he laughed and Beth laughed. Faith giggled, relieved. She said, 'They're all fed, Beth.' She received a grateful smile.

Then Beth turned her head to the window. She sighed. 'What a jerk I am,' she said.

'That's right,' said Ben Warren. 'You break for animals.' They both laughed again.

Beth turned serious. 'I'm not sure it's going to work, Ben,' she said. 'We get in each other's way so much.'

'I'll stick around for a while, lady,' said the cowboy gently. He put his big, tan hand over hers. 'We'll see . . .'

12

The summer horse shows were over. Beth, her arm still in a cast to protect her mending bones, began to plan for a gold cup event in Canada near Toronto. Standing in the centre of the ring, she shouted instructions at her students, barely hampered by her plaster-frozen arm.

Faith and Gem would be leaving in a few days. Gem still took lessons, but her drive had gone out of it. Faith had begun to take lessons once more and she was just getting into it. Unburdened by her former fears, she was advancing quickly. Beth shook her head in surprise or looked thoughtful. She had Faith jump some low cross poles and then the two-foot coop.

Since the accident, Faith had often ridden Cloud cross-country and through the woods with other riders. She had felt easy and comfortable, as if she'd been doing it right along. But Beth no longer discussed the horses with Faith and Gem as before or included them in the planning. She was pressed for time. She ran late all day, and had begun to fall alseep in her chair at the dinner table again.

Ben Warren had finally finished the sheep's bathroom. It still smelled cleanly of new wood. Faith took her first bath in the beautiful tub. In front of the new three-way mirror she combed out her red hair, grown way below her shoulders over the summer. Maybe I'll try a ponytail, she thought. Then she felt sad. Now that she truly belonged here, it was time to leave.

Gem was in a slump. She had enjoyed the difficult riding within the confines of a ring. She had done well this summer. Now she had to leave Rambler and jumping over fences, her borrowed riding coat and blue velvet hunt cap. She had to leave Owen, her new conquest, before she had time to savour the romance.

They had returned Rackity to the woods. He was almost full grown. Beth said to just leave his door open. At first, the raccoon wouldn't leave his cage. Then, one morning, he was sitting on the porch roof. The next day they saw him slowly enter the woods. He didn't come back.

'Good,' said Beth wistfully. 'He's found his real home. Maybe he'll come visit.'

Now, in the evenings, Faith and her sister sat on the back porch or walked the rail fence sorrowing together. While Gem moaned about leaving Rambler and Owen, Faith thought about losing Cloud. But she also tried to imagine the strangers at home, their mom and dad, their new brothers.

The day before they were to leave, Beth brought up some of their fresh-laundered clothes, which Ben had neatly folded. She set them on top of the bed.

The girls' suitcases were half packed. Beth stood watching them a moment, her head cocked to one side. Her shirt was crumpled and dusty and her dark-honey hair straggled from her scarf. She had a funny, sad little smile on her face.

'If you want to ride, go on ahead. There won't be any more lessons the rest of this week. We're busy with shearing the rams. The horses could use a little workout. Take the ones that suit you. You know which tack to use. Let me know before you go.'

She turned to leave but stopped at the door and looked back at them.

'I'm really going to miss you two,' she said. 'You've been good company – great helpers.' She eyed Faith and raised her eyebrows. 'I've learned some new things, too.' The words didn't leave Beth easily, she began to look uncomfortable. She turned quickly and thumped down the stairs with her heavy boots.

'I'm going to miss this place, the classes – everything,' said Gem. But she opted for a last date with Owen instead of a ride on Rambler.

On her way down to the stables alone, Faith said to herself, 'Not a real animal person.'

She thought about Beth and Ben. Beth imposed her will on things, on horses, students. Ben never forced or pushed . . . 'You wind up cutting yourself.' They argued all the time. Ben organized chaos to make things run smoothly. Beth moved mountains. Faith admired them both. Somewhere in between, she thought, is the road for me.

Beth had said she could have her pick of the

horses for her final ride. It wasn't a difficult decision. She would take Cloud out one last time before she bid the farm good-bye.

The big black horse came to her in the field. Flattered, she pushed her face into his neck before she clipped on the lead line. 'Cloud, my friend,' she said.

She picked a route along the hedgerow and up toward the woods. By the tree where Blackie White-face was buried, she stopped for a moment and said good-bye to the summer and to the place. But Cloud was eager and pawed impatiently at the earth. She pressed him into a trot.

Trees were heavily green and familiar as parents. There weren't many deerflies left to pester them as they trotted along the path.

Somewhere in the woods was an overturned boat, rotting between two trees. Faith had watched Cora and Gem jump it before. She found it with little trouble.

They paused, she and the horse, she gathered the reins, making certain Cloud saw the obstacle. He stirred beneath her. She held him, waiting, until she felt his eagerness, the excitement running up his legs and into hers.

Then she urged him forward with her calves, sitting erect until the last stride before the boat. Her hands softened forward, her legs asked. Her eyes reached out into the corridor of trunks ahead.

They soared over the boat and cantered away between the old and fragrant trees.

THREE TO RIDE

Christine
Pullein-Thompson

GOOD-BYE

Mrs. Smith packed for David.

'You'd better take all your clothes; it's not as though you've so many,' she said.

'Yes, I suppose so,' he replied.

Now that the moment had come, he didn't want to leave. He was filled with doubts. He couldn't believe that Major Seely would find him satisfactory, that he could ride well enough to become a working pupil in such a distinguished stable.

He went to the familiar mirror above the old wash-handstand with its faded jug and bowl patterned with roses and smoothed his hair. He was on the small side for his sixteen years, and with his dark hair, which fell naturally and persistently over his forehead, and his brown eyes he looked kind, a little bewildered, someone unsure of himself, and perpetually in a dream.

It was his last afternoon at home. Outside the cottage carefully tended flowers bloomed; he could smell them now as he moved to the window, and in every tree there seemed to be a bird singing. May had come with a west wind, and now she warmed the cottage's thatched roof, and the dry soil outside.

It was and always had been a wonderful month, thought David, letting his thoughts wander back, trying to remember himself as a little boy first learning to ride at the Riding School across the Common. Afterwards there had been Sinbad, the bad-tempered pony he had been lent by Colonel Lewisham, and the beginning of his friendship with Pat Lewisham. But that was over now; even the Elm Tree Riding School which they had run together was finished. Standing there, he didn't want to remember that part of his life, but a hundred images came rushing to his mind – the first time he had ridden Folly, their success together at the Royal Windsor Show, the wonderful feeling of knowing that she was his own; Pat and himself riding together, hunting together, having tea together in the Hall. Planning the Riding School, their first pupils, buying Tornado at a sale, realising that Pat was tired of their riding school, the beginning of the end. . . .

'I'll have to darn these. You're so hard on your socks, David. And the leathers need sewing on your jodhpurs,' his mother said.

They had sold their ponies – all of them except Tornado, Folly, and Pat's Swallow. The selling had been the worst part of all. Colonel Lewisham had insisted that Sinbad and Mistletoe must go; and there seemed no point in keeping little skewbald Suzy. They hadn't sold them very well, and Pat had cried into Mistletoe's mane, which David couldn't understand, because, if she hadn't preferred to be a debutante, nothing need have changed. But then he never had understood Pat.

And now she was going to London and he was going to his first job, and the sign which read The Elm Tree Riding School was in the shed behind the cottage, because David was sentimental and couldn't bear to imagine one of the gardeners at the Hall chopping it for fire-wood.

'We're going to miss you, David; it'll be funny not to hear you clumping down the stairs in the morning. It's like we're getting old,' said Mrs. Smith, shutting the suitcase he had bought to take with him.

He turned to his mother, who stood looking at him, her hair pinned behind her ears, wearing a faded pinafore. She had always backed him whenever he had made a decision. She had shared in his joys and sorrows. She had the wisdom of someone who has lived for many years in the country, observing other people, bringing up a family.

'It'll be quieter,' David said, searching for words to express what he felt.

'Are you going to say good-bye to *her*?' asked Mrs. Smith with a sniff.

Pat Lewisham had become 'her' to Mrs. Smith from the moment she had decided to become a debutante. Mrs. Smith couldn't forgive her for letting down David.

'Might as well. I've got to feed Tornado.' He turned away from the window and his mother. Much still remained to be done. There was his tack to be given a last polish, everything to be put ready for the horse-box which would come in the morning to take himself and Tornado from the gentle fields and dreaming rivers of Oxfordshire to Devon, which he knew nothing about, but which he imagined abounded with tea-shops and amenities for tourists.

'It's such a long way,' said Mrs. Smith for the twentieth time. 'But we'll be thinking of you, your Dad and me. It'll seem funny without you.'

'You'll get used to it in time. You'll have less to do; that's one thing. No dirty jodhpurs and dungarees to wash.'

'I wonder who'll do your washing,' mused Mrs. Smith.

'I'm lodging with one of the grooms,' said David, and wondered whether he would have a room to himself. He went down the stairs ahead of his mother, who was talking about his socks again.

'I'd better go and see Tornado now,' he said, looking round the cottage, at its shining black range, at the large scrubbed table, and the mantelpiece, where the cups he had won stood, polished by his mother so that you could see your face in them.

'Don't be too late,' said Mrs. Smith.

He crossed the Common living old memories. Here he had first learned to vault on to Melody's narrow brown back; here he had hurried in a thunderstorm praying that all his pupils were safe after a runaway. How often he had crossed the Common on his way to the Hall, thousands and thousands of times, and perhaps, except for tomorrow morning this was the last time for many months.

He reached the road, and presently passed the lane and the notice which said *To The Kennels*, which brought back other memories of himself, much younger, working among the hounds as kennel boy. He felt now that he had lived a great many years; yet the days before he started riding remained an insignificant blur. What had he done then? He couldn't even remember. He turned down the stable drive. There were few hoof-prints now on the gravel. Nothing seemed to stir. . . . Once he had seemed to belong here, but now, because Pat had grown tired of their Riding School, he felt quite alien, as he had the first time, when as a small boy he had gone to tea at the Hall.

Only one horse looked over the loose-box doors, and that was Tornado. The Hunt horses were out. Austin, the stud groom, was having an easy time; the other groom was helping on the farm.

He had hoped that Pat would be in the yard waiting for him. But there was no sign of her anywhere, and the saddle-room they had used looked empty with only three saddles and a couple of bridles.

Tornado was lonely and restless. She was sound now after her fall at the One Day Event where David had met Major Seely. David stood looking at her and felt a sense of happiness creep over him; at least he still had a horse, and Folly was only on loan, so she was still his too. He fetched a rubber and polished her bay coat. She was very fit, though since the One Day Event she had had no oats. She was a difficult horse; she trusted David, but if a stranger rode her she lost her head and became a bucking bronco.

'We go tomorrow,' David told her now. 'And you've got to behave, do you hear?'

In reply she nuzzled his pockets.

'It's the beginning of a new era for us,' continued David. 'Perhaps our big chance.'

Outside there were footsteps on the gravel.

'Hullo,' said Pat. 'I thought you would be here.' She had blue eyes, and chestnut hair which glinted copper in the sun; but David hated to look at her now, because she had changed. Once she had had an uncared-for, windswept look. Now she made him think of people in shiny magazines, people who moved in a different world than his. There was a barrier now between them, which he often felt nothing would break. And because they had spent so much time together he missed the old Pat.

'Are you all packed?' she asked.

'Yes. Mum's packed.'

'Excited?'

They were making conversation like strangers.

'Yes and no,' he said.

'I'm going to look out for you in *Horse and Hound*. You know: *Promising young David Smith is now riding for . . .*' she said.

'Don't kid yourself,' he cried, suddenly wishing that Pat would go, so that he could forget that once there had been horses of their own in the yard, not just Tornado, and pupils, and a telephone in the saddle-room; that once it had been alive, seething with activity, instead of shut up, dead till the hunting season started, as it was now.

'You're miserable, aren't you?' Pat asked.

'No; I'm not,' he said, suddenly determined not to care.

'That's all right, then.'

He fetched Tornado hay and water. Pat was wearing a flowered cotton dress and high-heeled, sling-back shoes. He supposed that was how she would always dress now – no more dungarees and open-necked shirts.

'Well, I really came to say good-bye – you know, good-bye, good luck and everything. And I brought you this,' she said, pressing a small parcel into his hand. He started to open it, but she said, 'Not now. Later. Good-bye.'

A moment later Pat had disappeared and it seemed another chapter of his life had ended. Inside the package he found a small statuette of a horse in beaten copper.

He stood and looked at it for a long time before he put it in his pocket and started for home.

And now there was twilight on the Common, and he saw two rabbits bobbing among the gorse bushes, the first he had seen since the myxamatosis epidemic. He met several people he knew and they all stopped to talk.

'We hear you're leaving us then, David,' they said.

And 'Well, best of luck in your new job,' or simply, 'All the best, son.'

David had never left home before, and because of this he couldn't imagine himself living anywhere else.

He shook all these people seriously by the hand, saying, 'Thank you very much,' and 'Good-bye.'

He found his father was home.

'Well, your last night in the old home. How do you feel, son?' asked Mr. Smith.

'Okay.'

'You'll make out all right. Time you left home, though we'll miss you. We'll be thinking of him, won't we, Mother?'

'That's what I keep telling him,' said Mrs. Smith.

'I hope Tornado settles down all right. She's so highly strung,' said David.

'You and that horse!' cried Mrs. Smith.

It was like any evening at home really, thought David, glancing round the kitchen again, and yet it was his last evening; and in a way he was glad, because now he would be standing on his own feet, learning his own worth; finding whether he had the talent to become a first-class rider, perhaps the best in the land. The future awaited him like a precipice waiting to be climbed, and as his mother passed him a cup of tea he felt capable of climbing it.

'Now, eat a good tea. Remember you've got a long journey in front of you tomorrow and only sandwiches for lunch,' said Mrs. Smith.

'Yes, Mum,' he said, and saw himself arriving – a

stable yard with pigeons fluttering on tiled roofs, Major Seely coming to greet him with outstretched hand.

ARRIVING

He said good-bye to his mother; she looked suddenly older as she said, 'You'll write, won't you? We'll be thinking about you.'

'Yes. I'll write,' he promised.

He was wearing his best jodhpurs. He had two pairs now, the worst patched all over by his mother. It was early. His parents had risen to say good-bye.

'Remember hard work never hurt anyone, son, but them what's afraid of it; and it kills them,' said his father.

'I will.' He was impatient to be gone by this time. He was the last of the Smith children to leave the cottage where they had all grown up. Susan worked now as a secretary in London, and seemed almost a stranger when she came back, smart and efficient, talking about films and nylons. His brothers had both won scholarships to Cambridge and held responsible jobs. He felt like the last fledgeling to leave the nest. He kissed his mother, said, 'Good-bye, Dad,' and walked away without looking back, carrying his suitcase.

He had packed the horse Pat had given him;

simply to remind him of old times, he told himself. Otherwise, he was determined to forget Pat.

A mist hung over the Common, and the same two rabbits were playing among the gorse bushes. He could hear hounds singing as he passed the lane to the kennels, and he thought: That'll fetch Bert (the Huntsman) from his bed.

He had said good-bye to the Hunt staff a couple of days back.

They had wished him all the best, and Bert had said, 'We'll miss you, David,' like his mother.

He wondered now what it felt like to live in a place where you are new and don't belong. It'll be a new experience, he thought, turning down the drive to the stables.

Tornado whinnied to him. He fetched her a feed – the last of the Riding School's bran and crushed oats.

He stood his tack with his suitcase in the yard. The mist was clearing. Cocks were heralding another day.

Presently he could hear the horse-box. By this time Tornado had finished her feed, so he led her out into the sunlight. He felt quite funny now, looking round the yard; perhaps for the last time, because he would never return unless Pat invited him. He could hear the horse-box coming up the drive and there was a lump in his throat, and he wished that there was someone to say, 'Come back soon, David. Don't worry; you'll be a success. There's no doubt about that.' But there wasn't; there was just the yard he loved and Tornado turning this way and that in the sunlight. Major Seely had sent the horse-box, and it was large and sumptuous, with a chromium horse on the bonnet.

'Well, David, aren't you going to say good-bye, just for old times' sake?' called a voice, and there was Mr. Austin, half asleep, coming to greet him. And coming towards him from the Hall was Maudie, the Lewisham's help, who had always had a soft spot for David.

'I had to say good-bye,' she told him and, leaning forward, kissed his cheek. 'Now behave yourself,' she added.

Standing there, he felt that these were his real friends.

'Well, if you don't like it, come back. We'll always be able to find you a job in the Hunt stables,' said Mr. Austin.

David had never been able to make Mr. Austin understand that, although he loved the hunting field, it was to the show rings and cross-country events that he belonged.

Now he said, 'Thank you. I'll never be out of a job, then.'

They loaded Tornado. 'Okay, then?' asked the driver.

'Best of luck,' called Mr. Austin.

'Be good,' said Maudie.

The horse-box was moving now. They were leaving; the yard was growing smaller. He was on his way to begin his new life. He stood in the groom's compartment talking to Tornado. He didn't feel strange any more, only determined to succeed.

They turned left when they reached the road. There were people bicycling to work, milk being delivered. The day had really begun. He remembered the days when he had delivered papers, and had belonged to this early-morning world. He had travelled a long way since then, and he meant to travel further. You get what you deserve from life, he thought; one must never blame circumstances for failure; there is always a way round. He had always felt that, though often he was completely devoid of confidence in himself.

He turned to Tornado. 'We have great days ahead of us,' he said. He leaned out of the window watching familiar fields pass, until they reached country he didn't know – the Vale of Pewsey, vast and open, Swindon – and as they travelled he rode across the landscape, galloping carefree across the Vale, clattering through the busy streets of Swindon.

They stopped at Frome for elevenses.

'We'll be there just about two, mate,' said the driver.

'What's the place like?'

'Pretty good.'

Tornado was restless, tired of the narrow confines of the horse-box. David was anxious to arrive. Supposing he hated the place? Couldn't get on with the grooms? He was filled with anxiety now.

They drove on through Glastonbury, past small

farmsteads, luscious fields, orchards, through stone villages. It looked very different from Oxfordshire to David, and he didn't see many horses, though plenty of prosperous milking cows. What are the people like? he wondered, and found that he was missing Pat. It seemed funny to travel so far with no one to talk to.

They were in Devon when they stopped to eat their sandwiches. It was very hot even for May. The countryside had changed. There were little rolling fields fenced by banks, and most of the villages had one wide street.

'Soon be there now, mate,' said the driver.

David fed Tornado, and they fetched her water from a tumbling river nearby. He imagined his mother at home eating by herself in the kitchen, most likely cold meat and pickles and bread and butter, because she never bothered to cook if she was by herself.

What was Pat doing? he wondered. When would she go to London? He supposed she would be visiting Wimbledon, Henley. Would she go to the Royal Windsor Show? he wondered.

'Better get going now, mate,' said the driver.

The climbed back into the horse-box.

'Wouldn't you rather ride in the cab?' asked the driver.

'No, thanks. I think I'd better stay with the mare.' Tornado was very restless now; she chewed the partition, and several times set into the back of the compartment with her heels. And David wanted to keep his eyes glued to the window, because any place might be Major Seely's Hampton House. A great many old fears came back to him now; he started to doubt his riding ability; to wonder why he had ever accepted the job. He felt he would have done better to become nothing more than a groom, under a good stud groom.

Then they were turning down a drive and he could see a clock tower, rows of loose-boxes, horses looking across a sunlit yard. He felt quite sick then. Everything seemed bigger than he had expected, smarter. He could see the chimneys of the house, an elegant garden. I'm here, he thought. I'm making a new beginning. This is my testing-ground. Here I shall know whether I will ever become a first-class rider or whether I belong for ever to the ranks of mediocrity.

The horse-box stopped.

'Here we are, mate,' called the driver.

All around were horses looking at them with inquisitive eyes. As David stepped out on to the gravelled yard, a groom emerged from a loose-box.

'Hullo. So you're David,' he said. 'How's the mare? Did she travel all right?'

'Not too badly.'

The driver was letting down the ramp. The fair girl David had seen at the One Day Event appeared.

'Hullo. You've arrived, then,' she said.

Tornado came out of the box with a rush. Her tail bandage had slipped; she had rubbed one of her hocks against the back of the partition.

'Useful sort of mare,' said the groom.

'She's lovely, isn't she?' asked the girl. They put Tornado in a box which stood ready.

The driver said, 'All the best, mate,' and got into his cab and drove away, leaving David's suitcase standing small and forlorn in the yard.

'Have you had some dinner?' asked the groom.

David had time to look at his companions now. The girl was slim, with a great deal of fair soft hair. She was taller than David and, he guessed, about his own age. The groom wore breeches and gaiters, braces, a flannel shirt without a collar, and working boots.

'Well, you'd better come along and see the Missis. You're lodging with us,' he said.

There was no sign of Major Seely; and now David could hardly remember what he looked like.

'I'm Bates, Jimmy Bates,' said the groom. 'The girl you were talking to is Sheila; then there's the stud groom, Mr. Booth. He runs the place when the governor's away.'

'Is he away now?' asked David.

'No. But he'll be going away later on.'

They had been walking behind the stables. Now they came to a small, single-storied building.

'My place,' said Mr. Bates. 'Olive, 'ere's our lodger come to see you.'

Olive was younger than Mr. Bates, David thought, with dark hair which was still in curlers.

'Pleased to meet you I'm sure,' she said, shaking his hand.

His room was small, with lino on the floor, a modern bed, a small mat, and an armchair.

'I hope you'll be comfortable here. Would you like a cup of tea? Have you had dinner?'

They all had a cup of tea in the kitchen. Then David and Mr. Bates returned to the stables.

'Have a look round the horses. I must be getting on. The governor should be here any time,' he said.

The horses were large, well built, except for one dun mare who was little more than fifteen hands. There was a chestnut-stallion, who stood in a box apart from the others. There was a hunter mare with a foal which David judged to be little more than a week old.

He couldn't help wondering which horse he would ride. Or would he try all the rideable ones?

'Feel strange?' asked Sheila. 'The stallion's called Royal Majesty – Majesty for short. Don't you think he's lovely?' Her hands were full of grooming kit. 'Here comes old Booth,' she cried suddenly and fled.

David didn't like Mr. Booth; some instinct in his being warned him against him, though why exactly he couldn't have said. He didn't like his small grey eyes, which didn't look at you. Nor the way he said, 'So you're David Smith.'

'You look as though you need a job. There's a pile of dirty tack in the saddle-room. What about getting down to it?' asked Mr. Booth.

'Yes. Right you are.' David found the tack.

'There's a hot tap outside on the right,' called Sheila from across the yard.

There were seven dirty saddles and nine dirty bridles. He started to work. Outside Mr. Booth was feeding cut grass to the horses. Jimmy Bates was taking a skip round the boxes. Sheila appeared to be dressing a black horse's off fore.

Tornado was walking round and round her box. The clock in the tower said two forty-five.

Presently a Scottie, a poodle, and spaniel came across the yard, followed by Major Seely. He spoke to Mr. Booth, looked across to the saddle-room. David had forgotten how nimble he appeared, and he looked every inch a horseman.

'Hullo, David. So you've arrived. Had a good journey?' he said, coming across the yard.

They looked at Tornado together. 'Nice little mare; but she needs to be a bit fitter,' he said. 'Has Jimmy showed you where you're lodging? Is it all right? Do you think you'll be comfortable?'

'Yes, thank you, sir.'

They stood for some time in silence, leaning over the loose-box door looking at Tornado.

'Well, we'll have a little school this evening – see how you ride,' said Major Seely. 'The horses will go better when it's a bit cooler.'

He walked round the rest of the horses with Mr. Booth. David returned to the dirty tack, and Sheila appeared and said, 'This is really my job.'

They worked in silence for a time until Sheila said, 'I wouldn't be in your shoes.'

'Why? I like the look of everything,' David answered.

342

'Major Seely yells like anything. He'll have you bumping round the paddock without stirrups. He'll lunge you for hours. I'd rather be just a groom, thank you.'

'I don't care so long as it improves my riding.'

'If you're a fanatic, that's all right. I like other things – dancing, the cinema. I've heard Major Seely say to people, "If you've enough energy left after two hours in the school with me to want to dance, it simply means you haven't been working enough." I have really.'

David felt his heart sinking. He longed suddenly now for the freedom of the Elm Tree Riding School, for the days when he and Pat had stood in the middle of a school instructing pupils. In spite of being poor, he had always been more or less his own master. Now he was a working pupil with pocket money of a pound a week and lodgings paid for by Major Seely.

He realised now that he had never valued his freedom enough. He thought, I can always leave, but at the same time condemned the thought, because how could he return home and admit failure? He imagined his parents' faces, though soon enough they would be on his side, his mother condemning Major Seely as she now condemned Pat.

He thought: I shall have to stick it out for a bit, for a month at least.

'That's finished. Are you going to help me fill up the water-buckets?' asked Sheila, hanging up the last bridle.

THE FIRST DAYS

He rode two horses that evening, big, honest, bay Jolly Roger and the dun mare, Sandstorm. As he rode the bay, he imagined his father calling, 'You look like a tomtit on a round of beef, son,' a favourite saying of his; and the bay did feel large, his ears seemed miles away, and David's heels only reached halfway down his enormous sides. The first time he jumped he fell off, banging his nose and jarring his back, but remembering to spring to his feet and run after the bay calling, 'Sorry, sir.'

Major Seely stayed where he was leaning against his shooting stick watching David. Jolly Roger halted and stood snorting. He'll never want me to stay on here now, thought David. Why did I ever come? I knew I wasn't good enough. He caught the bay and struggled back into the saddle with an effort.

'He feels big, doesn't he? You're not used to big horses?' asked Major Seely.

'No. I'm not really.' He hated to admit it.

He jumped the bay again, staying on, but only just, and feeling more depressed each moment.

'That's better. Now we'll try Sandstorm,' said Major Seely.

She was an easier ride and very clever. He enjoyed jumping her.

'She suits you better. Tomorrow we'll do some work on the flat,' said Major Seely.

They put Sandstorm away, and stood talking for a time about Oxfordshire, about shows, about Sandstorm's possibilities.

'I'd like to see you on your own mare tomorrow,' said Major Seely.

They walked round the horses saying little. Tornado whinnied to David.

It was still a lovely day, warm and tranquil, more like early September than May.

'I'm keeping you from your supper. Leave the tack till the morning.'

David had had tea with Jimmy Bates and Olive. There had been pilchards in tomato sauce as well as bread and butter, strong tea and little fancy cakes. He had complimented Olive on the cakes, though he preferred his mother's. Now he said, 'Well, good night, sir.'

He felt rather lonely as he wandered in the direction of the Bates's bungalow. It made him think of walking home across the Common after a happy day at the Riding School, imagine his mother in a faded overall pouring him tea, his father coming in. He felt nostalgic suddenly for familiar things, and was certain at the same time that nothing would ever be the same again. When he returned home he would see everything through new eyes because he had been away. How would the cottage look then? he wondered. He imagined everything would look smaller – his bedroom, the kitchen, the cottage itself.

'Well, how did it go?' asked Jimmy as he entered the bungalow.

'Did you fall off?'

The Bates were consoling.

'That's always the way,' said Jimmy.

'Never mind. Major Seely will understand. Won't he, Jimmy? I expect you were nervous,' said Olive.

There was bread and cheese, pickles, a little cold meat, tea again.

'Make yourself at home,' said Olive.

He realised now how tired he was; it seemed to come over him like a wave. Years might have passed since early morning.

'The governor's a good sort,' said Jimmy.

'Would you like a bath? We have a bath,' said Olive with pride.

He had always bathed at home in a tin bath in front of the range.

'I lit the copper specially,' said Olive.

They sat for a time after supper. Then David found his way to the bath, which was in the wash-house, and baled water from the copper. He felt too tired now to imagine anything. He only wanted to be in bed, to sleep and sleep.

Jimmy and Olive called, 'Good night' through the door. 'Don't stop there too long. We'll call you in the morning.'

He switched off the lights on the way to his room. It was dark outside now. One of the horses was neighing and he wondered whether it could be Tornado.

He clambered into his bed, which was modern with a walnut headpiece, and switched off the light. What a fool I was to fall off. I wish Major Seely had said something, he thought. He felt now that he would like to take a look at Tornado. Did she feel strange? he wondered, but before he could summon strength to get out of bed, cross the yard in the dark and find her box, he fell asleep.

The next day he rode a little better. He spent a long time bumping round the school without stirrups, just as Sheila had prophesied. As he schooled Tornado, instructed by Major Seely, he could feel her going better each moment, and Major Seely was encouraging.

'That's good. That's very good,' he said, and, 'You're sitting better now. Drive, more drive, drive.'

In the afternoon he was told to hack Jolly Roger, and Sheila was told to escort him on Parisian, an excitable thoroughbred. He felt much happier now. He was certain that his riding had already started to improve. Immense opportunities seemed to lie ahead. For the first time he could remember running the Riding School with Pat without pain.

'Well, do you like it here?' asked Sheila as they turned out of the yard, beneath a dappled sky.

'Yes; and I'm learning a lot,' he said.

'Gosh, you are keen, aren't you?'

'I suppose so. I've always been keen on riding ever since I was a little boy.'

'I'm too lazy. Besides, I'm going to get married next year,' she said.

'Congratulations,' exclaimed David, remembering his brother Michael's wedding, himself throwing confetti, the reception afterwards in the Village Hall, how strange his parents were in their best clothes.

'I haven't a ring or anything yet. It's just an understanding, if you know what I mean,' said Sheila.

It wasn't like riding with Pat. Sheila talked without a pause; but the countryside was beautiful, and in the distance they could see the moors. And Jolly Roger was a calm, pleasant hack, well-schooled and well-mannered.

'Leonard was in the same lodgings as me; now he's at an agricultural college. When he's got his diploma, we're going to get married.'

'And have a farm?' asked David.

There were banks on each side of them festooned with flowers. How do you jump a bank? he wondered. Do people jump them hunting? What happens when a horse hits a bank?

He turned to ask Sheila, but she was still talking about Leonard.

'He's taller than you are,' she said. 'And he has lovely dark, curly hair.'

David didn't know what reply was expected, so he said nothing. The fields on each side of them now were filled with ewes and lambs. The clouds had gone and it was another warm day. David rolled up his sleeves.

'Let's trot,' suggested Sheila, pushing Parisian with her heels.

They trotted along a dusty lane, forded a river, walked up a slope strewn with boulders, trotted again, and all the time Sheila was talking. The horses were sweating now and David started to slow down Jolly Roger, but Sheila continued trotting, shouting remarks back over her shoulder.

'Booth's an old so-and-so. Jimmy's not so bad. The governor's fair, I'll say that for him, but he thinks too much of Booth,' she called.

By Parisian's behaviour, David guessed that they had turned for home. Sheila was sitting anyhow and Parisian was breaking into a canter at intervals and throwing his head in all directions. Sheila continued talking.

'He used to jump a lot – jumped for England, someone said. You should see his lounge; it's full of photos. What would you say his age was?'

And then it happened; one moment Parisian was tearing along in front, with Sheila bobbing about on top, her pale hair windswept like a galloping palomino's mane, the next they seemed to be pitching forward, folding up in front of his eyes. David wanted to cry, 'Hi, stop! Hold him together. Collect him . . . drive, drive, drive . . .' But it was too late now. Sheila had let Parisian tear along, unbalanced, throwing his head about, off the bit, all over the place, and now he was falling and there was nothing David could do but watch. Parisian fell on his knees. Sheila went on over his shoulder. For a moment time seemed to stand still. Then the dark brown thoroughbred scrambled to his feet, stepped on the end of his reins, threw his head in the air, trotted away, leaving a trail of blood behind him. His knees are broken, David thought; he's scarred for ever and ever. Why didn't I say 'Let's walk' to Sheila? I knew she was riding badly. Why didn't I do something?

He looked at Sheila now, who lay in a heap, groaning faintly. He wanted to catch Parisian first. But supposing Sheila was badly hurt? He couldn't simply leave her there and follow Parisian.

He dismounted, bent over Sheila.

'Are you hurt? Can you move?' he asked.

'I don't know. I feel awful,' she cried. 'What will Major Seely say?'

He didn't know. He didn't like to think. He wished that Sheila would get up. He couldn't see Parisian now.

'Try to get up,' he said.

She stood up. She wasn't hurt; he could see that now. He was seized by a wave of anger.

'You aren't hurt at all. You were simply pretending,' he cried, starting to follow the trail of blood, imagining joint oil leaking from gashed knees, trying to imagine how he would feel if someone had let Tornado stumble through bad riding and ruined her for ever.

He could hear Sheila calling something to him

from behind, but he didn't listen. He had eyes now
for only the trail of blood. He reached a road and
saw Parisian grazing on a bank fifty yards ahead.
Approaching him, he noticed how well he was put
together. He had tremendous depth of girth, a long,
sloping shoulder, beautiful limbs. He couldn't find
fault with his conformation, and it dawned on David
that Parisian was probably a show horse, and that
made everything ten times worse, because what use
would he be for a show horse with scarred knees?
Always he would be marked down – his career was
ruined.

Parisian raised his head and watched David
approach. 'Whoa, little horse, whoa,' said David.

Already there were flies buzzing round Parisian's
knees. David wanted to run, to drive them off. He
couldn't bear the thought of them sucking Parisian's
blood, perhaps infecting his wounds. But he
restrained himself, because if he ran Parisian might
trot away, and that would be disastrous.

Another moment and he had hold of the broken
rein, was bending down looking at two bleeding
knees, while Jolly Roger stood patiently watching.
One was worse than the other; one was very bad
indeed. David felt quite sick as he looked at the
worst. It was deep and full of grit and dirt, and bled
slowly and obstinately, but not fast enough to
warrant a tourniquet, he judged.

'It wasn't my fault,' cried Sheila, suddenly behind
him. 'I couldn't help him falling, silly horse.'

She was near to tears.

'How far are we from home?' asked David, suddenly calm.

'About a mile.'

'We'd better have a box, then. Can you take Jolly Roger and get someone to come with a trailer or something?'

'Is he very bad? What will Major Seely say? It wasn't my fault.'

'I'll stay with Parisian,' said David. 'Accidents will happen,' he added, recalling a saying of his mother's.

Sheila mounted Jolly Roger.

'Go carefully. Don't hurry,' said David, wondering whether she had ever ridden the bay before.

He talked to Parisian while he waited. 'You'll be all right soon,' he said, 'We'll get you home, and then you can have some lovely hay and cut grass. You'll be all right soon.'

But he thought at the same time: Will he? What will they do with him if he's stiff in front for ever?

Time seemed to pass very slowly. More and more flies gathered until they were swarming round Parisian as though they had their own form of telepathy and could send messages to one another, 'Injured horse on bank. Very tasty.'

I should have told Sheila to telephone for the vet, too, David thought. Perhaps Major Seely isn't at home. Perhaps Mr. Booth gives anti-tetanus injections himself; some stud grooms do.

At last he saw a car and trailer coming. He started to wave, and saw that Mr. Booth was driving, with Sheila sitting beside him.

'Here's the trailer. You'll be home soon now,' he told Parisian.

'Now what's 'appened?' asked Mr. Booth, getting out of the car and bending down to look at Parisian's knees.

'Done them good and proper, hasn't he? Clumsy beggar. We'd better get him home and have a proper look at them.'

Parisian was very stiff now. He would only move his forelegs with a great deal of persuasion. They had to push and coax him into the trailer.

'He'll never make a show horse now,' said Mr. Booth gloomily, starting up the engine. 'What were you two doing anyway? Racing, I suppose.'

'We were trotting,' said David.

'He just fell. I don't know why,' added Sheila.

'One can't trust anyone nowadays. All they want to do is tear about,' replied Mr. Booth.

David didn't say anything. He sensed that Mr. Booth didn't like him, and the thought filled him with gloom.

And he felt gloomy, too, because he had known Sheila was riding Parisian badly and had done nothing.

But nothing would silence Sheila's tongue.

'He was very fresh. He wanted to be in front all the time, didn't he, David? It excites him being in company. It wasn't my fault,' she said.

That's what small children say. They break things, fall down, forget to shut gates, and they always say, 'It wasn't my fault,' thought David.

'I don't like to think what the governor will say,' said Mr. Booth, turning up the drive.

Sheila was crying now. 'I wish Leonard was here,' she whispered to David. 'It wasn't my fault, was it?'

'No; it wasn't. It might happen to anyone,' said David. Jimmy Bates was taking a skip round the boxes. Tornado was munching a feed. The sun had turned a fiery red in the sky.

'I'm sorry for you two. What were you up to?' called Jimmy.

'They were only trotting,' said Mr. Booth with sarcasm.

'*He*'ll be back presently,' said Jimmy, crossing the yard to look at Parisian.

'Proper mucked himself up, hasn't he?' asked Mr. Booth.

'Doesn't look too good,' agreed Jimmy. 'Never mind, Sheila. Cheer up. It happens to the best of us. When I was a lad I lost a racehorse. Went right through Newmarket it did, the blighter . . .'

'Come on. Let's get him in a box,' interrupted Mr. Booth. They half carried Parisian out of the trailer, put him in a box, looked at his knees again.

'I'd better give him a shot,' said Mr. Booth.

Sheila made herself scarce. 'You get on and clean the tack. You've done enough damage for the day,' Mr. Booth told David.

He spoke to Tornado, found Sheila in the saddle-room.

'What do you think Major Seely will say? It's all right for you. No one can blame you,' said Sheila.

'Mr. Booth seems to think it's all my fault,' said David.

'Don't listen to him,' advised Sheila.

They cleaned tack and Sheila continued talking, but David didn't bother to listen any more. He saw himself being lectured by Major Seely, disbelieved by Mr. Booth, and life seemed very hard indeed.

SCHOOLING

But David didn't see Major Seely that evening, for when he and Sheila had finished the tack, Mr. Booth said, 'Now you two had better scram. I'll deal with the fireworks.'

He left the yard regretfully. He hated the thought of Mr. Booth telling his version of the accident; and he didn't want to go to bed with a cloud still hanging over him.

The Bates had gone out, leaving tea waiting on the table. He ate a little bread and butter, roamed round the room, wondered whether Major Seely had returned yet.

After a time he wandered outside, down a lane, across two fields, past a little cottage and a woman fetching water from a spring. He felt homesick now. He wanted to talk to someone about the accident, to ask them whether it was partly his fault; he remembered the saying, *A trouble shared is a trouble halved*, and wondered whether it was true.

When he went to bed he slept badly, and dreamed he was in Oxfordshire again arguing with Pat about Tornado.

He wakened with a start when Jimmy Bates,

knocking on the door, said, 'Six-thirty.' He couldn't believe the night had passed so quickly. For a moment he thought, Where am I? before he remembered.

When he reached the kitchen Jimmy had already made the early-morning tea, and passed David a cup and a biscuit.

'You look glum enough. What's eating you?' asked Jimmy.

'Nothing really,' David said.

It was a cloudy morning, but very warm. David found a fork and started to muck-out Tornado. Presently Sheila looked over the door.

'Was there a rumpus last night?' she asked.

'I don't know.'

'Have you spoken to Mr. Booth?'

'Not yet.'

Parisian's knees were swathed in bandages. He looked very sorry for himself.

When the mucking-out was done, David returned to the bungalow with Jimmy for breakfast. Olive was up by this time and their bacon and eggs was ready.

'How's the horse?' she asked.

'Pretty bad,' replied Jimmy.

'Poor thing.'

'David seems to think it was his fault. Don't ask me why. He wasn't on top,' Jimmy said.

There was a letter for David from his mother. She wondered whether he had arrived safely, because he hadn't written. He remembered now that he had promised to send a postcard on arrival.

'What you need is a bike; get out a bit,' Jimmy said.

There wasn't any news in his mother's letter. 'Everything is the same,' she wrote. 'But your room looks empty. We haven't changed anything.'

'Come on. Back to the stables,' said Jimmy.

David continued to dread meeting Major Seely, but when he did neither of them mentioned Parisian.

'I'd like you to ride Tornado first. Give her a bit of a school. I've got to go to the office now, but when I get back we'll have out Sandstorm. There's a show next Saturday I'd like her to go to.'

He called his dogs and went away. 'What did he say?' asked Sheila, appearing as though by magic.

'Nothing. Didn't mention it.'

'Old Booth says he carried on something awful last night,' Sheila said.

'I think Mr. Booth has a grudge against us,' replied David.

'He has against you with reason, I suppose. Didn't you know his son used to jump for Major Seely?' asked Sheila.

'No. No one told me.'

'He pinched some money or something. He's in Borstal or somewhere. Jimmy told me,' Sheila said.

'That explains a lot,' David said, and in a sense the news was a relief to him, because at least he knew now why Mr. Booth disliked him.

He schooled Tornado for an hour; then after putting her away he put some tack on Sandstorm

and waited for Major Seely. The vet had been to see
Parisian and had pulled a long face.

'I can't say what sort of recovery he'll make. He
certainly won't be fit to show after this,' he had said.

Sheila was gloomy, Mr. Booth in a bad temper.

'I should take the mare out, loosen her up a bit
before the governor comes,' Jimmy advised David.

Sandstorm was very fresh. Someone had put up
the jumps. Sheila was raking the tan in the school,
which was outside and fenced by high split oak, so
that the occupants couldn't be distracted.

Presently Major Seely arrived and David,
thinking, Take the bull by the horns, said, 'I'm sorry
about our disastrous ride yesterday.'

He noticed now that Major Seely looked very
tired and thought, I've probably chosen the wrong
moment, but Major Seely only said, 'Don't worry,
David. Things like that just happen. It's a shame, but
there it is.'

'I'm sorry all the same,' said David.

'I think we all are,' replied Major Seely.

When David jumped Sandstorm she performed
very well, jumping the put-up course clear, while
David sat still, letting her judge her own distance,
only once collecting her a little when he felt her
losing the rhythm of her stride.

'That's very good indeed. We'll enter her on Saturday. Well done. Now will you fetch your mare
and see how she does round the course,' said Major
Seely.

He put Sandstorm away. He felt much better now.

Jumping Sandstorm had brought back his confidence in himself. He felt capable of anything now.

Tornado jumped well, only knocking the oxer with her hind legs. David couldn't remember a time when she had done better.

'Excellent,' called Major Seely. 'Just jump the oxer again. Do you want to take her on Saturday too?'

'Yes, please, sir,' called David.

The next few days were happy ones: the sun shone, Parisian's knees began to heal. David's riding improved; he started to settle down. He met Mrs. Seely for the first time; she was tall and friendly, and she suggested that he should come to the house for tea when he had time to spare. He had saved his first pound and tried to decide whether to buy a dog or a bicycle when he had saved some more. The approaching show loomed high on the horizon, but Major Seely had said, 'Don't worry about it, David. It's just a try-out. We're not expecting brilliance this year. Next season will be a different matter.' And so he wasn't worried, but determined to take it in his stride like a daily event. He had written to his mother – a long, descriptive letter; so now his conscience was clear in that respect. And he was beginning to like Devon, to feel at home among the banks, to like the narrow roads, the shallow, rushing rivers, the quiet villages.

Sheila still talked incessantly when they were together, but he had discovered that she didn't expect an answer and wasn't offended if he appeared to ignore her.

Sometimes he missed the easy comradeship which he had enjoyed with Pat in the old days, but as time passed he missed her less, and there was always Jimmy to talk to in the evenings.

Tornado and Sandstorm continued to go well, and he felt more at home on Jolly Roger now, who was destined for One and Three Day Events the following year.

'I think he should do well. He's bold with plenty of endurance, and by then his dressage should be better,' Major Seely said.

On the Friday before the show Sheila helped him clean his tack. She was to go with him and Major Seely in the trailer.

'Aren't you nervous? I should be. It must be awful jumping someone else's horses,' she said.

'One has to keep a sense of proportion,' David answered. 'One can't do better than one can.'

He still wasn't nervous; he had eaten a good tea. He felt happier, happier than he had for months. Everything seemed to add up to what he wanted – to become a great rider, to ride for England. He could see himself forging ahead, improving every day, until next year he was riding Jolly Roger in all the biggest events – Badminton, Stowell Park, perhaps even abroad.

And his own horse Tornado should be in the first rank by then, and there was still Sandstorm. He felt like singing at the top of his voice as he cleaned his jumping saddle. I have three to ride, he thought. Three first-class horses.

'This is going to be a wonderful summer,' he told Sheila.

'Why on earth?'

'I don't know,' he replied. 'It just is.'

'You're a funny one – one moment gloomy, the next moment full of the joy of living. Now, Leonard . . .' began Sheila.

He didn't listen because he had heard all about Leonard already. He let his thoughts drift back home, to the day he returned for a visit, perhaps with his dog if he had one.

Once a month he had a whole week-end off. He would go home then, he decided, and saw the cottage, the familiar kitchen, his parents. He couldn't help wondering about Pat. Where was she now? When would he see her again? Would he bump into her at one of the shows?

'It's all done. Wake up, dreamer,' exclaimed Sheila.

He looked at Sandstorm and Tornado before he walked to the bungalow. Their tails had been recently pulled, their coats shone. Tornado looked completely different to the vicious mare he and Pat had bought at a horse-sale roughly nine months ago. Then she had looked sad; there had been deep poverty marks in her quarters; she had been almost unrideable. Now she appeared well fed, her eye was kind, her quarters round. She looked worth three figures, and she's mine, David reminded himself with a feeling of pride.

'All ready for tomorrow?' asked Olive as he entered the bungalow.

'Yes. All set.'

He went to bed early; it was a cloudy night, with rain in the air, which had made Olive say at supper, 'I hope it keeps fine for you. I wish we were going along too. Don't you, Jimmy?'

'It's only a little show. We'll wait till 'e's at the White City or Harringay. That'll be worth seeing,' Jimmy had said.

David thought about that when he was in bed – Harringay and the White City, jumping in a lighted arena. It was something which had belonged to dreams before; now it was within the realms of possibility. Everything seemed a little too good to be true. Wouldn't Mum be pleased? he thought, and imagined her talking to him before he went into the arena at Harringay, the familiar shopping-bag in her hand.

He had always placed the big shows far away in the future, but now his companions talked about them like any ordinary event.

'We must try to qualify Tornado and Sandstorm for the Foxhunter Event at Harringay in October,' Major Seely had said.

'I hope I go with you when you take the horses to the White City,' said Sheila.

As though it was all already settled. Only Mr. Booth remained sceptical, and now David knew about his son he didn't bother about Mr. Booth any more.

He fell asleep quite soon on the night before the show, and didn't hear the storm which broke in the small hours, the rain which lashed his window, the crashes of thunder; nor did the jagged flashes of lightning waken him.

In the morning when he got up, still optimistic, the sky was clear, a breeze stirred the gravel in the yard – everything seemed to point to a fine day.

WELL DONE!

'Still cocksure?' asked Sheila when he appeared in the stable yard wearing a thick, faded jersey knitted by his mother.

'Not cocksure. I don't expect to win. I'm treating today as a kind of trial, as a testing-ground,' David answered. He had learned by experience to expect little rather than much. He found that way he wasn't continually disappointed; more often he had a pleasant surprise.

Mr. Booth had already fed the horses. He was usually in the yard first. It was a matter of pride with him; he liked to feel that he was better than his inferiors.

'I'll see to Sandstorm. You get on with your own mare,' he told David.

Nothing reminded David of preparing for a show at Elm Tree Riding School; there he and Pat had risen in the small hours; pupils had arrived on bicycles and were difficult to recognise in dawn's murky light. There had been something unusual, almost festive, about the washing and the plaiting, the hurry and the flurry. There had been breakfast eaten hastily in the Lewishams' kitchen; the mounting excitement as the time for starting drew near.

But today the horses weren't even to be plaited. Their daily grooming was always lengthy, so there was little extra polishing to be done. Mr. Booth checked the belongings to be taken.

'Don't forget to put the screws in their shoes if it's wet,' he told Sheila. 'There are the feeds all weighed out.'

Once David had groomed Tornado, there was little left for him to do, so he wandered back to the bungalow and gave his clothes an extra brush over while Olive prepared breakfast.

'I've cut you some sandwiches. Do you want something to drink, or will you get something from the refreshment tent?' she asked.

He was ready far too early. After breakfast he stood about the yard feeling conspicuous in his best riding clothes. The sky was quite clear; it was difficult to believe that there had been a storm in the night.

Tornado was restless, as though she knew something unusual was to happen. Jimmy said, 'Well, best of luck. I must lunge the stallion now or the governor will create. Don't fall off. Anything but that.'

At last Major Seely appeared, and backed the car out of the garage, and with Mr. Booth's help connected the trailer. Sandstorm loaded without trouble; but Tornado was suspicious and ill at ease, until finally David rode her up the ramp, jumping off as she entered the trailer.

Mrs. Seely appeared, and David and Sheila climbed into the back of the car.

'How do you feel, David – nervous?' asked Mrs. Seely. She was dressed in a checked suit, and carried a picnic set. With her came the dogs, wagging their tails madly at the thought of an outing.

'Not very,' David admitted.

'Perhaps you're one of those lucky people who don't get nervous,' said Mrs. Seely.

The horses travelled well. Sheila and David remained almost entirely silent during the whole journey. David could only imagine that Sheila was overcome by shyness in the presence of her employer. He was feeling shy himself, but it was an old feeling: he had always been intimidated by people socially better off than himself, though after a time he had felt quite at home with Pat's father, who owned the Hall, and was a retired Colonel and a Master of Foxhounds into the bargain. But for a long time he had found it difficult to get on with the better-off children at the Pony Club; only after he had won the Juvenile Jumping at the Royal Windsor Show had he felt on equal terms with them. He had always found it necessary to prove his own worth to himself. Pat had maintained that he suffered from an inferiority complex. But he didn't think that was true; he was simply a cat which walked alone, as one of his brothers had told him; and because he had one ambition which meant almost more to him than anything else on earth, he hadn't much time for other people.

'A penny for your thoughts?' whispered Sheila as they reached the show-ground.

'Not worth the penny. I bet I know what yours were, though,' David replied.

'What?'

'You were thinking about Leonard.'

'How did you guess?'

'Because you nearly always are,' David replied.

The ground was bright with tents. Hunters were being judged in the ring. Horses were everywhere.

Major Seely parked the car under a clump of trees.

'Time for a look-round before we unbox,' he said, springing lightly from the car, looking less tired today, so that David thought: He's one of those ageless people, who drop dead quite suddenly and, to everyone's surprise, are found to be eighty or ninety.

'Come on. Let's hurry,' said Sheila. David looked at the horses before he followed Sheila and Major and Mrs. Seely across the show-ground.

He felt very much at home now; he loved the bustle, the thudding of hoofs on turf, the gleaming tack on the horses being ridden, the air of excitement and suspense. It seemed to lift his spirits, until he was filled with elation. Crossing the show-ground, he could only think, as he had on other occasions: This is my life. Here I belong. Success or failure, I shall never desert this world of horses and horsemen.

He wanted to stand and take it all in; to lean against the ring ropes and dream about his future.

'A good class for hunters; not often you see so many in the ring at once at this sort of show,' said Major Seely. 'What do you think of them, David?'

He didn't consider himself a good judge of a horse. His heart was in show jumping, cross-country events, hunter trials, 'Pretty good lot,' he replied.

'Not quite top class. But a nice little lot, all the same,' agreed Major Seely.

David kept forgetting that he was so far from home and expected to bump into friends – Pony Club officials, Merry, Richard, people he had met in the hunting field.

They all stopped, leaned against the ring ropes, looked at the hunters. Several times Major Seely met people he knew. Once he introduced David.

'This is my new rider. He's jumping today,' he said.

The Grade C Jumping was at twelve o'clock. Presently Mrs. Seely wandered to the Secretary's tent, taking the dogs with her, to collect David's number, while Major Seely, David, and Sheila went back to the trailer and unboxed Tornado, whom David had decided to ride first.

'I want you to ride her round for a bit before you take a look at the course. Sheila will walk Sandstorm around until you want her. You're fifth in the ring on Tornado, according to the programme,' said Major Seely.

David still felt quite calm – uncannily calm, he

told himself as he bridled Tornado. The hunters had left the ring, and had been replaced by ponies and children on leading reins.

More people were arriving all the time. David mounted Tornado, who felt fresh and ill at ease; her back was up, her neck like a ramrod, for a few moments all her schooling seemed forgotten. Then she relaxed, dropped her nose, went into her bridle like a dressage horse, which made David realise how much she had improved since coming to Devon.

Soon the jumps were being arranged in the ring – gaily-painted red and white bars, two gates, a wall, dark brush fences. The crowd was becoming thicker along the ring ropes, spectators were climbing on the roofs of cars, practice jumps were appearing. The elegant hunters had gone; instead, a great variety of horses was emerging from trailers, horse-boxes, and from the road – cobs, thoroughbreds with goose rumps, thickset jumpers, all sorts, all shapes. Riders in black coats were fewer; there were more martingales and odd contraptions to be seen.

Presently Major Seely took Tornado.

'Have a look at the jumps while you can,' he said.

It was a relatively simple course: the two brush fences had guard rails, the stile was on the flimsy side, but the combination of two gates was straightforward, and there wasn't a twist or a sharp corner to unbalance Tornado.

'Not too difficult, is it?' asked Major Seely as David mounted again.

'No, sir. The stile looks the worst fence to me,' David replied.

He still felt calm as he stood in the collecting ring waiting for his number to be called.

Everyone else there seemed to know each other, which gave him the feeling of an outsider. Tornado had been entered under his own name, so that there was nothing to tell anyone that he was Major Seely's new working pupil. Walking Tornado backwards and forwards across the collecting ring, he longed suddenly for Pat to be beside him; he couldn't remember a show without her; she had always been there, 'nannying' him, as she called it. But that's past, he decided, and the past should be nothing more than a signpost to the future. He turned his attention to the ring and refused to see the image which obscured the jumps of a girl with chestnut hair who said, 'You'll be a great rider one day, David. I know you will.'

A few more minutes and the collecting ring steward was saying, 'You next. Are you ready?' And he was collecting Tornado, riding into the ring, not seeing the crowd, but only the jumps, thinking. Nothing else matters. Steady, Tornado. Steady – turning towards the first brush fence, remembering the guard rails on each side, letting his mare judge her own distance. It's like poetry, he thought, approaching the stile; like beautiful music. There must be no rough edges, no wrenching. One's performance must be as smooth as running water. Tornado tipped the stile, but it didn't fall; she cleared the gates with ease, jumped the wall with care, lengthened her stride for the triple. The crowd was quite silent; leaning against the ring ropes, Major and Mrs. Seely watched. There was a slight turn before the second brush fence; Tornado changed legs, cleared the brush, increased her speed for the hog's-back. Nearly home, thought David, collecting his mare for the upright fence, feeling a rush of joy as they approached the last fence of all, a Sussex gate.

'He's certainly got something,' said Mrs. Seely.

'He's a lot better than Tony Booth,' said her husband. I've done a clear round, thought David. Oh, Tornado, you're wonderful, and I never thought you would make a show jumper.

'Jolly good,' called Sheila, running to meet him. 'Here. Take your second horse.'

He found some oats in his pocket for Tornado before he mounted Sandstorm. The groans from the crowd told him that a popular competitor had knocked a fence. For the first time he noticed that the day was unbearably hot.

'Well done, David. A very nice round indeed,' commented Major Seely.

'Thank you, sir.'

'Best of luck,' muttered Sheila.

He was anxious now; he wanted to do as well on Major Seely's horse as he had on his own. But another clear round seemed like asking for the moon. He remembered his father saying once, 'It's what you expect from life you get, son,' and he thought: Perhaps I'd better expect it. Sandstorm felt nervous.

She eyed the ring suspiciously. However hard he tried, he couldn't imagine her jumping a clear round.

He wished now that he had jumped her first.

'That's one of Major Seely's horses, isn't it?' asked a man on a large ugly black.

'Yes. Sandstorm.'

He didn't want to talk to anyone. He had always felt like that before going into the ring; it was as though he needed silence in which to collect all his energy and concentration, so that he could empty his brain of everything but the task ahead.

He tried to relax, but his sense of calmness had fled, to be replaced instead by a pit in his stomach, by a nagging doubt of his own ability.

But when his number was called again his calmness came back. He entered the ring as he had before, and again only the jumps counted. Somehow his calmness seemed to enter Sandstorm, who jumped the first three fences like an old hand. After the fourth jump each moment became an agony of suspense to David. Could she clear them all? It seemed too much to ask; and yet the dun mare didn't hesitate, but judged fence after fence perfectly, while David sat still, letting himself go with her strides.

He knew by a burst of clapping that he had done a second clear round. His first thought was: I wish Mum was here, because the moment would have meant so much to her – more, perhaps, than to anyone else.

He dismounted, stood shading his eyes with one hand, praising Sandstorm. Afterwards he would look back on the next few minutes as some of the happiest in his life, but at the moment it was a sense of relief he felt more than anything. Once again he had proved something to himself: he knew now that he was fit to ride Major Seely's horses; that show jumping was really his *métier*; that he was right in believing he belonged to the world of riding.

'Well done. That was really superb,' said Major Seely.

'Congratulations. I've never seen her go so well. She was transformed!' cried Mrs. Seely.

He came back to reality. 'She was wonderful. I just sat there,' he said.

'There have only been four clear rounds, so you're in the running on both horses,' said Major Seely. 'I can only say: do the same again.'

'In capital letters,' added Mrs. Seeley.

He felt in a dream as he handed Sheila Sandstorm, mounted Tornado. He couldn't believe that he was here in Devon, changing horses after jumping two clear rounds. Success had always come to him as an appalling surprise, probably because he had never been much good at school – until he took up riding, almost the dunce of a clever family.

'I suppose one day you'll get over your inferiority complex,' Pat had said once, 'and discover that you can really ride.'

But so far he never had.

He entered the ring again. The jumps were higher. Tornado knocked the stile, otherwise she jumped a clear round. He changed on to Sandstorm.

A band was playing now. People were opening picnic baskets.

'Good luck,' said Sheila.

Sandstorm was inclined to rush this time; several times she shortened her stride at the wrong moment; once she put her nose in the air and, taking command, jumped the triple at full speed. But because she was clever she always adjusted herself at the last moment and when she left the ring it was with another clear round to her credit.

He dismounted, but a moment later was called back for a jump off. This time there were only three fences and Sandstorm cleared them one after another.

He came out of the ring, thinking this is my day, one of those days when nothing can go wrong.

A moment later he was back riding Sandstorm, leading Tornado, being presented with first and third rosettes, his mind soaring into the future, imagining other rings, bigger shows, foreign stadiums.

When the congratulations were over and Major Seely had insisted that he and Sheila celebrated with a drink, he sat on the trailer ramp in a daze and ate the sandwiches Olive had made for him.

He felt quite limp, and too tired to listen to Sheila, who was talking as much as usual, now that Major and Mrs. Seely were having lunch in the refreshment tent.

In the trailer the horses munched feeds. David had taken off his coat, pulled down his braces and rolled up his sleeves. Later he would collect Tornado's prize, which Major Seely insisted should be his. He knew from the programme that she had won £5. He felt like putting it in the Post Office in her name, but was afraid that people would laugh at him. He had been brought up to save money against 'a rainy day.'

'It never hurts to have something put by, however little,' his mother had often told him.

Even so, sitting now on the trailer, more than anything he wanted to buy a dog.

He suddenly wanted possessions: a dog, a bicycle – who knows, perhaps later a car.

'Here comes the governor. We'd better pack up. I don't believe you've been listening at all,' complained Sheila.

He stood up and a wave of happiness came over him. The impossible had happened. He had won! Anything could happen now. Even his dreams might come true.

He thought of the letter he would write home, of how pleased the Bates would be, and his life seemed full of hope and opportunity, like the beginning of a perfect day.

THE SECOND SHOW

The day after the show was rather an anticlimax. Tornado and Sandstorm rested. David schooled Jolly Roger and was told to take the afternoon off, and wandered along the lanes, suddenly lonely and homesick for Oxfordshire.

Three days later there was another show. This one was further afield and there was more bustle about the preparations. Mr. Booth plaited both the horses. David rose at five. This time Tornado boxed without trouble. Mr. Booth came instead of Sheila, and drove the car, because Major Seely was to come later, after visiting his office and answering the morning mail.

David travelled with the horses, preferring their company to Mr. Booth's, which seemed always to hold an undercurrent of hostility. The day was wet. Mr. Booth instructed him endlessly and kept him running around for things like a stable boy. The course was tricky; David was wet to the skin before he entered the ring. All the same, both horses jumped a clear round and were finally placed second and third, this time Tornado above Sandstorm. It seemed to David then that his name was already half made. He could hear the experts talking about him, other competitors looking at him with envy, one rider saying, 'Who's the boy Major Seely's found? He's someone to be reckoned with.' He belonged now completely. The name of David Smith was on everyone's lips. In spite of the rain, and the fact that Major Seely hadn't arrived in time to see his performance, David was happy. Looking at Tornado, he kept thinking again: She's mine. And now he imagined riding her himself in foreign competitions, himself competing on his own horse, and it seemed that he could ask for no more, that once he had done that he would be at last content.

Travelling home through the wet afternoon, he thought of all the things Major Seely had said, and now there was a shaft of anxiety in the back of his mind, because next month Major Seely was going for a holiday in France, leaving Mr. Booth in charge.

'You'll go on just the same as usual. We'll work out a schooling chart for the horses before I leave; and you might go to a show or two. Then when I get back we'll start on the really big ones – the Royal, the Three Counties. You may have to sleep in the box. You won't mind that, will you?' Major Seely had asked.

The future had seemed like Paradise to David, until he imagined himself being organised by Mr. Booth. He wanted to say something to Major Seely, but what could he say? That he didn't like Mr. Booth? That Mr. Booth didn't like him? His anxiety hung over him like a cloud all the way home. He had a ghastly sense of foreboding. Now he realised that everything was working too perfectly, that life wasn't like that. He started to dread next month.

Sheila shrieked her congratulations. As they took off Sandstorm's bandages, he asked, 'Did you know Major Seely was going away next month?'

'Yes. It's doctor's orders, apparently. He's been doing too much again. You know he's got a weak heart.'

He hadn't known.

'That's why he doesn't ride any more,' Sheila said.

'He doesn't look like someone with a heart,' David said.

'Don't you like the thought of him going?'

'Not much.' She understood, which made David's fears seem all the more real to him, though if anyone had asked, 'What do you think's going to happen?' he couldn't have said.

'Well, don't let it get you down. Jimmy and I are behind you,' she said.

He said good night to Tornado, walked to the bungalow with his hands in his pockets trying to rid himself of anxiety. But he couldn't forget how he had felt about Pat, how he had known weeks before she had said anything what was in her mind. And he had been right. He could only pray that this time his premonition would be proved wrong.

The next week-end he went home. The journey took four hours. He read *Horse and Hound*, and as he reached Oxfordshire felt as though he had been away for months instead of a few weeks. The trees were no longer in blossom; a few farmers had started to cut their hay. When he had left Oxford and was travelling in the familiar 'bus past fields which held so many memories for him, he felt really home.

He could think now: This is where I fell off. This is where Tornado bucked. This is where we quarrelled. This is where I took the pupils. It made him feel very old.

His mother was waiting at the 'bus-stop.

'Had a good journey? You look well,' she said.

Everything was the same.

'Okay. Plenty of room. I had to change at Reading,' he replied.

Tea was waiting on the kitchen table.

'Is Mrs. Bates looking after you properly?' asked his mother.

She went through his clothes, found a button missing, a seam which needed stitching. It seemed funny to sit there after tea watching his mother, to have no horse looking for him over a loose-box door, to have nothing to do.

'You're doing all right, then?'

He handed her *Horse and Hound*. Inside there was a photograph of him jumping Sandstorm. They were described as *a promising combination*.

'I always knew you'd do all right,' said his mother.

He wanted to tell her about Mr. Booth, because he was still anxious about the future. But he didn't know where to begin.

'Tornado's won £20,' he said instead.

'Well done. But don't you go spending it. Put it

aside for a rainy day. You never know what may happen,' his mother said.

He sat on in the kitchen, and started to think: What shall I do tomorrow? He wasn't accustomed to leisure. The week-end started to look very long. He wanted to say, 'Heard anything of Pat?' But his mother didn't like her now, and, anyway, he was afraid to ask, because she might be abroad by now, or already engaged.

Presently his father came in, and there was a new pot of tea and they all sat round the table talking.

'Well, you've done very well, David. I can't say more, can I?' asked his father.

They were proud of him. He had given himself a reputation which he must live up to.

'Heard anything from Pat?' asked his father presently.

'No.'

'I don't think she's here much now. Spends most of her time in London,' his father said.

He saw Harringay, himself competing, Pat appearing from the stands to congratulate him. But that sort of thing only happens in books or films, he thought.

The next day was fine. He had no close friends in the village besides Pat, so he spent the day helping his father in the garden. In the evening he walked across the Common and remembered how he had schooled Tornado up and down the bunkers of the old golf-course.

He felt quite lost without a horse to ride. He had

no other interests. He sat down on a bunker and thought about Tornado and watched the few rabbits scuttling among the gorse bushes.

On Sunday he put on his tidy clothes and went to church, which was something he hadn't done for years.

By this time he was glad to be going back to Devon. He wanted to see Tornado, to school Jolly Roger, to hear when he would be jumping again. He found he couldn't live without excitement now. He whistled as he hurried back to Sunday lunch, because by nightfall he would be back in Devon.

There was beef, three vegetables, Yorkshire pudding, fruit and custard. It was very hot in the kitchen. They sat with the door open.

'Now don't be late,' said his mother. She had done his packing. He kissed her on the forehead when he left, nodded to his father.

His mother had packed him a carrier full of food.

'Just a few biscuits, and an apple or two, and your favourite sweets,' she had said.

He caught the 'bus, watched Oxfordshire slip past the windows. The train was late; he changed at Reading again. I wonder who's been exercising Tornado, he thought. I hope Olive leaves something out for me.

Mr. Booth met him at the station.

'Got back all right, then?' he asked.

David was the only passenger to get off the train.

The air felt very soft, and in the distance he could see the purple hills of Exmoor.

'Yes. It's easy,' he said. 'Just change at Reading once you're on the express.'

Tornado whinnied when he stepped out of the car.

'We turned her out to exercise herself,' said Mr. Booth.

The Bates were out, but there was a cold supper waiting for him on the kitchen table. He sat down, thinking: It's not so bad to be back. Home's all right if there's something to do. . . .

'Can I come in?' called Sheila.

'Of course.'

'I was wondering whether you still want a dog, because I've heard of one. The sheep-dog at the farm's got six puppies. Mr. Sellars says you can have the pick,' she said.

'Sit down and have a cup of tea,' said David.

'Of course, you may not want a sheep-dog,' began Sheila.

'But I do,' he said.

Presently they both went down to the farm, and he chose a puppy with a splodge of black over one eye and paid Mr. Sellars £2.

'I should leave it for another week. She's a bit small yet,' said Mr. Sellars.

Walking back to the stables with Sheila, he felt very happy.

'How have things been going? Do you know when the next show is?' he asked.

'Mr. Booth was on about you. Said you didn't clean the tack properly. There's a show on Wednesday and the Seelys leave for the Continent on Saturday,' Sheila told him.

'Then we're all at the mercy of Mr. Booth. Why doesn't he tell me if he doesn't like the way I clean the tack?'

'Because you're neither fish nor flesh. You're not really under him at all, because you're a pupil, not an employee,' explained Sheila.

He couldn't see what difference it made, but quite suddenly he felt cold.

'He simply doesn't like me,' he said.

For a moment the future looked bleak. He knew he couldn't stand a great deal of disapproval; it destroyed the confidence he possessed in himself, which wasn't much.

Then he shrugged his shoulders. There's not much he can do really. Major Seely's completely satisfied with my riding. He won't be away long, he decided.

'I must rush or I shall be locked out. See you tomorrow,' called Sheila, disappearing into the dusk.

I wonder what I'm entered for on Wednesday, thought David. I really can't hope to do so well a third time. What shall I call the puppy? Thinking about his puppy, he went into the bungalow, cleared away the supper things and washed up.

Then lying back in a chair, he turned on the wireless and imagined himself riding with a sheep-dog at his heels.

THE THIRD SHOW

The next show was a large one. There were agricultural exhibits, a huge variety of animals, vegetables, fruit, flowers – even a shoeing contest. There were two rings, and David was to jump in the main ring at three o'clock.

He felt nervous today, though he couldn't have said why. He had slept badly the night before and arrived late in the yard in the morning. Sheila and Mr. Booth had come. Major and Mrs. Seely were to follow later in their second car. Tornado was nervous too; she didn't like the smell of the other animals, the bleating of the sheep, the squeaks from a pen of piglets. Sheila led her round while David rode Sandstorm. It was another hot day, and the smell of the animals, the clank of machinery, the hot mass of humanity milling round the tents seemed to consume all the air until there wasn't any left.

They had left early in the trailer and travelled without a break until after one o'clock; now it was twenty to three and David couldn't rid himself of anxiety, couldn't stop thinking: Supposing we do badly today? Supposing I make a muck on both horses?

Major Seely arrived in plenty of time, and stood in the collecting ring with David, giving him advice. There was a thin corridor of space between them and the ring; the rest of the space round the ropes was packed six deep with people, except on one side, where the grandstand loomed large, filled to the brim.

The first prize was £50 and a cup. The entries were limited, but Major Seely had entered a long time ago, in the days when he still had Tony Booth.

'It's quite a simple course really; nothing tricky,' said Major Seely, and David thought: People always think that if they're not competing. It's a different matter when you're about to meet the jumps one by one yourself. He had walked the course, one of the few riders without breeches and boots. He was to be the first competitor.

Nearly everyone seemed to know each other in the collecting ring, except himself. He felt conspicuous and a little lost – the first competitor, one of the youngest, the only one in sight in jodhpurs.

If I could win today with Tornado, I could get myself some boots, go to that place in London where Colonel Lewisham goes, have them made to measure in real calf, thought David, watching the spectators settling themselves more comfortably in the grandstand, the judges entering the ring, feeling suddenly sick, thinking: It's such a big show. Really, it's awful riding other people's horses.

'Well, best of luck, David,' said Major Seely, going away to his car, while the Collecting Steward approached and they pulled back the rope which barred the entrance to the ring. He was ready now, all his energy concentrated on the effort he was about to make. His entrance was heralded by a fanfare. It was very hot in the ring; the grass looked parched. On all sides a sea of faces watched.

He cantered across the turf. People looked at their programmes; over all shone a sun from a sky flecked with the faintest, tiniest clouds. Sandstorm was eager. She took the first three fences a little fast, but fault-lessly, like a well-balanced piece of mechanism. They cleared the oxer, the double railway gates, the triple bars; David felt confident now and marvellously detached from everything but the job in hand. They approached the wall. They were half-way round the course. From somewhere in the crowd a little girl dropped a paper-bag, which fluttered across the ring. It was so small. Afterwards David could never decide what Sandstorm thought it was: A piglet? An enor-mous bloated insect? But now in the ring, she half stopped, dashed sideways, rushed on towards the wall, suddenly alarmingly close. She hit it full square in the centre, pecked, half recovered her balance and fell.

David seemed to be toppling in a world of bricks; then for a moment he was out, another second and he was in the midst of hoofs and tangled reins, thinking What's happening? where am I? He was up before the stretcher arrived, saying, 'No, thank you. I'm quite all right,' calling everyone 'sir' rather aggressively.

He looked round for his mother, before he remembered that he was in Devon, and, more dimly, leaving the yard in the morning. Presently he seemed to be sitting in the Seely's car drinking tea with sugar in it, about which he kept complaining. His head ached and the most important thing seemed to be the time and that he still had Tornado to ride.

He couldn't remember the time, not even when someone had just said 'Four o'clock' or, 'Nearly five.' He couldn't remember whether it was Friday or Saturday, though it actually was Wednesday.

A doctor examined him, while he protested feebly, saying, 'I'm all right. There's nothing wrong.'

Presently he travelled home with the Seelys and was received by Olive, who seemed to be expecting him and hustled to bed, still asking the time.

He fell asleep at once and dreamed that he was jumping Tornado. When he wakened it was dark, but there was a plate of biscuits and a glass of milk by his bed. He couldn't remember very much. But he knew that he had met with catastrophe, and he guessed that he had concussed himself.

He was filled with gloom when he wakened in the morning. By the amount of light streaming through the curtains he knew that it was late. He tried to remember yesterday, but all he could recall was the bustle in the yard in the morning. The rest was a blank: only dimly did he recall travelling back with the Seelys.

Supposing I hurt one of the horses? he thought, climbing out of bed, pulling back the curtains, letting the sun into the room. He looked at himself in the mirror above the mantelpiece. He looked distraught, his hair was on end, but there was no mark on his face. He dressed and found Olive in the kitchen.

'So you've woken up at last,' she said.

'What happened? Did I fall off?' Standing there, he had to know at once; the suspense was unbearable. Olive put down her duster. 'Sandstorm fell with you,' she said, and started to explain.

He didn't want to eat, but Olive had kept some breakfast for him in the oven – fried potatoes, sausage.

'You must eat something. Horses all fall sometimes. Surely you know that.'

'Well, how are you feeling this morning?' called Jimmy when he entered the yard. 'Proper silly you were last night.'

Tornado was looking over her box door.

'How's Sandstorm?' he asked.

'Nothing wrong with her,' said Jimmy.

He was teased all day.

'You certainly did go up the pole yesterday,' said Sheila.

'Crackers by all accounts,' agreed Jimmy.

'Never seen anything like it. The way you spoke to the governor . . .' said Mr. Booth.

He wasn't allowed to ride. 'You're to take it easy today, according to the governor,' said Mr. Booth.

He went down to the farm and looked at his puppy, wrote to his mother. He still felt gloomy. It had to happen at the biggest show, he thought. Why couldn't it have happened to Tornado after I had jumped Sandstorm? He couldn't help thinking that his luck had changed. He hated having nothing to do. In the afternoon he helped Sheila clean the tack.

'Cheer up. It happens to the best people. Now, take Leonard . . .' she said.

On Friday, Major Seely worked out a schooling chart for the three horses with David.

'There's just one show I want you to go to while I'm away. Both horses are entered. If Sandstorm wins it'll upgrade her, and after that you'll be in the open classes,' he said.

David had never ridden in an open jumping event. It would be another rung in his ladder to success.

'And don't worry about last Wednesday. It happens to the best of us at times,' added Major Seely.

He walked round the horses with Mr. Booth, discussing their feeding problems.

Sheila and David stood together in the saddle-room.

'I wish he wasn't going. The moment he's gone, Mr. Booth will start throwing his weight about, you'll see,' said Sheila.

'It's a horrible thought.'

'The only thing is to have a sense of humour. Once you start fretting and fuming, you're finished,' said Sheila.

The next morning the Seelys left at dawn. At first there was a sense of relaxation hanging over the stables. No one hurried; David schooled the horses in a more leisurely manner than usual; Sheila found time to scribble a line to Leonard during the morning.

But by the afternoon Mr. Booth was running them all off their legs, most of all David.

'You may be a pupil, but you're a working one,' he said once.

David didn't mind being corrected and harried in his stable work, but when next day Mr. Booth started to take an interest in Sandstorm's schooling, he began to feel uneasy.

'It's all worked out, Mr. Booth. The governor and I talked it over together before he left. Today I'm working her on the flat, tomorrow we're hacking, the next day schooling and jumping,' he said.

'She's too fresh. You're not riding her enough. Take her out this afternoon. Let her have a pipe-opener,' said Mr. Booth.

'I'm schooling Jolly Roger this afternoon,' said David.

Mr. Booth watched him ride Jolly Roger. He seemed to have all the time in the world, now that Major Seely was away.

'You want to get him more collected. He's all over the place. He'd go better in a double bridle,' said Mr. Booth.

'But the governor . . .' began David.

'That doesn't matter. I'm in charge now.'

A cold shiver travelled swiftly down David's spine.

He began to dread the next few weeks; they loomed ahead full of awful possibilities.

'And what I say goes,' said Mr. Booth, leaving the school. The horses will be ruined quite quickly, thought David. I shall have to stand up to him. One must have a few principles. He was filled with a sense of futility. How will it end? he wondered.

Mr. Booth returned with a double bridle under his arm.

'But I have Major Seely's instructions,' began David.

He thought: Everything's going wrong very quickly. First I concuss myself, then this happens.

'Are you in charge or am I?' asked Mr. Booth.

'I'm in charge of Jolly Roger's schooling.' David rode Jolly Roger out of the school, down the drive, into the road without looking back, though he wanted to very badly indeed. He knew now that he had as good as declared war on Mr. Booth. It would be a fight between them now to the bitter end. He didn't expect to win; but one has to stick to one's principles whatever the cost, he told himself, and remembered his mother saying once, 'If you do what's right, David, everything will come right in the end.' He believed that now as he hacked Jolly Roger round the outside of a field. Somehow, everything would come right; Major Seely would understand. He remembered that he was to go to a show with Mr. Booth, that he had to work with him; the future looked complicated, and to forget it he sent Jolly Roger into a gallop, and switched his thoughts to cross-country events and imagined himself riding at Badminton.

He hacked slowly home. Mr. Booth wasn't to be seen, but Sheila seemed to be waiting for David.

'Whatever's happened? Mr. Booth's in an awful state. I thought he was going to throw a fit or something!' she cried.

'That's all right,' said David, sliding to the ground. 'He tried to make me ride Jolly Roger in a double bridle. I have my orders from the governor, and I'm sticking to them.'

'Well, you've certainly put him in a mood. It's not much fun for the rest of us.'

'One must have a few principles. I'm not employed by Mr. Booth,' replied David.

'Have it your own way, but I wouldn't be in your shoes.'

Jimmy wasn't encouraging either. 'It's never good to quarrel with your superiors,' he said.

'But David's only a pupil,' said Olive.

'That don't cut any ice with Fred Booth,' replied Jimmy.

'But Major Seely said . . .' began David.

'That don't make no difference neither. Fred Booth's in charge,' said Jimmy.

It sounded very illogical.

'Anyway, the horse might go better in a double. Major Seely isn't always right,' continued Jimmy.

'I see David's point of view,' said Olive.

'You don't know nothing about it,' replied Jimmy.

'I've had my orders from Major Seely, and I'm sticking to them,' announced David.

'No need to get on your high horse,' replied Jimmy.

David was suddenly sick of the subject. He was still certain he had done the right thing.

'Well, I shall stick to the chart, whatever anyone says,' he said stubbornly.

'Okay. But you'll be heading for deep water,' replied Jimmy.

'Don't frighten the boy,' said Olive.

David stood up, put his cup and saucer on his plate. 'I think I'll go for a walk now,' he said. Outside it was still sunlit, and the air caressed his cheek as only Devon air does, and from the fields came the gentle baas of sheep.

He didn't feel like visiting the stables again. He felt as though he was slowly burning all his boats one by one. For the first time he thought: Supposing I lose my job? – tried to imagine himself returning home a failure. And it was too awful to contemplate. Better take a look at my puppy, he thought, turning towards the Sellars' farm, while in the bungalow Jimmy said, 'He's heading for trouble all right, rubbing Booth up the wrong way.'

THE LAST SHOW

The next few days were some of the worst in David's life. Mr. Booth ignored him completely; he seemed to be walking under a perpetual cloud. No one but Olive was sympathetic.

'You've brought it upon yourself,' Sheila said when he complained. 'If you'd had as many jobs as I have, you would have learned to take things as they come. After all, you could have told Major Seely when he came back what had happened.'

'But Jolly Roger might have been spoilt by then,' replied David.

'Not likely. Booth's schooled horses for Richmond.'

'But Jolly Roger isn't a show horse.'

Gradually things grew worse. Mr. Booth cut the horses' oats. Sandstorm's jumping deteriorated; David lost confidence in her and in himself. He tried to place her at her fences, which he had never done before, and she, muddled by a method she didn't understand, began to rush. Tornado with far less oats lost her speed and dash, which had stood her in such good stead in time competitions. She began to tip fences. This was the moment when David needed help and advice; someone to stand and call. 'Leave her alone; sit still,' to share the responsibility for the training of two show jumpers and a promising One Day Event horse.

He thought of writing to Major Seely; he tried to remember everything he had ever read or been told about show jumping. He stopped jumping Sandstorm and Tornado for two days. Then Mr. Booth spoke to him.

'We'll be leaving at nine tomorrow. I'll do Sandstorm. You can look after your own mare,' he said.

David replied 'Yes, sir' without thinking, and immediately began to dread the morrow. He wanted to run after Mr. Booth, to cry 'Need we go?' like a child who doesn't want to go to a party.

He didn't know the name of the show, where it was, how long they would have to travel. He felt quite lost, and each moment the future seemed to grow blacker.

'Well, aren't you pleased? Show tomorrow,' called Jimmy.

'No. The horses are off their form,' David shouted.

He thought: If only they were both mine; then nothing would drag me there. Why didn't I stay at home, take a job as a labourer and school Tornado in the evenings? At least I should have had some freedom then.

He thought: Probably Sheila's right, I was a fool to stand by my principles. If I hadn't quarrelled with Mr. Booth, he would have helped me school the horses, and if they were in bad form we needn't have gone.

He thought: When one comes down to brass tacks, it's generally one's own fault.

'Cheer up,' said Olive when he went in to tea. 'You look as though you'd just come back from a funeral.'

'I feel like it,' he answered.

He had no appetite for the potted meat-paste, the little fancy cakes, the large piece of yellow cheese, the sliced bread from the Co-op. He thought: I should have written to Major Seely. Why didn't I? I could have got his address from somewhere.

Olive poured him some tea. 'Aren't you going to eat anything?' she asked.

He shook his head. He sat looking at the stained white tablecloth and saw his world of dreams toppling like a pile of bricks before his eyes.

He saw Sandstorm refusing three times in the ring; Tornado somersaulting over the wall. And everyone will say I lost my nerve the day I concussed myself, he thought.

'He's got cold feet about tomorrow,' Jimmy told Olive.

'Can you tell me why Mr. Booth's been cutting the horses' oats?' he asked.

'Couldn't say,' replied Jimmy, cutting himself a piece of cheese and reaching for the butter. 'Why don't you ask him?'

Yes. Why haven't I? wondered David. Really,

everything's my own fault. He stood up and, muttering, 'I must clean my shoes,' left the room.

'What's the matter with him?' asked Olive.

'Can't get on with Fred Booth. First of all he was cocky; now he's the opposite.'

'I'm sorry for the kid,' said Olive.

Much later he decided to visit Tornado. An awful feeling of loneliness hung over him, a black shadow separating him from friends and foes alike; his old sense of inferiority had come back. He felt empty inside, but couldn't bear the thought of food. Olive and Jimmy had gone to the local. He might have read a book to escape from reality if there had been one in the bungalow, but the only reading matter besides the *Daily Mirror* was Olive's magazines, which concerned themselves with romance and knitting patterns and occasionally babies.

He could hear Olive and Jimmy coming back as he walked to the stables. The night was clear. Another fine day tomorrow, he thought.

He crossed the yard, spoke quietly to Tornado, before he noticed that the light was on in the forage-room, though the door was shut.

'Back in a moment. I'll get you a handful of oats,' he told Tornado.

He was about to open the forage-room door when he heard voices inside.

'I can't let you have another bag till next week,' said Fred Booth.

'That's all right. The same price then – a quid?' asked his companion.

David stood frozen. 'Yes. Okay by you?' asked Fred Booth.

'Okay. The chickens are laying fine on it.'

David wanted to flee, but now the door was open, the light dazzling his eyes, Mr. Booth saying, 'Hullo, who is it?' He couldn't speak. He realised a great deal now. He knew that he and Mr. Booth could never be anything but enemies for ever. He stood there feeling like an eavesdropper, and guilty, though he knew that right was on his side. He's a thief, he thought. He's selling Major Seely's oats. That's why the horses' rations have been cut. Do any of the others know? Sheila? Jimmy?

'So it's you. What are you doing roaming about at this time of night?' asked Mr. Booth.

David could move now. 'Just taking a look at the horses. I saw the forage-room light was on,' he answered.

'This is a friend of mine. I should get along to bed if I were you,' said Mr. Booth.

He noticed a van parked by the yard entrance as he walked back to the bungalow. His mind was in a turmoil. He saw a hundred possibilities. Should he write at once to Major Seely? Send a telegram? He had no proof. Would Sheila support him if he told her?

He longed for Pat's company now. She would know at once what should be done. Perhaps he should write home for advice. The problem was still unresolved when he went to bed, not to sleep, but to lie tossing and turning till the small hours.

He wakened feeling like a limp rag. He got out of bed thinking: I wish there wasn't a show – longing more than anything to be able to go back to sleep. He didn't bother to comb his hair or wash his face, simply dressed and plunged out into the cool morning air in his oldest jodhpurs, a shirt, and braces.

Mr. Booth was already up. Jimmy and Sheila were starting to clean the loose-boxes. He was the last, unwashed, feeling too tired to care.

The events of last evening seemed far removed from reality in the morning light. Much more real and of greater importance was the approaching show.

David started to groom Tornado. 'You'll have to do all the work today,' he told her.

Because he felt untidy, Sheila appeared unusually spruce. She had curled her hair and her face was freshly made up.

'Feeling better?' she called to him across the yard.

'Okay. I'd like a chat later with you,' he said.

He felt he had to tell someone what he had seen and overheard. Sheila wasn't reliable, but she must have an opinion one way or the other.

'Okay by me, if there's time,' she said.

He was ready by nine o'clock. He found Mr. Booth already loading the horses when he appeared in the yard, his jumping hat and stick under his arm.

'Here you are, then,' said Mr. Booth.

He travelled with the horses. No one had suggested that he should ride in the car, and he preferred their company. He knew now that they were competing in a reasonably large show sixty miles away. He had learned that much from Sheila before he left. He had had no opportunity to discuss his discovery of the evening before with her.

But when he left she had called, 'See you tonight.'

Travelling, he could only foresee disaster – refusals, fallen fences, himself falling off. Mr. Booth drove carefully and the journey seemed to drag on unbearably like a hideous, endless dream.

They were late when they reached the showground. David knew that as they entered the ground, by the loudspeaker calling his number, by the riders in the collecting ring, and by the competitor jumping the large, well-planned course. He found that he was sweating, that the dream had become a nightmare from which there would be no awakening except to the fact that it was reality.

'There's plenty of time,' said Mr. Booth, getting out of the car.

But David knew there wasn't. His hands were shaking. He couldn't buckle Sandstorm's throat-lash; and the loudspeaker was still calling his name.

'Plenty of time,' said Mr. Booth.

David wanted to scream 'There isn't!' as he sprang into Sandstorm's saddle, cantered across to the collecting ring.

'You're late,' said the steward. 'Better go straight in.'

His hands felt clammy on the reins. It was worse than a nightmare. Sandstorm was still stiff from the journey in the horse-box.

He rode straight in, saw the usual horde of faces, women clutching bags, children sucking sweets, here and there a knowledgeable face mixed up with the crowd. Everything was the same, yet different, because for the first time he was afraid.

He turned towards the first fence, felt Sandstorm settle into her stride. He hadn't been able to study the course, he could only hope to follow the numbers. He let her choose her own pace, saying to himself over and over again, 'David, don't interfere. Sit still. Leave her alone.'

They cleared the first three fences before he lost his way. He realised too late that he was jumping No. 5 and heard the judge blowing his whistle with a sudden feeling of sickness.

'Will No. 46 leave the ring,' announced the loud-speaker.

He felt like a whipped cur as he left the ring.

'Whatever happened to you?' asked Mr. Booth.

He couldn't answer, because he could only have screamed, 'It's all your fault!' and he had been brought up to believe things were his fault, not other people's.

He mounted Tornado. Somewhere a band was playing Elgar's *Pomp and Circumstance*; in the ring a competitor was jumping a faultless round.

'Better do better this time,' said Mr. Booth.

There was time to ride Tornado round the show-ground, to look at the other competitors, to remember that she was off colour, to pray for a clear round.

The feeling of sickness came back as he entered the ring. Tornado eyed the jumps without enthusiasm. There was a tightening in his throat, as though something was winding itself round his neck, slowly throttling him. He let Tornado go as she liked; she tipped the second fence, the third, the fourth.

He didn't care – didn't care about anything any more. No one clapped as he left the ring; he was the last competitor; the loudspeaker was calling numbers for the jump-off.

'Well I never,' said Mr. Booth.

David thought he caught a gleam of satisfaction in his eye. He dismounted on to legs which felt as shaky as stilts. Now we can go home, he thought. It's over. The worst has happened.

They boxed the horses in silence.

'No point in staying,' said Mr. Booth.

What will happen now? thought David. I'll lose my job, I suppose. But it's not as bad as losing your legs, going blind, becoming mad. Lots of people live without realising their ambitions. He felt calm now, rather as though he had just emerged from fighting a rough sea – exhausted, glad only that he had survived. He thought: There are other jobs. Major Seely must give me a reference of some sort. He can say I'm honest, that I have enthusiasm – at least that.

He remembered the incident of the night before,

403

and for a second it seemed that he held Mr. Booth helpless like a fly in the palm of his hand. Then he thought: But supposing no one believes me? I haven't any proof. Why should anyone believe my word against his?

They were travelling again now – much faster this time, it seemed to David.

I suppose Mr. Booth will write to the Seelys, he thought next. Probably he does regularly. Had we been friends, he might have found excuses. As it is, he'll write the worst he can.

They passed the moors, and lonely cottages standing by themselves like lost people who have pitched their tents in exposed places, unable to go on any longer. They passed through a town. The horses stood calmly munching hay. David remembered suddenly that he hadn't eaten. He couldn't remember breakfast, and he hadn't eaten the night before. Probably Olive had put out a large package of sandwiches, but he hadn't seen them. He remembered his puppy. What could he do with her if he lost his job? What with Tornado?

I can go home, he thought.

Presently he saw the drive. The yard with its clock tower, the grey pigeons. They turned in. We're back, he thought, and braced himself to meet Sheila and Jimmy, while in one of the loose-boxes a horse neighed.

'I'M BACK'

'Don't be so gloomy,' said Sheila later as she and David stood together in the saddle-room cleaning tack. 'You make the governor into such an ogre. He'll just think you need some more instruction. After all, he's show-jumped himself. He knows what it's like.'

'If only I knew what Mr. Booth was going to write,' sighed David.

He felt very tired. He wanted to sleep and sleep. He had found Olive's sandwiches and eaten them. Jimmy had handed him a letter from his mother.

'Write soon,' she said. 'People are always asking after you.'

But he knew he wouldn't write until he had good news. Or until the news was so bad it couldn't be worse.

'Anyway, if you do lose your job you can always get another one,' said Sheila with the voice of experience.

'But what about Tornado and my puppy?'

'They're a handicap, it's true. I suppose at a pinch you could sell Tornado.'

But he knew he couldn't. It would be like selling

405

a part of himself. She was tied up with his successful past, and he couldn't let that go. Looking at her, reminding himself that she was his, he could remember that once he had been a success, and what he had achieved once he might achieve again.

'Well, I'm knocking off. It's been a long day. Only three weeks now and then Leonard will be back,' said Sheila.

She combed her flaxen hair, shrugged her shoulders.

'Well, good night, David. Don't always look on the black side.'

He felt worse when she had gone. The awfulness of the day came rushing back and he had to remind himself again: It would be worse to lose my legs, to go mad, to be blind.

Tea was waiting in the bungalow.

'So you didn't do so well today,' said Olive. 'Never mind. You can't always win, you know. You mustn't be a bad loser.'

She doesn't understand, he thought. She doesn't know how badly I rode. If only it was simply a matter of being a good or bad loser – if that was all.

'Better luck next time. That's what I always say,' continued Olive.

It was a relief to find that Jimmy was out. He could let his mind wander crazily like a sleep-walker through the last month while she talked.

'What about the washing-up?' he asked when they had finished tea.

'It'll keep.'

406

'I'm going to bed, then.'

'What about supper?'

'Don't bother about me. I've had lots of tea, thanks all the same.'

It was wonderful to climb into bed; to pull the bedclothes up to his eyes, to feel like a wounded animal returning to its lair, a long journey over, to feel oblivion, to sleep and sleep.

Nothing happened for nearly a week. David rode the horses. His despair ebbed away. Perhaps Mr. Booth hadn't written, he thought.

He had told Sheila about Mr. Booth selling the oats.

'Gosh! Lots of grooms do that. If you'd seen some of the things some stud grooms do when the boss is away! Why, at one place the head groom was letting out the horses for seven-and-six an hour,' she said.

'But didn't you do anything?'

'What could I do?'

'Well, write to the boss,' said David.

'But I hadn't his address. Besides, what's the point of stirring up trouble? He was a jolly good stud groom, all the same,' Sheila replied.

Sandstorm and Tornado were back on their proper rations. Mr. Booth spoke now to David, though not more than to give orders or to comment on the weather.

Then on a sunlit day when flaming June was living up to her name, and a cuckoo had been calling 'Cuckoo, cuck, cuckoo' since early morning, and

David had fetched his puppy and decided to call it Tina, his world collapsed.

Mr. Booth found him in the saddle-room.

'I've had a letter from the boss,' he said. 'He's not pleased by the way you're riding the horses. He can't come back for a month, and so he thinks it's better if you leave. I have a week's wages for you here.'

For a moment everything seemed black. Is this really happening? thought David.

He couldn't think of anything to say – could only stand, seeing the future all too clearly, repeating to himself again and again: He thinks it's better that you leave.

'Of course, we're all sorry. That goes without saying,' said Mr. Booth.

He wanted to shout, 'You know that's not true. You've always disliked me because of your son, and later because I knew about the oats.' But instead he muttered, 'Thank you for telling me,' as though it was a moment for politeness!

He thought: I've got the sack – and felt the shame which it had brought to his forebears to have to say the same thing. He took the money offered by Mr. Booth without noticing. The future held nothing but disgrace.

Presently David noticed that Mr. Booth had left. He had been fetching Jolly Roger's tack; he had planned a long ride; there seemed no point in riding now. He found he still had an egg-butt snaffle bridle slung over his arm. He hung it up, stood looking round the saddle-room, thinking: I've lost my job. What do I do next? Where do I go from here?

He wandered aimlessly round the yard, before he walked the half-mile to the nearest kiosk and found himself saying, 'Is that the station? I want to box a horse to Oxford tomorrow. Is that possible?'

It took a long time, but when everything was fixed for seven-thirty in the morning, it was still only three o'clock.

'So you're leaving,' said Olive when he went in to tea.

'That's right. Seven-thirty in the morning.' He couldn't help feeling ashamed. None of his family had ever lost a job before. It was a matter of pride; it was possible to leave of your own free will, but to be given the sack was something which didn't happen to the Smiths.

'I'm ever so sorry. Never mind. Don't be miserable,' said Olive.

She helped him pack. 'Are you taking your horse?'

'Yes; and the puppy.'

'Got anywhere to keep the horse.'

'Not yet.'

'I can't understand Major Seely. It's not like him. I don't trust Mr. Booth myself. Jimmy says he's all right, but . . .'

But what? thought David. 'Mum's always said if you do what's right everything comes right, but I can't see it. Not now, anyway,' said David suddenly.

'Well, there's still time,' answered Olive. 'I wish I'd known before that you were leaving. I'd have ironed some of your things. They look a proper sight, really they do.'

The morning was grey, as grey and dismal as David's mood as he put his tack on Tornado.

Mr. Booth had offered to take the puppy and David's suitcase to the station in the car, an offer David could gladly refuse, since he had ordered a taxi for the purpose.

Olive had handed him a parcel of sandwiches and a thermos of tea.

'Don't bother to send back the thermos; we've got another,' she said.

Jimmy and Sheila had said good-bye as a sort of greeting when they arrived. Now he had only to leave.

He mounted, looked at the yard, rode out into the greyness of the morning. Tonight I shall be home, he thought. If there's nowhere else for Tornado, I shall have to ask permission to put her in the Hunt stables. He saw himself arriving at the cottage, his mother looking up from her cooking, crying out with surprise. Tomorrow I can buy *Horse and Hound* and start looking for another job, he decided. He came to the station, and there was the taxi with Tina looking out of the back window wriggling her behind. It was sleepy as country stations are in the early morning. Nothing seemed to stir; over everything hung the greyness of the morning which was soon to clear giving place to a perfect day.

He tried to forget that he was going home. Tornado could smell the smoke of trains and advanced in leaps and bounds. A porter emerged from a door marked *Parcel Office*. 'Your truck's ready for loading,' he said.

Presently he was sitting in the groom's compartment with Tina on his knee licking his face. Tornado watched him with large eyes. His suitcase lay beside him on the seat.

He wished now that he had written home. There would be so much explaining to do, and he didn't feel like explaining. He wanted simply to make another start.

He could see his father beginning, 'Well, son . . .' His mother upset, but behind him with her bottomless faith in his ability to ride as well as anyone in England.

It was a long time before the horse-box left the station. When it did it was on the end of a long train, and swayed and jolted, while outside the sun dried the hay lying in cut fields and gilded hurrying rivers gold, and lit the countryside with brilliance, giving beauty to everything it touched.

David sat, going back over his past; remembering past failures, past mistakes, past catastrophe. He had no confidence in himself now, and there was no Pat Lewisham to cheer him, because she was in London or at Henley or Wimbledon being a debutante. He half-envied her now; to have no need to work for anyone, to be able simply to enjoy yourself, seemed to him at that moment the most important thing in life. A paradise which he would never reach, because he had very little money and no talent.

It was a long journey, or, rather, it seemed so to David. Tina shared his sandwiches, but he had nothing for Tornado except crusts of bread, and could sense her growing hungry as the hours passed.

As they drew into Oxford Station past the cemetery and the gasworks, he began to panic. Supposing no one will have Tornado? Supposing I drop Tina on the way home and she cracks her skull? he thought frantically.

But when he was out of the town riding with Tina perched in front of him on the saddle, he felt calmer. He remembered the popular song, *What will be, will be*, and at that moment believed it. It was evening now; the hottest part of the day had passed. Farm implements rested in fields he knew, had hunted across, loved. Cows grazed, no longer besieged by flies. In farmyards motherly hens took their chicks to bed.

I'm going home, thought David, and saw the cottage soft in the evening light, his room the same as always, the Common framing a sunset of red and burnished gold.

It was a long ride; Tina fell asleep quite soon and lay across his knees, her lips drawn apart, showing small baby teeth. Tornado smelt the countryside, walked easily with a swing to her stride, as though she knew that she was going home.

They passed the Hall, the drive to the Hunt stables, where Tornado hesitated; they came to the

Common and saw the sunset, and that the gorse was still in bloom.

They rode down Church Lane, saw the cottage, Mr. Smith digging the garden, the back door open, smelt the flowers in the front border.

The church clock chimed the hour; among the graves an old man sharpened his scythe.

'Hullo. I'm back,' called David, thinking: What will they say? Will they mind? Where shall I put Tornado?

HOME AGAIN

'It's David!' cried his mother, leaving the hot iron she was using on a snow-white pillow case, so that presently a smell of scorching arose and she had to flee indoors again. 'Whatever's happened now? And you've brought Tornado too. Not that I'm not pleased to see you. Don't think that.'

His father put down his fork, dusted his hands carefully on the seat of his trousers. 'Been in a scrape?' he asked.

David dismounted. 'This is Tina,' he announced, holding out his still-asleep puppy for both of them to see. He felt the weight of the whole world hanging round his shoulders. It was one of those moments which would be with him for always, one of the worst in his life.

He couldn't look his parents in the face. He stood in the road shuffling his feet, a small boy again caught in the middle of a forbidden escapade.

'It's a long story,' he said at last. 'Do you think Mr. Jackson down at the farm would put up Tornado for the night?'

'You haven't done nothing terrible? Stolen or anything?' asked his mother with a tremble in her voice.

David was hurt by the suggestion. He thought: She should know me better than that.

'Of course not. What do you take me for?' he asked.

'I don't know what I'm saying,' she cried.

'It's worth trying Jackson,' said Mr. Smith.

David kissed Tina, buried his face in the tiny ruff of fur round her neck.

'I've lost my job. That's all,' he said. 'It's a long story.' Tornado stood eating the Smiths' neatly trimmed thorn hedge. The smell of half-dried grass drifted gently towards them from the churchyard.

'Well, I'm sure it wasn't your fault,' said his mother, rushing indoors to save her pillowcase.

Presently David was down at Mr. Jackson's farm, holding Tornado, knocking on the back door, while Tina ate bread-and-milk in the Smiths' kitchen.

He had crossed the Common, ridden down the slopes where once he had schooled Tornado.

'Well, I'm willing to help you out for a day or two,' said Mr. Jackson, and led David to an oblong paddock behind his house.

'She won't hurt the calves, will she?' he asked.

'No. She's never hurt anything,' replied David.

He watched the bay mare roll. He didn't want to return to the cottage, to have to explain, to talk and talk, to listen to his parents' opinions, his mother's indignation; though in a way he was glad enough to be home.

He crossed the Common slowly, stood looking at the landscape, before he turned down Church Lane.

He found supper ready on the table.

'I expect you'd like to eat first and talk after,' suggested his father.

His mother had found a cardboard box for Tina, in which she had put an old blanket folded four times. The puppy was asleep again, and David wished for a moment that he was Tina, well fed, asleep, with no worries and nothing to explain.

He ate the plate of fish his mother passed him with bread and butter. He drank three cups of tea.

'Well, this is how it happened . . .' he began, determined to tell his parents every detail.

The next day he caught a meandering country 'bus into Oxford and bought *Horse and Hound*. He still couldn't believe he had really lost his job. When he thought about it, his knees felt weak, and there would be a tight feeling in his throat and he'd think: But it's true, I have. I've had the sack – and the thought would make him stop in his tracks, so that once an old lady tripped over his feet in the High, and a little later he held up all the traffic in the Cornmarket.

On the way home he scanned the columns of *Horse and Hound*, marking two or three situations with a pencil.

It was another perfect day – too perfect for anxiety or sorrow. There wasn't a cloud in the sky, and Oxfordshire was a tranquil land of quiet, sunlit fields of cut hay, baled hay, hay being cut and baled and carried.

'Any luck?' asked his mother when he was home, slightly dazed from reading in the 'bus, from the crowds in Oxford, and from the journey which had revived so many old memories.

Sitting on the kitchen table he read out the advertisements he had scored with a pencil:

'Groom wanted for well-known show stable. Must be lightweight and able to school ponies. Good wage for right applicant. Wilts.'

'That's not so far away. You could come home on your day off,' said Mrs. Smith.

'Boy or girl wanted to assist in busy London riding school. Some experience essential,'

continued David.

'Groom wanted to help on farm in summer. Sole charge of point-to-pointers during winter months.'

'They simply want a labourer. You would find you were doing the whole lot winter and summer,' said Mrs. Smith. 'Milking the cows and all.'

'It's a bad time of year really,' said David. 'There's lots of jobs if only I could drive a horse-box. Otherwise most of them are for girls. If it was August I could get one in a Hunt stable tomorrow.'

He sat looking out of the window, trying to

imagine himself in London, schooling ponies in Wiltshire, hay-making.

'Isn't there another paper?' asked his mother.

'Not with the same sort of advertisements.'

'Why don't you stay here a while? You know we like having you.'

'I can't do that,' replied David, jumping off the table. 'There's Tina and Tornado to be considered too.'

'Well, Tina's all right here . . .' began his mother.

'But Tornado isn't. Mr. Jackson only wants to have her a few days,' cried David.

He climbed the stairs to his room, and in a mood of desperation replied to all three advertisements, stuffed them in his pocket and hurried to the post. He had written very little, simply stated his experience, mentioned Tornado and Tina, and said that he would only require pocket money and keep for his horse.

He felt a little happier when the letters had disappeared into the red letter-box at the end of Church Lane. But presently he met a friend of his mother's, who cried, 'Well, David, it's good to see you. Your mother said you were home on holiday. How does it feel to be back?'

His first thought was: So Mum's ashamed of me losing my job – and he felt himself reddening and all the beauty seemed to have gone from the day.

'Okay,' he muttered, hurrying away down Church Lane.

If I don't get any replies to my letters by Tuesday,

I shall go to an agency, get anything, work in a builder's yard, on a farm, anywhere as long as I can keep Tornado and Tina, he decided.

During the afternoon he took Tina with him to see Tornado. The day seemed endless. Hours seemed to have passed since he was in Oxford, yet it was the same day, and there would be tomorrow and Monday – no chance of a reply to his letters till Tuesday. And then he would have to write to say, 'Yes' or 'No.' He couldn't simply send a telegram saying, 'Coming.'

And by Tuesday Mr. Jackson might be tired of Tornado grazing in his paddock. And there would still be a great many tiresome arrangements to be made about trains . . . about an insurance card, because he had never had one, and there would be the long hack to Oxford Station again.

He felt very depressed, probably more depressed than ever before, though there had been plenty of bad moments in his life.

He remembered one of his brother's favourite quotations:

Not by Eastern windows only
    When daylight comes, comes in the light;
In front the sun climbs slow, how slowly
    But westward, look! the land is bright!

But it gave him no more hope now than his mother's 'If you do what's right, David, everything will come right. You'll see.'

That evening his father said, 'Why don't you write to Major Seely yourself? Stand up for yourself. Tell him the truth.'

'But I haven't his address,' began David.

'It can be forwarded. He must have left an address. Stands to reason a busy man like Major Seely wouldn't go away leaving no address.'

Why didn't I think of that before? wondered David.

'It seems like telling tales,' David said.

'There's nothing wrong in telling the truth,' replied his mother.

So he sat down and wrote:

'DEAR MAJOR SEELY, – I am very sorry indeed that I have lost my job, because I was very happy riding your horses and liked staying with the Bates. I am very sorry that I rode Sandstorm so badly at the last show. I think it may have been because we were very late arriving, and the night before I saw Mr. Booth selling oats and was upset.

'Thank you for teaching me so much.

'Yours very sincerely,
'DAVID SMITH'

He took the letter straight to the post because he was afraid otherwise he might change his mind and throw it on the kitchen range.

When it was safe in the box he thought: I wonder what ructions that will cause, if any – and started immediately to think of things he might have said which all sounded much better than what he had said. But now, of course, it was too late to write another letter, so he walked back along Church Lane for the fourth time that day, thinking: I'll let Tina out. Then I'll go to bed. Thank goodness today's over.

Tuesday brought him a reply from the London riding school.

'DEAR MR. SMITH [the letter ran], – We were very pleased to hear from you. We have a spare box, so could take your bay mare, and your puppy could sleep with you or in the saddle-room.

'We have a stable of thirteen at present – four at livery, the rest our own – and you would be expected to escort rides as well as doing all the usual duties. We are shorthanded, so could you start some time this week, if you like the sound of the job? We suggest a starting wage of £1 and keep for the three of you.

'Yours very sincerely,
'MURIEL PAGE.

'PS. – If you could travel to Paddington, we would provide transport for the rest of the way.
'M. P.'

David passed the letter to his mother and tried to imagine himself in London, and started to think about Pat and wonder whether he would meet her one day in one of the parks when he was escorting pupils.

'They sound in a great hurry. Are you going to take it?' asked his mother.

'Well, the others haven't answered, and Mr. Jackson wants Tornado gone by Wednesday,' replied David.

'Couldn't you put her anywhere else?'

'But the others haven't answered. I can't wait till next week's *Horse and Hound*.' He could see himself now in London, the bustle in the streets; he would be in one of the greatest capitals in the world; there must be compensations to be found for the loss of peace, fresh air, and dreaming villages.

'I can always leave if I don't like it.'

'That's no way to talk,' retorted his mother sharply. 'I don't like to hear a son of mine talking that way. Get a bad name, you will. You're lucky to get a job as it is without a reference. When I was young, if you had no reference you were as good as finished.'

He didn't listen, though. He could only think: I've got a job, anyway. For a second he forgot completely the thrill of the show ring, of the feeling that came over him waiting to go into the ring, that competing had always meant more to him than almost anything else.

Then it came to him with a rush, and, standing there, he thought: I'll never jump for England now. It's farewell show jumping. But I know now I'm not good enough. I probably never was. Devon was my testing-ground and I failed.

He sat down and wrote accepting the job at a weekly wage of £1. He looked up the trains, rang up the station from the kiosk and booked a box for Thursday. He added a postscript to his letter giving his time of arrival and posted it.

And then at last he felt free of anxiety. It's settled now. I can't go back on it, there's no sense in worrying any more, he thought, and with an effort shoved all his ambitions into the back of his mind, and thought: From now on I'm a groom in a London riding school, and that's good enough for me.

LONDON

Thursday found David in a train again, determined to like his new job, 'looking on the bright side,' as his mother said.

Tornado had been difficult to box this time, imagining, no doubt, another long journey without food and water. But David had made plans in advance, and now she munched mixture hay from a hay-net, while Tina lay on the seat watching David. His mother had packed him plenty of food. Because he had only been to London once before, to the circus in the Pony Club 'bus, he was excited. He saw it as a city of pageantry, a place where anything could happen, but most of all as a city of opportunity.

There was no one to meet him at Paddington. The horse-box was shunted down a siding and left. The station was unbearably hot; people hurried by with cases, with umbrellas and newspapers under their arms. Trains were announced over the loud-speaker. To David it all seemed very far from Oxfordshire and Devon.

He longed for a drink of lemon squash, but didn't dare to leave the box for fear of missing Muriel Page. He fell to thinking about her. Was she young or old?

Fat or thin? He imagined her slim, with neat, short hair, but when she came at last she was large, with her hair in a net.

'So you've arrived. You are David Smith? Good. The trailer's just outside the station. We'd better unbox your mare,' she said.

She looked Tornado over. 'Nice-looking mare,' she said.

The trailer was a ramshackle affair, towed by an ancient Buick which had evidently known better days. The trailer ramp swayed under Tornado's hoofs.

'We don't use it a lot now. We used to when we went to shows, but we haven't time nowadays for gadding about,' said Muriel Page.

David tried to smile; but there was a sinking feeling in his inside. Climbing into the Buick, he realised for the first time how hard it was going to be to say farewell to his ambitions.

'She'll be useful for some of our gentlemen,' said Muriel Page, starting the engine.

For a second he couldn't think who she was speaking about; then he knew it was Tornado.

'You mean my mare. But she's difficult; she was vicious when I bought her. Didn't I mention her in my letter?' asked David. He knew he had: he had written very firmly, 'She is only suitable for escorting rides.'

'Oh well, we'll soon knock some sense into her,' replied Muriel Page.

Tina looked out of the window at London. Thunder rumbled in the air. David felt stifled, too horrified by everything to speak. Gone was the golden city of opportunity. Instead, he saw Tornado becoming a tired, overworked hireling before his eyes; himself no more than a groom working among listless, overworked horses.

Lightning flashed, thunder crashed; Tina tried to hide under the seat. In the streets people ran for cover as the first rain fell.

David decided to speak. 'I'm thinking of your gentlemen's necks. The only time she was ridden by anyone besides myself, she bucked him straight off, and he was a well-known judge,' he said.

'Oh well, we'll see. But in my experience work cures most things,' replied Muriel Page.

David didn't speak again. The further they drove the drearier the streets seemed to become; then at last they turned into a mews and Muriel Page said, 'Here we are.'

Washing hung in one corner of the mews. David couldn't see any horses looking over loose-box doors; but there was a smell of horse and the sound of hoofs kicking against a wall.

'You've got a little room next to the harness-room,' announced Muriel Page.

They stepped out of the Buick into the hot afternoon. David couldn't bear to think of Major Seely's stable-yard now, though he saw for a moment the large, clean loose-boxes, the shining heads and necks and remembered the air of spaciousness and comfort which seemed to hang over everything.

'We've got a stall ready for Tornado,' said Muriel Page.

The stables were on all levels. There was electric light, peat bedding. The horses were not thin, but they looked as though they never had quite enough to eat. Tornado's stall was approached by a cobbled slope along which she walked gingerly, eyeing her surroundings with disdain. David's room was small, with a narrow bed covered by a dingy eiderdown. A wash-handstand stood in one corner, an old rickety chest-of-drawers in another.

'There's a gas-ring in the harness-room if you want to make yourself a cup of Nescafe or cocoa at any time. You have breakfast and lunch with us,' said his employer.

He combed his hair in front of the cracked mirror above the wash-handstand, while Tina explored the room. He didn't want to think any more now. He could understand Sheila's attitude at this moment: a good job was worth everything in the world; he knew that now. He remembered someone saying to him once, 'Never quarrel with your bread and butter,' and he had quarrelled with his.

He called Tina. Muriel Page was saddling a big bony grey.

'Here. You must meet my husband. Sid, come and meet David,' she called.

Sidney Page reminded David of a pointer dog; long and lean, with a nose which never missed a chance; he shook David by the hand. 'I hope you like it here,' he said.

The harness-room was full of dirty tack. The stalls needed cleaning. Tornado stood looking lost and bewildered. Her eyes seemed to reproach David when he looked at her, so that he turned away, hurrying to help his employers saddle horse after horse with dirty tack while outside the day seemed to grow hotter and fresh thunder rumbled louder even than the ceaseless roar of traffic.

At six o'clock clients started to arrive. First two girls straight from office stools. They changed in the harness-room into slacks and fashionable blouses. They were pushed on to the big grey, who stood patiently with drooping ears, and on to a roan cob which had pigeon toes and a mane which needed hogging. The horses left the yard reluctantly as a large car turned in.

'Here's Mr. Carruthers. One of our wealthiest clients,' said Muriel Page.

Pupils continued arriving until eight o'clock, when at last the yard was empty except for David, Tornado and Tina.

David had his instructions: he was to clean the fourteen stalls, fill the water-buckets, put hay in the racks. Working, he lost all sense of time, though quite soon clients started to return, handing him their mounts, saying, 'We'll be back the same time next week.' Or 'Are the Pages still out? Well, I'd better ring up.' Or 'You're new here.'

A tall girl in jodhpurs walked round the stalls until she saw Tornado.

'Huh, a new horse by the look of it. A good-looker too. I'd like to try her next week,' she said.

'She's mine. She's not for pupils, I'm afraid,' replied David.

'But I'm not a pupil. I've ridden for years. You ask Mr. Page. I ride all the horses here,' she replied.

David couldn't think of anything else to say. The day seemed suddenly unbearably long; the future stretched ahead of him, too awful to contemplate.

He began to clean another stall, and tried to remember when he had last eaten, and wondered why he had been stupid enough to take the first job offered him.

Presently the Pages came back with the beginners they had been escorting. David had finished the stalls; dusk had come, heavy with petrol fumes; the buckets were filled with water, the racks with hay.

No one suggested cleaning the tack. The horses were brushed over quickly with dandy brushes. The lights were switched off.

'I expect you're hungry. I'm afraid we can't offer you a meal, because we're going out, but there's a very good fish bar just down the road,' said Muriel Page. Her husband stood in the saddle-room drinking beer.

'Bit young to start swilling this stuff yet, aren't you, David?' he asked, showing a row of pointed decaying teeth.

David took Tina with him. The fish bar was

crowded, but presently he was seated with a plate of fish and chips, a cup of tea, vinegar, bread and butter.

He sat eating looking at the other people, with Tina on his knee sharing his supper. And I imagined I might meet Pat, he remembered, and tried to laugh, but felt only a choking sensation in his throat and a piercing sense of loss which seemed to penetrate his whole being, leaving him without hope. Sitting there with Cockney voices calling to one another, while outside 'buses passed the window, and the street lights came on to compete with the fading summer sun, he thought: All these years I've been living in a kind of dream world, where people have helped me, found me horses, given me a start. I've never realised how lucky I've been, never appreciated the meal waiting for me every evening at home, never understood that the world was really quite different; that one must fight for everything in life. Sitting there, he felt that he was seeing life as it really was for the first time; he lost all sense of time watching the people come and go, until at last a woman in a white overall tapped him on the shoulder. 'We are closing now,' she said, pointing to the clock.

It was eleven-thirty. He plunged out into the street. People walked along the pavement arm in arm; shops were lighted. Two policemen passed and stopped further down the street to try a door.

David found his way back to his room, gave Tina a drink from a bucket, undressed, fell into bed. Somewhere below him a late Tube train rumbled, from the road came a screech of brakes. He slept, dreaming he was at home, at school again, being teased by the other boys for his love of horses, until suddenly the scene changed and two policemen pursued him through the streets of London waving truncheons.

THE MEETING

The next afternoon David escorted two children on the only ponies at the Mews Stables, Cherry and Dicky.

Cherry was a chestnut mare of twelve-two and Dicky a little grey pony of just eleven hands. They were both quiet and elderly. David rode Tornado and took his pupils Timothy and Jean in the Park, around which ran a tan track provided for riders.

They were meek, well-washed children who had come accompanied by a nanny. Their riding clothes fitted perfectly and each carried an elegant riding stick. They answered politely when David spoke to them, but neither began a conversation on their own account. Tornado was strung up after nearly twenty-four hours in her stall; she was difficult to manage and started to buck the moment they reached the Park.

When she had settled a little David started to question the children.

'Do you know where the withers are?' he asked Jean.

She looked bewildered and answered in a whisper. 'No. No, I don't.'

Timothy had never heard of a throat lash, and neither knew that both their ponies were wearing snaffles.

In the evening the big grey was discovered to be lame.

'We'll have to change everyone round and use your mare. He'll do for Carruthers,' Mr. Page said.

David put down the two water buckets he was carrying.

'She isn't reliable. Really she isn't.' He knew he sounded unconvincing. He thought: What will Mum say if I lose another job? I can't go home again this time.

'Mr. Carruthers is quite a fair rider. He'll manage her all right,' replied Sid Page.

There seemed nothing more to say. David picked up the water-buckets again, and presently with a dismal heart saddled Tornado with his own saddle. Further down in another stall the big grey, who had been given by someone the unsuitable name of Imp, stood resting a swollen foreleg.

Tina followed David like a shadow, small and tireless, but with a worn look on her puppy face which made David feel guilty, because he knew now that London was no place for a sheep-dog puppy, that she didn't belong to the noisy mews and dusty streets, but to hills and wild valleys and windswept moors. He picked her up and stood stroking her until Muriel Page appeared and said, 'Seven more sets of tack to go on yet, David.'

He saddled more horses. He tried not to think

about Tornado, to forget about the prizes she had won, but quite suddenly he thought, I'd much better sell her. Perhaps Major Seely would be interested if I advertised her in *Horse and Hound*.

'Which animal did you say I was to ride tonight?' asked Mr. Carruthers, walking through the stables.

'Lead her out, David,' said Muriel Page.

He put down Tina, who was in his arms again. He felt very small suddenly looking at Mr. Carruthers, who was tall, and looked taller because he was smoking with a long cigarette-holder. He wanted to say something and was overwhelmed by a desire to cry, 'You can't ride her! She's mine!' But he felt suddenly like a small boy again, and forced back the words rising to his lips, and led out Tornado without a word.

'Quite a good sort. Where did you pick her up, Mrs. Page?' asked Mr. Carruthers.

Muriel Page answered in almost a whisper, so that David knew at once that she was telling a lie, most likely pretending she's theirs, he thought with a rush of bitterness.

'She's not an easy ride,' he told Mr. Carruthers, pulling down the stirrups.

'Don't worry about that,' replied Mr. Carruthers confidently. 'I've ridden a good many.' He mounted while David held the offside stirrup, felt in his pocket, handed David a shilling. 'Odd sort of saddle you've put on her,' he said.

'It's a jumping one,' replied David.

'Would you like it changed? We can easily change

it, sir,' said Sid Page, coming forward all bows and obsequious smiles because Mr. Carruthers was the stable's richest and most regular customer.

'No. Don't worry, Sid,' said Mr. Carruthers, kicking Tornado, riding out of the yard, while David thought: Perhaps she'll behave all right – and didn't know whether to be glad or sorry, because if she was good he was afraid she'd take more customers, more and more until she was just a tired hireling like the other horses.

'You see, David. All she needs is a little work,' said Muriel Page.

David was suddenly too sad to speak. He picked up Tina; stared at the stables, but saw only rows of jumps, himself on Tornado; the One Day Event, the last few shows he had ridden in.

'If you keep on picking up that dog, she'll give up walking altogether soon,' said Sid Page.

Three hours later the Pages and David stood in the mews yard together. Every horse was home except Tornado.

David's face was devoid of all colour. He looked like a ghost; he felt too tired to talk, too tired for anything. He could only think: Something's happened to Tornado. Imagine her galloping through London traffic riderless, see her slipping, falling, hear the screech of brakes.

'It's not the first time Mr. Carruthers has stayed out late. If he likes a horse, he's inclined to go on and on, look up his friends, get a drink from a pub. Isn't he, Muriel?' asked Sid Page, going to the harness-room to pour himself a glass of beer.

'I'm going to look for them,' said David, walking straight out of the mews, ignoring what Muriel Page called after him.

He ran to the Park, stood scanning the riding track without much hope. Why didn't I stop Mr. Carruthers riding her? Why haven't I more spirit? What's happened to me? he thought, hurrying across the Park to the West Gate, standing staring at the constant flow of traffic passing outside, suddenly deciding: I'll hand in my notice. I'm not going to stay with the Pages any longer. I've still got some of Tornado's prize-money left. I'll manage somehow. Nothing could be worse than life as it is at present.

He looked so odd standing in the gateway staring at the traffic, that a woman asked, 'Are you all right, dear? Not ill or anything?'

'I've lost a horse,' said David.

The woman looked at him as though he was mad and hurried on.

David ran into the street. The shops were closed. Workers hurried home. Outside a cinema there was a queue. David felt a little mad. His life, his whole world, seemed quite shattered. Supposing I never find her. Supposing she's already dead? he thought.

I've been too proud, he thought. I was afraid to stay at home for fear of people learning the truth. I needn't have quarrelled with Mr. Booth. At that moment he nearly walked under a 'bus.

'Why don't you look where you're going?' the driver shouted.

'It's boys like you what cause the accidents,' called a woman.

He was lost in a world which wasn't his. He didn't know where to go next, who to ask, 'Have you seen a loose horse, please?'

He started to run, dodging people on the pavement, knocking over a bicycle which leaned against a kerb. Sweat was pouring down his face now. He was wearing his old clothes; he was beginning to look like someone on the run, someone hunted.

He stopped to ask a woman selling newspapers, 'Have you seen a loose horse, please? Or a tall man riding a bay mare?'

'A horse, dearie? No I'm afraid I haven't. Thank you, sir,' she added as someone pressed threepence into her hand and took a paper. 'I should ask the police, dearie. They'll know if there's been an accident.'

He glanced at her pile of papers to make sure there wasn't a paragraph headed: *Well-known business man killed in riding accident*. But though a baby had been murdered, a woman strangled and a Countess divorced, there was no mention of an accident.

'I should. Really, I should,' added the newsvendor.

David said, 'Thank you.'

'There's a police station on the corner three streets down. Thank you, madam. Good evening, sir.'

He left her still selling papers. He stopped to wipe

his face with a handkerchief. Why didn't I think of going to the police before? he wondered. When I get back to the mews I'm going to hurl Pat's bronze horse away, he decided a moment later. It's brought me nothing but bad luck. And I'll never believe my mother's saying about if you do what's right everything will come right, not ever again, he swore to himself, looking frantically for a police station.

I must have missed it, he thought a moment later, entering a residential area, where large houses stood in gardens and the street was lined with trees. I'll look a fool if Mr. Carruthers turned up at the stables half an hour ago looking as cool as the Thames in winter, he thought.

A pram stood chained to basement railings. Two people in evening dress passed in a taxi.

'But it is,' cried a voice. 'I thought it was. Hullo, David. Whatever are you doing here?'

There were feet running towards him from behind. He didn't want to turn round; he was so afraid of being disappointed.

It can't be Pat, he thought. It can't.

'Whatever are you doing? I thought you were in Devon,' cried Pat, halting beside him, out of breath from running, looking not a day older, just the same as always except for the clothes she was wearing, which were elegant compared to the patched jeans she so often wore in the old days.

'I've lost Tornado,' replied David, and felt suddenly like breaking down altogether.

'Why are you here? Are you competing at the White City or something?' asked Pat.

'It'll take too long to explain now. I must find Tornado. Do you know where there's a police station?' David answered.

'No. But we can easily dial 999. Look. There's a kiosk just down the street,' cried Pat, and started to run ahead of him, crying back over her shoulder, 'We won't need any money if we dial 999.'

They reached the kiosk. 'You'd better do it,' said Pat.

David dialled 999. 'Fire, Police, Ambulance?' asked a voice.

'Police,' replied David, thinking suddenly: But supposing she isn't lost after all. I should have rung the stables first. But he was through now, explaining, saying, 'I've lost a bay mare. Yes. I think there's been an accident.'

Presently he was outside again talking to Pat. 'It's awful supposing she isn't lost after all,' he said.

'I think you had better tell me the whole story,' suggested Pat.

Walking along the street towards the Park, he told her everything; and as he told her a great deal of his despair ebbed away.

She listened in silence until he had finished. Then she said, 'I think you've had a perfectly awful time. I feel like ringing up Major Seely this very moment. I can't believe things like that really happen.'

'And what have you been doing? Oughtn't you

to be going somewhere? Weren't you on your way somewhere? I don't want to delay you,' said David, who felt much calmer now.

'No. I'd been out to supper. That's all. I'm not much good at being a debutante really. I'm not pretty enough. I want to see your puppy. She sounds sweet,' replied Pat.

'I'm afraid she'll get distemper. That's another thing,' he said.

'Haven't you had her inoculated?'

'She isn't old enough.'

'What did the police say?'

'They're going to make inquiries. They'll notify the stables if they discover anything,' replied David.

'Poor Tornado. London can't be her cup of tea.'

'It isn't. She's beginning to look like a captive animal. And her coat's dull. A few more weeks at the Mews Stables and you would hardly recognise her,' David said. 'But I'm going. I decided that about an hour ago. I'm not staying. It's too awful. I'm going to get another job,' he added.

'A jumping job,' cried Pat. 'You can't take another dead-end job. You're going to jump for England. You know that.'

His confidence was coming back. He was certain now that he could never say farewell to show jumping. He was determined now to make another beginning.

'How much farther is it to the stables?' asked Pat.

'Are you coming the whole way?'

'Of course.'

He was ashamed to let her see his squalid room. He didn't want her to see how low he had fallen. He didn't want her to see Sid Page with his fingers stained with nicotine and his beery eyes; nor fat, bossy Muriel Page; nor the thirteen tired hirelings.

'Oughtn't you to be somewhere?' he asked again.

'I'm coming to see your puppy and to find out about Tornado. Don't forget she was once more or less half mine,' replied Pat firmly, as though she could read David's thoughts.

They hurried across the Park, and to David life was suddenly worth living again, though he couldn't understand himself. How had he got into such a mess? Why had he stood calmly by while Mr. Carruthers had ridden away on Tornado? Why had he ever taken the job, for that matter?

'I've been mad, haven't I?' he asked Pat.

'You mean getting in such a mess? Yes. You have rather.'

He had time to look at her now. She was wearing a checked summer dress, toeless sandals; her hair was casually done. She wasn't so different from the Pat who had run the Elm Tree Riding School as his partner.

'I've done silly things too. I suppose it's all part of growing up,' she said.

'But I've been so feeble, sort of lukewarm,' he said.

She didn't contradict him. They reached the other side of the Park. The roads were much quieter. The sky was streaked with red and gold. At that moment

London looked beautiful – dreamy, mysterious, touched with gold, almost the capital David had imagined when he took the job at the Mews Stables.

They passed the fish bar where David had eaten on his first evening.

'I hope Tina's all right,' said David, remembering how she had sat on his knee and shared his supper. 'I left her in my room.'

'It would be awful if she was lost too,' Pat replied.

And now the awfulness of the whole day came back to him: the dreary ride in the afternoon round and round the Park, the endless stalls to be cleaned, the moment when the Pages had decided that Mr. Carruthers was to ride Tornado. How he had felt watching Tornado go out of the yard; the hours of waiting for her to come back, the realisation that something had happened, the moment when he had left the mews, ignoring the Pages, hating the whole world.

He could see the entrance to the mews. Children were playing outside, though it was dark and quite late. Somewhere music drifted from an open window.

'We're nearly there. I don't know what sort of reception I shall get. I left without a word,' he said.

'I suppose they're paying you almost nothing. You always have needed someone nannying you. You're hopeless on your own,' said Pat with a grin.

They were there now. He could see the lights were on in the Pages' little untidy flat above the stables, which always seemed to smell of stale tobacco smoke, gas and wet clothes.

'Be prepared for the worst,' he told Pat.

'I am,' she said.

If only Tornado's there already, he thought, turning into the mews. With Pat to back me up, it'll be easy enough to give in my notice. If only she's there.

'I'M NOT STAYING'

But she wasn't. Her stall stood dirty and empty. The harness-room was piled with dirty tack and smelt of beer; a dirty glass stood on the window-sill.

David let out Tina. 'Oh, isn't she sweet?' cried Pat.

'I'm not going to show you my room; it's too awful,' said David.

He felt exhausted again now. His exaltation at meeting Pat was wearing off. Reality stared him in his face.

'Was Mr. Carruthers the sort of man to steal a horse?' asked Pat.

'Gosh! No. Look. That's his car,' replied David, pointing to the enormous Jaguar which stood parked in the mews.

'Well, I suggest we start on the hospitals. The London Clinic first.'

'The hospitals?' cried David.

'Mr. Carruthers must be in one. And as he's rich, if he had any choice, he most likely chose the London Clinic. Where's the telephone?' replied Pat.

'What about the Pages?'

'I'm not going to bother about them,' cried Pat.

'But what are you going to say?'

'I'm going to find out exactly what did happen.'

The London Clinic said that they had admitted Mr. Carruthers, who was suffering from slight shock after a riding accident. He had left at nine o'clock. They knew only that he had been thrown by a dangerous horse. They refused to disclose his home address.

'Now we'll have to find his telephone number,' said Pat, replacing the receiver and picking up one of the Pages' directories. 'By the sound of him, I should say South Kensington.'

David couldn't understand Pat's remarks. But he was happy to have her take charge.

'Here we are. I bet that's him. Do you happen to know his initials?' she asked a few seconds later.

'No. He called Mr. Page Sid, but he was very much the gentleman – at least, the Pages seemed to think so.'

'Well, I don't. If he had any manners at all, he would have rung up here from the London Clinic.'

'But perhaps he did.'

'Well, you said you waited three hours, didn't you?' asked Pat, dialling a number on the dial David couldn't understand at all, since it seemed to be composed mainly of letters.

'He's gone out – obviously night-clubbing. The maid says he's had a nasty accident. A nasty horse bucked him off in a Park somewhere or other. I expect he's night-clubbing by now,' said Pat a few minutes later.

'Where do we go from here?' wondered David.

Pat started to walk round the saddle-room biting her nails. 'I'm surprised the police haven't found her by now,' she said presently.

David could hear footsteps outside.

'Is that you, David? Wherever have you been?' called Muriel Page.

'Looking for Tornado.'

Muriel Page was in her dressing-gown.

'I can't understand what's happened to her,' she said in an exasperated voice. 'I shall never forgive you if she's thrown Mr. Carruthers.'

'And we'll never forgive you for letting him ride her,' cried Pat.

'Who's this girl?' cried Muriel Page.

'Miss Lewisham,' replied David stiffly. Standing there, he suddenly discovered that he hated Muriel Page to an extent which shocked him. 'As soon as I've found her I'm leaving,' he announced, feeling suddenly strong enough to face anything.

'You have to give a week's notice.'

'Well, I am not going to. I'm not staying another hour once I have my horse.'

'You'll have no reference.'

'I don't care.'

The telephone rang. Pat picked up the receiver. 'Yes, it is. Oh good. You've found her, then. The Brewery Stables. Where did you say? Yes. I know. I'm sorry to have given you so much trouble. Yes. Well, that's something. Thank you very much.'

She put down the receiver. 'The police have traced

Tornado. She's in a brewery stable roughly seven miles from here. She seems to have crossed most of London. They want us to leave her there till morning,' she said.

'Is she hurt?' cried David.

'They don't think so.'

He stood there in a daze, anxiety ebbing away. He picked up Tina.

'Well, that's something. Now perhaps you'll change your mind about this nonsense about leaving,' said Muriel Page.

David was too tired to argue. He felt now that he only wanted to sleep on a comfortable bed, but his bed wasn't comfortable. He hated his room. He had risen at six that morning; he had worked all day; now he only heard Pat talking through a mist.

'He certainly is. He's coming to spend the night at my aunt's. I'm ringing for a taxi now,' she said.

After that there seemed to be an argument. And at some time Mr. Page appeared.

'He can't leave, can he?' cried Muriel Page. 'I won't have it.'

'A week's notice is the rule,' agreed Sid Page.

'Go and pack, David. Would you like me to help?' asked Pat.

He took Tina with him, bundled his few belongings into his suitcase. Pat was waiting outside the door. 'What awful people they are. Come on. Here's the taxi.'

A moment later they were travelling through an almost deserted London.

'Won't your aunt mind?' asked David.

'No. She's the best-natured person in the world. Nothing upsets Aunt Jill,' Pat replied. 'You can have the spare room. It's always ready for guests.'

He wanted to thank Pat for everything. He tried to make up a little speech beginning, 'But for you . . .' But words wouldn't come. Nothing made sense any more. For a moment he imagined himself home, then he fell sideways asleep. He was too tired to eat. Aunt Jill appeared through a mist in a dressing-gown.

Pat shepherded him up lushly carpeted stairs into a room with flowered chintz curtains. She put Tina in an armchair, placing a blanket on it first.

'I should fall into bed,' she said.

'But I haven't washed.'

'Do it in the morning.'

The room made him think of rooms he had seen in films. He undressed, put on his pyjamas. Once in bed, he seemed to be floating on a cloud. He felt Tina jump on to his feet before he fell asleep.

The sun wakened him. The room bewildered him until he remembered. He lay then feeling like someone in a book, out of this world, staring at the elegant dressing-table, seeing for the first time that there was a green basin, feeling like a millionaire, a king, a film star.

Tina had gone. He imagined Pat walking her, London alive outside, Tornado champing in the brewery stables.

Ten minutes later he was walking downstairs. He could smell bacon cooking and realised suddenly that he was ravenous. He thought: What do I do now? I wish Pat would appear. I can't even remember what her aunt looks like.

He had put on his best riding clothes, looked out of the window of his room, and seen that in this part of London there was little traffic besides a horse and milk trolley, taxis, an occasional car.

He thought: What a lot I shall have to tell Mum when I get home. Perhaps she'll stop hating Pat now. Or will she be furious at me giving up my job?

Pat came in with Tina as he reached the hall. 'Hullo. You're just in time for breakfast. Tina was whining, so I took her out for a run. She *is* sweet.'

Aunt Jill presided over the breakfast table. 'You look better this morning,' she told David.

'You were hardly *compos mentis* last night,' said Pat.

'What dreadful people you've been working for,' remarked Aunt Jill, pouring David an enormous cup of coffee.

He didn't want to be pitied, so he changed the subject.

'How do we get to Tornado?' he asked.

'On a 'bus. We've worked it all out,' replied Pat.

He ate a great deal, though he felt like sticking halfway through the coffee, because until now he had always had tea for breakfast.

'How are you going to manage to get the horse home? I'm afraid I haven't got room for it here. Pat darling, I must fly if I'm going to call at Fortnum's on my way to that fashion show,' said Aunt Jill.

David tried to work out a plan.

'You can do anything you like except stable your horse in my house, David. Stay as long as you like,' said Aunt Jill as she left.

'We'd better ring up the station and see what they can do about a train for Tornado,' said Pat. 'Then I'll ring up home and say she'll be in the park till further notice. Swallow's there, so she won't be alone.'

'Will that be all right?'

'Why on earth not? Come on. Let's telephone.'

They managed to arrange a horse-box for three o'clock that afternoon. Then David collected his suitcase and they set off for the brewery stable, taking it in turn to carry Tina.

'It's lucky I met you,' said David.

'I've been hoping you'd write for ages. I thought you'd write to say "Thank you" for the horse. I thought of calling on your parents once to ask how you were, but I know your mother doesn't like me,' replied Pat, staring away down the street along which they were walking. 'I wanted to know how you were doing; then I saw the piece about you and Sandstorm in *Horse and Hound*, and knew you were all right, that you were going to jump for England one day just as you always said. You can imagine the shock I got when I met you last night looking on the verge of suicide. I couldn't think what you were doing. Here's our 'bus stop,' she added, stopping.

'I've been pretty stupid really. Somehow I didn't think you wanted to go on knowing me. You going to London and all,' said David.

'That wasn't all me. My parents have wanted me to for ages. They were afraid I'd turn into a Muriel Page,' replied Pat.

'But you couldn't. Nothing could make you look like her,' cried David.

They climbed on a 'bus, clambered up the stairs.

'I love travelling right on the top,' Pat said, thinking: He's changed. I don't know how quite, but he has.

I still don't understand her, decided David, but then I never have.

'Until I met you I had really said farewell to show jumping. Now I know I never can,' David told her. 'I thought I was no good.'

'Even after you'd seen that bit about you in *Horse and Hound*? Major Seely's the man I can't understand. Surely he must realise Mr. Booth's crooked,' Pat answered.

They changed 'buses. The day was warming up. Tired shoppers turned homeward laden with baskets, shuffling aching feet.

'I never got to know him very well, you know. I wasn't there long enough,' David said.

They sat in silence, each thinking about David's adventures, until Pat said, 'Anyway, if you want a reference, Daddy will give you one. Surely you've always known that. For that matter, I bet he could find you a jolly good job if you asked him.'

'I'll remember that.'

'This is where we get off again,' said Pat.

The stables were at the end of a dead-end street. Clean and airy, high-ceilinged and well-ventilated, they were a pleasant contrast to the Mews Stables. A little man in breeches and gaiters greeted them. 'You've come for the little mare, then. We put her in the box at the end. She seemed a bit reckless. I'm afraid your saddle's in poor shape,' he said.

My saddle! thought David. He had forgotten about it, never considered that it might be damaged beyond repair.

'The girth's broke on one side too,' said the stableman. Tornado looked very small in the old fashioned box obviously built for an enormous dray horse. She was turning round and round, churning up the straw. She whinnied when she saw David.

'I'll get her harness for you,' the man said.

'She's been beautifully groomed,' Pat said. 'Have you any money? We must give the stables a pound. Look at all the hay she's got.'

They mended the girth with string. The tree of the saddle was broken; the reins had lost their buckle; one saddle flap was torn.

'Poor David, your lovely saddle,' said Pat.

They thanked the stable-man, gave him a pound and said, 'For her keep and your trouble and everything.'

David mounted, rode out of the yard feeling like a free man. Tornado was sound; she walked with pricked ears. He had met Pat again and they were

friends. He was never going back to the Mews
Stables; with Colonel Lewisham's help, he'd find
another job; hope ran through him like water down
a thirsty throat, giving him strength to begin again.
Third time lucky, he told himself, beginning to
whistle softly.

'Hi! Wait for me,' cried Pat. 'Remember I've got
your suitcase as well as Tina, and I'm not on the
'bus yet.'

He took the case. 'If you hadn't put on a dress,
you could have ridden,' he told her.

'I've only got dresses in London. How was I to
know I was going to meet you and Tornado yesterday?'

'I'm like a bad penny. I always turn up again.
We're both bad pennies, aren't we, Tornado?' he
asked his mare, leaning forward to stroke her neck.

Pat thought he looked like he always had again
now. Last night he had seemed suddenly old, but
now the furrows had gone from his forehead, his
hair was falling forward as it always had, and he was
laughing, smiling like he had in the days when they
had started their riding school.

She thought of him riding home from Oxford
and how quiet the landscape would be after
London, and how untroubled.

She thought of the cottage kitchen, which always
seemed to smell of pastry, and saw Mrs. Smith
rushing out to greet him. She remembered all the
good things Maudie had said about David when he
had gone, and how her father's stud groom said,

'The yard isn't the same place without David. He's a good lad, and that's no mistake.'

'I don't like to ride while you walk,' David said.

'Here's my 'bus. See you at Paddington,' cried Pat, seizing the suitcase and dashing away down the road, thinking: Everyone likes David except awful people like the Pages, and even they didn't want him to leave.

A LETTER

They met at Paddington. The horse-box was waiting down a siding.

'I seem to spend all my time putting poor Tornado on trains,' David said.

'While I was waiting for you I rang up home. It's all right. You can put Tornado in the park, and Daddy says of course he'll write you a reference,' Pat said.

'Thank you very much.'

'So I shouldn't rush into a job. You've got your prize-money. Surely you can stay at home for a bit.'

He didn't like to admit that he was bored at home after a few days, or that his parents liked to think all their children were working, that they would be worried if the neighbours started to talk, saying, 'I wonder why David Smith's at home. Why, only a few days ago he was on holiday. Don't say he's lost his new job already.'

David knew Pat had never lived in his world. Nobody bothered whether she was working or not. Nobody cared. She doesn't really know what life is like, he thought. She's never wondered how she's going to buy the next meal. He felt much older than her now, almost grown-up as he boxed Tornado.

She gave him Tina, his suitcase.

'Thank you for everything. I don't know how to thank you enough,' he said.

'Don't then. It's nothing. I may come down next week-end; if I do, perhaps we can ride together,' she answered.

He saw them riding together down lanes they had both known since childhood.

'Oh, good. It'll seem like old times,' he said.

'Exactly,' replied Pat.

They stood together saying nothing until an engine was hooked to the horse-box.

'Time to say good-bye. All the best,' said David then.

'Yes. Regards to your parents. Let me kiss Tina good-bye,' answered Pat.

She said good-bye to Tornado and Tina, pushed her chestnut hair back from her eyes.

'Well, look after yourself,' she said.

He climbed into the groom's compartment. 'Pity you aren't coming too. It'll be cooler at the Hall than up here,' David said.

The box was moving now. Pat stood waving.

'Thanks again,' shouted David.

'Don't mention it,' cried Pat.

He watched her out of the window, still waving, standing quite alone on the siding now.

Then he started to think of arriving home. What would his mother say this time? Would his father be furious? I've lost two jobs in a very short time, he thought, and nobody else in the family has ever lost a job. I shall soon be the black sheep. He looked at his saddle again, at his broken reins, and the wave of elation on which he had ridden all morning became less buoyant.

He thought: Pat is such an optimist. She brushes aside the difficulties in life as though they don't count. His future looked very ugly to him now. He was beginning to dread his approaching appearance in his home village, and he started to wonder how he was to set about acquiring another job.

So while Pat rushed back to her aunt's to change before a lunch date, David sat glumly in the horse-box, watching his future grow blacker each moment before his eyes.

I ought to sell Tornado. I should never have bought Tina, he thought. They're both a handicap when it comes to jobs. If you're a girl it's different. You can help a little in the house, look after children, have pocket-money, and your horse is welcome. People expect girls to have horses, but not someone like me. Travelling swiftly between Slough and Maidenhead, he started to feel bitter.

One needs money to get on, the right background, he thought angrily. The dice have always been loaded against me. One can't pretend not to notice the fact for ever when it's staring you in the face all the time.

The train stopped at Reading. He got out, bought himself chocolate, potato crisps, a pork pie, which he shared with Tina. Pat's got people like her Aunt Jill behind her, he thought, and saw his mother's work-worn hands kneading pastry. It's different for her.

He had never thought like that before. His successful elder brothers despised people who blamed circumstances for failure in life. But sometimes his father would say, 'Oh, well. It's different for them,' alluding to someone like the Lewishams. Now he agreed wholeheartedly with his father, ignoring the fact that he had Tornado and his pony Folly to call his own, that he had started from scratch and yet been able to jump his own horse at some of the biggest shows in England.

When they reached Oxford, he thought again: Yes. The dice have always been loaded against me. All my life I have had to fight.

Riding once more through Oxford with Tina on his knees again he admitted defeat. He was too angry and miserable now to enjoy the sunshine, or the well-remembered fields they passed presently. The horrible reality that he was jobless stared him in the face, obscuring the sun, killing the beauty of tall trees against blue sky, making the whole landscape hideous to David, making him think for the second time in about two weeks: I'm returning home a failure.

He tried to imagine jobs he might take, but now he couldn't think anyone would wish to employ someone like himself, plus a dog and horse.

I shall have to sell Tornado, he decided, and it

was a relief to have made the decision. But that will take time, he thought a moment later. I shall have to advertise her. People will want to ride her. And supposing she bucks them all off? Whichever way he turned, there seemed to be an obstacle facing him; and each moment Church Lane was drawing nearer and he would have to tell his parents what had happened, and hear the comments of his neighbours. He could imagine them saying things like, 'Fancy you back already, David' and 'When are you going to get fixed up with another job? Why don't you try the Labour Exchange?' as the weeks passed and he was still at home.

And once Mum was proud of me, he remembered. How she used to boast! Now people will be able to have their own back.

Presently he turned down the drive to the Hall. Swallow grazed alone in the park. He took off his broken saddle, called to Swallow, let Tornado go, watched the surprise in her eyes, until she rolled, over and over, again and again as though to shake the dust and dirt of London from her bay coat for ever and ever.

He thought: Lucky Tornado, living in the present, never dreaming that she may be sold. He turned back along the drive, because suddenly there were tears blinding him and he was ashamed of them, because he was almost grown up. Something told him then that if he sold Tornado he would give up the struggle, fade into obscurity, whatever Pat might say.

He watched Tina running ahead, smelt the rhodo-
dendrons on each side of the gravelled drive,
thought: Dad will have just got in. They'll be having
tea.

He met no one as he walked home, and the nearer
he drew to Church Lane the slower his steps became.
The cornflowers were out in the garden. Today the
back door was shut, but from the kitchen came
the smell of fish cooking.

London seemed far away now. He could hardly
believe that he had spent the morning with Pat. He
picked up Tina. He could hear the wireless now
blaring out music into the summer's evening.

They'll never understand what it was like at the
Mews Stables, he thought. He walked up the path,
opened the back door, said, 'I'm back again.'

They both jumped up; his mother upset her cup
of tea.

'What have you done?' she cried.

'Where have you sprung from?' asked his father.

He kissed his mother's forehead, said, 'I'm sorry.
I couldn't stand it. You've never seen such a place,
and they started to use Tornado for the pupils . . .'

'Well, sit down and have some tea,' his mother
said. 'I'll make a fresh pot.'

'No. Don't bother.'

'You'll be getting a bad name, David. Couldn't
you stick it any longer? You mustn't put your horse
before yourself,' said Mr. Smith.

'Well, now I'm going to sell Tornado. I've made
up my mind,' David said, and felt like weeping as he

sat down at the familiar table between his bewildered parents.

'Sell her? But she means more to you than anything, that horse,' cried Mrs. Smith.

He remembered buying Tornado, breaking her in, her first show; he saw her bay head and large, kind eyes watching for him in the mornings, whinnying when she heard his footstep; he remembered hunting her, her speed, her scope in jumping. But I'm going to sell her, he decided. Life isn't like I thought. There's no room for Tornado in my life any more.

'Switch off that darned wireless, Mother,' said his father.

'Are you short of cash, then?' he asked David.

'No. Not yet, anyway.' David wanted to be alone now; he wanted to think things out, reshape his life.

'Your puppy's grown,' said his mother.

'Well, eat something, David,' said Mr. Smith.

He forced himself to eat. Outside the church bells pealed. 'Bell-ringing practice,' said his father.

He was home, but in a sense it wasn't home any more. The air was sad with disappointment. At this moment his parents seemed almost like strangers. The same clock ticked on the mantelpiece; the same flowered curtains met the same brown window-sill; the same black kettle sang on the black range. The cottage was the same as it had always been as long as he could remember, but always before his parents had been behind him. Now he could sense their disapproval; they were ashamed of their youngest son.

Forcing fish down his throat, he thought: Why did I come home? There must be somewhere else I could have stayed. Where do people go who have no home? I could have pretended to my parents that I was still in London, invented a story.

'Well, what are you going to do now? Where's Tornado?' asked his father.

'In the park. I met Pat in London. She's been wonderful.'

'What, Pat Lewisham?'

'Yes.' He realised now how wonderful Pat had been. 'She took me to stay with her aunt. She saw me on the train this morning,' he said, and now the whole episode seemed like a dream, a fairy tale. Pat thinks life should be beautiful, he thought; soon she'll be my only friend, or, rather, the only person I can turn to for help, the only one who will understand.

'How did you meet? Did you look up Susan while you were in London?' asked his mother.

It never occurred to him to look up his sister, probably because they had nothing in common.

'You might have gone to her for help.'

'But I didn't go to Pat. I met her in the street.' How fantastic it all seems now, thought David.

'Don't bother the boy, Mother. He looks to me as though he needs a good night's rest. Everything will look different in the morning,' said Mr. Smith.

'I'm sorry. I couldn't have stayed there even if the Pages hadn't put Mr. Carruthers on Tornado. Mum, you should have seen what I had for lunch and breakfast — cold pilchards, corned beef and old spuds. And I had to get my own supper. I never finished till ten o'clock at night, and was up at six each morning. I couldn't have stuck it,' David said, seeing all the horrors of the Mews Stables before his eyes again — the endless stalls to be cleaned, the dejected horses, fat Muriel Page and her lean, shifty husband swilling beer. 'Their place smelt like a pub does in the early morning,' he added.

'Then you were right to come home. I wasn't happy about you going, was I, Dad? I can't help wondering what the neighbours will say, though — you back in less than a week and all,' said his mother.

David had Tina on his knee now. He couldn't eat any more. He fed his puppy with bits from his plate.

'Let them talk. Some of them haven't so much to talk about anyway,' said Mr. Smith.

In a sense, the worst was over now: he had told his parents. But he was still jobless. Dreadful days stretched ahead; tomorrow he must begin: advertise Tornado, perhaps advertise himself.

'Young professional rider seeks post. Experienced. Good worker. Excellent reference. David Smith, 10 Church Lane.'

He needn't mention Tina till everything was almost settled — that is, if anyone answered his advertisement.

Tornado, he could say, was a promising jumper and One Day Event horse. He could list her winnings. People must have seen her. The trouble would start when prospective buyers desired a ride. But perhaps he could sell her over the telephone. He had heard of people buying horses like that without seeing them. But would that be honest? he wondered, seeing himself boxing Tornado once more, but now for the last time. He could feel tears rising behind his eyes; in a moment he would be crying; he stood up ashamed, clutched Tina, while an awful wave of despair engulfed him completely, leaving no room for anything else. Once he had believed that dreadful things didn't happen as long as you were honest, worked, told the truth. Now he didn't believe anything – least of all that if you did what was right everything came right in the end.

He felt his mother put her arm round his shoulder. 'You're ill, David. That's what you are,' she said.

But he knew he wasn't – not physically, anyway. He just felt as though there was nothing left of his dreams. 'I'm all right, Mum.'

The church bells had stopped ringing now. He thought of Tornado with Swallow in the park; like old times, he thought. If only we had never given up the riding school. I could have gone on alone. Why didn't I?

'What are you going to do next?' asked his father.

'Advertise myself and Tornado, I suppose.'

'I've just remembered something,' said his mother. 'That letter for David. Where did we put it, Dad? We didn't have your address. You never left it.'

A letter, thought David. Nobody ever writes to me.

'It had a Devon postmark,' said his mother, routing among the collection of vases, David's past trophies, and a mug saying *From Bexhill* which stood in a cluttered disorder on the mantelpiece.

It won't be good news, thought David. It can't be from Major Seely. Perhaps Sheila's invited me to her wedding. All the same, his heart had started pounding with excitement and with the first gleaming rays of hope.

'It came just two days after you left. Perhaps I put it on the dresser,' said Mrs. Smith.

David started to search too now – frantically, as though his life depended on the letter.

Tina, imagining a game was afoot, began to rush round the kitchen yapping joyfully.

'Did you take it upstairs, do you think, Mother? Maybe you put it in his room,' said Mr. Smith.

David ran upstairs with Tina yapping at his heels. Then he heard his mother call:

'David, I've found it.'

I mustn't hope, he thought. It's sure to be bad news. He ran downstairs, took the letter, looked at the postmark.

'I think it's from Major Seely,' he said.

His hands were trembling. He tore the envelope open and read:

'DEAR DAVID, – I was shattered to receive your letter. But first let me apologise for not having

465

written to you before. Unfortunately, I was rather ill on first arriving in France and I could make neither head nor tail of Mr. Booth's letters. My wife and I were very surprised, however, when we received one from him saying you had left of your own free will.

'As you may guess, we came to the conclusion that you didn't like being at Hampton House and that there was nothing we could do about it.

'But, to cut a long story short, now we're home and, with the co-operation of Jimmy and Sheila and Olive, have got to the bottom of things. Mr. Booth has gone, and if by any chance you're free and can forgive me for the shocking way you've been treated, would you consider returning at increased pocket money of £2 a week and, of course, with your puppy and Tornado?

'Hoping you'll say yes, I've entered Jolly Roger for a One Day Event and I've been jumping Sand-storm on the lunge and she is in great form.

'Kindest regards from us both,

'Yours very sincerely,
'RICHARD JOHN SEELY.'

'Look,' cried David. 'Look,' handing the letter to his parents, thinking: Everything's all right. I needn't sell Tornado. I'm not a failure after all. I can go on show jumping, One Day Eventing. . . . I can begin again.

'It's just as I always say. If you do what's right

everything will come right in the end,' said Mrs. Smith, handing back the letter with eyes full of tears.

'Well done, son,' said his father, reading the letter slowly, reading it twice, three times, looking at David as though he was seeing him for the first time.

THE VISITOR

Next morning David rose early and, with Tina at his heels, ran to the nearest kiosk to put through a call to Devon.

Major Seely was fetched from his bath.

'I'm sorry to telephone you so early, sir,' said David, 'but I only saw your letter last night.'

'Are you coming back to us?'

'Yes. I'd like to very much.'

A great many pleasantries followed.

'Well, come as soon as you can. I'll put a cheque for your horsebox in the post this morning,' said Major Seely as the pips sounded for the second time.

David walked back to the cottage seeing himself, as he had so many times before, riding for England. Nothing seemed too difficult for him now, nothing impossible.

The past few weeks were nothing to him now except a bad patch in his life which was over. When he met Mrs. Emmett, whom he had known as long as he could remember, he found it easy to smile and ask after her health and tell her that he was returning to Devon very soon.

He felt free — freer than he had for months. He

thought: While I'm here I'll go over to Milton and have a look at Folly. How lucky I am to have a horse, a pony and a dog!

His mother had cooked an extra-special breakfast when he returned to the cottage, and the sad atmosphere of the evening before had gone, to be replaced by a feeling which David could only describe as similar to that which always hung over them at Christmas or on a birthday.

After breakfast, when he was upstairs combing his hair before he walked across the Common to the Hall, his mother called, 'There's a visitor to see you, David.'

And now he could hear Pat laughing in the kitchen.

He ran downstairs.

She was standing talking to his mother. 'I've heard your good news. Isn't it wonderful? I came back last night. London was stifling,' she said, turning to David.

She was dressed in riding clothes. To have her there was like putting the clock back six months.

'I thought we might go for a ride this morning. What do you think?'

A moment later they were walking across the Common together.

'I couldn't believe Major Seely had really given you the sack when you told me. Now you'll be all right,' Pat said.

'What about you?'

'I shall stay a bit longer in London. Then I may

take a job. I don't know really. I haven't decided,' Pat said, starting to chew a blade of grass. 'Perhaps I'll go abroad. We might meet at a horse show. Wouldn't that be fun? Supposing we met in Paris? I should feel so smart knowing you if you were jumping for England. I should feel very proud.'

'Do you remember me schooling Tornado up and down here?' asked David.

'Yes. Doesn't it seem years ago?'

'Yes. Years.'

They walked on together, and it seemed to David, that he had almost everything he could ask for in life, that in a matter of a few hours his life had somersaulted from disaster to success.

And I nearly gave up, he remembered, but, as Mum would say, everything has turned out for the best in the end.

'I shall come and see you some time in Devon. I've got friends near you I can stay with,' said Pat.

'That'll be lovely,' replied David, imagining Pat 'nannying' him as she had in the old days, biting her nails and tearing her hair with excitement.

Part **1** of the City Cats Series

Colin Dann

King of the Vagabonds

By the creator of the award-winning
THE ANIMALS OF FARTHING WOOD

Incredible animal adventures starring
furry felines, Sammy and Pinkie...

'Don't stray into Quartermile Field. Any animal with sense avoids the spot,' warns Sammy's mother. But Sammy is curious - about the Field, and about his father, the fierce, wild father he's never met.

  Then one day Sammy discovers that his father has returned. And determined to track him down, Sammy sets off towards the strange, wild land of Quartermile Field - and into a very different and dangerous world...

THE CITY CATS SERIES by Colin Dann
in paperback from Red Fox

KING OF THE VAGABONDS
ISBN 0 09 921192 0   £3.50

THE CITY CATS
ISBN 0 09 921202 1   £3.50

and coming soon!
COPYCAT ISBN 0 09 21212 9

Part **2** of the City Cats Series

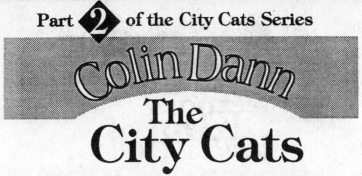

The City Cats

By the creator of the award-winning
THE ANIMALS OF FARTHING WOOD

Incredible animal adventures starring
furry felines, Sammy and Pinkie...

Scavenging for food in the back of a van leads Sammy
and Pinkie into trouble when they suddenly find
themselves trapped - and travelling. They arrive in a
scary place, full of fast cars and strange people, but a
park provides shelter and a fat pigeon makes a fine meal.
Sammy's still the proud King of the Vagabonds and
Pinkie's looking forward to having a family. As big city
cats they've finally found the good life. But how long can
it last...?

THE CITY CATS SERIES by Colin Dann
in paperback from Red Fox

KING OF THE VAGABONDS
ISBN 0 09 921192 0   £3.50

THE CITY CATS
ISBN 0 09 921202 1   £3.50

and coming soon!
COPYCAT ISBN 0 09 21212 9

Redwall Map and Riddler
BRIAN JACQUES

Get ready to take the Redwall Map and Riddler challenge - it's the ultimate Redwall adventure!

The Redwall Map is a perfect reading companion for all fans - old and new - of the legendary Tales of Redwall by Brian Jacques. Beautifully illustrated in full colour, it lavishly charts all the places, landmarks and sites made famous by the Redwall stories.

And there's more!

With the map comes The Redwall Riddler, a quiz book crammed full of riddles to unravel, quick-fire questions, baffling word puzzles and cryptic conundrums. So now you can test your Redwall know-how with tricky brain-teasers like these:

✿ In REDWALL, Cluny the Scourge only has one eye. How is he reputed to have lost the other?

Answer:
✿ In battle with a pike

Redwall Map and Riddler by Brian Jacques
Red Fox, £4.99 ISBN 0 09 925611 8

THE MENNYMS
BOOKS
SYLVIA WAUGH

'Brilliant' *Independent*

'Weird, witty and wonderfully original' *Guardian*

'Extraordinary' *Sunday Telegraph*

Sylvia Waugh's extraordinary debut novel about the Mennyms, a family of life-size ragdolls, won the 1994 Guardian Children's Fiction Award.

The Mennyms - Granny and Granpa, Vinetta and Joshua and their five children - are far from ordinary. They've kept a secret hidden for forty years, a secret to which nobody has even come close. Until now...

THE MENNYMS   ISBN 0 09 930167 9 £2.99

MENNYMS IN THE WILDERNESS ISBN 0 09 942421 5 £2.99

MENNYMS UNDER SIEGE   ISBN 0 09 955761 4 £2.99

MENNYMS ALONE   ISBN 0 09 95577 1 £3.50

and coming soon!
MENNYMS ALIVE   ISBN 0 09 955781 9 £3.50

The MENNYMS books by Sylvia Waugh
Out now in paperback from Red Fox

❖ Tales of Redwall ❖
BRIAN JACQUES

'Not since Roald Dahl have children filled their shelves so compulsively' *The Times*

An award-winning, best-selling series from master storyteller, Brian Jacques.
Discover the epic Tales of Redwall adventures about Redwall Abbey - and beyond!

- **Martin the Warrior** 0 09 928171 6
- **Mossflower** 0 09 955400 3
- **Outcast of Redwall** 0 09 960091 9
- **Mariel of Redwall** 0 09 992960 0
- **The Bellmaker** 0 09 943331 1
- **Salamandastron** 0 09 914361 5
- **Redwall** 0 09 951200 9
- **Mattimeo** 0 09 967540 4
- **The Pearls of Lutra** 0 09 963871 1

❖

Tales of Redwall by Brian Jacques
Out now in paperback from Red Fox priced £4.99

ADVENTURE

The Adventure Series by Willard Price

Read these exciting stories about Hal and Roger Hunt and their search for wild animals. Out now in paperback from Red Fox at £3.50

Amazon Adventure

Hal and Roger find themselves abandoned and alone in the Amazon Jungle when a mission to explore unchartered territory of the Pastaza River goes off course...
0 09 918221 1

Underwater Adventure

The intrepid Hunts have joined forces with the Oceanographic Institute to study sea life, collect specimens and follow a sunken treasure ship trail...
0 09 918231 9

Arctic Adventure

Olrik the eskimo and his bear, Nanook, join Hal and Roger on their trek towards the polar ice cap. And with Zeb the hunter hot on their trail the temperature soon turns from cold to murderously chilling...
0 09 918321 8

Elephant Adventure

Danger levels soar with the temperature for Hal and Roger as they embark upon a journey to the equator, charged with the task of finding an extremely rare white elephant...
0 09 918331 5

Volcano Adventure

A scientific study of the volcanoes of the Pacific with world famous volcanologist, Dr Dan Adams, erupts into an adventure of a lifetime for Hal and Roger....
0 09 918241 6

South Sea Adventure

Hal and Roger can't resist the offer of a trip to the South Seas in search of a creature known as the Nightmare of the Pacific...
0 09 918251 3

Safari Adventure

Tsavo national park has become a death trap. Can Hal and Roger succeed in their mission of liberating it from the clutches of a Blackbeard's deadly gang of poachers?...
0 09 918341 2

African Adventure

On safari in African big-game country, Hal and Roger coolly tackle their brief to round up a mysterious man-eating beast. Meanwhile, a merciless band of killers follow in their wake...
0 09 918371 4

It's wild! It's dangerous! And it's out there!

Other great reads from **Red Fox**

Top new fiction

LETTERS OF A LOVESTRUCK TEENAGER
Claire Robertson

'I'm Gilly Freeborn and I'm nearly fourteen and I've got problems . . .' Her chest is as flat as a pancake, her sister's a mean, selfish man-eating piranha, her best friend's turned traitor and – *argh!* – she's fallen in love with The Vision. What's a girl to do? Turn to Alexa Deehart of course, agony aunt of *The Bizz* magazine . . .

0 09 94252 1   £3.99

SWITCHERS
Kate Thompson

Tess is a Switcher – she can change shape to become any animal she chooses. She always thought she was unique, but not any more. Tess meets another Switcher, Kevin, and together they have powers they never dreamed of . . .

0 09 925612 6   £3.99

MIDNIGHT'S CHOICE
Kate Thompson

With Kevin gone, Tess is feeling ever more lonely and isolated from everyone around her. Then she senses a call to which she has no resistance, and finds herself in the middle of a dilemma. For now she has found a new friend, and has a very difficult decision to make – a choice to change her life forever.

0 09 925613 4   £3.99

CHILD OF THE MAY
Theresa Tomlinson

No one is ever going to crush fiery Magda's independent streak. She yearns for the thrill of adventure and when her chance comes . . . she's going to take it. This stirring sequel to The Forest Wife continues Theresa Thomlinson's compelling account of life amongst the outlaws in Robin Hood's Sherwood Forest.

0 09 969231 7   £3.99